THE
GOODBYE
CAFÉ

MARIAH STEWART

THE
GOODBYE
CAFÉ

GALLERY BOOKS

New York   London   Toronto   Sydney   New Delhi

G

Gallery Books
An Imprint of Simon & Schuster, Inc.
1230 Avenue of the Americas
New York, NY 10020

First Gallery Books trade paperback edition March 2019

GALLERY BOOKS and colophon are registered trademarks of Simon & Schuster, Inc.

For information about special discounts for bulk purchases, please contact Simon & Schuster Special Sales at 1-866-506-1949 or business@simonandschuster.com.

The Simon & Schuster Speakers Bureau can bring authors to your live event. For more information or to book an event, contact the Simon & Schuster Speakers Bureau at 1-866-248-3049 or visit our website at www.simonspeakers.com.

Manufactured in the United States of America

10 9 8 7 6 5 4 3

Library of Congress Cataloging-in-Publication Data

Names: Stewart, Mariah, author.
Title: The goodbye café / Mariah Stewart.
Description: First Gallery Books trade paperback edition. | New York : Gallery Books, 2019. | Series: The Hudson sisters series ; 3
Identifiers: LCCN 2018055861 (print) | LCCN 2018058972 (ebook) | ISBN 9781501145162 (ebook) | ISBN 9781501145124 (paperback)
Subjects: LCSH: Sisters—Fiction. | Female friendship—Fiction. | Domestic fiction. | BISAC: FICTION / Contemporary Women. | FICTION / Romance / General.
Classification: LCC PS3569.T4653 (ebook) | LCC PS3569.T4653 G66 2019 (print) | DDC 813/.54—dc23
LC record available at https://lccn.loc.gov/2018055861

ISBN 978-1-5011-4512-4
ISBN 978-1-5011-4516-2 (ebook)

For Camryn Jane Maybaum,
with much love

ACKNOWLEDGMENTS

Telling this story—*writing* this story—was just the first step in getting my characters out into the wide world. By the time I finished my (sometimes frustrating but eventually satisfying) journey with the Hudson sisters, my manuscript was touched by dozens of oh-so-talented people. Editorial people, production people. The art department, the marketing department, publicity and sales and other people I don't even know about. Sometimes when I think about all that goes into making a book, I wonder if my part isn't the easiest. Okay, maybe the least complicated. When I'm working on that first draft, I don't answer to anyone other than my characters. Of course, all that ends when I send that draft to my editor and she gets her hands on it! My editor, Lauren McKenna, can be a demon—she's so often right in her comments, suggestions, and revisions, and I try not to whine too much about it. I don't always remember to say it, but many thanks for always steering me in the right direction and pointing out where I could go deeper and where my characters could be stronger. You're the best, and I'm grateful to call you mine!

I'm grateful, too, for the professional staff in production that works so hard; the art department folks, who have always come up with just the right look for my covers; the marketing and publicity staff, who find the best ways to showcase my books; and the sales department, which gets my books from the warehouse to the bookstores and distributors. I appreciate all your hard work.

My agent, Nick Mullendore, always has my back, and I thank him for picking up the pieces when our beloved Loretta Barrett left us to read some heavenly manuscripts on a higher plane.

The Writers Who Lunch bunch keeps me sane by getting together once a month for conversation and support and the best kind of friendship. Cara, Gwen, Helen, Terri, Gail, Martha, and Kate—I look forward to seeing you every fourth Thursday of the month and thank you for the collaboration that resulted in the Brandywine Brides anthology.

My Facebook community of friends and family is the best! I appreciate and thank every one of you who have supported my books over so many years, and who have followed me from my contemporary romances to my romantic suspense to my women's fiction.

Jo Ellen Grossman, Chery Griffin, Helen Egner, and Robyn Carr—I'm more grateful than I can say for your friendship and support. Love you all.

Our family keeps expanding! This year, 2019, will see the birth of our fifth grandchild. Rebecca and David's first baby will join Kate and Mike's three boys—Cole, Jack, and Robb—and their brand-new baby girl, Camryn. Bill and I are waiting with open arms and open hearts to meet her!

THE GOODBYE CAFÉ

CHAPTER ONE

At the earliest light of a summer day that promised to be even hotter than the record-breaking heat of the day before, Allie Hudson Monroe made her quiet way through the otherwise deserted streets of Hidden Falls, Pennsylvania. She strode with purpose, a large canvas bag over her shoulder, toward the intersection of Hudson Street and Main, where she crossed, and once on the other side, entered the Sugarhouse, the 1920s Art Deco theater that was her family's legacy.

Built by her great-grandfather and bequeathed to her and her two sisters by their father, Franklin "Fritz" Hudson, the Sugarhouse had been boarded up for years. Since Fritz'd specified in his will that his three daughters had to live together in the family home on Hudson Street and restore the theater before they could receive their generous individual inheritances, his "wish" had actually been more of an ultimatum. Only the thought of receiving the promised windfall could have coaxed Allie to leave her California home and face the heat and humidity of a summer spent in the Pocono Mountains along with her estranged sister, Des, and her newly discovered half sister, Cara. Fortunately, life in Hidden Falls had turned out to be much more interesting than Allie'd ever imagined. She and Des were on their way to burying long-held resentments on both their parts, and she'd found Cara—whose mother may or may not have been married to their father, the paperwork on that being a little shady—to be amicable and open to their new relationship. Best of all, perhaps, was discovering their father had a sister they'd never met. Their aunt—christened Bonnie but called Barney by just about everyone who knew her—was delightful, welcoming, and loving to her nieces. While Allie was still finding her way, navigating carefully through these new relationships, she was also finding untapped riches within herself.

She'd even found herself a little short on the snark that had been one of her least endearing personality traits. Maybe even a kinder, gentler Allie, though nothing was a sure thing.

As she'd done for the past week, after stepping inside the theater, Allie left the front door unlocked for the contractors who were working on the building. She turned on only enough lights to guide her to her destination: the scaffold that had been erected in the middle of the lobby. Shingles blown off the roof during a fierce summer storm had resulted in a leak in the ceiling and caused considerable damage to its hand-painted motifs. Allie had accepted the challenge of restoring them, and she would, one way or another.

One way would have been to hire an artist with sufficient talent to repair the intricately painted designs on the ceiling. Another would be for Allie, who wasn't completely lacking in artistic ability, to make the repairs herself. Since there were no funds for the former, the latter was going to have to do. Though she'd majored in art and had had some training, she'd never fully tapped into her innate artistic talent. This was her chance to prove to herself—and everyone else—that she had more going for her than just a pretty face and a stunning figure. Only to herself did Allie admit she'd skated on her appearance for far too long. She was eager to find what else she had to offer, especially now that her fourteen-almost-fifteen-year-old daughter was with her for the summer and striving to find herself as well. It was suddenly more important than ever to be the kind of mother, the kind of role model, she wanted for Nikki: the happy, loving mother, and the strong, self-reliant woman Allie and Des had never had in Nora, their own mother.

The air inside the theater was hot, close, and dusty from the work the contractors were doing in the basement: repairing a recently discovered section of concrete wall that had been weakened by the same storm that had damaged the ceiling. Allie stifled four sneezes that followed in quick succession as she made her way into the lobby.

She took a really deep breath, then sneezed several times more, before staring straight up.

"It's fine," she whispered to herself as if encouraging a small child. "It's not all that high. Not high like, oh, a twenty-story building might be. You've done this before. All you have to do is put one foot in front of the other and climb." She straightened her shoulders before adding, "Just don't look down."

She shifted the canvas bag higher up on her shoulder before latching on to the lowest rung. One by one, sweating hand over sweating hand, one uncertain foot at a time, her heart crazily beating in her chest, Allie climbed the rungs until she reached the top platform. She couldn't remember what had precipitated her fear of heights, she only knew it had always been with her. Des shared the same fear, one of the few things they acknowledged to have in common other than their parents.

"Don't look down, girl, just don't look down." Allie sang softly to the tune she'd made up earlier in the week. "Everything's okay as long as you don't look down."

She eased herself onto the edge of the platform, then carefully swung one leg over until she was straddling the plank. She wiped her palms on the red shorts she'd borrowed from Cara, still slightly annoyed that her sister's size-six clothes actually fit her. Allie had always worn a four. She hadn't been conscious of having gained weight, but there was no Pilates studio in Hidden Falls, no spin classes, none of the fixtures of her life in L.A. Walking trails (in this heat, are you *kidding*?), a track at the middle school (so not her style), and a gym if you wanted to drive two towns down the highway and work out with a bunch of sweaty strangers (no, thank you) were not an option. So when she needed a pair of old shorts to wear while she painted at the top of the theater, she'd had to borrow. She'd fully expected the pair Cara proffered to bag on her and require a belt to hold them up. She was appalled when she'd had to inhale to zip them. Since she was a full five inches taller than Cara, the shorts were *really* short. Which really wasn't much of a concern because who did she see in Hidden Falls she'd like to impress with her mile-long legs? No one, that's who.

She slowly lowered herself to sit on the edge of the plank, then paused to readjust the pins that held the coiled braid of her long, thick blond hair. She knew it was messy, but she'd never worn a braid until yesterday when she realized she had to come up with something better than the ponytail that skimmed the tops of the paint jars every time she moved her head. Nikki had suggested the braid, and at that point, Allie barely cared, as long as she could keep her hair out of the paint. For possibly the first time in her life, Allie was unconcerned with her appearance, her focus totally on her work.

She scooted forward to position herself directly under a white patch where a plaster repair had been made. There were areas where moisture had destroyed entire sections of the beautifully painted ceiling. Allie felt sick every time she looked at it, knowing it had been the handiwork of an artist who had known some limited fame during his lifetime, but who'd become well known as time went on. That he had a close personal relationship to Allie's own family had made him even more of a favorite of hers: he'd courted and married a great-great-aunt.

When the theater was still quite new, the first Reynolds Hudson had employed Alistair Cooper, a young artist from the local college, to design and hand paint the ceiling. No one knows exactly how long it took Alistair to complete the work, but it was universally agreed that it was a thing of beauty. Geometric shapes, painted in vibrant yellow, green, gold, blue, and red, wound together, radiating out from the chandelier to create a glorious spectacle on the ceiling's background of peacock blue. Alistair'd met the lovely Josephine Hudson and fallen in love, and once her parents had determined he was bound to be a famous artist, they'd permitted the two to marry.

"I'm not worthy," Allie murmured as she prepared to go to work, lining up the jars next to her on the platform. Just the fact that she was attempting to re-create the beauty Alistair had envisioned made her feel like an impostor. "I seriously am not."

She'd never try to restore the work freehand; she wasn't so arrogant as to think she was Alistair's equal. But she'd cleverly made tracings of his designs, then turned the tracings into stencils, which she then placed over the missing areas of the ceiling. She'd had the original paint colors matched as closely as could be done, so any minute difference was imperceptible from the floor below.

Allie cleared her throat before sliding a stencil from her bag. After carefully positioning it directly over her head, she taped it lightly to keep it in place.

"I feel like such a fraud," she grumbled. "I can't believe I have the audacity to even attempt this. Yet here I sit . . ."

She searched her bag for just the right brush, then opened the first jar. Taking a deep breath, she touched the brush to the paint, then leaned back as far as she could and began to fill in the center of the design with the pale yellow.

When the paint dried, she'd begin the border of blue, then outline it in gold to match the original. Taking her time, she painstakingly copied Alistair's work. Ignoring the oppressive heat at the very top of the room, Allie focused all her attention on her task. She was so absorbed she didn't hear the door of the theater open and close.

"Mom." Allie's daughter, Nicole—Nikki—stood at the bottom of the scaffold. "Can I come up?"

"I don't know, can you?" Allie replied without looking down. Even from the top of the scaffold she heard Nikki's deep sigh.

"*May* I come up?"

"You may if you wait a minute. Let me finish this one section." Allie remained focused on the diamond shape she was completing.

A few minutes later, she called down, "Okay, now you may climb up, but take your time and be really careful."

She'd barely gotten the words out when Nikki was scrambling across the platform, her long blond hair, so like her mother's, flowing over one shoulder.

"You climb like a monkey."

Nikki grinned. "Thanks. I've been practicing."

"Oh really? When?" Allie moved her head slowly from side to side, trying to work out the kink that had settled in her neck.

"Mark and I raced up to the top the other day. I would have won but his arms and legs are longer than mine. I should have made him give me a handicap." Nikki swung her legs over the side of the platform, making it sway slightly and forcing Allie's stomach to flip.

"When were you and Mark in the theater together?" Allie frowned.

"Last week. Aunt Des was showing Mark's uncle Seth the section you already finished. He was gobsmacked." A smile spread across Nikki's pretty face—so very much like Allie's—as she looked up. "Everyone knows you're doing an awesome job. When the paint dries, no one will be able to tell the difference between what you've done and the original."

"I doubt that's true, but thank you, sweetie." Allie knew she was doing as good a job as anyone could possibly do, but all the same, her daughter's words warmed her heart. Still, she harbored no illusions about her work: not freehand but with the use of props. But the bottom line was that it looked pretty darned good from the floor of the lobby. "So what are you up to this morning?"

"Mom, it's almost noon." Nikki was still looking up, her eyes studying the sections her mother had already painted.

"Seriously?" Allie frowned. It felt like she'd only been in the theater for a short time. And yet almost six hours had passed, which probably accounted for the fact that her neck and back were burning from the stress of having kept the same position all that time.

"You were up really early. I heard you leave but I was too tired to get up and go downstairs and have breakfast with you."

"I wanted to get some time in here before it got too hot." Allie wiped the back of her neck with a tissue she pulled from her bag. Her skimpy tank was stuck to her, front and back, so wet she could wring the sweat out, and now that work was no longer a distraction, she felt like a sticky wet mess. "I had no idea I was here so long. I've had enough for today."

She glanced at her daughter.

"So what *are* you up to?" Allie repeated the question as she began to repack her bag.

"I wanted to ask if I could go out to Seth's farm this afternoon."

Allie raised an eyebrow. "Let me guess. Mark's working with Seth today."

Nikki nodded. "They're making frames for the new grape plants Seth brought back from France last week. They worked over the weekend to get the plants into the ground, but now Seth wants to get the frames up before the plants start to grow."

"And this would involve you how?"

"I offered to help paint the frames." Apparently anticipating resistance from her mother, Nikki hastened to add, "Mark's sister, Hayley, and their friend Wendy will be there also. I just met her yesterday. She's really nice and wanted to help, so I asked Aunt Des and she said sure. I could go with Aunt Des. She's going to be helping, too."

"I guess it's all right."

"Yay! Thanks, Mom." Nikki's phone immediately appeared in her left hand and she began to type with a speed only the young have mastered. Seconds later, they heard a ping. Nikki swiped her screen, then smiled. "Mark is already out there. He's been working since early morning with Seth." She pocketed the phone.

"What's going on back at the house?" Allie stretched her

shoulders, grateful for a few minutes looking straight ahead rather than up.

"Not much. Aunt Barney's going over to Tom's house to help him sort through some stuff of his mother's. He said he doesn't know what stuff's valuable and what's not."

"Shouldn't Tom's sister be doing that?"

Nikki shrugged. "She lives in London."

"Oh. Right. What's Cara doing?"

"She got up early, not as early as you, though. She packed a picnic. She and Joe are spending the day out at the lake. They're going to kayak and stuff."

Nikki's phone pinged again.

"I gotta go." She looked up at Allie. "Aunt Des is ready, and she wants to leave by twelve thirty and it's twenty after." Nikki leaned forward as far as she could to kiss her mother's cheek. "You're the best mom. See you later. And thanks again."

"You're welcome." Allie watched Nikki work her way down, nimble as an elf, before adding, "I think."

She continued to pack up her things, fighting off the feeling she got whenever Nikki spent time with Mark. Oh, of course everyone said what a good kid he was. He was smart, he was athletic, he was polite, he was hardworking, and he was adorably cute. He'd volunteered to build houses in Haiti with a group from his church. Rationally, Allie knew Nikki'd hit the boyfriend jackpot. He was the son of Seth's cousin. Did it make her a bad mother that she knew Nikki'd be returning to California at the end of the summer and that would probably be the end as far as Mark was concerned?

Mothers weren't always rational where their young teen daughters were concerned when it came to boys. Allie knew she was overprotective sometimes—some might say overbearing—but Nikki was her world. Her only child. The only good thing that came out of a fifteen-year marriage to a man who one day decided he didn't want to be married anymore and cut her loose. Clint, her ex, had made a big thing out of giving her the house they'd bought years ago in L.A. Everyone said how generous he was—but she was the one who had to pay the insanely high taxes on the place. Clint had moved to a community that was close to an hour away from Allie, then enrolled Nikki in a very toney—and pricey— private school, for which Allie ended up paying half the tuition, an expense she couldn't really afford but insisted on contributing her fair share. Which of course Clint had known she'd do.

Allie'd been working as an assistant director on a TV series that had been canceled and was rapidly running out of funds when her father died. The conditions of Fritz's will had infuriated her—if ever she'd needed that inheritance, it was then—and his demands that his daughters move to Hidden Falls and rehab the theater had been puzzling. But in retrospect, she recognized there'd been a financial silver lining. She could rent her house while she was gone and have enough income to continue paying her share of Nikki's school expenses, since she, Des, and Cara were living expense free in the family home with their aunt while they worked on the theater.

Allie swung her bag over her shoulder, preparing to start her descent, thinking how much her life had changed since she'd arrived in Hidden Falls. There were days when she felt like a different person from the one who'd boarded the plane at LAX and flown to Scranton, Pennsylvania, rented a car, and driven to this tiny nowhere town. At first she'd hated it. Now she was growing accustomed to the slow pace and the fact that everyone in town knew who she was and where she came from simply by virtue of her being Barney Hudson's niece.

She dropped one leg over the side, singing softly to herself, "Don't look down, girl, just don't look down. Everything's okay as long as you don't look down," when she did exactly that.

She bristled at the sight of the man who stood at the foot of the scaffold staring straight up.

"What are you doing here?"

"I was looking for Des. I stopped over at the house but no one answered." His arms were crossed over his chest, and instead of wearing his usual chief of police uniform, Ben Haldeman—the very bane of Allie's existence, the gigantic thorn in her side—was dressed in cutoff jeans and a light blue tank top, flip-flops on his feet. He didn't bother to smile at her—why pretend he liked her any more than she liked him?—but he didn't blink when she stared down at him, either.

"I'll let her know when I see her."

"Then I'll just leave this little guy here and you can take him home with you. How 'bout I just tie his leash up to the scaffold?"

"What little . . ." Allie leaned over the side of the platform, just far enough to make her head spin and her stomach flip. She pulled back, but not before she saw the little black dog on the red leash that Ben was tying to the bottom rung. "Wait, where'd that dog come from? You can't leave it here."

"Found him out on the highway running loose. Tell Des to give me a call." Ben patted the dog on the head and turned toward the door.

"Wait. Ben. No, don't . . ."

He waved as he walked away. "Have a nice day."

With a deep sigh of exasperation, Allie sat back on the platform. The man had given her a hard time before she'd even gotten out of her car the night she arrived in Hidden Falls—she'd just barely turned into Barney's driveway—and he hadn't let up since. Oh, there'd been a time when he'd seemed to be lightening up on her, but she'd killed any mellow feelings he might have started to have on the Fourth of July when she'd inadvertently—not to mention publicly—reminded him that his only child had died.

Not exactly, but close enough.

He'd been teasing her about being overprotective where Nikki was concerned. Was it being overprotective to want to know where her fourteen-year-old daughter was going and with whom? She didn't think so. Her comeback had been quick and thoughtless.

"Said the man who—" She'd stopped herself before she finished the sentence, but it was pretty clear she'd been about to say, *Said the man who has no children.* She hadn't said it, but the unspoken words had hung in the air between them—and everyone around them had heard.

Ben had gone white, then turned on his heel and left, and it was obvious he'd been cut to the quick.

She knew she could be a first-class pain in the ass, and God knew she had her moments, but she would never—*never*—purposely say something like that to anyone, not even her worst enemy. It had made her sick to her stomach to know she'd hurt Ben in the worst way possible. She'd gone to his apartment that afternoon to apologize, but the damage had been done. He'd shown her a photograph of his beautiful son, who along with his mother had been killed when their car had been hit by a drunk driver. The picture of the sweet dark-haired boy had broken Allie's heart. She'd tried to tell Ben how terrible she felt, how she'd never intentionally say something so horrible, but he'd turned her words against her, accusing her of making it all about her. Her feelings. Her embarrassment.

The last words he'd spoken to her before today had been, "Nice, princess. Guess you told me, right? Way to get the last word." And then he'd slammed the door in her face, leaving her speechless and tearful on his doorstep.

The feeling she'd had that day swept through her, a chronic sense of self-loathing she was pretty sure she'd never be able to shake, every time she thought back to that day.

"Damn." She looked down at the dog. From the top of the scaffold, she couldn't tell what kind of dog it was, just that it was small and all black and was moving nervously around the limited space Ben had left it in. Of course he'd bring a stray to Des. She was the dog whisperer. She'd funded a rescue shelter back in Montana, where she'd been living, and it appeared she was now doing the same thing here in Hidden Falls. Seth had lots of room for a shelter on his farm, and he'd made it clear he was okay with Des bringing abandoned and lost dogs there since the town had no other provisions for strays. The fact that Seth was in love with Des probably had something to do with his offer.

Another heavy sigh, and Allie began the climb down. When she reached the floor, she stood several feet away from the dog and stared at it. It had perky ears that stood away from its head and big round eyes, a stocky body, short legs.

"So, I, ah, guess you got lost." She set her bag down on the lowest plank of the scaffold and reached to untie the dog, which backed away as if in fear. "Oh, no, no. I'm not going to hurt you. I just want to untie your leash so we can leave."

She stopped to consider how Des might handle this situation. She tried to remember how her sister spoke to Buttons, the white dog she'd rescued—and kept—several months earlier.

"So maybe you're hungry." She stared at the dog, which made no move but continued to stare at her with its oversized eyes. "Or maybe thirsty. Want some water?"

The dog didn't move, nor did it look away.

"All right, look. We're going to go for a walk, okay? Wouldn't you like to be not tied up anymore?"

She leaned closer and reached for the leash. The dog growled.

"Oh crap. Was that a threat? Are you going to bite me? It figures he'd bring me a vicious dog." She stood with her hands on her hips, trying to figure out what to do next. "Look, I'm hot and starving, and I want to go back to the house. I have to take you with me. I can't leave you here tied up, all alone."

She reached again for the leash—and once again the dog growled.

"Okay, you've gotta stop doing that. I'm trying to help you. You don't look like a puppy, so you should know the difference between someone who's trying to help you and someone who means you harm."

Another growl, this one from deep in the dog's throat.

"I give up. I get that you don't like me, but I still can't in good conscience leave you here." She searched her bag for her phone, then speed-dialed Des's number.

"Des, we have a situation," Allie said when her sister answered.

"What kind of situation?"

"The canine kind. Ben dropped off a dog at the theater. He found it running loose on the highway. He brought it in here and tied its leash to the scaffold so I could bring it home to you. Which would have been fine except the dog growls at me every time I reach for the leash. What do I do?"

"Does the dog appear to be injured or hurt in any way?"

Allie walked around the dog, giving it a wide berth even as she gave it a once-over. "Not that I can see."

"Did you speak to it nicely, or did you talk to it the way you talk to Ben?"

"What difference would that make?"

"Dogs are very sensitive creatures. They recognize hostility. If you've been snarling at it, it's going to snarl back."

"Des, I didn't snarl. I was actually very nice. I asked if it was hungry or thirsty and told it I was going to take it for a walk, but it won't let me untie it." Frustrated, she added, "Ben knew the dog wasn't friendly. He still hasn't forgiven me for—"

"Ben's past all that," Des interrupted.

"No, he isn't."

"Let's focus on the dog. Ask it if it wants to go for a walk. Most dogs know *walk*."

"Okay. Wait . . ."

"Allie, say it nicely."

Allie groaned. She lowered her voice and said slowly and sweetly, "Hi, doggie. Want to go for a walk? Walk, doggie?"

"What's it doing?"

"Glaring at me with these big eyes."

"Sit down and talk to it. See if you can get the leash loose."

"He's going to go right for my bare legs, I just know it." Allie flinched, imagining those sharp little teeth buried in her calf.

"Do you have any food?" Des asked.

"I don't know. Let me look in my bag." She rummaged for a moment, then found a cookie encased in plastic wrap.

"I have a cookie, but I don't know how old it is."

"It's not chocolate, is it? Chocolate's not good for dogs."

"It's a sugar cookie." Allie took a closer look through the cellophane. "Not much sugar on it."

"If he's hungry, he won't care."

"Okay, here goes." She unwrapped the cookie and broke off a piece. "Here, boy. Want a little snack?"

The dog's nose began to twitch as he sniffed the air. He took a few tentative steps toward her.

"Come on, it's for you." She lowered her voice as she'd heard Des do when she was talking to Buttons, then lowered it again to almost a whisper. The dog came closer, then stretched out its neck. Allie extended her arm so the dog could take a bite. She broke off another piece, then while she fed it with one hand, she untied the leash with the other.

"Yes!" she said triumphantly. "The dog has the cookie, I've got the leash, and we are outta here. Thanks, Des."

"I'll meet you at the house in about ten minutes and check out your new friend."

"Why didn't you just meet me here and do your thing with him? He could have bitten me. Attacked me."

"But he didn't do any of those things. You're fine. He's fine. See you soon." Des was gone.

"Come on, boy. I'm guessing you're a boy. Can't really tell and I'm not gonna look. Not taking a chance of losing a finger. Besides, it doesn't really matter, right? You're not staying with me, so frankly, my dear, I don't give a damn." Allie tugged gently on the leash, and to her surprise, the dog followed her through the lobby and out the front door.

"It was the cookie, wasn't it?" She paused to lock the front door. "It's not me, right? You just wanted a snack." She tucked the key into the pocket of her shorts. "Dad always said the way to a man's heart was through his stomach. Appears that applies to dogs as well."

They stood on the curb and waited for the light traffic to pass, then crossed the street. Once on the other side, Allie picked up the pace and the dog kept up, stride for stride. When they reached the Hudson family home, Allie let the dog sniff around the yard before going into the house, as she'd seen Des do with Buttons.

"I think you're supposed to be doing something right about now, buddy. Like watering the plants, if you get my drift." The dog continued to sniff the grass and the plants that framed the front porch steps, but that was about all. "So maybe you're okay, then. I guess Ben took you on a walk or something?"

She went up the front steps, the little black dog right on her heels.

"Here's the deal, pal. You may not do your business in this house. Uh-uh." She shook her head and opened the front door. "Good dogs leave it all outside, do we understand each other?"

The dog dashed past her, running the straight length of the hall to the kitchen.

"Well, I guess you know what the kitchen is for. Let me see if I can find something for you to eat." She dropped the leash and went to the refrigerator and hunted through the contents until she found a container of leftover pork from two nights prior. "If you sit like a nice doggie, you can have some of—"

The dog jumped up and snatched the meat out of her hand.

"That was rude. Didn't anyone teach you manners?"

She started to take another piece of pork from the container, then paused. "Dear God, I'm having a one-sided conversation with a dog. I'm turning into my sister."

"Not that there's anything wrong with that." Des came into the kitchen with Buttons on her leash.

When the little white dog saw the newcomer in her house, with one of her humans, she stopped in her tracks and glared.

"It's okay, Buttons," Des assured her. "He's a new friend. We're going to take him to the vet, have him checked out, and if he gets a thumbs-up from Dr. Trainor, we'll take him out to Seth's farm to play with the other doggies."

The black dog's tail began to wag slowly, then Buttons approached him, stopping to sniff his butt.

"Gross. Why do dogs do that?" Allie made a face, and Des laughed.

"Why do you shake hands with someone you've just met?" Des asked.

"So much more civilized than—you know." Allie pointed to the two dogs, which were engaged in the canine equivalent of getting to know you. "What kind of dog is he, anyway?"

"Looks like a French bulldog. Nice breed. Come here, little guy. Let me look at you." Des knelt next to the dogs and ran her hands gently over the newcomer's back. His tail continued to wag. "You've very cute, you know that, right?"

Allie rolled her eyes, and Des laughed again.

"Don't pretend you weren't talking to him when I came in, girl. I heard you."

"I wasn't carrying on an entire conversation as if I expected a verbal response."

"Were, too." Des grinned.

"Was—wait! Did he just . . ." Allie pointed to the puddle around the leg of one of the kitchen chairs. "He did. He lifted his leg and peed on that chair."

"Aw, that's sweet, Al. He peed on the chair you usually sit in. He's just marking his territory, and he's made sure it includes you."

Des gathered up both leashes. "You might want to clean that up before Barney gets home."

"Wait. Where are you going?"

"To the vet's. He closes early on Saturday. Then I'm going back to Seth's. See you later." Des disappeared down the hall. Seconds later, Allie heard the front door close.

"Nice way to thank me for bringing you home and saving you from a life on the streets." Grumbling, Allie grabbed the nearby roll of paper towels and soaked up the puddle on the floor. "This is why I will never have a pet. If I'd wanted to clean up after someone, I'd have had another child. Which I have no intention of doing. Ever."

She tossed the paper towel into the trash and washed her hands. She made a sandwich, then hunted in the fridge for a beer, but they were out, so she settled for a glass of Barney's freshly made lemonade and went out to the patio in the backyard. She ate at the bistro table, then stretched out in the sun on a nearby lounge. After about twenty minutes, she grew hot and bored.

She took her plate and empty glass inside, refilled her lemonade, and went up to her room.

The bed was still unmade and the shade still completely down, so the room was dark. She pulled the shade halfway up, then opened the window a little more to let in whatever breeze might drift through from the trees behind the house. Stripping off her clothes, she headed for the shower. Fifteen minutes later, wrapped in a towel, she wandered back into the bedroom and sat on the room's only chair to dry her hair.

The house was so quiet, felt so empty when there was no one else there. How did Barney stand it, all those years she lived here alone, after her only sibling had taken off with his girlfriend for California and their parents passed away? Any empty house might feel lonely, but the Hudson house was large enough to take up the entire block on its side of the street, so there was no such thing as a next-door neighbor. With seven large bedrooms and baths on the second floor, and a number of spacious rooms on the first, it definitely qualified for mansion status. And rightly so, since the Hudsons had all but founded the town. They'd made their money in coal and had set the bar high for the treatment of their workers: They paid decent wages, provided medical care for the sick and injured, and founded a college that the miners' children could attend free of charge. The college had been named for Allie's great-grandmother, and Althea College had continued to grow and expand in the years since. The Hudsons had donated the land on which the first elementary school had been built and donated money for the first hospital in the area. It was no surprise that the family that could afford to do all that would have the grandest house in town. Even Allie, jaded though she'd been after living in Los Angeles for so many years, had been impressed with its Victorian turrets and wraparound porch and all the gingerbread trim, the generous rooms, high ceilings, and more than a few ornately trimmed fireplaces.

Hudson House was impressive, all right, though Allie was pretty sure she wouldn't want to live there alone for any length of time. But being a Hudson in Hidden Falls came with a legacy, one Allie was just beginning to appreciate. She was proud of what her ancestors had accomplished and of their philanthropy.

Her father's infidelity aside, she was proud of him, but she was most proud of Barney, who'd fought to be the first woman president of the family's bank, who'd seen the town through troubled financial times, and had approved the loans with which residents had purchased homes and kept their businesses afloat in times of trouble and sent their kids to college. Would it be overreaching to say that Barney was the backbone of Hidden Falls? Maybe, but not by much.

In Hidden Falls, it was good to be a Hudson.

Unless you were alone in the sprawling house on a hot afternoon when everyone else was out doing their thing.

Did it seem everyone had found a partner of one degree or another? Cara had found Joe when the sisters hired him as the general contractor on the theater project. Des had met Seth when she rescued several stray dogs from the boarded-up theater and he'd volunteered to foster one, and later helped her dream of a rescue shelter there in Hidden Falls come true. Nikki had Mark to hang out with, and even Barney had found a would-be partner in Tom Brookes, who'd been a neighbor and best buddy of Gil Wheeler, her late fiancé.

So, everyone but Allie. Not that she was looking for an "other," but suddenly she felt like the ultimate fifth wheel.

Unexpected loneliness swept over her, a harbinger, she thought, of the years ahead of her. She knew she'd only have a few more years with Nikki before her daughter went off to college. Then—blink!—Nikki would be starting her career, whatever that might be. Then—poof!—marriage to some guy Allie might not even know, and the one person in this world Allie would willingly die for would be gone. Intellectually, she knew that the bottom line was to cherish the moments she had.

And I have those moments now, this summer, she reminded herself.

But when the summer came to an end, Nikki would be back with her father, who lived only a few blocks from Nikki's school. Well, her father and the woman he's seeing. Who just happens to be the mother of Nikki's best friend, Courtney. Allie hadn't brought up that dating situation to Nikki since she was unsure if her daughter was aware. What if Clint hadn't shared that with Nikki? As much as it wouldn't bother Allie to see Clint uncomfortable, she would never do anything that would damage his relationship with their daughter. Whatever else Allie could say about Clint—and there was plenty—she had to respect the fact that he was a terrific father, one who loved his child very much.

I am going to take every bit of this kid I can get this summer, she told herself as she searched her bag for her phone. *I'm not going to feel sad about what's going to happen after the summer is over. Seize the moment and all that.*

She hit the icon for Nikki's phone.

"Hi, Mom." A giggling Nikki answered on the third ring.

"Hey. You sound happy. What's happening out there, silly?"

"Oh, Mom, it's been so much fun. Aunt Des and I painted so many of those frames for Seth's grapevines. And it's so stinking hot. So we went down to the pond and jumped in. And now we're doing—" Nikki screamed, turning Allie's blood to ice before she started laughing.

"Nik?" Allie held her breath.

"Seth has water balloons. He exploded them on the ground in front of us and we're soaked!" Nikki dissolved into a fit of laughter as apparently another balloon had hit close by.

"Well, when you come home to change into dry clothes, why don't you and I get dressed up a little and drive into High Bridge and have dinner, just the two of us. Then maybe we could go see a movie in that new theater out on the highway, just like we used to do back home."

"I would except Aunt Des and Seth are going to barbecue and they invited us—me and Mark and Hayley and Wendy—to stay and eat with them since we worked so hard today. I didn't think you'd mind, but I was going to call and ask."

"Oh. Well. Okay." Allie felt more than a little deflated. She tried to keep the disappointment from her voice, but she was pretty sure she'd failed. It hadn't occurred to her that Nikki would have made plans on her own without letting Allie know.

"Can we do it another night?"

"Of course. Sure. Well . . . I guess I'll see you when you get home." Allie's philosophy had always been, when you don't know what else to say, hang up.

"Mom, wait. Aunt Des said you're welcome to join us."

"Oh, no, that's okay. Sounds like she's got a full house. I'll stay here and grab something with Barney."

"I guess with us here and Aunt Cara doing that picnic with Joe, Aunt Barney wouldn't have anyone to eat with, so that's nice of you." Nikki shrieked again as apparently another water balloon burst.

In the background, Allie could hear laughter.

"Look, it sounds like you have a lot going on there, so I'm going to hang up. Tell Aunt Des I said thanks for the invitation, but I'll pass."

"Okay, bye, Mom." Nikki was laughing as the call ended.

Allie sighed, and tried to ignore the wave of sadness that began to creep around her. Except for the weekends, when she had Nikki to herself, Allie'd lived alone for almost a year in L.A., but she'd never felt as lonely as she did after disconnecting that call. She tried to decide what to do with herself when she noticed the ice had melted in the glass of lemonade she'd left on the table. She thought about the half-empty bottle of vodka in the small linen closet in her bathroom.

Since Nikki arrived, Allie'd kept her drinking to a minimum: Even she'd had to secretly admit her nightly "cocktails" were becoming a problem, though she never drank when Nikki was around.

"Well, she isn't here now, so why not?" she murmured.

She went downstairs for ice and was about to refill the glass when she heard the front door open, then close.

"Hello, anyone," Barney called.

"In the kitchen," Allie called back.

"Oh my, but it's a scorcher, isn't it?" Barney came into the kitchen, her face glistening with perspiration. "I can't remember being this hot. Ever. I am calling Joe and telling him I want that central air-conditioning put in ASAP. I don't care if he has to put one unit upstairs for the second floor and one unit in the basement for the first. I just want it done and I want it done now and I don't care what it costs."

"Yay for that. We're all dying."

Barney dropped her bag on a kitchen chair, then poured herself a glass of water from the tap and took a long drink. "I'm too old to sweat this much."

"I felt that way when I got back from the theater. A shower works wonders."

"I'm on my way upstairs right now." Barney swept the sweat from her brow. "Where is everyone?"

"Des and Nikki are at the farm with Seth and some of Nikki's friends, and Cara is still with Joe."

"Will anyone be here for dinner?"

"Looks like you and me."

"Well, then, let's just take ourselves over to the Goodbye. Judy had a sign out earlier that they have Pocono Mountain trout tonight, and I'd love to dig into one of those."

Allie debated between the bottle upstairs and the trout in the café on Main Street.

"Come on, Allie. Just you and me. We never have any time together, just the two of us."

"All right. Sure. Thanks, Barney."

"I'm going to run upstairs and take that shower and you go on and change into something pretty."

Barney's smile as she left the room assured Allie she'd made the right choice. Even as the desire for a drink had started to play on her nerves, she took a deep breath, tried to push that need away, and followed Barney upstairs, grateful she'd been able to beat back the dragon at least for a little while.

Chapter Two

Allie sat in one of the rocking chairs on the front porch, waiting for Barney. Changing into a soft navy T-shirt dress hadn't taken her long, and since she kept her makeup to a minimum these days, mascara and a swipe of dark pink on her lips would do. She wore hot pink sandals on her feet, big gold hoops in her ears, and two inches' worth of gold bangles on her left wrist. Her hair was pulled back into a high ponytail in an attempt to keep it off her neck, but it still hung past her shoulder blades. She was thinking it might be time for a trim when she heard the door open.

"I always said we Hudsons clean up real good." Barney grinned as she stepped out onto the porch, her white cardigan folded over her arm. She wore a pretty black-and-white sundress, gold earrings, and black strappy sandals. Her still-blond hair was blunt-cut and came to her chin to frame her face. Even in her seventies, Barney looked darn good. "Shall we go?"

"We shall." Allie followed Barney down the steps and onto the sidewalk. "What's your buddy Tom doing for dinner tonight?"

"He's driving into Scranton to see a cousin. He invited me to tag along, but I didn't feel like going."

"Sounds like things are moving pretty quickly between you two."

Barney made a face. "Maybe that's why I didn't want to go. Though it's been nice, having someone my age to spend time with."

"You have a lot of friends your age in town and you spend lots of time with them," Allie reminded her.

"Yes, but Tom is different. He left Hidden Falls a long time ago. I don't remember him coming back very often. I'm not sure we have a whole lot in common anymore."

"He must have come back to visit his parents, and his mother after his dad passed away."

"If he did, I didn't notice."

"How could you not have noticed? You live right across the street," Allie pointed out.

"Maybe I was just too caught up in my own life. For so many years I was so wrapped up in the responsibility of being president of the bank. I knew what just about everyone in town was doing financially. I knew who hadn't saved enough for their retirement, who had a child in college and two more kids right behind, who'd lost his job, who had another child on the way and couldn't afford it. I can see it now, but I couldn't see it then. I felt like I had the weight of the entire town on my shoulders."

"Because you wanted to solve everyone's problems."

"Like my dad before me, and his dad before him, and his . . . well, you know."

"That's a heavy weight to carry, Barney."

"Don't I know it. I lost twenty-two pounds after I retired."

"Because you were getting more exercise? Not sitting all day?"

"Sitting all day?" Barney rolled her eyes. "I've never sat all day. But after I retired, I realized I was a stress eater. Once I eliminated the stress, I didn't feel like snacking all the time. Plus retiring cut out all those birthday, retirement, wedding, and new baby parties in the break room. I bet I ate the equivalent of twenty whole cakes over the course of my working years."

"Do you ever miss it?"

"I miss the structure my days used to have. I miss the interaction with the other employees. I miss seeing all the folks who came into the bank, the new babies, the retirees, the little kids clutching their savings books in one hand and a fistful of birthday money in the other. I don't suppose there's much of that anymore, what with online banking and such." She paused as if reflecting. "But I don't miss the responsibility. Or the stress."

They crossed Hudson Street at its intersection with Main, passing the corner drugstore, a vacant storefront that had housed the town's only bookstore, a sporting goods store where one could purchase everything from guns and ammo to pink Wellingtons and flowery Laura Ashley garden gloves, the beauty salon, and the Hudson Diner, in that order. Traffic was light after four thirty in the afternoon on any given day, so there were few cars on the street.

"I heard the bookstore is reopening in a few months," Barney said as they passed the empty store. The sign on the large glass window in front read HUDSON BOOKATERIA. "I hope they change the name. The last two owners have carried over the original and it hasn't seemed to bring either of them any more luck than the first owner had."

"What would you change it to?" Through the window, Allie could see a long row of shelves along one wall that went all the way to the back of the store.

"If I owned it, it would be Barney's Books."

"Catchy." Allie nodded slowly. "Not to mention original."

"You asked."

Moments later they arrived at the Green Brier Café, known to the locals as the Goodbye due to its reputation as the place in town to take that special person who was no longer all that special. It'd been rumored that many a breakup had taken place there, though no one could name anyone who'd admitted to having been dumped at one of their tables.

Allie grabbed the door and stepped back for Barney to enter. The hostess station was vacant, so they stood and waited for a minute or two before a waitress approached.

"Hey, Miss Hudson." The young woman smiled. "I'll have a table for you in just a minute."

"Thanks, Degan." Barney looked around. "Where's Judy? Don't tell me the owner actually took a night off?"

"She's in her office. I'll let her know you're here." Degan gathered two menus and led Barney and Allie to a table.

"Not too crowded yet," Barney noted as they sat.

"That's because it's barely five thirty. Who eats dinner this early besides really old people?"

"Watch it, girlie." Barney's eyes were fixed on the menu. "And I shouldn't have to remind you that you're eating dinner 'this early.'"

"Only because I'm with a"—Allie covered her mouth to cough—"senior citizen."

"You may say senior. You may not say old, elder, or advanced age. And never geriatric if you know what's good for you." Barney put the menu down. "I'm going with the trout."

"Is it boney?" Allie asked.

"It's a fish, Allie. Fish have bones. You watch for them, you pick them out. Should one get into your mouth, you remove it."

"No, thanks. I'll go with the coconut shrimp." Allie held the menu in both hands. "And for the record, I never think of you as being old. Or senior, even."

"Well, thank you. In that case dinner's on me." Barney looked to be about to say something else when Degan returned to the table.

"Miss Hudson, Judy asked me to ask you if you'd come back to the office," the waitress said.

"Of course." Barney handed her the menu. "I'm having the trout and a large iced tea." She looked at Allie. "I'll be back in a few."

"Iced tea for me as well," Allie told Degan. "And the coconut shrimp."

"I'll put that in for you." Degan took Allie's menu. "I'll be right back with your teas."

She was true to her word, and Allie was just about to take a sip when the café door opened behind her. She turned, more from reflex than from curiosity, in time to see Ben Haldeman come in with a pretty dark-haired young woman who was chattering away. It appeared to Allie he was hanging on every word. She turned away from the door and focused way too hard on her iced tea. Degan led Ben and his date to a table in the back. When Allie looked up again, she realized he was seated directly in her sight line.

She inwardly groaned. Was she really going to have to be looking at him all through dinner?

The only good thing was that he hadn't seemed to notice her at all.

Allie sensed the exact moment when he did. She could feel his eyes boring into her and made herself busy checking her email and her Instagram account on her phone lest she make eye contact with him. She put the phone down when she realized she'd read the same email four times.

What, she wondered impatiently, was keeping Barney?

Degan brought salads for her and Barney, and Allie kept her eyes on her plate, pushing around the lettuce and tomatoes and cucumbers until she finally began to eat. A few minutes later, Barney came bustling out from the office, in such a hurry she failed even to see Ben, who'd been about to greet her. She pulled out her chair and sat, her face white, her expression grim.

"Barney, what's wrong?" Allie asked.

"The worst. The absolute worst." Barney's breath came in quick bursts.

"What? Are you all right? You look like you're about to start hyperventilating."

"It's Judy. She's leaving for New Mexico and—"

"Whoa. Slow down. Start over." Allie reached a hand across the table to rest on Barney's. "Take a deep breath."

After Barney was able to collect herself, she took a big breath. "Judy's parents are in New Mexico. Her father's had a stroke. Her mother is in the early stages of dementia. She has to leave Hidden Falls. She's going to go out there to stay and care for them herself rather than put them in a senior care center."

"Oh, that's too bad. I'm sure she's terribly upset, but I don't see—"

"She's going to close the Goodbye, Allie. Do you know what this place means to this town? It's the place to go for breakfast or lunch with your friends or where you meet them for coffee. It's where you and your family pop in for dinner on those nights when you don't want to cook. It's Hidden Falls, Allegra Jane Hudson Monroe. Closing the Goodbye is going to change everything." Barney looked like she was about to cry.

"Well, I understand that you love the place, but there is the diner right across the parking lot."

"No one *meets up* at the diner. It's always been the Goodbye."

"So maybe it's only temporary. Maybe it'll only be closed for a short time."

"She's going to sell it. She has no idea how long she'll be in New Mexico, or if she'll ever come back." Barney was obviously distressed.

"Maybe Judy has a sister or a brother who could take over and keep it running until she gets back."

"Her brother is out in New Mexico now, but he can't stay forever. He has a family and a business to run in Michigan. Judy's children are scattered all over the place and they all have young families, and none of them have ever had any interest in the restaurant business. Oh, I just can't imagine Hidden Falls without the Goodbye." Barney shook her head. "It's been my favorite place forever."

"Well . . ." Allie tried to think of another solution. "Has she thought about maybe hiring someone to live with her parents and take care of them?"

"You don't treat family that way when there's a crisis like this. You don't push your responsibilities off on someone else. You take care of it if at all possible." Barney appeared personally offended. "How is it that you don't understand that?"

"Oh, I don't know. Maybe being the daughter of a woman who drank herself to death and wanted nothing to do with her children could have something to do with it. Or maybe having a father who died without telling his daughters he was sick, who arranged to be cremated before we even knew he'd died, who had two wives— though we're not really sure what Susa's legal status was—and children who never knew about each other." Allie added pointedly, "Who never even told us about you."

Barney sighed. "It's hard to argue with any of that. God knows you didn't have very good role models." She tapped her fingers on the side of her glass. "There has to be some way to fix this."

"Maybe she could hire someone to run it for her," Allie suggested. "Surely there's someone around who's capable of running a restaurant. She could keep the same staff and just have someone acting like a kind of overseer. I mean, how hard can it be?"

"I'll suggest that to her, though she may have already thought of that herself." Barney started to rise from her seat, but Allie reached across the small table to place a hand on her arm.

"Wait until after you've finished eating."

Degan appeared with their meals, and the two women ate almost in silence, each with her own thoughts, Barney obviously still perturbed about the status of her favorite restaurant and Allie focusing on not looking over Barney's shoulder in Ben's direction.

Who was the dark-haired woman? Allie hadn't seen her around before. An old girlfriend? A new girlfriend? She tried to push the thought away by telling herself she really didn't care whom he was with or what he did. She'd made a mistake—yes, she had—and she'd been the first to admit it. She'd done everything she could to apologize, but he'd thrown her apology back at her. He'd forfeited his right to her friendship, if that was what had been building between them. He could date every woman over the age of consent for all she cared.

She unconsciously flipped her ponytail and savagely speared a green bean on her plate while she thought about how little she cared.

"I'm going to run in the back and talk to Judy again." Barney pushed back her chair.

"You finished that whole thing already?" Allie stared at the remains of Barney's fish, which consisted of the head, a long string of bones, and the tail.

"It was a small trout. I won't be long. Order me a coffee, please. And take a look at the dessert menu and order us something from there."

"Wait, I don't know what you want."

"But you know what I like." Barney got up and headed to the back room.

Allie finished her dinner, once again resorting to her phone lest she glance at the third table from hers. Degan stopped by to clear their dishes and bring the dessert menu. Allie ordered their coffees, and moments later, Degan returned with two dark green mugs with the Green Brier logo. Allie took as long as she possibly could to look over that night's offerings.

What was Barney doing back there with Judy? How long could it possibly take to make a simple suggestion?

After Degan's third stop at the table to see if Allie'd made a decision, she ordered two peach cobblers and hoped Barney'd hurry back. Allie added cream and sugar to her coffee and focused on drinking it for another five minutes or so. Finally, when she was just about to go to the office herself to see what was going on, Allie glanced up to see Barney coming her way. This time, how-ever, her aunt was smiling—glowing, even.

She must have talked Judy into keeping the restaurant open. Good for her, Allie thought.

"Success?" Allie asked as Barney took her place at the table once more.

"Yes. And it's going to be a wonderful adventure." Barney's eyes were sparkling.

"What? A wonderful adventure for who?" Allie slowed her at-tack on her cobbler so Barney could catch up. "This is delicious, by the way. Do they make this here?"

"An adventure for all of us," Barney told her. "Judy pays a local woman to make the desserts and bring them in. Always delicious."

"Go back to *us*." Allie's fork stopped halfway to her mouth. "Define *us*."

"Us. We." Barney took a bite of the cobbler. "Oh, this is fabu-lous. We'll have to keep her on."

"Barney." Allie pushed her plate to one side and rested her forearms on the table. "Us? We? Adventure? Please tell me you didn't offer to babysit the Goodbye while Judy's in New Mexico."

"Of course not." Barney took another bite. "I bought it."

"You *bought* . . ." The words died in Allie's throat.

"This wonderful café." Barney waved her fork around. "Well, I haven't actually bought it yet. We have to go through all the things one does when one buys a property. But yes. The Goodbye Café is going to have a new owner. Me."

For a moment, Allie thought her head was going to explode, and she fought to put words into a coherent sentence.

"Barney, why would you want to do this?"

"Because someone has to, and the sooner the better. I'm here. I can do it sooner."

"Judy could sell it to someone else. It doesn't have to be you."

"If she puts it on the market, it will sit vacant until a buyer is found." She spoke slowly and deliberately as if addressing a young child. "Which will not only deprive the town of the café for an undetermined amount of time, but will also drive the price down. Judy has owned the Goodbye forever. She's worked very hard to make it the wonderful place it is. She should get fair market price. She should not have to take a loss."

"Why are you assuming no one else would pay her what it's worth? Maybe there are other people in town who value the café as much as you do."

"Well, I'm sure there are many who value it as much, who have as many good memories here as I have. The difference between them and me is that I can afford to pay cash for the place and Judy can leave without a sale hanging over her head."

"But are you sure you want to do this at—" Allie stopped in midsentence. The words on the tip of her tongue would not be well received.

"At my age?" Barney arched an eyebrow and quietly placed her fork on her plate. "Seriously, Allie?"

"I didn't mean . . . well, it's a lot of work, I'm sure. I just meant are you sure you want to take on all that work and responsibility after we just talked about how good it feels for you not to have the responsibility, that's all."

"I'm quite capable of running a business. I ran a bank for many, many years, and did so quite successfully. If I want to spend some of my money to buy something that will bring me a great deal of pleasure, I'm going to do it." She pushed her chair back from the table. "Besides, I have three able-bodied nieces living with me. I'll have all the help I need."

Barney stood and lifted her bag off the back of her chair. She signaled Degan. "You can give the bill to my niece."

And with that, Barney swept from the Goodbye.

"Oh crap," Allie muttered as she dug her wallet from her bag. "Me and my big mouth."

Degan handed her the bill, and Allie did a quick calculation of the tip. Before she could count out what she owed, a shadow fell across the table.

"You just can't seem to help yourself, can you?"

Allie didn't need to look up to know it was Ben. While he may not have heard everything, he'd apparently heard enough to know she and Barney had had words.

"And it would be your business because . . . ?" She opened her wallet and took out the appropriate cash without looking up.

"Barney is one of my favorite people. I hate to see her upset."

"Family business, Sheriff. Butt out." She knew her insistence on deliberately misstating his title no longer amused him—of course she knew he was chief of police—if in fact it ever had, but she didn't care.

"Allie . . ." His voice lowered and deepened at the same time.

"Excuse me. I need to go and you're in my way." She stood, and until he took two steps back, they were almost face-to-face. They stared at each other for a very long moment.

"Ben?" Ben's date had apparently been headed to the door but doubled back when she realized he wasn't with her.

"He's all yours." Allie stepped around him, handed Degan the check and the cash, and left without looking back.

Anger and frustration quickened her steps, so she arrived at the house before she cooled off. Rather than go inside and face an angry Barney, Allie walked up the driveway and into the backyard and plunked down on one of the lounges. Her first impulse was to go up to her room and take a few quick sips from her vodka stash. But Nikki would be home sometime soon, and there was no way she was going to let her daughter see her tipsy or worse. As hard as it was to resist that deep-seated pull, even knowing how a few drinks would take the edge off, she wasn't going to risk it. Besides, she would be back at the Sugarhouse in the morning, painting the intricately traced designs, and that was no work for shaking hands.

And there was some small amount of pride in feeling she'd overcome something that was so strong, yet so destructive to everything that was important to her. Not just Nikki, but her relationships with Barney—such as it was at that moment—Des, and Cara, who was the only one who shared her secret. She hadn't intended on showing that side of her to anyone, but one night a few months ago, she'd overdone it, and when Cara tried to awaken her, she'd been unresponsive. Eventually Allie had come around, but Cara had warned her in no uncertain terms that if it ever happened again, she'd call 911 without hesitation, and whatever the repercussions might be, Allie would have to deal with them head-on, alone. Since then, Allie'd been very careful about what she drank, and when.

She'd also noticed that she was better able to reason when she was sober. Who would have guessed?

Right now she needed her wits about her. She'd offended Barney and wanted to apologize before the wound caused by her unintended remarks began to fester. Allie wasn't accustomed to apologizing, but she was learning that there were times when you had to put your own feelings aside for the sake of people you cared about. And she cared very deeply for Barney.

Allie stared up at the back of the beautiful house her aunt had opened to her and her sisters, the house she hadn't known about before they'd arrived on her doorstep, suitcases in hand. Barney'd known they were coming, of course, but she hadn't met them, and couldn't have known what she was getting into. Allie and Des had grown up in a mansion in Beverly Hills, where luxury was a given, due to her father's success as an agent to the stars, and her mother's own stardom when she was young, before alcohol had gotten its teeth into her and her reputation among the producers in Hollywood had gone from "difficult to work with" to an automatic "don't even bother." But Allie'd never lived in a house like the Hudson mansion. A glorious Victorian, with all the frills and delightful touches of that era, it was also a warm and welcoming home thanks to Barney. There were always fresh flowers in the house and piles of books everywhere, and comfortable furniture that even Buttons, the dog Des had rescued, was invited to curl up on now and then. There were meals around the kitchen table—mostly prepared by Barney herself—where the conversation flowed from one topic to the next, no limitation on subject or point of view. Barney had opened not only her home but her heart to her nieces and had shared her life with them.

In the home Allie and Des had grown up in, there'd been a cook who prepared adult meals even when the girls had been small. There'd rarely been anyone other than the two of them at the table at mealtime, and when their mother was present, there was little conversation, because their mother had very little interest in her children, very little interest in anything that didn't directly pertain to her. Except, of course, when Des had her own TV show and Nora got to be the stage mother in charge of the girl who starred in *Des Does It All*. By that time, Nora's own career was nonexistent, and her only tie to the stardom she so desperately craved was through her young daughter. The fact that Des hated being on TV had never been a concern to Nora, nor had she even noticed Allie's growing resentment of Des's success. It was the height of irony that Allie would have given anything to have had her own TV show, but she'd been born without a lick of talent, while Des, so very talented, hated everything about it. The resentment had driven a wedge between the two sisters that they'd only recently dealt with. The Hudson home West Coast style was far from a happy one.

Allie watched the light in the kitchen go out and moments later a lamp's glow shine through the sitting room window. She thought about Barney's life until now. Years before, her fiancé, Gil Wheeler, had died when he'd fallen from the rocks overlooking the falls for which the town had been named. She'd been single all her life, and as far as Allie knew, no one had ever shared that house once her family was gone. Barney had many friends, and even now gave her all to the community. But there must have been times when loneliness set in, nights when she wandered from room to room, unable to settle herself, much the way Allie herself had done after Nikki left their home to live with Clint during the week. How had Barney coped? How had she spent her holidays and whom did she turn to in the middle of the night when she needed comfort or guidance? Had she been happy? Would she have been more content had she sold this place and bought a smaller home for herself?

Allie sighed as she watched the fireflies dance through the increasing darkness, knowing she couldn't avoid going inside and doing what she had to do to try to make things right with Barney. She just wished the right words would come to her, and so far they hadn't.

She turned at the sound of a car in the driveway and flinched. She should have gone straight into the house and apologized while it was just the two of them. She craned her neck to see who was the first of the crew to arrive home.

Joe's pickup truck came into view and parked next to the carriage house. Allie was pretty sure it would be a while before Cara jumped out and headed for the house. Lately, Cara had spent as many nights at Joe's house as she'd spent at the family home. It would be no surprise to anyone if Cara decided to stay in Hidden Falls with Joe once the theater was ready to reopen.

Besides, though Allie and Cara had not discussed it, there was talk about Cara turning the first floor of the carriage house into a yoga studio much like the one she'd owned in Devlin's Light on the Delaware Bay, where she'd been born and raised.

Allie started to rise, the window on private time with Barney closing rapidly, but she'd underestimated how long it would take Cara and Joe to say good night. Before she could stand, Allie was making her way along the path to the house, stopping once to wave goodbye to Joe as he turned the truck around.

"Hey, whatcha doing out here alone in the almost-dark?" Cara asked when she spied Allie sitting on the lounge. "Allie? You okay? What are you doing?"

"Hiding."

Cara laughed. "From what?"

"From Barney. And it's not funny."

Cara sat on the edge of the lounge cushion. "What's going on?"

"I stuck my foot in my mouth. I know. Shock, right?"

"There are some things you do better than most people, agreed." Cara pulled a leg up under her and asked, "What happened?"

"Judy Worrell's moving to New Mexico to take care of her parents." Allie blurted, "Barney's buying the Goodbye Café."

When Cara didn't respond, Allie poked her leg with her foot. "Say something."

"My mind is still trying to wrap itself around Barney wanting to buy the Goodbye."

"Not *wanting to*. She's agreed to do it."

"What? For real?" Cara's eyes grew wide.

Allie nodded. "We went there for dinner tonight. She went into the office with Judy, and when she came out, Barney was grinning from ear to ear. She told me 'we' were in for an adventure. *We*. As in *us*. You, me. Des. Nikki. We're going to have some swell fun running a restaurant."

"Why would Barney do that? You'd think at seventy-something—do we even know how old she is?—she'd want to stay retired and not have any daily obligations again."

"That's pretty much what I said that got me into so much trouble. She snapped at me and left the restaurant and stuck me with the check."

"So unlike her," a dismayed Cara said.

"I know, right?"

"But did she say why she did it? She must have had a good reason."

"Pretty much that she feels she owes it to the community to keep the restaurant open. You know how she's always felt this heavy civic responsibility."

"Yes, but buying a demanding business . . . unless she's planning on hiring someone to run it." Cara paused. "Which would be so uncharacteristic for Barney, who's used to being in control. Who *thrives* on control."

"It's the responsibility thing. She doesn't want the café to be closed while Judy tries to sell it—she says the town needs the Goodbye open, it's everyone's favorite place to eat and to meet up with friends, yada yada. The other part of that is she's afraid Judy won't get what she deserves from the sale if the place sits on the market for however long it would take to sell it. That the price will drop, and Judy will end up taking whatever someone is willing to pay for it."

"And she doesn't think anyone else in town would step up?"

"Apparently she isn't willing to take that chance."

"Boy, that Barney." Cara bit a cuticle thoughtfully. "Have you ever known anyone like her?"

Allie shook her head. "It's hard to believe anyone is that altruistic, isn't it? I mean, she could wait a few months and get a better price, but she's more concerned about being fair to her friend."

They sat in silence for a moment, both contemplating the mystery that was Barney Hudson.

"She said so many of the town's memories are there."

"Then there's the answer. She's going to protect the Goodbye the way she's protected this house and Hudson Lake and the bank and the park and the rest of the town. The way Reynolds Hudson protected the men who worked in his coal mines and their families." Cara smiled. "And us, now that she has us."

"Well, she's planning on using us to work at the Goodbye, so don't get too sentimental. When was the last time you waited tables?"

"When I was sixteen. And I wasn't very good at it," Cara admitted. "You?"

"You're kidding, right? How 'bout never?" Allie pulled her knees up on the lounge. "Before you came home tonight, I was thinking about Barney living alone here for so many years. Why didn't she sell this big house, move into something smaller, more manageable for a single woman?"

"Because she understood what it meant to the town to have a Hudson living here," Cara said without hesitation.

"That's what I think, too. She understood her place in Hidden Falls. She still does." Allie swung her legs over the side of the lounge and stood.

"So what are you going to say to her?"

"What I should have said back at the Goodbye when she told me she'd just bought it."

Allie went into the house and followed the trail of light down the long hallway to the sitting room. She stood at the threshold, her hand poised to knock, when Barney looked up at her expectantly.

"May I come in?" Allie asked.

Barney nodded and closed the book she was reading after marking her page with a folded piece of paper.

"I owe you an apology." Allie stepped into the room and sat on the chair opposite Barney.

"Yes, you do." Barney's voice held no reproach, no animosity, no bitterness. Just her usual matter-of-fact, speak-the-truth tone.

"I'm sorry. I had no right to question you. Not what you do with your life, nor what you do with your money. I think it's admirable what you're doing for Judy and for Hidden Falls."

"What exactly do you think I'm doing?"

"I think you're taking care of business, like you always have done."

At that, Barney smiled. "I couldn't have said it better myself. Thank you for understanding."

"It took me a while to see the light. But I get it, and while it doesn't excuse what I said earlier, and it probably doesn't matter, but for what it's worth, I'm really proud of you." Allie swallowed a lump in her throat. "I'm proud to be your niece."

Barney looked down at her hands that gripped the book. A moment later, she raised her head, her eyes moist. "That may well be one of the nicest things anyone has ever said to me."

"Thank you. Am I forgiven for tossing in my two cents where they weren't needed?"

"Of course you are." Barney opened her arms and beckoned Allie into a hug. "Which doesn't mean that you won't be working your butt off at the Goodbye."

"Barney, I don't know anything about restaurants or waiting tables or cooking."

Barney smiled broadly.

"Neither do I, dear. So unless one of your sisters has some experience we can draw from, we'll all be learning together."

CHAPTER THREE

"Really? We own the Goodbye Café?" Nikki squealed when she heard the news, which Barney shared as one by one everyone arrived home and filed into the sitting room. "I *love* the Goodbye! They have the best fries!"

Nikki immediately hugged Barney around the neck.

"Aunt Barney, you are the coolest person in the world. I love you so much! You are the best!"

"Well, I love you, too, Nikki." Barney laughed. "And I hope your enthusiasm is contagious, because it's a done deal as far as I'm concerned."

"When is it ours?" Nikki wanted to know.

"Well, there are legal issues to be dealt with, but I feel I can safely say the Goodbye Café will be the property of the Hudson family within two weeks. There's no mortgage because I'm going to pay cash. Of course, there will be inspections to be made and certificates to be issued, but we'll work all that out as quickly as possible. Judy's kept up with the maintenance and the kitchen inspections and whatnot, so we should be able to close on it rather quickly." Barney's optimism was showing.

Nikki, Allie noticed, had no trouble including herself when it came to the ownership of the popular café.

Cara had also hugged Barney after she'd been told. "What a

wonderful friend you are to Judy. I'm sure she appreciates you stepping right up and making an offer. And good for you for finding an outlet for all that energy of yours."

Allie wanted to smack her. *Way to make me look like the family bitch. Which, on second thought, I probably am.*

Des, on the other hand, not having had the benefit of speaking with Allie ahead of time, stared blankly at Barney.

"What?" She frowned. "No. Why?"

Allie could have kissed her. *Way to take the onus off me.*

After Barney went through the events at the restaurant earlier that evening, Des said, "Oh. Well. Congratulations, I guess."

The five settled into the cozy sitting room making their plans for the café. Barney being Barney, she drew all of them into what she referred to as Project Goodbye. Allie sat in one of the wing chairs Barney recently had re-covered in a lively floral print, Cara in the other, while Des and Nikki sat on the floor in front of the love seat occupied by Barney and Buttons. On the hearth in front of the stone fireplace sat an old stone crock filled with deep blue hydrangeas from the backyard. Family photos in silver frames—several taken since Barney's nieces had arrived in Hidden Falls—graced the mantel next to several sets of tall brass candleholders. Cara had turned off the overhead light—a small crystal chandelier—in favor of the table lamps with their deep rose silk shades.

"Of course, I'm going to need help, girls." Barney hadn't even tried to deny the facts. "I ran a bank for years, but I have no clue how to run a restaurant."

"Café," Nikki interjected. "It's small and pretty and friendly, and *restaurant* sounds big and impersonal."

"All right, then. We'll refer to it as the café." Barney smiled. Nikki always went to the heart of every matter, and Barney obviously thought everything the girl said was golden and brilliant. She never even tried to pretend otherwise. "So I think we need to start out this venture with everyone knowing what part they're going to play."

"Wait, didn't we just do this with the theater? Des, you're the money girl, Cara takes care of the physical renovation, and I got to do the artsy décor stuff?" Allie frowned. She knew what Barney was doing by trying to draw them all in. "And aren't we all free to leave and go back to our lives once the theater is declared fit to open?"

Barney shot her a dirty look. "Of course. But right now you're all still here, and you're going to be here for a while yet, so you might as well pitch in and help an old lady out."

"Wait, did you just call yourself an old lady?" Allie's eyes widened. "After the lecture about never old, senile, geriatric? That was you, wasn't it?"

"I said *you* couldn't say it. However, I'm not above playing the age card when I need to," Barney said dryly. "To continue, I'm having a meeting with Judy at the café tomorrow morning around nine. I'd like you all to be there." Barney's gaze went around the room, pausing on each of her nieces. "Des, I'd like you to take notes on the financial end. The expenses, payroll, how to reorder stock items. We'll have to hire an accountant, but I think we need to know all the ins and outs first. Cara, I'd like for you to take note of the physical layout and see if there are areas that need some attention. Especially the floor." Barney paused. "I've always hated that yellow vinyl floor. See if there's anything we can do about that and how much it will cost. Ask Joe to look at the roof and the mechanics. I'm pretty sure everything's in proper working order, but let's get that confirmed. Also, I always thought something could be done to make the outside a little more appealing."

A somewhat awkward pause followed. Finally, Allie said, "So what plans do you have for me?"

Barney smiled broadly. "I'm glad you asked. You're going to be in charge of personnel."

Before Allie could respond, Des laughed. "You're kidding, right? You want to put Miss Personality, Miss I-Never-Met-a-Person-I-Didn't-Want-to-Insult, Miss—"

"Thank you, Des, for breaking down my people skills so succinctly." Allie glared at her sister from across the table.

"Sorry, Allie, but even you have to admit you . . ." Des cleared her throat. "Come on a little strong sometimes. Suffer fools, oh, not at all. Have no patience with anyone who isn't you."

"That's not fair, Aunt Des," Nikki said softly. "My mom is not like any of those things."

"Maybe not to you, but, honey, the rest of the world isn't her offspring." It was obvious Des was trying to walk her words back just a little for her niece's sake, but it was too late.

"My mom is the greatest." Nikki got up from the floor to walk around the table and stand behind Allie's chair, then draped her arms around her mother's shoulders. "My mom is the best mom and I love her."

"Love you, too, sugar." Allie's heart melted and dripped into a huge puddle on the floor.

"Honey, we all love your mother, but that's not what we're discussing here," Des told her.

"All right. Enough." Allie threw her hands up. "I accept the position of being the people-pleasing person at the Goodbye. But only after my painting in the theater is done for the day." She turned to Barney. "And I want to go on record here and now that as soon as the ceiling is done, as soon as the renovations are completed, I am outta here."

"Understood. Of course, Allie. We all know you have no intention of staying in Hidden Falls any longer than you have to." Barney's face was unreadable, but her voice held a tinge of resignation. "But since you're going to be in charge of the waitstaff, I want you to learn how to use that newfangled ordering thing they have. It's like a computer that sends the orders directly into the kitchen. I'm not sure what else it does, except that Judy said she paid a fortune for it."

"I'll try not to scare the help," Allie said.

"I appreciate that," Barney replied.

"So what exactly do you want me to do as far as the staff

is concerned?" Allie patted Nikki's hands, and Nikki bent down and kissed her cheek before returning to her spot on the carpet.

"I'd like you to interview all the employees, from the cooks to the waitstaff. I want you to analyze what they do and what we need, review Judy's performance reviews—assuming she did them and knows where she put them—watch to see who could use a little reminder about manners and that sort of thing. I want every one of our customers to feel comfortable from the moment they come into our place. Just like our home." Barney hastened to add, "Not that I don't feel that way when I'm there, but I've been going to the Goodbye for many years, so maybe I don't notice things that could use improvement."

"What does that leave for me to do?" Nikki asked. "What's my job going to be?"

"Hmmm, well, I'm not sure you're quite old enough to actually work, Nikki. The legal age used to be sixteen but that may have changed."

"I'll check that out. I'm going to be fifteen soon."

"I know, sweet pea. I'm sure we can find things for you to do." Barney reached over to squeeze Nikki's hand.

"I'll do whatever you need," she said as she typed a note into her phone. "I want to be part of it. I'll do what no one else wants to do. I'll take inventory on stuff. I'll help clear tables and wash the floor. I'll iron napkins."

Barney smiled once again. "I imagine there will be a laundry service for such things, but we can check it out. I'm positive you will make an important contribution, and you will of course be a part of whatever we do. Always."

"This is so exciting." Nikki's phone was still in her hand and she began texting wildly. A moment later, her phone pinged, and she grinned. "Mark thinks you're so cool, Aunt Barney. He said he'll help out in any way he can." She looked around the room. "He's the nicest guy I ever met. He's so kind and thoughtful."

Allie felt the stab of concern she always felt when Nikki's boyfriend was mentioned. It wasn't that she didn't want her daughter to have a normal teenage life. She just wished she could postpone all that girl-boy stuff until Nikki was, oh, maybe twenty-five or thirty.

"He is a very dear boy. Please tell him we'll certainly call upon him if we need him." Barney turned back to the others. "Any questions?"

"Probably a million, but I'm still processing the fact that you're actually buying that place," Des said.

"'That place' represents a special part of Hidden Falls history. One I hope you'll come to appreciate." Barney stood and stretched. "Well, there's that early-morning meeting tomorrow and it's way past my bedtime. Anyone who thinks they might learn something from coming with me is certainly invited. Up to you. Good night, girls."

"Night, Barney." The chorus followed her out the door, leaving her nieces behind.

"Anyone else really think that invitation was optional?" Cara said.

"I think she made it pretty clear once she started handing out assignments," Des agreed. "So I guess I'll see you all bright and early."

"You'll definitely see me," Nikki said. "I am going to learn everything there is to know about running the café. Maybe someday I'll even run the Goodbye. Wouldn't that be so cool? If I stayed in Hidden Falls and ran the café when the rest of you are too . . ." The word "old" hung over the table. "Too *tired* of doing it and want to do something else."

Without waiting for comments, Nikki kissed her two aunts and her mother and dashed out of the room.

"There goes a future president of this fine country," Cara said.

"She's got that diplomacy thing down pat, that's for sure," Des agreed. "That last-minute substitution of *tired* for *old* was pretty damned slick."

"Agreed, but do you really think Nikki's going to be spending her entire life in Hidden Falls when she has the whole world to choose from?" Allie'd stood, and before Des or Cara could respond, she said, "Yeah. Me, neither. See you tomorrow, girls."

Allie set her alarm for even earlier than usual, even though she and Nikki'd sat up talking until two in the morning, not because the weather forecast called for more record heat, which it did. She simply wanted to avoid all the chatter about the Goodbye Café and who was doing what. She promised her daughter if she finished painting that day's section of the theater's ceiling early enough she'd join them. But she didn't expect the meeting to run that long. After all, she figured there couldn't be much to talk about. You have the menu and the cooks take care of that. You take the receipts to the bank and then you write checks to cover your expenses. You figure out how many servers you need for each shift and you hire that many. You smile when someone comes into the restaurant and get them seated. She was pretty sure all that couldn't take more than two hours at the very most, so they'd be finished before she left the theater.

She was wrong.

The section of ceiling she'd planned to work on had three major components, two of which had been badly damaged and consequently had been obliterated when the plaster was repaired. It took time to perfectly position the stencils she'd made and to paint each detail to match the original. It was tedious work, and her focus was on that bit of the ceiling directly over her head, but when she was finished, she leaned back as far as she safely could to assess her work. It was, she decided, as close to the artist's free-hand as anyone could get, and she felt a flush of accomplishment and pride. Other than her daughter, nothing in her life gave her the thrill of doing what she'd known she could do. The theater's ceiling would be lovingly repaired, and her work would stand as long as the theater.

Or, she thought wryly, until another hundred-year storm blew shingles off the roof again.

After selecting the next day's area of concentration, Allie packed up her supplies and started down the side of the scaffold. She still broke into a sweat and her heart still pounded wildly, much to her annoyance. She'd convinced herself that after she'd made the climb up and down several times the height would no longer bother her. She'd been at it for over a week and there'd been no sign her fear was diminishing. Hence the "don't look down" song.

"Maybe tomorrow," she said aloud as her feet touched the floor. She took a deep breath and headed for the exit without looking at the ceiling again. The less time she spent thinking about how far up she'd been, the happier she'd be.

It was already late morning when she emerged into an overcast day. She glanced up the street to the café. Surely the meeting was over by now. She should just go home. But there was no harm in checking. At least she could say she'd stopped by.

The hostess—not Degan today, she noted—recognized her as being a customer who'd been in several times before, so she greeted Allie with a welcoming smile and a menu.

"Oh, I don't need a table. I was just checking to see if Barney—er, Bonnie Hudson was still here," Allie told her.

"She and several others are still in the office."

"Oh great. I'll just go on back."

"I'm sorry. Mrs. Worrell said she didn't want to be disturbed by anyone for any reason unless the building caught fire or the cook walked out." The hostess—a woman in her late twenties—wore a name tag, and Allie glanced at it

"Look, Ginger, I may be late to the party, but I'm part of that group that's meeting back there in Judy's office. So I'd appreciate it if you moved aside."

Ginger shook her head. "Mrs. Worrell didn't mention that anyone would be coming late."

"Oh, for the love of . . ." Allie pulled her phone out of her bag and sent a text to Des, who immediately poked her head out and beckoned Allie, who walked around the hostess. "Honestly," she told Des, "you'd think you guys were working on the nuclear code, or the formula for turning straw into gold, the way that woman is guarding the door."

"She's doing her job." Des closed the door behind them. "Judy told her not to disturb us. We didn't think to leave word that you might be coming. But she's doing what you want your employees to do: She's following her boss's instructions. I'd think that would be a big plus for Ginger when it comes time to evaluate her. Which you will be doing sooner rather than later."

"Maybe."

Allie greeted Judy, then took the only unoccupied seat before accepting the offer of iced tea from Judy, who poured into a glass from a pitcher that sat on the sideboard next to a tray of baked goods. Everyone, even Nikki, had a notebook in front of them. Allie dug around in her bag hoping she had something to write on, but finally gave up. She felt like she was back in college and had just failed the first basic requirement of her first class on day one.

"So you always order from the same food distributor?" Des eased back into the conversation they'd evidently been having before Allie's arrival.

Judy nodded. "Though in the summer and fall, I buy as much as I can from the local farms. There's a list of the farmers I've been doing business with in that packet I gave each of you."

"You must have stayed up all night putting this together," Barney commented as she shuffled through the folder Judy'd had ready for them.

"Pretty much," Judy admitted. "I'm concerned about getting to my dad before something dire happens, so I wanted to give you as much information as possible. Of course, you all know you can call me anytime if you have questions or concerns about, well, about anything." She turned to Barney and touched her arm. "I can't even begin to tell you how grateful I am that you decided to buy the café. I'd hate with all my heart to see it closed or to sell it to someone who doesn't have an attachment to it, or someone who'd open something unsavory in this space. Like a massage parlor where they offer more than massages. I know that's silly. It's just a building, but . . ."

"It's not silly, Judy. The Goodbye has been part of my life for as long as I can remember. This was the first restaurant my parents ever took me to." Barney wiped an emotional tear from her face. "Gil and I had dinner here the night before he died. You can talk to anyone in town, and they'll have a special memory here."

"I'll bet they're not all good memories, though," Nikki piped up. "Otherwise, it wouldn't have been called the *Goodbye*."

"Oh, that's mostly just local gossip," Judy said, suppressing a smile. "There might have been a few couples over the years who broke up here, but that's all."

"Then who decided to call it the Goodbye instead of the Green Brier?" Nikki asked.

Judy thought for a moment, then laughed. "Probably one of those who did break up over dinner."

"We're going to keep the original name, right?" Des asked.

"The sign out front says the Green Brier Café, so yes, we're keeping the name for the sake of the tourists and the newcomers to town," Barney said. "But it'll still be the Goodbye to the locals."

"Tourists?" Allie frowned. "Do tourists ever come to Hidden Falls?"

"Only if they're passing through on their way to one of the lake communities, or the ski lodges in the winter," Judy admitted.

"That's going to change once the theater reopens." Barney spoke with confidence. "Maybe we'll even do something with our lake eventually."

"Oh, like maybe a campground?" Nikki's imagination went to work. "We could do so many cool things at a lake!"

"Perhaps someday, dear, but right now we have to focus on the café." Barney turned to Judy. "How do you decide which waitresses work which shifts?"

Judy began to answer as Allie's mind began to wander in the

direction of her daughter. It had always been Nikki's nature to jump into everything, feetfirst. Allie could see how her daughter would be excited about being a part of planning something like a campground that had some form of attraction. It had been on the tip of Allie's tongue to remind Nikki she'd be back in school in California by the end of the summer, but there was no need to remind her.

". . . don't you think, Allie?" Barney was asking.

"I'm sorry, what?" Allie snapped back into the meeting.

"I said today would be a good time for you to meet the staff. Well, today and this evening. Judy wants to leave as soon as possible, so there's little time to waste. I suggested that you dash home, clean up, then come on back and take the hostess shift for the afternoon and evening."

"Oh, well . . ." Allie felt trapped. All eyes were on her.

"I'll come, too," Nikki told her without waiting for Allie to fully respond. "We can talk to all the people and let them know that we're going to be the new owners."

"I think we should leave that part to Judy, dear." Barney glanced at her old friend, who once again had tears in her eyes. "People are going to want to know what's going on, and I think Judy'd like to have the opportunity to explain why she's leaving and that the reins had been passed into other hands."

"But everyone knows you, Aunt Barney. It's not like you're a stranger," Nikki said.

"True, but we're going to let Judy handle what she wants to tell people. It's still her place until the papers are signed."

"I appreciate that, Barney. It's going to be hard enough, but you're right. Longtime customers are going to want to hear it from me." The palms of Judy's hands smacked lightly on the table. "So. We'll do this. Allie, Barney's right. The sooner you start as hostess, the sooner you'll get to know the regulars, where they like to sit, which waitresses they prefer. That's going to take some time, because different folks make a habit of coming on different days. And since repeat business is what a restaurant is built on, you're going to need those people to keep coming back. Best to get to know them as soon as possible. I'll be here with you, so I can show you the ropes."

Allie nodded and tried not to convey the feeling that she'd just been sentenced to a form of punishment she'd rather avoid. She got up and poured a glass of iced tea, lingering over the plate of brownies and lemon squares.

Allie'd tasted a lemon square and took a second bite. They were the perfect blend of tart and sweet. "Judy, did you make the lemon squares?"

"Oh, no." Judy turned to Barney. "You know Justine Kennedy, Barney. She married Stephen Kennedy and they moved to Clarks Summit. He died a few years ago and she moved back here to her parents' house on High Street after they passed away."

"I do know who she is, but I can't say I *know* her, though I do recall she married Stephen," Barney replied thoughtfully. "I wasn't aware she did all the baking."

"You went to school together, though, didn't you? Weren't you in the same grade?" Judy asked.

Barney shook her head. "Justine was two years younger. She was Justine Mitchell then. Her sister, Sharon, was in my class." Barney paused. "Sharon and I were friends in grade school, but not so much after we got into high school."

"Why?" Nikki asked. "Why weren't you friends in high school?"

"Oh, some petty nonsense. Silly high school drama." Barney dismissed the matter with a wave of her hand.

"Like, you both liked the same boy?" Nikki persisted. "And he liked one of you better and you stopped talking to each other and then she talked behind your back?"

"Something like that. It was a long time ago. I don't recall all the details."

Allie watched her daughter's face as Nikki seemed to think through Barney's high school social drama. It occurred to her that Nikki hadn't mentioned her best friend in California, Courtney, in at least a week. *Could mean something, could mean nothing.* She'd have to ask, but discreetly lest Nikki feel interrogated. Allie was finding it was a thin line to walk between caring parent and *prying* parent.

"Anyway, Justine does all the baking except for the breads. I get those from Zehren's Bakery. That's all on the list I made for you. But I'll talk to Justine when she comes in this week and fill her in on what's going on. I'll tell her she can expect to hear from you, Barney."

"Great. I hope we can continue the relationship. I'd hate to have the clientele depend on me for their brownie fix. I'm afraid I'm not very good." Barney turned to her nieces. "Girls? Any bakers here?"

"Nope." Allie finished the lemon square.

"Don't look at me," Des told her.

"Granola is about all I know how to make," Cara said. "I'd be happy to make some of that for breakfasts if you wanted, but that's the extent of it for me. Sorry."

"I've made brownies lots of times, Aunt Barney. I can make them for the café," Nikki volunteered. "They're really easy. The mix comes in a box and you just add water and an egg."

"I think we'll be wanting baked goods made from scratch, sweet pea, but thank you. And we'll certainly keep that in mind should we have a brownie emergency," Barney assured her. "But yes, Justine Kennedy it is, then. Judy, I'd appreciate it if you let her know she'll be hearing from me."

"I'm adding it to my list of things to do before the end of the week." Judy jotted something down on the tablet, then looked up. "She usually brings in whatever she's made twice each week. Tomorrow would be her day. Sometimes she drops things off the night before if she has something else to do, but it's usually first thing in the morning. I'll have to remember to call her."

The meeting lasted another fifty minutes, and when it became apparent they weren't going to be able to cover everything in a few hours, Judy suggested they reconvene later to finish going over the business end of things.

"Good idea. I've been sitting so long my legs are stiff." Barney rose.

"Mine, too." Judy stood at the same time. "How about we meet back here at around six, so you can meet the staff that's working the dinner shift?"

"We'll be here." Barney gathered her folder and her notes and looked to the others.

"I can be back," Cara said.

Des nodded. "Me, too."

"Then we're good." Barney followed Judy from the room.

Des turned to Cara. "I thought you were seeing Joe tonight."

"I am. He's coming over around eight with his HVAC guy to give Barney an estimate for the air-conditioning, but we should be back by then. I can call him if it looks like we'll be longer than that. After the HVAC guy leaves, Joe's going to take a walk-through of the carriage house with me."

Allie's head shot up. "Ah, so it's happening."

Cara smiled. "I'm playing with the idea of maybe—I said *maybe*—using it for a yoga studio. Barney said she didn't care since she wasn't planning on using the space."

"So you're staying." Allie grinned. "Looks like Barney'll have one of her girls sticking around after all."

"I'm not sure. I still have some reservations, but I thought maybe I should just see if the building could be retrofitted at minimum costs. It doesn't have heat or air-conditioning and the floor is concrete."

"I'll bet Joe will do it for the cost of materials. Anything to keep his sweetie in Hidden Falls." Des winked at Allie. "So when did you make the decision?"

"I haven't, I'm just exploring the possibility, that's all." Cara stuffed her folder into her tote bag. "I miss yoga. I do it every day in my room or in the hallway, but it's not the same as having a whole group. Plus I like teaching, and if I stay after the theater's finished, I'll need an income."

"What about your studio in Devlin's Light?" Des asked. "And your house?"

"I don't know. I can't sell that house. I never will. It was my mother's pride and joy. If nothing else, if I stay here, maybe I'll keep it for a summer place since it's at the beach. The studio . . ." Cara shrugged. "I could sell that. My assistant, Meredith, has been running it by herself since I've been here, and she's done a great job. I know she'd be first in line to make an offer, so maybe . . ." Cara covered her face with her hands. "I just don't know. It's too big a decision to make. What if no one in Hidden Falls wants to do yoga? What if things don't work out with Joe? What if—"

Allie slipped a hand over her sister's mouth.

"But what if you and Joe end up together? What if droves of people in town come banging on your door, begging for yoga lessons?" Allie stage-whispered in Cara's ear.

"Oh my God, look at you, being all supportive and positive." Des pretended to faint into the chair she'd earlier been sitting in.

"It was an aberration." Allie grinned and released Cara and swung her bag over her shoulder. "It probably won't happen again."

It was an eight-minute walk from the café to the Hudsons' house if one moved briskly, which Allie was doing in order to get ready for her shift as hostess in training and make it back to the café in time. She still couldn't believe she'd agreed to be part of something she thought was crazy. Barney would be eighty years old in a few years. How long did she really think she'd be working at the Goodbye? But she felt she did owe Barney something more than loyalty, so she went back to the house, up to her room, and had showered and dressed in no time.

"How do I look?" she asked as she stepped into the sitting room, where the others were busy planning. She'd pulled her hair over one shoulder and had put on just enough makeup to lend a little polish. She wore a white cotton shirt with short sleeves and black ankle-length pants and black sandals.

Des looked her over. "Like the hostess with the mostess."

"Professional," Cara added.

"You always look beautiful, Mom." Nikki nodded.

"A bit severe, but you'll do," Barney said.

"Severe?" Allie frowned and looked down at herself. "All the restaurant hostesses I've ever seen dress like this."

"Maybe a pink lipstick instead of that shrieking red," Cara suggested.

"You think this shrieks?" Allie opened her bag and took out the lipstick she'd used. "The Devil Wore Red. You think it's too much?"

Everyone nodded.

"I have the perfect shade, Mom. I'll be right back." Nikki jumped up and ran upstairs.

"I've looked forward to the day when I'd be sharing makeup and clothes and stuff with her since she was born," Allie told them. "Now that it's here, I'm not ready for it."

"It's only lipstick, Allie," Des reminded her. "She told me she's been wearing lipstick for the past year."

"Today lipstick, tomorrow stilettos." Allie sniffed.

Nikki dashed back into the room. "Here you go, Mom. It's called Pretty Posy." She took the top off the tube and handed it to Allie. "It's gorgeous, right?"

"Thank you, sweetie. Yes, it's just right." Allie went into the hallway and stood in front of the large mirror to apply the hot pink shade.

Nikki stood in the doorway watching. "It's perfect, Mom. It goes on a little bright, but see, it deepens to a darker pink."

"Hmmm. Not bad," Allie conceded. She handed the tube back to her daughter. "Thanks again."

Allie poked her head into the sitting room. "I'm off to my first lesson. I'm guessing today I'll learn to say, 'Hi. Welcome to the Green Brier. I'm Allie, your hostess.'"

"I don't think you have to introduce yourself," Des said, "but that wasn't a bad start. Smiling when you say welcome might be a nice touch, though."

Allie rolled her eyes and left the house, Barney's "We'll see you down there later" in her ears.

The entire time Allie was walking she was wondering how she'd gotten into such a situation. She'd never worked in a restaurant, not even back in her school days when it seemed everyone tried their hand at waitressing over one summer or another. She supposed she could have said no, but just imagining how Barney would react—not to mention Nikki—was enough to make her swallow her pride.

"Taking one for the team," she muttered as she opened the Goodbye's door and stepped inside, where Judy was waiting for her.

"Allie, thanks for coming back. I want to introduce you to the staff, and then we'll position you right here at the front desk so you can greet everyone who comes in. Degan works the desk three nights every week but almost never on the weekends. The other nights she's at school, so I usually take that shift."

Allie looked around the café, where only one table was occupied, a bald man who appeared to be in his seventies who was engrossed in the newspaper's crossword puzzle. Judy took her by the elbow and steered her into the kitchen, where she met the entire staff. The only name she remembered was the big man Judy called Chef George, the head cook, who was just starting to work on the dinner menu. There were three others who filled out the rest of the cooking staff and two young men who were at the sink in the back of the room washing dishes.

Name tags could help, Allie decided, making a mental note to discuss that with Barney. She couldn't keep referring to the staff as *the guy with the mustache* or *the woman with the legs that need shaving*.

"Now, there's really nothing to this part," Judy was saying as they returned to the front of the café. "You just need to make people feel welcome and at home. But it's important to refer to the seating chart before you take them to a table."

"Seating chart?" Allie felt confused. What restaurant had a seating chart?

"Yes. It's so you can balance the number of tables assigned to the waitstaff. It's standard procedure." Judy opened the center desk drawer and pulled out a sheet of paper. "We do one of these for every shift. This one's for tonight. These circles represent the tables, and you can see each one has an initial in it; the initials correspond to the staff on board tonight. See these with the M's? Those are Maddie's tables. Maddie is the short girl with the dark hair over there filling the water carafes at the station." Judy pointed out the tables that had been assigned to the two other waitresses, Carolee and Penny. "You try to make sure each girl has the same number of tables, got it? So that Maddie isn't working her butt off while Carolee is so bored she's watching videos on her phone."

Allie nodded. "Got it."

Sounds easy enough. Welcome people with a smile. Each waitress gets the same number of tables. Piece of cake.

For the first hour, it was that easy. She gave the first customers a table in Maddie's section, the second went to Carolee, and the next to arrive would be seated in Penny's section. Allie could do this in her sleep. Hell, Nikki could do this in her sleep.

The phone rang, and Judy answered.

"Let me take this in my office." Judy put the call on hold. To Allie she said, "You're doing great. I have to take this call, but I won't be long."

"Take your time," Allie told her. "I've got this."

And she did, for three couples who came in, and a foursome. It was the single diner who almost did her in.

"Well, well. Look who up and got herself a real job." Ben Haldeman was waiting at the desk when Allie returned after seating the last couple. He lowered his voice and whispered, "Not really suitable for a princess, but at least you don't have to get your hands dirty."

"Get off my back." Allie picked up a menu, determined to ignore his digs. "Is someone joining you?"

"Is it your business?"

"It is if you're going to want a table for two."

"Are there tables for one?" He made a quick survey of the room. "Looks like they all can accommodate two people. Or one."

"This way, please." She led him to a table in Penny's section, which was right next to the kitchen door.

"I'd rather sit by the window," he told her.

"Sorry. That's Carolee's section, and right now it's Penny's turn." She placed the menu on the table without further explanation. "Enjoy your dinner."

She walked away knowing he was still standing next to the table, knowing, too, that he was watching her. Finally, Penny went to the table and filled his water glass, making what Allie assumed was small talk. It gave her a perverse sort of pleasure to know that every time the kitchen door opened, a wave of heat and cooking smells would waft in Ben's direction. It was petty on her part—she acknowledged that—but she was fine with it. Had any other customer made the request for a different table, she would have gladly honored it.

She was still feeling the glow when the door opened slightly, and she turned to see a woman struggling to juggle several boxes and the door at the same time. Allie rushed to help, grabbing one box as it began to fall.

"Oh, thank you." The woman was almost as tall as Allie but not quite as slender. She appeared to be close to Barney's age and wore her short graying blond hair tucked behind her ears. Her sunglasses were still on her face when she turned to Allie. The woman paused for a very long moment, staring at Allie, a curious expression on her face.

"You're new here," she said.

"I am," Allie replied. "I'm Allie."

"Where's Judy?"

"She's in her office. May I tell her—"

"I'll tell her myself." The woman placed the boxes on the desk, and with one last glance over her shoulder in Allie's direction, she headed toward the back of the café. After knocking twice on the office door, she disappeared behind it.

A family of three came in and Allie showed them to the table next to the window that Ben had apparently had his eye on.

She went back to the desk, wondering what was in the boxes. The one on top had foil over the contents, and she couldn't help herself. She lifted the end of the foil and found one fat layer of gorgeous frosted brownies. She poked into the middle box and found lemon squares. "Oh, yum!"

She was just about to look into the box on the bottom when the office door opened and the woman—she had to be Justine, the baker—stormed out. She approached Allie with fire in her eyes, snatched up the three boxes, and pushed past Allie to get to the door. Allie tried to help her open it, but she shoved Allie's hand away and balanced the boxes in such a way as to open the door herself.

Allie turned to Judy, who'd followed the woman into the dining room.

Judy rested a hip against the top of the desk. "I think you might want to call Barney and tell her to pick up a few of those boxed brownie mixes. That was Justine, the baker. She just quit and took the desserts I ordered for the week with her."

Chapter Four

Barney arrived at the Goodbye after the dinner rush had abated. "I don't understand. Did she give a reason?"

Judy's expression was both anxious and chagrined, and it was clear she really didn't want to repeat what Justine had said. Reluctantly, she told Barney, "She said, 'I wouldn't bake a crumb for Barney Hudson.' I'm sorry, Barney, but that's what she said."

Barney rubbed her face with her hand. "I can't imagine why she would say such a thing. Why she would . . . well, it just doesn't make sense."

"Aunt Barney, you did say you and her sister used to be friends, then you weren't," Nikki reminded her.

"That was so petty, I can't believe a grown woman her age— well, she's seventy if she's a day—would act like this, especially over something that had nothing to do with her. And Sharon doesn't even seem to hold a grudge. We always speak civilly when we run into each other."

"Are you sure you didn't have some misunderstanding with her at some time?" Des asked.

Barney shook her head. "I never had any dealings with her. I never really knew her." She turned to Judy. "She didn't say anything else?"

"No. Sorry. She stormed out of my office before I could ask her why."

"I guess the only thing you can do is ask her directly," Cara suggested.

"I bet if you ask her really nicely to bake for us, she'll say yes." Nikki. Ever the optimist.

"Of course, you're right. I need to speak with her myself. I'm sure we can work this out. If I slighted her in some way . . ." Barney sighed. "I can't imagine when I could have done such a thing, or why. But she clearly has a bug up her butt, and the only way to resolve it is to face it head-on."

Barney turned to Judy. "I'm sorry, I wanted to meet the staff tonight as much as the others do, but I feel I should take care of this right now."

"I agree. I can introduce the staff to Cara, Des, and Nikki, and maybe have time to make up a list of things we want to cover in the morning. You can meet the evening shift tomorrow night."

"That'll be fine," Barney agreed.

"Come along, then, ladies, and we'll start with the kitchen staff." Judy led the way. Over her shoulder, she said, "Good luck, Barney. I hope you can straighten things out with Justine."

"So do I." Barney still looked a bit bewildered.

"I'm sure it's a misunderstanding," Allie told her. "Something silly, and you'll talk it over and you'll end up best friends when the smoke clears."

"Pray you're right, Allie." Barney opened the door to leave. "Or there's going to be a lot of baking in your future."

I hope she was kidding about the baking, Allie was thinking as she straightened the pile of menus on the desk. But it could come to that. She could still see the look on Justine Kennedy's face when she grabbed the stack of boxes from the desk, the way she'd looked at Allie with such anger, such loathing. The more she thought about it, the crazier it seemed. Oh sure, Allie knew there were people who didn't like her, but those were people who *knew* her. In most cases, she'd earned that dislike honestly. However, this woman was a total stranger. Allie was positive she'd never done anything that would have merited the sort of disdain she'd seen reflected in the woman's eyes.

It was also puzzling that she'd have a grudge of some sort against Barney, who everyone in town seemed to love, if not revere.

Whatever. Allie suspected Barney would get to the bottom of whatever it was, and she'd make amends, and Justine Kennedy would be bringing back the goodies she'd left with in a huff.

"You're really on a roll, aren't you?" Ben said as he approached her.

"What?" She restacked the pile of menus. No need to look up. She'd suspected he'd find something snarky to say before he left.

"It looks like you're two for two."

"I have no idea what you're talking about. If you've paid your bill, you're free to go." She refused to look at him.

"It just seems like every time you're in here, you piss someone off. Last time it was Barney, tonight it's Mrs. Kennedy. I gotta hand it to you, you really put the 'goodbye' in the Goodbye Café."

"Go away, Ben." No need to tell him she hadn't been the one to inflame Justine Kennedy. It wasn't any of his business, and besides, he always believed the worst where she was concerned. Best to just ignore his attempts to get a rise out of her, because that was exactly what he was doing.

"You keep alienating the customers, the Goodbye is going to go out of business."

When she didn't react, he continued. "It must have been something really good to make Mrs. Kennedy leave and take her dessert stuff with her. She's been baking for Mrs. Worrell for as long as I can remember."

"Maybe she doesn't like that the ownership has changed, I don't know," Allie snapped. "Now, if you're finished insulting me, there's the door."

Ben's eyes narrowed. "What do you mean, the ownership has changed?"

Argh! She hadn't meant to say that. They'd agreed to let Judy tell her regular customers, and Ben was clearly one of those.

"Never mind. It'll be public soon enough." Allie could have kicked herself for not being able to resist slapping back at him in the first place.

"If it'll be public soon, why not tell me now?"

"Because I don't want to, okay? I don't want to talk to you until . . . Oh, just go."

"Until . . . ?" He gestured for her to continue.

Allie sighed and turned to face him, eye to eye. "Until you accept my apology. Until you acknowledge that maybe, just maybe, I'm not the evil, horrible, despicable person you think I am."

He stared at her, and for a moment she thought he was about to speak. But instead he shook his head, opened the door, and left.

Allie's eyes stung with tears she had no intention of shedding. There'd been times in her life when she'd admittedly tossed barbs with the sole purpose of leaving a mark. If an insult cost her a friend, she hadn't lost any sleep over it, mostly because she'd had few friends she'd miss. Yes, she'd been *that* girl once upon a time. So she couldn't deny the irony that the remark she'd *not* made to Ben would be the one to haunt them both. She wasn't a monster who'd throw a man's lost child in his face, and yet that's what he believed she'd been about to do with words she'd *almost* but not quite said. She'd tried in any number of ways to make him understand, but he'd closed his mind the moment it happened, and he hadn't spoken to her since except to berate her.

She checked her seething emotions and greeted the latest customers, led them to a table and said all the things she was supposed to say with the obligatory smile on her face, but she felt the same shame she'd felt on the Fourth of July when Ben had shoved the photo of his son at her, then all but tossed her out of his apartment.

Allie knew she shouldn't let it get to her. She knew she hadn't meant to hurt Ben, her family knew she hadn't meant to say anything hurtful, but it was his choice to believe what he wanted to believe and there was nothing she could do to change his mind.

She shouldn't let him get under her skin. And what did his opinion about anything matter?

"It doesn't," she muttered. "Who needs Ben Haldeman anyway? Not this girl."

Over the course of the next hour, customers came and went, and she fulfilled her hostess duties admirably. Her daughter and sisters had made the rounds to meet the waitstaff before disappearing behind closed doors once again. Allie mentally redecorated the dining room, changing the somewhat dull white walls to a pale buttery yellow. She'd keep the photographs that, taken as a whole, told the story of Hidden Falls, but she'd paint all the frames black. She'd paint the wooden chairs black as well, and the tables white. She'd add touches of color with vases that held small bunches of whatever flowers were in season. Thinking about the café as a project helped drive Ben out of her mind for a while.

The dinner crowd had pretty much thinned out when Barney returned, looking a bit shaken.

"Are you all right?" Allie was unaccustomed to seeing Barney in such a state.

"Peachy." Barney declined to elaborate. "Is everyone still in the meeting with Judy?"

"Yes, but . . ."

Barney moved past her, weaving around the tables until she came to the office. She walked in and closed the door behind her.

Allie sighed. *Well, thank me for my concern.*

What a strange night this had been. First Justine Kennedy's tantrum and Ben Haldeman's chiding, and now Barney looking like the sky had fallen. Allie felt like the world had tilted slightly, making it a more confusing place than it had been a few hours ago. Suddenly there was nothing she wanted more than to go back to her room in the house on Hudson Street and pour herself a healthy helping of vodka to ease out the wrinkles that had emerged since she'd entered the Goodbye earlier that afternoon. She could almost feel the heat of the drink in her throat and in her gut, feel it sailing smoothly through her veins. She licked her lips, which had gone suddenly dry, and she wondered how much longer she was going to have to stay there.

She asked one of the waitresses for a glass of ice water, and she sipped it steadily, trying to keep the urge to drink something much stronger under control.

Then the office door opened and her daughter and sisters spilled into the dining room, laughing, a jumble of smiles. When Nikki saw her mother across the room, she made a beeline for her.

"Mom, I said we should change the names of some of the things on the menu. Like the Green Brier Burger. Mrs. Worrell says everyone calls it the Goodbye Burger, but I said we should call it the Hello Burger. Get it? Goodbye? Hello? 'Cause we're new owners?" Nikki dissolved in a fit of adolescent giggles. "I'm taking a menu home so we can sit up and make up names for stuff. Like Cara's Crab Cakes."

"Des's Deviled Egg Salad." Cara came up behind Nikki.

"Allie's Avocado Toast." Nikki laughed. "Barney's BLT."

"Nikki's Nachos," Des added.

Allie took one look at her daughter's shiny, happy face and knew there'd be no sitting alone in her room with only a half-filled bottle of vodka for company tonight. She took another sip of water, knowing she'd be drinking nothing stronger. If she had to choose between laughing with her daughter and anything else in the world—even the relief she found in a bottle—Nikki would win. Every time.

"Barney, are you going to tell me what Justine Kennedy's problem is?" Allie asked after she arrived home. She'd stayed later than she'd expected, meeting customers and learning the computer system.

She seated herself in the kitchen, which had become the family's gathering place, taking a place next to Cara on the window seat. The room was spacious and cozy at the same time, with a stone fireplace and a window seat piled with comfy cushions. The room really was the heart of the family home, especially after the girls had given it a face-lift, banishing dated stenciling and painting not only the walls but the cabinets as well. Barney'd been delighted with the refresh.

Allie turned to Cara. "I thought Joe was coming over to look at the carriage house."

"He just left," Cara told her. "He said there'd be no problem making the few simple changes I'd been thinking about. So we'll see." Cara leaned forward on the table. "So, Barney, what happened when you went to Justine's?"

"As I told the girls earlier, I rang her doorbell and she answered. The fact that she blocked the doorway with her body and didn't invite me in was my first clue that things weren't going to go well." Barney got up, turned her back, and began to fill the teakettle with water. She set it on the stove, turned on the burner, and went back to the table and sat.

"Did she tell you why she won't bake for us?" Allie asked.

Barney shook her head. "She thinks I know why, but I don't. I swear, I have no idea what her problem is. She was rude. I tried to appeal to her in every way I could imagine, but she wouldn't budge. The last thing she said before she slammed the door in my face was, 'I don't want anything to do with you or your family. I wouldn't cross the street to help anyone whose name was Hudson.'"

"That's . . . that's like really so mean, Aunt Barney." Nikki gazed around the table. "We're nice people. How could she not like us?"

"It was definitely personal," Barney concluded.

"Did something happen at the bank?" Des said. "Like maybe she or someone in her family applied for a loan or a mortgage and was turned down?"

Barney shook her head. "Not that I know of."

"Maybe she applied for a job there that she didn't get," Nikki suggested.

"I don't recall her or her sister or anyone else in her family applying for a job at the bank."

"How 'bout her husband's family?" Allie suggested.

"No. We always had a good relationship with the Kennedys. My dad approved the mortgages on their house and their business." Barney shook her head again. "Honestly, I swear I have gone over every single interaction with her and her family and her neighbors and I can't think of one thing that would cause her to behave like this."

"Okay, then, we put Justine aside and we move on from there." Cara came to the same conclusion everyone else apparently had, because they all nodded in unison. "So we have to decide what we're going to do about the desserts."

Allie heard the whistle of the teakettle and got up to turn it off.

"People who come to the Goodbye on a regular basis do so because they like the food. They've come to expect a certain quality and I'm not going to have anyone complaining that Justine did a better lemon square or anything else," Barney declared. Allie prepared Barney's tea and set the mug on the table. "Thank you."

"You're welcome." Allie took her seat again. "So what do we do?"

"Our first choice, obviously, is to find someone else to bake for us," Barney said. "In the interim, I guess we're going to have to pitch in."

"Pitch in how?" Allie asked.

"By baking something we can serve until we can find someone else," Barney said. "Allie, how would you like to be our new baker? On a temporary basis, of course."

"I spend hours on my back painting the theater ceiling every day," Allie reminded her. "Did we forget I'm still doing that?"

"You're only at the theater in the morning. You can come home, bake something, and get to the café by four," Barney told her.

"What? When did we talk about me being the night hostess?"

"Judy called a while ago. Degan is taking a full load of classes at summer school this semester and can only work a few mornings."

"If the hostessing thing is so important, who's doing it until four?" Allie asked.

"I will, when Degan can't," Barney replied. "I can ask Ginger to come in early when I can't make it, but most days I'll be there from breakfast until you get there. Then I'll go home and soak my old, tired feet, and maybe come back later to have dinner with you all."

"No offense, Aunt Barney, but that's not fair." Nikki was suddenly all attitude. "It's not fair that my mom has to be the baker and do all that other stuff, and I don't get to do anything. Why can't I bake?"

"Oh. Well." Barney appeared to consider that. "I don't see any reason why you couldn't. Do you think you could make brownies?"

"Yes! I can do that." Nikki immediately whipped out her phone and began typing.

"You might want to find a few recipes and test them out till you find one you can live with." Barney sipped her tea. "Just in case."

"Guys, there are videos online that teach you how to do stuff," Nikki told her, and after more serious typing, she held up her phone. "Look, see? It goes step by step."

Allie leaned closer to her daughter and watched the instructive video for a few moments.

"You guys, I'm going to make the most kicking brownies anyone ever had," Nikki announced with confidence. "Who needs old Justine Kennedy's brownies, anyway? Not the Goodbye Café."

Allie took a quick shower. Afterward she pulled on a tank top and a pair of sleep shorts, then opened the window as far as she could to let a bit of night breeze blow in to cool the room. She'd meant to ask Barney if she was going to have air-conditioning installed in the house anytime soon. Before the summer ended would be good.

Until now, she'd successfully avoided her stash of vodka, but she couldn't say she wasn't thinking about it. If she went downstairs now and got a glass of ice with a little lemonade, she could make a cocktail before she turned in. One little drink wouldn't hurt anything, right? And she was working her tail off these days between the theater and now the Goodbye.

She'd convinced herself she deserved a nightcap when she heard a light tapping on the door.

"Mom?"

"Come on in, Nik." Obviously the nightcap was going to have to wait.

Nikki came into the room wearing a short pink nightshirt, her phone in her hand.

"Were you in bed?" she asked.

"Just thinking about it," Allie told her. "What's up?"

Nikki shrugged. "Just wanted to see what you were doing."

Allie knew her daughter. She never just wanted to see what her mother was doing. Something was up.

"Come in and sit." Allie sat on the bed. "Did you find a recipe for your brownies?"

"I did. They're going to be awesome. I'm going to test them tomorrow morning, and if they're really good, I'll make more and bring them to the Goodbye." She drew up her legs and hugged them. "It's exciting, isn't it, owning a restaurant? I was happy Aunt Barney gave me my own assignment. I promise I will make the best brownies ever, and no one will say that Mrs. Kennedy's were better."

"I'm putting my money on you, kiddo." Allie leaned forward and tucked a long strand of hair behind Nikki's ear.

"Thanks, Mom." Nikki tapped the cover of her phone and looked around the room. "You have more fresh air in here. The rooms in the front of the house don't get the breeze like you do."

Allie leaned back against the headboard and slid under the sheet. The day was starting to catch up with her, now that she'd slowed down.

"Mom, what happened to all the pretty jewelry you used to wear? Those gold bracelets and the diamond earrings?"

"They're over there in the dresser in a little jewelry case."

"Can I see them?"

"Of course."

Nikki got up and went to the dresser, then returned to the bed. She took out Allie's bracelets and put them on, then held them up to the light. "Why don't you wear these anymore?"

"They'd get in my way when I'm trying to paint, and besides, Hidden Falls isn't a very fancy place. I'd feel overdressed if I wore them every day." Allie watched her daughter switch the bracelets around. "Is everything okay, Nik?"

Nikki nodded, but a moment later asked, "Why can't we stay here in Hidden Falls?"

"Because our lives are in California. Your father. Your school. Your friends."

Nikki lay down next to Allie. "They have a good high school here. Dad can get on planes and fly everywhere for his job or for his vacations, so he can get on a plane and come and see me." She paused. "And I have better friends here."

Allie raised an eyebrow. "Does that include Courtney?"

"It includes everyone." She scooched closer to Allie, curled up, and closed her eyes. "Can I stay here for a while, Mom?"

"Of course you can." Allie leaned over and turned off the lamp on the bedside table. "All night, if you want."

"Just maybe for a few minutes." Nikki yawned.

Within minutes, her daughter was sound asleep, the bracelets still on her arm, but wondering what had happened between Nikki and her longtime best friend kept Allie awake for a while longer. Eventually she chalked it up to normal teenage drama, closed her eyes, and gave in to sleep.

CHAPTER FIVE

"Barney, what did Tom say when you told him you were buying the Goodbye?" Allie filled her travel mug with ice and water to help keep her hydrated while she was in the hot theater. She was usually on the scaffold and well into painting by now, but she'd stayed in bed a little longer because she hadn't wanted to disturb Nikki. It had been eons since her daughter had crawled into bed next to her, and Allie had wanted to savor every minute, because she didn't know if there'd be a repeat anytime soon.

"Oh, I haven't discussed it with him. Been too busy." Barney opened a cupboard and looked over their selection of boxed cereals. "Maybe we should serve Cara's granola and yogurt with fruit for breakfast at the café. What do you think?"

"I think it would be great, if Cara can fit in making granola while overseeing the rest of the renovations at the theater. Oh, and checking out the Goodbye for potential repairs and possibly retrofitting the carriage house for a yoga studio."

"The granola's a great idea. But big news: We got lucky. Judy sent me a text earlier. She found some of Justine's baked goods in the café's freezer this morning. What with so many people going away on vacation last week and the week before, Justine made too much of everything, so Judy put the extra in the freezer, so we're covered for at least a while."

"Better pray Justine doesn't get word of that. She might storm in and raid the freezer."

"I wouldn't put it past her," Barney muttered. She pulled a box from the shelf and closed the cabinet door. "Honestly, Allie, I don't know what is wrong with that woman. If you could have seen her face . . ."

"Oh, I saw her face when she came out of the office after Judy told her you'd bought the place. She was loaded for bear." Allie wasn't going to forget that expression anytime soon.

"Well, there's nothing we can do about her. We have our own game plan. Judy's saved her order sheets, so we'll know just how much of each item we have to make for a week if we can't find someone else, which is probably the best thing to do. So let's forget about Justine and whatever her problem is, and we'll just move forward and do our thing."

"Excellent idea, Barney."

"I'll be happy if I never hear her name again," Barney said.

"Might be tough, since we're all living in the same small town, but I agree. She's history." Allie took a bite from a banana and searched the dishwasher for the lid to her travel mug.

"Hi, Mom. Morning, Aunt Barney." Nikki made her appearance yawning. She opened the refrigerator and took out the milk, then searched the cereal cabinet.

"Looks like someone could have used a little more sleep," Allie said.

"I couldn't sleep in today. I have too much to do."

"I have your favorite right over here." Barney held up the box of oat cereal.

"Thanks, Aunt Barney."

"Nik, you look like you're sleepwalking," Allie said.

Nikki proceeded to prepare her breakfast. "I'm testing brownie recipes this morning. Aunt Cara said she'd drive me to the grocery store to pick up the stuff."

Allie told her about the stash in Judy's freezer, and Nikki turned up her nose.

"We don't need her stuff, Mom. I'm going to be aces at baking brownies."

"I'm sure you will be."

"I'm making more than one kind, too."

"I think it's a great idea for you to try out different things. There must be a million recipes for different kinds of brownies, but you can't make them all."

"Hundreds. Maybe thousands, but yeah, I need to nail down maybe two or three different ones." Nikki sat at the table and began to eat her breakfast. "Like, a plain chocolate one that we can frost sometimes, a special chocolate like peanut butter or mint, and a blondie."

"Sounds like someone has been reading recipes," Barney said.

Nikki nodded. "Many recipes."

"Whatever you decide, I'm sure they'll be terrific." Allie kissed the top of Nikki's head, then paused before planting a kiss on Barney as well. While the older woman didn't acknowledge the gesture, the tiny smile that curled the side of her mouth assured Allie that she'd gotten the message: Barney was loved.

"I'll see you later." Allie picked up her bag and stuffed her water bottle inside.

"Oh, and Mom, that new dog that you found is adorable. He's just the kind of dog I want. Aunt Des said he's a French bulldog. So cute." She glanced at her mother hopefully. "And he's just so sweet."

"Your father would have a fit. He never wanted a dog, not even when you were little and I practically begged him to let you have one."

"He might say yes if I beg him." Nikki grinned. "I can be totally irresistible when I have to."

"There's no arguing that."

"He could stay with you during the week when I'm at Dad's."

The picture of the dog peeing on the chair leg in the kitchen had stuck in Allie's mind.

"I'm not sure I'm ready for that." Allie laughed and headed out.

The walk to the theater was a brief one, and before long, Allie was seated on the top plank of the scaffold, her paintbrush in her hand, filling in the stenciled design she'd sketched. Today she was focused on the green geometric shapes that formed part of the border radiating out from the base of the chandelier. Next would come the shiny gold paint that outlined the border. It was a gloriously colorful design, and not for the first time she marveled at the originality and creativity of the original artist.

"Alistair Cooper, you were one talented dude."

The music from the basement level wafted up the stairwell, and from time to time she heard the voices of the workmen who joined in singing along with Journey and Bon Jovi—someone downstairs was stuck in the eighties—or who taunted one of the others working on the wall. As loud as they often were, the sounds faded into background noise as she painted. She applied the paint in painstakingly small strokes, making sure to blend it with the existing color.

Secretly Allie missed painting. Once upon a time, she'd fancied herself an artist, and had taken several classes in technique and style. But then she'd met Clint, who'd swept her off her feet, and she soon found she hadn't time for anything that didn't include first him, then Nikki. When she was offered an assistant director's position by an old friend from the days when Des's show had been a huge hit, Clint had talked her into accepting the job, convincing her that she missed the excitement of working in television. The truth was that Nikki had started school, Clint had a new job that required him to travel, and Allie was bored to death. If she missed standing in front of a canvas with a brush in her hand, seeing the image in her head take shape as she brought it to life with bold colors, she hadn't admitted it even to herself. They'd just decided to build an addition onto their house, and the extra money would go a long way toward paying for the new family room and larger master suite.

Now she held a brush every day, and the smell of the paint took her back to a time when she was experimenting with color and technique and searching for her own style. She'd found the greatest freedom through expressing herself with vibrant colors, but she'd only begun to explore what she might do with that knowledge. The job at hand required more structure than she was inclined to follow, and more and more she had to fight an urge to paint wide swaths of bright reds and yellows and purples across the ceiling. Not that she would—that would have been desecration in her view—but the thought of painting freely was never far from her mind.

Best to save those for when she had a canvas in front of her instead of a ceiling. And she would have a canvas and paints of her choosing as soon as her work at the theater was finished. When she got back to California, she was going to do things differently. The money from her father would go a long way to supporting her for a long time, and she'd be able to explore whatever talent she might have.

She let her mind wander. Maybe someday she'd even show her paintings in a gallery like the one that snotty Merille Ann Jefferies had in L.A.

Voices directly below brought her back to the moment. She glanced down and saw Cara walking through the lobby with two women dressed casually.

Oh crap! She'd forgotten there was to be a meeting this morning about the theater seats with the upholsterers, Rita and Elsa Werner. She momentarily froze. Should she reveal herself or stay quiet and let Cara handle it?

She eased her phone out of her pocket and dialed Cara's number.

It rang four times before her sister answered.

"Cara, it's me. I'm on top of the scaffold." The whispered words spilled out in a jumble. "I forgot those people were coming in today to look at the seat cushions."

"Oh, it's fine, Allie. Not to worry. I'll get back to you on that."

"Are you sure you don't mind? I know the décor for the theater is supposed to be my gig, but—"

"Of course not. I totally understand."

"You're the best. Thank you."

"You're welcome."

Allie tapped *end call* and breathed a sigh of relief.

When they first went through the theater, they'd carefully inspected every seat cushion, and while many were faded and showed wear on the velvet nap they'd had when they were new, most had faded from their original red to a sort of rose color the sisters had liked.

"They look authentic. The color goes with the rest of the interior," Des had said. "You can tell they're original and they suit the theater without looking shabby. Like they've aged but aged well."

"I agree. I say we keep them and save ourselves a small fortune, which we don't have anyway," Cara had agreed. "Allie? It's your call."

"I like the muted shade. And I like the fact that they're original. But there are a few that are frayed, a couple that have rips in them, and those do look shabby. This is one instance when shabby doesn't look chic." Allie'd pointed out the seats under discussion. "If we can find someone—an upholsterer, I'm thinking—who can match this dark rosy shade, I'd prefer to just redo those and keep the others as they are."

"I like the idea," Cara said.

"Me, too," Des said. "I guess the internet is the place to look."

"I'll start there and see what I can come up with. I hate the thought of spending so much money to replace every cushion on every seat, when what we have is so pretty and so right for the building. I'll let you know what I find."

Allie had begun her search that night and found several upholsterers in Scranton who'd sounded intrigued when she'd called them the following morning. The two women now with Cara looking over the seats were from the third place she'd called. They'd been enthusiastic and seemed to understand exactly what Allie wanted. From her perch high above the theater she could hear voices, but nothing distinct enough to understand what was being said. It was forty-five minutes before Cara and the two women emerged from the audience section and went straight to the front door. A few minutes later, Cara came into the lobby.

"How'd it go?" Allie called down to her.

"Wait, I'm coming up." Cara kicked off her sandals and climbed the scaffold to the top. She sat a few feet away from Allie and immediately looked up. "That's gorgeous. The colors match so perfectly. I can't get over that you're able to do this, Al. You're so clever."

"Aw, thanks." Allie slowly turned around on the plank. "It's tedious, but we're getting there."

"It's amazing what you're doing. What you've *done*. The ceiling is the centerpiece of the theater. If we'd had to leave it with those big, bold ugly patches of plaster showing, it would have taken so much from the overall beauty of the building. You saved our bacon, 'cause there's no way we could have hired someone else to do this."

"It would have drained us," Allie agreed. "So what's the verdict with the seats?"

"They think they might be able to find a fabric that's compatible. Their first choice would be to find some vintage velvet that's in good shape, so that's where they're going to start. They have a few sources they're going to call, and we'll see where that goes. They're interesting women, both in their fifties. Sisters who took over when their dad passed away. He'd taught them everything he knew about fabrics and upholstery. They're willing to work with us to find the right match and with the pricing because they're totally behind the idea of preserving old buildings. They loved the Sugarhouse and want to be part of the revival."

"Sounds like a perfect match for us."

"Yeah. They're really nice ladies."

"Thanks for meeting with them. I really appreciate it. I can't believe I forgot that they were coming today." Allie rolled her eyes. "I should have looked at my calendar first thing this morning."

"No big deal. I was glad to do it. And besides, you have your hands full right now. Painting the ceiling. Playing hostess. Being

Nikki's mom, which is a full-time job in itself. You're holding up admirably."

"Well, you've got a lot on your plate, too. Who knew we'd be walking into all this because of Dad's will?"

"When I found out that Dad died, I felt like the bottom had fallen out of my life. I mean, coming on the heels of my husband abandoning me in favor of one of my best friends—having a child with her!—it was a lot to take at one time." Cara swallowed hard. "I felt like I had no one. My mom was gone, my husband, my dad. My *life*. When Uncle Pete told me about the will and having to come here, I thought it was odd, maybe even a bit silly, like a cliché, that Dad would do such a thing. I came mostly to get away from Devlin's Light and all the gossip about Drew and Amber and the divorce and their wedding and their baby . . ." Cara shivered.

Allie reached out a hand to squeeze one of Cara's.

"You definitely had the most on your plate. I came for the money, pure and simple, because I needed my inheritance. Otherwise, I never would have left California."

"You had a life there. My life in Devlin's Light wasn't a very happy one. But if Uncle Pete hadn't made Dad's will so tight, I'd never have known what was waiting for me here."

"Like Joe."

Cara laughed. "Yes, Joe, and a second chance. But more than Joe, I found a family, which was something I didn't have." Her eyes glistened. "Now I have two sisters. I have an aunt. I have a niece. I wouldn't have known any of you existed if Dad hadn't forced us here, if he hadn't made Uncle Pete write his will so it could not be challenged."

Uncle Pete was Peter Wheeler, their father's best friend and lawyer, and brother of Barney's lost love.

Cara added, "And I don't mind saying I adore all of you."

"Oh, Cara . . ." Allie moved to hug her, and the platform swayed. "Oh crap, I'm going to kill us both."

Cara laughed through her tears. "I don't know why I got so

sentimental all of a sudden. Maybe because I'm starting to see the end of this project. There isn't all that much more to do. Of course, there's the ceiling. The restrooms. The seats, the stage lighting. Oh, and the guys have to finish shoring up the wall downstairs and then paint it. Joe said they're doing a great job and might even finish ahead of schedule."

"That would be a first. But we do still need to refinish the stage and have new curtains made."

"That's something the ladies who were here mentioned. They think they can clean the old curtains. I'd love for them to try. The color almost matches the shade of the seats," Cara said. "And Joe said he, Seth, and Ben will refinish the stage and the backstage area."

"How are they going to do that?"

"They'll rent floor sanders and whatever else they need from some contractors' supply place Joe buys from. He knows what equipment to get and how to use it, so that's one less expense and one step closer to the end."

Allie could feel Cara's eyes on her.

"So? Aren't you happy? Maybe we'll be done in time for you to go back to California sooner than you thought."

Allie nodded. "It'll be great, yeah. I can't stand not being able to see my kid every week. I know she has to live with her father during the week now, but I'm going to change that when I get back. If I can find a house closer to Nikki's school, I'm going to insist on returning to our original custody agreement: Nik lives with me during the week, and Clint on the weekends." Allie'd already thought this through. "You know she's only been living with him during the week this past year because his house is so close to her school and mine is almost an hour away. It's better for her to be there during the week, even though it damn near kills me."

"You think he'll be willing to do that? Give her up during the week?"

"He's going to have to. That was the legal agreement. I'll go back to court if necessary, but she belongs with me during the week."

"Well, I wish you luck with that. I hope it happens for you. Anyone can see how close you and Nikki are."

"We are. She's my entire world."

"Obviously. And she should be. She's spectacular, amazing, brilliant, adorable, bighearted, funny . . . What did I miss?"

"You covered it well enough, thank you." Allie tapped her fingers on the side of the paint jar. "How much more time do you think before we're completely finished?"

Cara shrugged. "It's tough to tell. Maybe two months? I don't know. It depends on how quickly everything falls into place." Cara swung her legs over the side of the scaffold. "I'll let you get back to work, and I need to get back to the house. Nikki and I went to the supermarket and bought everything she needs to make brownies. There's going to be lots of taste testing later, so be ready."

"Ready to pack on the pounds," Allie said.

"It comes with the territory. Besides, you're the thin one. You could use a few more pounds on that tall frame of yours."

Allie bit her tongue. She'd been about to complain that she'd gained so much weight since she arrived in Hidden Falls, she could fit into Cara's shorts. There was a time she wouldn't have hesitated to mention it.

"I'll see you back at the house," Allie said. "And thanks again for meeting with the upholstery ladies."

"It was nothing. Glad to do it." Cara reached the bottom and hopped off the rail and into her sandals. "See you."

Allie watched Cara cross the lobby floor, and seconds later, she heard the front door close. She sat back and exhaled. The conversation with her sister—when had she stopped thinking of Cara as her *half* sister?—had touched her more deeply than she'd allowed herself to show. Allie was being honest when she said she came to Hidden Falls only because she had to, but she was having a more difficult time than Cara expressing what the past few months meant to her. She, too, had felt abandoned and alone, had felt that way for a very long time. After her mother removed herself from her daughters' lives so she could drink herself to death, and the self-imposed estrangement from Des, and her father's distancing himself—though now she understood the reason for that—Allie had no one until she'd met Clint. She'd fallen deeply, totally in love with him, and thought his love would make up for all she'd lost. Then they had Nikki, and for a time, Allie's life felt like it had been mended and made whole, all those empty places filled. But once Clint had left, and Nikki'd gone to live with him, Allie realized how little she had to hold on to. She had few friends—maybe no real friends, when you got down to it. The cancellation of the TV show she'd been working on and the loss of her job had been the last straw.

The hours she'd spent alone had become hours she'd spent drinking and watching old movies on television. Her world had become smaller and smaller, shrinking down to the weekends when she'd spend time with Nikki. She had nothing else to look forward to. Nora had died, and once Fritz had passed away, Allie'd felt anchorless. His demand that she pick up and move across the country had seemed ridiculous, and she'd looked for a way to fight it, but his will was ironclad, and if she hoped to get herself out of the financial mess she was in, she had to comply with his wishes.

All of which led her to Hidden Falls and the Sugarhouse. Barney and the house on Hudson Street. Cara, whom she'd been determined to dislike, but who'd won her over with her open heart. Cara had a seemingly endless capacity to love freely, and gave of herself without being asked. Miraculously, Allie and Des had been able to talk through their resentments and their long-held anger toward each other. They'd cleared the air after a knock-down, drag-out yell-fest some weeks ago, and were on their way to becoming the sisters they'd been when they were children.

Like Cara, Allie'd found her family. And like Cara, she adored every one of them.

"Better not let that get around. I have a reputation to protect,"

Allie said aloud, then went back to the task of painting one small design element on the vast ceiling. She'd finish one more, then she'd pack up and head home.

The kitchen was in a state of total disarray when Allie arrived. It seemed every bowl that could be used to mix something was on the table or one of the counters. Barney's old stand mixer was whirling away, Nikki peering into the bowl to watch, and there was chocolate everywhere, including on Nikki's face when she turned to greet her mother. Cara was sorting through Barney's collection of baking pans.

"Hi, Mom. I'm on the second batch of brownies. Aunt Cara showed me how to measure stuff the right way and how to melt the chocolate without burning it. You should try one of those." Nikki pointed to a baking pan that sat on a wire cooling rack. "They are so good. Just chocolatey and gooey. I think that's going to be one of the finalists."

"You look like you're having fun." Allie placed her bag on the window seat, then wiped a smudge of chocolate from her daughter's cheek.

"I am. But it is work, you know." Nikki nodded as if she'd imparted an important truth.

Allie cut a sliver of brownie, tasted it, then gave Nikki the thumbs-up sign. "It's delicious, Nik."

"I know, right?" Nikki beamed.

"You're doing a great job." Allie looked around. "Where's Des?"

"Oh, she took my car and drove over to the vet's," Cara said. "Someone left a litter of puppies in a box on their doorstep and the vet didn't know what to do with them. He called Ben 'cause he's the chief of police, and Ben called Des. She's going to pick them up and take them out to Seth's if they look like they're old enough."

"Isn't the mother dog with them?" Nikki asked.

"Apparently not. I think whoever had them only left the puppies," Cara said.

"That's so awful," Nikki said. "What kind of person separates puppies from their mother?"

"Someone who doesn't want puppies," Allie said.

"I don't like people who do things like that." Nikki was visibly disturbed. "What's going to happen to the babies?"

"I'm sure your Aunt Des will think of something, and whatever it is, it will be best for the pups, don't worry," Cara assured her.

"And where's Barney?" Allie asked. "I looked for her in the sitting room and in the office when I came in, but she wasn't there."

"She and Judy are meeting with their lawyer today to work out the agreement of sale," Cara said.

"They're using the same lawyer? Is that ethical on his part?"

Cara shrugged. "It may not be the ideal, but they've both used the same lawyer for years, and since they both agree on every one of the terms of the sale, they're pretty much writing the agreement as they want it."

"Boy, when Barney decides to do something, there's no getting in her way."

"That's the truth," Cara agreed. "And why not? She has the time and can afford to do as she wishes."

"Well, once the theater is completed, you'll be able to afford to do what you want, too," Allie said. "Any idea what that might be in the long run?"

"Nothing set in stone yet, but more and more I can see myself staying here. Joe says it won't take much at all to get the carriage house ready. Cleaning it might be the biggest project."

"Ready for what, Aunt Cara?" Nikki asked.

While Cara explained her plans to open a yoga studio, Nikki poured her latest batch of chocolate into the baking pan, then washed the mixer's bowl.

"I'm running up to the shower," Allie announced. "I need to get over to the Goodbye."

Nikki sat still as a stone on the window seat cushion, her phone in her hand, her face unreadable. Allie knew that look well.

It was Nikki's expression when faced with something she didn't understand but knew she didn't like.

"Nik?" Allie walked toward her.

"What?" Nikki looked up from her phone, then turned it off quickly and stuck it into her pocket.

"I asked if you still needed the mixer. Otherwise, I'd clean it and put it away."

"Oh. No. I mean, yes, I need it. Thanks." Nikki got up and walked past her mother, her expression never changing.

"Is something wrong, sweetie?" Allie asked.

"What? Oh. No. Everything's fine." Nikki forced a smile.

"You sure?"

"Sure. Everything's great, Mom." Nikki picked up her recipe and appeared to be reading.

Having been dismissed, Allie went up to take her shower. She knew everything wasn't "great," knew something was bothering her daughter, but she also knew that when Nikki didn't want to talk about something, wild horses couldn't pull words from her mouth. For now, Allie had to let the matter drop.

If nothing changed by tomorrow morning, she'd try again.

CHAPTER SIX

"So you're my new boss?" Ginger was at the hostess desk when Allie arrived early at the Goodbye, Barney and Judy apparently still at the lawyer's office.

Allie could tell by the woman's posture that she wasn't pleased. "No, my aunt is the boss. Of both of us. *All* of us."

"I heard you were going to be the one who decided who stays and who goes." The attitude had not softened.

Allie took a deep breath. It would be so easy to trade attitude for attitude. But this was Barney's business, and she wasn't going to start alienating the staff right off the bat.

"No. My aunt asked me to talk to everyone so we know what you all do and how well you do it. It's always going to be her decision."

"But you're going to tell her what you want her to hear." Ginger placed one hand on her jutting hip. Her expression hadn't changed one bit.

"Look, if you're doing your job well, why does it matter who makes the call? We're not—that is, my *aunt* isn't out to fire anyone. We—*she'd* love to keep the staff exactly as it is. If you're good, you stay. If you suck, you're out. Does that make it easier for you to understand?"

The woman appeared to be in a staring contest with Allie.

Sorry, girl. You'll never get me to blink.

"Do you do your job, Ginger? Are you good at it?" Allie asked.

"Yes. And yes."

"Then you have nothing to worry about. Now, if you'll excuse me, I'm on at four."

When Ginger didn't move from her post, Allie walked around her and dropped her bag behind the desk and tried not to show that the woman had gotten on her nerves. She smiled at Ginger— a forced one, but still—and began to stack the menus into a straight pile.

She thinks I'm here to interrogate her. I suppose I am. Well, no time like the present.

"Ginger, why don't you get yourself a cup of coffee, and while there's no one here, you and I will sit down and have a little chat." This time, Allie didn't even bother to force a smile. She'd never interviewed anyone before, and her own experience with being interviewed had been very limited. Her being hired on her last TV show had been a given. She'd worked with the director before, but when she'd gone into the HR department, she'd still had to fill out an application. She tried to remember what was on it.

In the end, she'd remembered all she needed. Experience, education, work ethic, attitude. Ginger had worked for Judy for almost seven years, and she finally, tearfully, admitted that as a single working mother, she'd been terrified she'd be let go when she'd heard the café had been sold. They'd both dropped their posturing after that, and Allie realized the woman was a dependable, valuable employee who liked her job and desperately wanted to keep it.

"Of course, it's my aunt's decision, but there's no reason for her not to keep you on," Allie told her. "I think you're a valuable member of the staff, and that's what I'm going to tell her."

From that moment on, Ginger's attitude changed. She got Allie an iced coffee without being asked, and she cheerfully covered for her when Allie wanted to hit the ladies' room.

Hmmm. There might be something to that old saying about catching more flies with honey than with vinegar.

"I hope they're all that easy," Allie'd murmured when she returned to the desk alone just as the first customer arrived.

She couldn't wait to see Barney so she could tell her how the interviews had gone, but she'd had to wait until later that night because her aunt never showed up at the café. With Ginger's help, Allie closed the restaurant, and after counting the receipts and not knowing what to do with them, stuck the cash and the credit card slips into her bag. She'd had to walk home alone in the dark, carrying more cash than she'd seen in a long time, and while she wasn't afraid, she'd felt a little spooked once she'd turned onto Hudson Street, which was not as well lit as Main.

"Barney, I thought you were going to come down to the Goodbye and play hostess once you finished up with the lawyer," Allie said when she opened the front door to find Barney just about to go up the stairs.

"I was waylaid." Barney appeared slightly unstable on her feet. Allie looked down to see if she had on high heels, but nope. She was wearing her usual flats. "I probably should have called, but we—that is, Judy and I and Leo—were having such fun and I lost track of time. How were things at the café? I assume you took charge of the kitchen and the dining room?"

"I did."

"Thank you, dear. I don't know what I'd do without you."

"Sooner or later, you know, you're going to have to." Allie felt it necessary to remind her from time to time, since Barney seemed determined not to consider that any or all of her nieces would be leaving Hidden Falls once they were no longer required to stay there.

"Piffle." Barney waved away the comment with one hand.

She was clearly in denial about Allie's future.

"Who's Leo?" Allie asked.

"Leo Jones. He's our lawyer. Handsome devil. Way too young for either Judy or me, but still, a girl can dream." Barney grinned and wavered a bit. Had her words been just a little slurred?

"How come Uncle Pete didn't handle it? I thought he was the one anointed to handle all things legal for the Hudsons."

"If he were here in Hidden Falls, he would have. But he's at his office in Philadelphia this week, and it didn't seem fair to ask him to come all this way when Leo was perfectly capable of doing what we'd wanted done."

"Afraid he'd try to talk you out of it, eh?" Allie grinned.

"He may have tried. Wouldn't have worked. Thought I'd spare him the trip. He'll find out about it soon enough, and I suppose he'll have something to say. And I'll remind him that it's really none of his business." Barney's eyes seemed to have a strange glow. "Anything I missed at the Goodbye tonight?"

"I did my first staff interviews today." Allie watched Barney carefully. "I think Ginger is a gem and we need her. She knows the menu, the staff, the customers. You may want to think about promoting her to manager at some point. Like before I leave so that she can get used to the job."

"Again, I say piffle. I don't want to think about that. The others?"

Yeah. She was in deep denial.

"Okay. So, other than Ginger, I only was able to speak with Alice and Kelly because it got pretty busy between six and eight and we closed at ten. They've both been there for three years, right out of high school. Everyone Judy hired seems to know their jobs. I wouldn't rock the staff boat if I were you. At least, not now."

"Good. Glad to hear it. Raises for everyone. See you in the morning." Barney started toward the steps a bit unsteadily.

"Wait." Allie dug in her bag for that day's receipts. "I didn't know what to do with the money we took in today. I didn't want to leave it in the cash register, so I brought it home."

"Oh, keep it till the morning, Allie. I don't want to deal with that now."

Allie walked a little closer to Barney and caught a whiff of something that smelled suspiciously like bourbon. Could Barney be . . . ?

"Barney, have you been with Judy all this time?"

"Of course. Leo, Judy, and I stopped at the Bullfrog for a drink to celebrate the sale of the Goodbye." Barney turned and faced Allie and pointed a finger directly at her niece's nose. "Don't judge."

A stop at the Bullfrog Inn explained both the wobble and the fact that Barney'd been a no-show at the Goodbye. You'd think Allie, who'd wobbled and slurred on many an occasion, would have immediately recognized the signs, but it was so out of character for Barney.

"Then Judy made the announcement—about the sale, you see—and everyone wanted to buy us drinks. My, what a friendly crowd." Barney's smile was crooked, and so were her glasses, which sat just slightly sideways on her nose. "If you can imagine, it was almost like, the queen is dead, long live the queen."

"Barney, I believe you're drunk." Unlikely, but true.

"I believe the term is 'shit-faced.'" She patted Allie on the cheek. "Good night, dear."

Allie stared at her aunt in disbelief. She'd never seen Barney drink more than a glass of wine or one beer.

"Barney, let me help you." Allie took her arm.

"No need. I'm steady as a rock," Barney assured her.

Allie rolled her eyes. "Right. Here's the stairs. Pick your foot up."

"Which one?" Barney appeared confused.

"Doesn't matter. Whichever one you like."

"I think I like my right foot best. That's the one I use to drive Lucille with."

"You didn't drive Lucille tonight, did you?" Allie held her breath. They'd all come to love Barney's vintage Cadillac convertible. Barney drove it like she was in the Indy 500 when she was sober. God only knew what she'd do to that gas pedal in her current state.

"Oh, no. That lovely young girl who's bartending at the Frog called a ride for us. Wasn't that nice of her?"

"Very nice. Who'd she call? An Uber?"

"Uber? Like we have one of those in town." Barney made a face. "No. She called Ben, of course. He's the guy who watches out for all the drunks in town, you know."

"All too well," Allie muttered.

"He can't tolerate drunk drivers. It's because of what happened to his family. So tragic."

Allie'd heard the story so many times since coming to Hidden Falls, she knew it by heart. Which wouldn't stop Barney from repeating it.

Barney stopped on the bottom step and placed her hand over her heart. "I remember like it was yesterday. That terrible accident. Joe's father drunk and driving like a bat out of hell. Hit poor Sarah's car broadside. Killed her and little Finn outright. Horrible, horrible thing to happen. And worst, Ben had gotten a call about an accident, but no one knew at the time it was his wife and baby boy."

"Barney, you don't have to repeat all the details."

But Barney was on a roll. She took one more step, then stopped again to wipe away the tears that ran down her face.

"Joe's father killed, Sarah and Finn, too—and all because Joe Senior couldn't control his drinking. Left his wife and daughter without a dime."

Another step, and, "Thank God Joe is the man he is. Took over his father's business, which was failing, and turned it around. Made sure his mom and sister were okay. So grateful that he and Cara found each other.

"And Ben, so forgiving. He's never held it against Joe, not for one second. They're still as close as brothers. Closer." Almost made it to the landing. "Poor Ben. You shouldn't be so hard on him."

Allie stopped short of the step. "Me, hard on him?"

"I've heard you snipe at him, don't deny you do." Barney had reached the top, holding on to the newel post with both hands to steady herself.

"Because he baits me. He insults me every chance he gets.

He's been on me since the very minute I arrived in this town, and—"

"What the heck is going on out here?" Cara came out of her room and went to the landing.

"Barney's turning in early," Allie told her, "but she does not go quietly."

"See you in the morning, girls." Barney stumbled on the end of the rug at the top of the steps, caught herself, and straightened her back, reclaiming some small bit of dignity as she headed to her room.

Her eyes wide, Cara pointed to Barney silently, then looked at Allie, who shrugged.

"She and Judy celebrated at the Frog," Allie explained.

"Is she drunk?"

"She prefers 'shit-faced.' And right at this moment, I envy her. It's been a really long day." Allie turned and started back downstairs.

"Wait, are you just getting back from the Goodbye?" Cara asked.

"I am. And I'm exhausted, so I'm going to run downstairs and turn off the lights and lock up for the night."

"No, don't. Nikki isn't back yet," Cara called after her.

Already on the first floor, Allie looked up. "Back from where?"

"She was invited to go with Mark's family—Mark and Hayley's, that is—to their church picnic, so Des dropped her off on her way to Seth's. Apparently it was a last-minute invitation. Mark's mother, Roseanne, called and Des talked to her, and we thought it would be okay." Cara paused, then asked tentatively, "Was it okay?"

"It would have been nice if someone had thought to ask me." Allie stood in the hallway below the landing, her hands on her hips.

"We didn't want to bother you." Cara stared down over the railing. "Sorry. Next time we'll call. We didn't think it would be a problem, Allie. Sheesh."

Cara's bedroom door closed with more force than usual.

It had less to do with Mark in particular than with the fact that he was a boy. A nice boy who seemed to have his head on straight—as straight as any sixteen-year-old boy could—who didn't wear ripped pants or low-slung jeans, who never looked anything less than clean-cut, who was very polite and always spoke courteously and who was an honor student. But when you got down to it, he was still a teenage boy. And everyone knew that teenage boys were interested in one thing.

Allie was pretty sure Nikki didn't have much experience with boys her age outside of going places as a group as she did with her friends from school. Not that she trusted any of them, either.

She groaned. Why was parenting so hard?

Nikki would probably say why is being a kid so hard.

Allie went into the kitchen and poured herself a glass of lemonade. She couldn't wait to get back upstairs to doctor it a little.

The clock in the front hall chimed ten. Early by anyone's standards. She was trying to decide whether she should go upstairs and proceed to have her private party or wait until Nikki got home. How long does a church picnic last? And who was bringing her home, and were they coming right home afterward or going somewhere else? If Cara'd had that information, she'd have shared it, right? Which to Allie meant neither Des nor Cara had asked.

Allie sat on the window seat and pulled her legs up under her. The lemonade was good straight, but a little enhancement would go a long way toward making it even better. But she was too tired to go upstairs and doctor her drink, then come back down to wait for Nikki, and of the two, Nikki was more important. She closed her eyes and rested her head against the window frame. The day had lasted forever—up early to paint in the theater, a walk in the sweltering heat to the Goodbye, hours on her feet, then walking back to the house, though thankfully the temperature had begun to drop a lot since the morning.

Allie mentally revisited her interview with Ginger. It hadn't occurred to her until sometime after they'd concluded that she and

Ginger had something in common: They were both single mothers of a daughter. Nikki was older than Ginger's little girl, whose name, Allie learned over the course of the evening, was Ava, but both she and Ginger'd had financial issues that demanded their current work situations remain stable.

Things were dicey when Allie was in California, but currently, she had it so much easier than Ginger. Allie had basically no living expenses, since Barney wasn't charging her nieces room and board, she had the rent coming in from her house in L.A., and she had the prospect of a very large inheritance looming in the future. Ginger had none of those things. She needed her job at the Goodbye every bit as much as Allie had needed her job with the television show before it had gone south.

Allie began to doze off, the glass still in her hand, so when she heard the front door open, she startled awake, spilling half her drink on herself.

"Ugh. What a mess." She got up and went for the paper towels while she called to the hallway, "Nik? Is that you?"

"Yes. Me and Mark and Hayley and Kayla and Mrs. O'Hearn."

Who are all those people? Allie wondered. The only name she recognized was Mark's.

The entire group crowded into the kitchen while Allie was in the process of sopping up lemonade from her shirt.

"Sorry," she said to no one in particular. "I spilled lemonade."

"Hi, Mrs. Monroe," Mark said. "This is my mom."

Allie glanced over her shoulder at the woman upon whose shoulder Mark had placed his hand. His mother was average height and weight, with brown hair styled casually. She wore denim ankle pants and a light blue shirt with the shoulders cut out. Allie was still dressed in her white shirt and black pants from having been at the Goodbye.

"Nice to meet you." Allie held out a hand to Mark's mother once she'd dried it off. "I'm Allie Monroe."

"Roseanne O'Hearn." She was pretty when she smiled, Allie decided. "I think you've met my daughter, Hayley, and this"—she indicated a dark-haired girl—"is Seth's niece Kayla. His sister Amy's daughter."

All three girls were dressed similarly in khaki shorts and crew-neck T-shirts, as if required by the dictates of summer fashion.

"Hi, girls." Allie gave them her biggest smile. She hoped it looked spontaneous and natural, though it was anything but.

"Thanks so much for letting Nikki join us tonight at the picnic. We all enjoyed having her with us," Roseanne said. "And what a singing voice. Wow. She was terrific, but I'm sure you know that."

Allie turned to look at her daughter, who was blushing under the praise.

"Nikki, what did you sing?" she asked.

"Oh, just some show tunes we learned in chorus last year for the musical in May." She shrugged. "And it wasn't just me. Everyone else sang, too."

"Well, like what?" Allie really was curious.

"Like 'I Dreamed a Dream,' from *Les Misérables*. And 'Memory,' from *Cats*, 'A Day in the Sun,' from *Beauty and the Beast*," Nikki said.

"And Nik and Hayley sang 'For Good' from *Wicked*," Kayla said. "That was definitely the best. You guys rocked."

Roseanne and Mark both nodded in agreement.

"Totally rocked," Mark said.

Nikki looked at her mother. "We did all those at the spring musical, remember? Mrs. Parry made us learn new show songs and old ones, like 'The Surrey with the Fringe on Top,' from *Oklahoma*?"

"You started that one and everyone picked up. It was fun." Mark turned to Allie. "Nikki's very good. She has a really pretty voice, Mrs. Monroe."

"She certainly does," Roseanne said. "The next Taylor Swift, right here. And not too far from where Taylor grew up."

Allie nodded in agreement, though she couldn't remember hearing Nikki sing any of the songs that had been mentioned. She must have been at that program in May, but apparently she'd forgotten. Had she self-anesthetized before she left the house that night, knowing she was going to see Clint with Courtney's mother? Because even back then, she'd had her suspicions.

"It would be so fun to put on a real musical at the theater someday," Nikki was saying. "I'd try out for it, wouldn't you guys?"

The other three kids nodded.

"Absolutely."

"Sure."

"Of course."

Right, Allie was thinking. Because nothing said *damn I'm cool* like belting out a few choruses of "The Farmer and the Cowman" or "Officer Krupke."

"Well, that would be nice for Hidden Falls," Allie said. Not that she and Nikki would be around for that, but no need to remind her daughter she'd be back at school in California when—if—such a thing ever happened. "Roseanne, thanks for taking Nikki along with you tonight. It looks like she enjoyed herself."

Nikki was smiling at Mark and not listening to a word Allie was saying.

"Anytime." Roseanne ushered the three kids she was taking with her into the hallway. "Nice meeting you, Allie. I hope we see you again."

"Same here." Allie followed the group to the front door and walked out onto the porch with them. "Beautiful night," she said, looking up at the stars.

"It'll be fall soon enough. You can almost smell it in the morning air." Roseanne waved and walked across the lawn to her car, a silver minivan, the three kids trailing behind. They got into the car, Roseanne giving the horn a light tap before she backed down the driveway.

Allie had lived in Southern California all her life. She had no idea what fall smelled like on a Pennsylvania morning.

"Thanks for letting me go tonight, Mama." Nikki wrapped her arms around Allie's waist.

Allie felt her daughter's breath on the side of her neck, just like when Nikki was little. But the arms were no longer soft and chubby, dimpled at the elbows, and those were not the pudgy fingers of a toddler, but of a girl who was growing into womanhood. Allie tried to push back the bite she felt at her heart whenever she thought about Nikki growing up, but the knowledge had become more and more insistent, more difficult to tuck away. Nikki would be fifteen soon, a few days after she returned to California, and that date was closing in on them quickly. Allie would have to push harder to get the theater ceiling finished, to get the seats and the stage curtains taken care of, to make sure the rest of the restorations went as quickly as possible. She'd get back to Cara and find out when Joe could refinish the stage floor and the backstage area. The last thing they'd have to do was remove the wooden boards from the marquee and bring the ticket booth up from the basement. Both had been carefully restored by the owner who'd bought the theater from Fritz, then later sold it back to him. Allie would make a list and try to keep everything on track.

Allie followed Nikki back to the kitchen, hunting for the plate of brownies she'd made earlier in the day.

"I took some to the picnic." Nikki opened first one, then another cabinet until she found what she was looking for. "Everyone said they were the best. Mrs. O'Hearn even said they were better than the one she had last week at the Goodbye. I mean, I didn't even ask for a comparison. She just said it." Nikki's eyes were shining. "You know what this means, right, Mom?"

"What does it mean, Nik?"

"It means our brownies are better than that mean old Mrs. Kennedy's." Nikki took a bite of one, rolled her eyes as if in ecstasy, then held it up to Allie to taste.

"Wow. That really is good. I think I'll have one of my own."

She was just about to ask Nikki what they did at the picnic besides eat and sing when Nik's phone pinged.

"Oh my God. Is that Mark already?" Allie teased. "He just left a minute ago."

Nikki glanced at her phone. "It's not Mark." She tucked the phone into her pocket without reading the text. "It's Courtney."

"Aren't you going to look at it?"

"Maybe later." Nikki got up and poured herself half a glass of milk. "I always want milk when I have something really choco-latey, don't you, Mom?"

Allie nodded. "What's going on between you and Courtney?"

When Nikki didn't answer, Allie said, "I thought she was your best friend. BFFs and all that."

"Yeah, well, so did I." Nikki drained the milk from the glass and rinsed it in the sink, effectively turning her back on her mother so Allie couldn't read her face.

"Are you going to tell me what's happening with her?"

Nikki shook her head, her body language clearly closed. "Please don't ask me again." She kissed Allie on the cheek. "Good night, Mom. See you in the morning."

The matter was still eating at Allie the next morning while she worked at the theater and after, when she made her way back to the house. Barney had a hair appointment and Nikki was still asleep when Allie checked in on her around ten thirty. She took a quick shower and tossed on an old T-shirt and a pair of running shorts and went downstairs, where she found Des and Cara lingering over coffee.

"You guys are going to have to help me out here." Allie came into the room.

Cara leaned back against the counter. "What's the problem?"

"Nikki," Allie said.

Des scoffed. "Nikki's never a problem."

"Something's bothering her and she won't tell me what it is."

"Al, you're her mother, and she's almost fifteen. Teenage girls don't tell their mothers everything." Des found the brownies Nikki had made the day before, selected one, then passed them around.

"She's always told me everything," Allie complained.

"If I were you, I'd consider those days gone forever. Look back nostalgically but say goodbye." Des nibbled on her brownie. "She's not a little girl anymore. She's not going to want to confide in you."

"Something is wrong, and I can't help her if she won't tell me what it is."

"What makes you think something's wrong?" Cara asked. "Or—and don't take this the wrong way—maybe she doesn't want your help. Maybe whatever is on her mind, she wants to handle it herself."

Des nodded. "She's going to want to make more decisions on her own, and solve her own problems, the older she gets. Do you think it has something to do with Mark?"

"No. I think it's about her best friend back home."

"Courtney," Des said.

"The one whose mother is dating Clint," Cara said.

"Which Nikki may or may not know about, but that's not the issue." Allie frowned. That hadn't occurred to her. "At least, I don't think it is. Could be, though."

"Where is this going? Not that I mind talking through problems with you," Des said, "but I promised Barney two days ago I'd pull weeds out of her flower bed and I want to get started before the vet calls me and tells me to come over and pick up those puppies. Then I'll be hauling them out to Seth's, and I'll be there forever."

"Which we know you'll hate having to do," Allie teased. "We can give you a hand with those weeds. Maybe the physical activity will get the blood moving through my brain and I won't need either of you to tell me what to do."

They all grabbed their garden gloves from the shelf near the back door where Barney kept them and went out into the yard. The air had grown cool overnight and stayed that way, much to everyone's relief.

"Let's work together and do one bed at a time," Des suggested. "Start with the first bed and move to the roses on the side of the house."

"Good plan." Cara pulled on her gloves and started to yank

weeds from around a clump of black-eyed Susans. "So tell us why you think something is going on with Nikki and that it has to do with Courtney."

"Nik and Courtney text back and forth all day and call each other all the time. Over the past couple of days, I've noticed Nikki getting texts she's not responding to, at least while I'm around. Maybe she responds later, but I just see her read, then put the phone in her pocket. And she gets this look on her face, like she's angry, or hurt or confused. I'm not sure which."

"Allie, you know damned well girls argue. They get mad at each other, they fight, they make up, they're BFFs again." Des dragged over an empty trash can to hold the weeds. "That's probably all there is to it. I wouldn't worry."

"It's the look she gets on her face, guys. I'm telling you, something is going on and it's upsetting her. I know my kid."

"Why don't you just ask her?" Cara suggested.

"I did. She all but told me to butt out. And not to ask her about it again." Allie worked alongside Des.

Des frowned. "That doesn't sound like the Nikki I know."

"Guys, that's what I'm trying to tell you."

"She didn't give you any clues?" Cara shook dirt from the weed she'd pulled, then tossed the stems onto a pile on the grass.

Allie shook her head. "Nothing. Zilch."

"I don't know what to tell you." Des started pulling at some grass that had planted itself alongside the monarda.

"What does your gut tell you?" Cara stood up.

"My gut's telling me to check her phone," Allie said quietly, as if afraid of being heard outside the garden.

"You mean spy on her?" Cara shook her head. "I don't know if I'd go that far. If she found out . . ."

"She'd be royally pissed off, and with good reason," Des said. "That's not cool, Al."

"Either of you have a better idea?" Allie looked from one to the other. When neither of them spoke up, she said, "Didn't think so."

"That's a serious breach," Des said. "It's an invasion of her privacy."

"Look, you're going to do what you want, but I would think long and hard before I did something like that. The repercussions when Nikki finds out that you went through her phone without her permission could be brutal," Cara said. "And you know she'll find out, because once you know what's going on, you're going to want to discuss it with her."

"Cara's right. She's going to see this as you snooping on her because you don't trust her, which of course is exactly what you'd be doing. It's like if our mother went through our diaries when we were kids."

"Des, our mother didn't care enough about either of us to snoop through our diaries," Allie said.

"That's probably true," Des said. "But the point is that it would be a long time before she'd trust you again."

"I agree with everything you've both said, and I thank you for listening and for your advice."

"Good. Then you'll leave it alone and we'll be spared the drama when she finds out." Des glanced at Cara. "I don't know about you, but I'm relieved."

"Wait, I didn't say that. I appreciate your input, but I don't know what I'm going to do. I need to think this through."

"It's your life," Des muttered. "But if you're going to look at her phone, I don't want to be around when she finds out. Just give me a heads-up first, because I'll want to go out to the farm before it hits the fan."

"Does Seth have an extra room?" Cara asked.

"I know I speak for him when I say you're always welcome," Des assured her.

"Very funny." Allie went back to pulling weeds. "Now could we change the subject? I think we've exhausted this one."

"How'd you like playing hostess at the Goodbye?" Cara asked.

"It was okay. Not fun, but not awful. I'm getting to meet people I haven't seen around town before, though." Allie thought

back to the crowd that had come through the café the night before. "We were really busy last night. I had to take names and start
a waiting list."

"Look at it this way." Des stood, weeds gathered like scruffy
bouquets in each hand. "Maybe J will come through one of these
nights and the mystery will be solved."

Allie snorted. "Right. Like she's going to walk up to me and
say, 'I dated your father while he was dating your mom, back in
the day. Yeah, he dumped me for her. But I'm over it now.'"

"Wow, things have been so busy around here I'd pretty much
forgotten about the letters," Cara said.

"'Dear Fritz . . .'" Allie began to recite from memory the letters
Cara'd found hidden in the carriage house that had revealed a ro-
mantic relationship between their father and a woman in Hidden
Falls who'd signed her letters J.

"No, she didn't say, 'Dear Fritz,'" Cara reminded her. "She
started her letter with just *F*."

Allie nodded. "Right. 'F. You're a liar and a cheat and I will always hate you for what you've done to me.' Or something like that."

"That was pretty much the gist of it." Cara nodded. "I hope
she went on to find someone wonderful who loved her. I feel a
little sad every time I think about those letters."

"Me, too," Des agreed. "No doubt about it, Dad was a cad."

Allie worked along with her sisters to clean up the flower
bed, watching the pile of weeds grow larger and larger, until
she needed to get ready to go to the Goodbye for her shift. She
cleaned up and dressed and peeked in on Nikki before she
headed downstairs. Her daughter was still sleeping, and next to
her pillow was her phone.

The temptation was overwhelming. Allie's hand itched. All she
had to do was reach out and pick it up, slip into the hall, turn it
on, and scan the texts. She knew Nikki never locked her phone
when she was in the house. Allie stood there for a very long moment, staring at the device that held all Nikki's secrets, debating
her right as a mother against her daughter's right to privacy.

Allie sighed. She needed to decide whether it was worth possibly alienating Nikki for a long time to come. Maybe if she thought it was a matter of life or death she could justify it, but for an argument, the invasion into Nik's privacy wasn't worth it.

Nikki turned onto her side, her long blond hair spreading over her face much as it had when she was a toddler. It took all of Allie's willpower to not tuck the hair behind Nikki's ear and kiss that precious face. She left the room and closed the door behind her as quietly as she could, then went downstairs.

She walked past the sitting room on her way to the front door, then paused before going in. On the shelf where they'd left it was the small wooden box that contained the letters between her father and the woman they knew only as J. Allie opened the box and took out the two letters Cara had found and shared and read them for possibly the fiftieth time.

J. ~

It's really hard for me to write this letter. I don't know how else to say it, so I'll just say that I'm leaving for California on Tuesday morning with Nora. I know you will hate me now and that is the worst thing about this. I know you will think I lied to you, but every word was true. You are the best girl I ever knew. I'm sorry I can't stay and be with you.

F.

F. ~

I'm sending back your letter. I don't ever want to see you or hear from you again. Not that I would anyway, since you're leaving Hidden Falls with her. You're just a liar and a cheat and I will always hate you for what you've done to me. I never should have believed you when you said you and she were just friends. It was just another lie, like "You're the only girl for me." I should have listened to my sister.

J.

Allie hadn't shared with the others how many times she'd gone back to reread the correspondence between the long-ago lovers. The story the letters told was so poignant, so sad, it always made her throat tighten. She refolded and returned them to the box, which she returned to its exact place on the bookshelf, then quietly left the house.

CHAPTER SEVEN

Barney arrived at the Goodbye around six, which meant Allie only had to serve as hostess for a few hours, which was all she could have taken. Three minutes before Barney came through the door, Ben Haldeman and his date du jour arrived. Tonight's feature was a short, bouncy redhead who was wearing a cute but revealing sundress, sandals (which Allie coveted) tied around her ankles, and a stack of silver bracelets that clanged into each other every time she moved her arm. She was also slightly loud.

"I really like this place, Benny," Red was saying when they came in. "It's so cute."

Allie turned from the desk, a broad smile on her face, and greeted them in her most pleasant, saccharine voice. "Welcome to the Goodbye Café, *Benny*. Table for two?"

"Thanks. Yeah." Ben looked away.

"This way, please." Allie led them to a table next to a family with four young children who were having a food fight. She handed Ben and Red menus. "Enjoy your meal, Sheriff."

As she turned from the table, she heard Red say, "You should tell her you're the chief of police, not the sheriff."

"She knows," Ben replied.

"Then why did she call you—"

"Because she likes to be annoying." From the corner of her

eye, Allie saw Ben shift in his seat. "Let's see what the specials are tonight . . ."

Chuckling to herself, Allie stopped on her way back to the desk to pick up a few french fries that had been tossed by one of the toddlers, ignoring the nip of what felt strangely like jealousy. *Impossible.* She dismissed the thought.

"I see Ben has a new girl on his arm tonight." Barney was studying the specials sheet on the desk.

"Second one this week," Allie told her. "That I know of, anyway."

"Well, he's young, single, good-looking, well employed, and an all-around nice guy," Barney said. "I'm sure he has no problem getting dates. And frankly, I'm happy to see him getting out there and dating again. He needs to move on with his life. Not that he'll forget Sarah, but he can't live the rest of his life alone."

Allie sort of grunted noncommittally and greeted the next couple who came into the café. After she'd seated them, Barney tapped her on the arm.

"Would you mind staying on the desk a little while longer? I invited Tom to come down and have dinner with me." Barney paused. "Have you eaten?"

"Yes, I'll hang in here until you and Tom finish dinner, and no, I haven't. I'll grab something at home."

"There is nothing at home. I haven't gone grocery shopping this week because of all the rush to get the sale resolved. If you don't want to eat here, at least take something home. Oh, and you might want to check with Nikki. She and Mark were sitting on the front porch when I left. They may want something as well."

Before Allie could ask, Barney added, "Yes, they're there by themselves and they're fine. They're looking at pictures Mark took in Haiti when he was building houses, bless his heart. Cara and Joe went to pick out paint for the redo she's orchestrated for his kitchen cabinets, and Des took puppies out to the farm and I'm pretty sure she's staying there overnight." Barney smiled. "As would I if I had a sweet man like Seth MacLeod in love with me."

Tom arrived five minutes later, looking his dashing self. Tall, thin, with a shock of thick white hair, Tom Brookes was handsome. His face seemed to have a perpetual tanned and weathered appearance, and Allie wondered where he'd been stationed all those years in the army.

"So how do you think you'll like being part owner of the best eatery in town?" he asked Allie.

"It's all Barney's," Allie said. "I'm just along for the ride."

They chatted for a few moments until a table was cleared and set, then Barney grabbed a few menus, and after stopping at Ben's table to chat and introduce Tom, she led the way to their table.

"That's Miss Hudson, the new owner?" Penny leaned across the desk to whisper to Allie.

"That's right," Allie replied.

"And she had to sit at one of my tables." The waitress grimaced.

"She's the nicest person you'll ever meet," Allie said. "Really. Nothing to worry about." Allie tried to make a joke, saying, "Unless you spill soup in her lap."

Penny's face went white. "Oh God, you heard about that?"

The waitress grabbed a copy of the specials sheet and hustled to Barney's table, leaving Allie wondering who'd had to wear their soup home and when.

Allie noticed Ben and Red getting ready to leave. She stood near the doorway watching him approach, his eyes on her, sporting that tiny bit of turned-up-at-the-corner smile he seemed to wear more and more lately.

"Hope you enjoyed your meal. Good night, *Benny*." Allie held the door open for them, and a heartbeat later, Ben chuckled as he passed by, his eyes still locked on hers.

That wasn't the reaction she'd been expecting. As if he knew, he turned on the sidewalk outside the café and saluted her. Allie smiled, feeling somehow a truce of some sort had been negotiated. On the one hand, it warmed her. On the other, she wondered what he was up to.

When Barney was ready to take over for the night, Allie made a quick call to Nikki.

"I'm going to be leaving here in a few minutes," Allie said. "Have you had dinner? Could I bring something for you?"

"Yes, please. A burger would be great. And maybe we could share a salad?" Nikki said.

"Sure. I think I'll do a burger as well." Allie paused. "Would Mark like me to bring something for him?"

Nikki asked, and Allie heard his, "Tell your mom I said thank you, but I've had dinner."

When Allie got home, Nikki and Mark were sitting on the front steps, deep in conversation, Buttons between them working over a chew bone. When they finally noticed her, Allie was half-way up the walk. Mark rose immediately, walked to her, and took the package containing dinner from her hands.

"How are you, Miz Monroe?" he asked.

"Great, thanks, Mark. What's new?"

"Well, I've been practicing my driving. Tonight my mom's taking me out to Seth's farm to let me practice on his access road."

"Are you old enough to drive?"

"I'm sixteen, so I have my learner's permit. But I can drive farm vehicles. Seth taught me how to drive his truck, which has been good practice."

"Is that legal?"

Mark nodded. "You have to be at least thirteen to drive a farm vehicle."

"Thirteen? Have you been driving since you were thirteen?"

"Since I was fourteen, and only Seth's old truck. It has a special farm-use license plate. I don't drive it around for fun, if that's what you're asking. And I don't drive it at night. I'm pretty sure that wouldn't be legal. I can only drive it for farm business." They'd reached the porch. Nikki's eyes were on Mark, and she was taking in every word, a smile on her face.

Dear God, Allie thought, that's what young love looks like.

"Like if Seth wanted me to drive some of his produce to one

of his customers, I could do that, but it would have to be within a hundred and fifty miles of his farm."

"I guess that's the law so that farmers' kids could help out," Allie said.

"Right. Delivering produce or chickens or whatever the farmer was selling."

"Well, you learn something new every day." Allie took the package from Mark and thanked him. "Nikki, you want to come inside and eat while your dinner's still warm?"

Nikki looked up at Mark.

"I need to get home. I told my mom I'd be back while it was still light so I could practice driving for a while." To Allie he explained, "You have to have so many hours with a licensed driver before you can take your driver's test, so we try to get in an hour or so every day. Nik, I'll see you later."

"Tomorrow maybe." Nikki stood.

"Nice seeing you, Miz Monroe."

"Same here. Night, Mark."

Nikki stood on the step and watched Mark walk down the sidewalk, cross the street, and head up toward Market at the far end of Hudson. Once he was out of view, she turned and took her mother's arm. "Let's eat outside on the patio at that cute little table."

"Good idea." Allie pushed open the front door and Buttons sped inside.

"I'll get drinks and bring them out," Nikki said.

"Thanks. Just water for me. Grab paper plates if there are any left." Allie trailed behind the dog through the house and out the back door.

The patio was in the shade of two large beech trees. While she waited for Nikki, Allie left the package on the table and inspected the progress Des and Cara had made in the flower bed. The pile of weeds had increased dramatically, and the garden was much tidier for it.

"I like those pink flowers," Nikki said as she joined her mother outside. She'd placed plates and forks and Allie's glass of water on the table and joined Allie at the edge of the garden. "Those." She pointed to small hot pink flowers that stood on sturdy silvery stems. "What are they?"

"I have no idea, but Barney probably knows. She planted the beds."

"Those red things are nice, too." Nikki bent to take a whiff of the flowers that grew in a large clump. "Hmmm. No fragrance."

"I guess all flowers don't have a heavy scent. I was helping Barney out in the garden a little when I first got here, but lately I've been so busy at the theater, and now at the Goodbye, I haven't had time." Allie reflected for a moment. "I enjoyed it. Maybe when things slow down, I'll get back to it. When I get home to California, maybe I'll start a garden."

"Someday I'm going to have a big flower garden just like this," Nikki said. She tugged on her mother's hand to draw her back to the table. "I'm going to have flowers in my house all the time like Aunt Barney does. But not the stuff you buy in the store. I'm going to only have flowers like these."

"In the winter you might have to rely on the store-bought bouquets," Allie said. "Though I think you can grow year-round in California."

"It's nice to be able to come outside and gather up whatever looks pretty and bring it inside and put it in a vase where you can see them. I'm going to ask Aunt Barney if I can pick some for my room."

"I'm sure she'll let you do that." Allie unwrapped their food, placed some on Nikki's plate and some on her own, sharing the salad equally. "So what's going on out at the farm?"

"Seth is taking some stuff—like lettuce and beans and carrots, that kind of stuff—to some restaurants, and Mark's going with him."

"You like Mark a lot, don't you?" Allie knew it wasn't really a question.

"I like him so much, Mom. He's the nicest guy I ever met. He's not all about himself. We talk about all kinds of stuff. He reads a lot, and so does Hayley. We're going to start a book club, us three and Jack, who's a friend of Hayley's, and this other girl, Wendy. She lives next door to Mark and Hayley, and she and her mom are here for the rest of the summer. Her grandma went on a trip and Wendy and her mom are house-sitting. She said it was sort of like a vacation for them because her grandma has a pool. She said we could all come over and swim on a day when her mom is there."

Nikki stopped to take a bite of her burger.

"Did you stop to eat or to breathe?" Allie asked.

"Both."

Allie couldn't help but contrast the Nikki who sat before her, merrily chatting away, with last night's Nikki. Whatever had been bothering her must have been resolved.

Thank God, Allie thought. She'd been saved from making a decision she did not want to have to make. Des and Cara were right. Snooping in Nikki's phone would not have worked out well.

They finished eating and went inside once it began to get dark. Allie remembered having heard a story about Joe Domanski being attacked by a bear in the woods behind the house, somewhere near the falls. While the attack had occurred in daylight, once the shadows grew dark out back, Allie headed inside.

She was loading their glasses into the dishwasher and Nikki was leaning against the counter, talking away, when Nikki's phone pinged. Allie glanced over her shoulder and watched her daughter swipe the screen. She appeared to read for a moment, her eyes narrowing as she began to type furiously. It was evident in her expression and her body language that Nikki was fighting mad. She finished the text and shoved the phone into the pocket of her shorts, still obviously fuming.

The storm Allie assumed had passed—hadn't.

The tears of anger gathering in her daughter's eyes finally sent Allie into action.

"Courtney again?"

After a moment, Nikki nodded.

"Nik, what's this all about?"

"I can't tell you." Nikki stared at the floor.

"Baby, there's nothing you can't tell me. I'm your mom."

"That's why I don't want to talk to you about this."

"Why not?" Allie put her arms around her daughter, and at first, Nikki seemed to freeze. Then she began to cry.

"I don't want to tell you because it would hurt you," Nikki sobbed.

"Sweetie, the only thing that hurts me is knowing that something's hurting *you*." Allie held Nikki and let her cry. Finally, when it appeared the worst of the tears had passed, Allie said, "Spill."

"But Mom . . ."

"No buts."

"You don't know . . . Are you sure . . . ?"

"I'm positive."

Nikki pulled the phone from her pocket. She located the text she was looking for, then held up the phone.

"Court sent this to me two days ago."

It was a picture of Clint and Courtney's mother in a very tight embrace, kissing as if they'd invented it. Under the picture, Courtney had typed, *Tell your father to keep his filthy hands off my mother!!!!!*

Allie cleared her throat.

"I didn't want you to know about Dad and Mrs. Davenport. I was afraid it would make you sad." Nikki sniffed, and Allie thought she might be revving up for another round of tears.

"Why would it make me sad?"

"Because you and Dad . . . maybe . . ."

"Are you thinking that Dad and I might get back together someday?"

Nikki hesitated, then nodded.

"Sugar, that's never going to happen. Your father and me divorcing has been best for both of us. I know it's been hard on you, but we're really happier apart, and that's better for everyone." Allie smoothed back long strands of blond hair from Nikki's forehead. "As far as Courtney's mom and your dad are concerned, I figured that out a while back."

"Then why didn't you tell me?" Nikki pulled away abruptly.

"Because I thought that was a conversation your father should have with you. I didn't know how he wanted to handle it and I tried to respect that. But when did you find out?"

"When Courtney sent that picture." Nik pointed to the phone in Allie's hand. "I knew they got along really well and they liked each other and we spend a lot of time together, me and Dad and Court and her mom. I thought it was because Court and I were friends and we live close and we go to the same school. But I didn't know they were . . . *like that*." Nikki wiped her face with the back of her hand as a younger child might do. "How did you know? Did Dad tell you?"

"No, but you sent me all those pictures of the four of you together, and I thought you looked like a family. I saw your father with Marlo—that's Courtney's mother's name, right?"

Nikki nodded.

"And I could tell by the way they looked at each other that there was something there beyond friendship." Allie tried to keep it simple and be gentle with her words, since she wasn't sure exactly how Nikki was picturing her father's relationship with her friend's mother. "So how did you respond to Courtney?"

"I told her to tell her mother to back off my father."

"How'd she take it?" Allie had a feeling Courtney hadn't taken it well.

"She got all mad at me and said if I didn't make him leave her mother alone, she was going to . . ."

"Going to what?"

"She was going to tell all the kids in school . . . things about me."

"Like what things?"

"Like things that aren't true." Nikki took a very deep breath and said, "Like that I'm having sex with Mark. And, Mom, we're not. I swear, we're not. We wouldn't . . ."

"Nik, I believe you. But what a horrid little . . ." The names that lurked on the tip of Allie's tongue weren't names she should use in front of her daughter.

"She's already told some kids that. I sent her a picture of me and Mark, and she's shown it around to the girls, who all texted me and said they thought he was hot and they'd be . . ." Nikki's face turned red. "They'd be doing him, too."

Allie could feel the anger rising inside her. How dare that little . . . But for Nikki's sake, she had to remain calm. In control. Rational. Mature. But *what a wretched little bitch!*

"Oh, Nik, I'm so sorry. That's a horrible thing to do to someone who's supposed to be a friend."

"I probably won't even have any friends by the time I go back home."

Deep breath, Allie.

"Look, if she sends another text, ignore it. Stop responding to her. And let me think this through."

"What are you going to do?" Nikki asked. "Don't do anything that's going to make things worse."

"Let me mull it over, okay? In the meantime, don't even open her texts. Just ignore her."

"All right. I should have come to you right away. I'm sorry I didn't. I thought if I threw it back on her mother, Court would leave me alone. But I guess not."

Nikki looked so unhappy Allie's heart just about broke.

"I also thought she was really, really my friend, but I guess not that, either."

She's an evil little witch, and that's exactly what Allie would tell Clint when she called him after their daughter had gone to her room. Allie went into the office on the first floor and speed-dialed Clint's number.

"Allie, is everything all right with Nikki?" Clint's way of answering the phone.

"No, Clint. Everything is not all right with Nikki." Allie proceeded to tell him everything Nikki had told her. Miraculously, she kept her temper. Clint did not respond well to hysterics. If she wanted him to step up, she had to deal with him in a very cool manner.

When she finished, Clint said, "What do you want me to do?"

"I want you to get your ass on the first flight from L.A. to Scranton, where you'll rent a car and make the hour-long drive to Hidden Falls, then sit your daughter down and tell her what's going on between you and Marlo. You should have done it months ago. You're also going to tell Marlo in no uncertain terms to have a little talk with her obnoxious child and make her tell every single one of those kids that everything she said about Nikki was a big, fat lie. And then Courtney's going to apologize to Nikki. And by God, she'd better mean it." Allie took a deep breath.

"Wait a minute, are you saying that Courtney told the kids out here that Nikki is having sex with some guy out there?" Clint's voice began to rise. "I put that on you. If Nikki is—"

"No. She isn't! That's what I'm trying to tell you!" Allie's control slipped and she reined it in. "Courtney made it up. It's a lie, Clint. Get it? She made it up because she's angry about you and Marlo."

There was a long silence on the phone.

"Clint, are you still there?"

Allie heard him exhale. "We thought it might be more problematic for the girls if they knew we were . . . dating."

"Why would you think that?"

"Because when we started, we had no idea where it was going to go. We thought if the girls knew, and we stopped dating, it might create tension between them."

More silence. Then, "All right. Yes. You're right. I should come out there and talk to Nikki. And you better believe I'm going to have a long talk with Marlo and with Courtney."

"Clint, you should probably leave the Courtney talk up to her mother."

"Not when she's spreading such viciousness about Nik." Another sigh. "Damn it. That little bitch."

"You might not want to lead with that when you tell Marlo what's going on."

"Point taken."

"You'll let me know when to expect you?" Allie asked.

"I will. Do you want to tell Nikki I'm coming?"

"I think you should do that."

"I'll call her now. Thanks, Allie. I'll get back to you as soon as I have a flight. And, Al." He paused. "You did the right thing by calling me."

A while later, Allie was in her room, looking at the photos she'd taken with her phone of some of the ceiling designs, when Nikki burst in.

"Dad called. He said you called him." There was a touch of accusation in Nikki's tone.

"I did, Nik. He's your father and he loves you, and he needed to know what was going on with Courtney. Just because he's dating her mother doesn't mean he's going to let Courtney off the hook. It doesn't work that way."

"He said he was coming out here on Saturday because he wants to talk to me."

"Which he should do, of course."

"He's going to talk to Court's mother?" Nikki asked.

Allie nodded. "Yes. Her mother needs to know what she's been doing. Someone needs to put that . . . *girl* in her place."

"That'll be a first," Nikki muttered.

"Maybe that's her problem. I bet it won't be the last time. Spreading lies about someone to ruin their reputation is an evil thing to do. She needs to learn that actions have consequences."

"What would you do if it were me, telling lies about Courtney?" Nikki asked.

"You'd be grounded for a very, very long time. After you made a sincere apology." Allie watched her daughter's face, but it was unreadable. "You haven't . . . ?"

"Oh, no. I was just wondering. Honest, Mom. I would never do that." Nikki sat on the edge of the chair next to the window.

"Nik, we need to understand that people who make up stories

to make other people look bad do it because they feel bad about themselves for some reason. I'm not sure what Courtney's problem is, but her parents are going to have to get to the bottom of it."

"If nothing else, it got Dad to come see me. So thanks for that." Nikki stood and hugged her. "I told Dad we'd show him the theater and he could have dinner with us at the Goodbye. Was that all right?"

"Perfect. I'm sure he'll love the theater, and we'll have to make certain there's something really good on the menu for Saturday night."

"Dad really likes meat loaf," Nikki said. "He makes it for us sometimes. But when we go out to dinner, he always orders fish because it's healthier. Maybe we should ask Chef George to make meat loaf for Saturday night."

"And if not, I'm sure there will be something wonderful."

"Mark and Seth caught trout in our lake and they were delicious. Maybe I should ask them to take me fishing on Saturday morning." Nikki's face lit at the prospect. Allie knew who Nik was texting as she walked through the door after kissing her mother good night.

Sure enough, before Allie left the house after breakfast the next morning, Nikki announced that Seth had agreed to take her and Mark to the lake on Saturday morning to fish for trout. It was obvious that Nikki wanted to not only show off her boyfriend but introduce her father to the wonders of the Pocono Mountains and have bragging rights to the fish they'd serve at the café.

Points to Nikki for being resourceful.

Allie was back at the theater a short while later. She'd sung her way to the top of the scaffold, set herself up, opened the first jar of paint for the day, and settled in to begin. She'd barely gotten one entire design traced when she felt the scaffold begin to sway.

"Whoa!" she cried, and grasped the sides of the plank she was sitting on.

"It's okay," Des called up to her from halfway up the scaffold. "It's not going to fall."

"No, but it could shake me right off the top. What are you doing?" Allie called down to her.

"Cara and I want to talk to you," Des said.

"It can't wait till I'm finished here?"

"It won't take long." Des was in a sweat by the time she reached the top. "God, Al, how do you do this every day? My hands are shaking and my heart's pounding. I can't even look down."

"Then don't. And for the record, that's how I get up here. I sweat, my hands shake, and my heart pounds. I was hoping if I did it every day I'd get over it, but nope."

Allie glanced over the side. Cara was almost all the way up.

"Guys, this might not be a good idea. I don't know if this thing is going to hold all three of us." Allie could feel her heart rate start up again.

"It held Joe, Ben, and Seth the other night. I think it'll hold us." Cara pulled herself up and sat carefully beside Des.

"What were they doing here?" Allie asked.

"Racing to the top. You know how competitive they are," Des told her. "Three little boys who never got over playing to win."

"By the way, Seth won," Cara said.

Allie put the lid back onto the paint jar. "So what's so important that the two of you had to make like monkeys and climb up here at ten minutes to eight in the morning?"

"We saw Nikki at breakfast. She looked like herself again. Happy, singing, making jokes," Des said.

"So we wanted to know what happened. You know, with the phone and her getting texts and all that."

"You just wanted an excuse to get a close look at my work." Allie nodded at the ceiling.

"Well, there was that." Des tilted her head back to look. "It's fabulous, and that was a brilliant idea. Now. Nikki."

Allie related the entire story.

"That girl said what?" Des said in disbelief. "About our Nikki?"

"She did."

"You really think Clint's going to take care of this?" Cara asked. "I don't know him, so I don't know how he'd react to something like this."

"Most things, he'd let go. He's not confrontational. He doesn't like arguments. Frankly, I think he's a bit of a wuss most of the time. But when it comes to his daughter, he can be Papa Grizzly. It remains to be seen how he'll handle this, because Marlo's involved. I told him he had to come out here and tell Nikki where his and Marlo's relationship stands, and he had to come ASAP. He hung up with me and called Nik and told her he'd be here on Saturday. So. Done. Still not his biggest fan, but I have to give him props for showing up this time."

"Sounds like Clint's grown a pair," Des said. "I never liked him very much. But if he stands up for Nikki now, he might earn some respect."

"Now that you know—and of course you're not going to breathe a word to Nikki that you know, she'd be so embarrassed—the two of you may resume your previously scheduled . . . whatever it is you were going to do today." She shooed them away with both hands. "Go. Now. I have work to do."

Des and Cara climbed down, but before they left, Des looked up and said, "Does Barney know about any of this?"

"I haven't seen her to tell her."

"You might want to fit that in before Saturday when Clint shows up," Des said. "She might wonder what your ex-husband's doing in Hidden Falls."

CHAPTER EIGHT

Allie knew there was a problem when Barney came into the Goodbye looking like she was going to bite someone's head off.

"So when were you going to tell me?" Barney stood in front of the desk, eyes blazing, hands on her hips.

"Tell you what?" Allie looked up from the seating chart. "That Clint is coming on Saturday?"

"That, and the reason why he's coming. If I ever get my hands on that nasty little girl, I'll—"

"Whoa. Whatever you're going to say, I'm sure it qualifies as child abuse. Yes, she's an evil little demon, and I hope Nikki realizes that this girl is not her friend. Actually, I never liked her. Not that I spent a lot of time with her, but on the few occasions when I picked them up after a dance or something, she always seemed to be talking about one of the other girls, and I don't mean in a complimentary way. I remember one time asking Nikki if she wondered what Courtney says about her when she's not around, and she said Courtney would never do that, that she's her best friend. Her BFF."

"Hmmph. That must stand for *big faux friend*." Barney was still steaming. "You really think Clint is going to take care of this?"

"I do. He said he'd call Nikki, and he did, shortly after calling me."

"That doesn't mean he's going to confront the mother of this little beast and she's going to put her daughter in her place. Especially since he's sleeping with the mother."

"Clint loves Nikki. He might even love her more than he loves himself, and that's saying something. I can't see him letting this slide regardless of his relationship with Marlo—that's the mother's name."

"So why's he coming here?"

Allie explained to Barney that Clint's never discussed his relationship with Marlo, and he needs to do that face-to-face.

"I suppose that would be for the best," Barney agreed.

"Besides, he hasn't seen her all summer. I know Nik misses him, and she can't wait to show off the theater and the Goodbye."

"Oh, of course she would, and she should. I'm just feeling cranky because I felt blindsided when I got back from my library board meeting and Des and Cara were talking about that whole mess. Courtney telling the other girls vicious lies and Clint coming here on Saturday."

"I'd have told you myself, but you weren't up when I left this morning, and then when I got back from the theater, you'd already left for the library."

"Things might get a bit complicated on Saturday, though."

"What things?"

"Well, Judy had planned on flying to New Mexico on Friday, but I talked her into staying at least through the weekend. I wanted to have a little goodbye party for her at the café, but I thought we'd have more time to plan for it. But she's decided that since she's signed everything she needed to for now, she should go on out and spend a day or two with her brother. She figures she can sign anything else electronically, as they do now. She said she doesn't feel right hanging around Hidden Falls when she knows her brother has to go home. So the party has to be this weekend."

"That's short notice, isn't it?"

"Short notice? No problem." Barney grinned. "We're doing

flyers, and I've asked Nikki and her friends to take them around town to invite Judy's friends and customers to the 'Goodbye at the Goodbye' on Saturday night. Yes, I went there." Barney grinned impishly. "I couldn't resist."

"So what are you planning?"

"Don't worry, it's not going to be a free, all-you-can-eat buffet. I'm generous, but I'm not crazy. I've ordered a huge sheet cake from a bakery in Rose Hill. Folks can come in, say a few words to Judy, have a piece of cake, and then leave."

"How many flyers did you have made?" Allie asked cautiously.

"Nikki made them. I'm not sure how many, but she said they'd put a stack in the library, the pharmacy, the hairdressers. Places like that. We'll leave some for you to give out tonight at the Goodbye to the regulars who come in." Barney put one hand on her hip and returned Allie's stare, one questioning eyebrow raised. "What?"

"I'm just wondering how this is going to play out. I mean, we're going to be serving dinner while all these people are coming in and out, right?"

"I suppose. So?"

"So how are you going to get them to leave once they're there and chatting with Judy, and then they're chatting with someone else, then someone else, while diners are trying to find tables to order dinner? Get my drift?"

Barney appeared to mull that over for a moment. "Well, I guess I'll have to shoo some of the well-wishers along somehow."

"Or maybe come up with another idea." The door opened and the first of the dinner customers arrived. Allie counted out five menus. Leaning close to Barney, she whispered, "Otherwise, you're going to need more than one cake."

"Did you check with the town to see if it's legal to put all those tables and chairs out on the sidewalk?" Allie asked on Saturday morning after Barney shared her plan to have the "Goodbye at the

Goodbye" on the sidewalk outside the café to reserve the tables inside for customers who wished to order dinner.

Barney's look could have blistered paint.

"No, Allie, since I'm new to this town and I was born yesterday," Barney said.

"Just asking. I know you've been really busy this week, so I just thought I'd ask," Allie said. "I know how certain members of the town council feel about you and would love nothing more than a chance to take a swipe at you."

"You mean Irene Pettibone and Ross Whalen? Pfft. Those two. Why would I bother with them?" Barney brushed them away with the back of her hand. "I went straight to the seat of power."

"You called Seth," Allie said flatly.

"Of course. Who better than the mayor to decide such matters?" Barney's eyes narrowed and the corners of her mouth turned up just a tiny bit. "Won't that fool Whalen get a surprise when I announce I'm going to run for his seat next election?"

"You're going to run for town council?" Allie's jaw dropped. "Why?"

"Why wouldn't I?" Barney asked indignantly.

"I would think between the Goodbye and the Sugarhouse, you're going to have your hands full."

"I'll manage. I expect I'll have help. I'll catch up with you later. Tom rented the tables and chairs for me and he's going to pick them up and take them over. He'll set them up, too." She paused and added, "It can be nice to have a man around to help out after managing alone all your life. I rather like it. As long as he's not in my way."

Barney grabbed her cutting shears from a hook near the back door, then said as she went outside, "I need to cut some flowers for the front hall since we're having a visitor today."

Allie looked up as Cara came down the steps.

"She thinks we're all staying," Allie told her.

"You can't blame her for wanting us to. Des, for sure, I'd bet on her staying. She's got a rescue shelter going out at Seth's and you know she's not going to leave that for him to deal with, and she's not going to turn away any strays. She said last night she's going to try to set up a network with shelters in Scranton, Wilkes-Barre, and Stroudsburg." Cara reached the bottom of the stairwell. "Besides, she and Seth are crazy in love. They can't stop looking at each other. They finish each other's sentences. Des isn't going anywhere."

"And you?"

"Could go either way. On the one hand, I own a business in Devlin's Light. My mom's house is still there. But on the other hand: Joe." Cara sat on the bottom step.

"And you two are crazy in love and can't stop looking at each other. I got that."

"I am pretty crazy about him, and I know he feels the same way. We spend just about all our free time together, and it's always great. Like right now, I'm helping him work on his house. He has that darling Cape Cod, but it's so badly outdated. Needs everything, but it has a big yard and good-size rooms and it's in a nice neighborhood. We're working on the kitchen right now. He doesn't have a lot of money to spend on it, so I'm giving him the benefit of everything I learned from Susa, who was the queen of DIY long before it was a TV show. And watching a lot of HGTV, of course."

"That still kills me," Allie said, "that your mother was so thrifty and did so much herself, when Dad had more money than he knew what to do with."

Cara laughed. "You actually sound like Dad. He was always after her to hire a contractor to make the house bigger. *'Why?'* she'd say. *'It's perfect for the three of us just as it is.'* Or, *'Susa, hire someone to take care of that garden.'* And she'd say, *'But then it wouldn't be mine.'* Or, *'Susa, let someone else run that shop of yours.'* Then she'd almost but not quite raise her voice."

"I bet that drove him nuts."

"It did, but I don't think Mom realized how much money Dad had. I didn't, and she wouldn't have cared. He never flaunted it in Devlin's Light. I guess because he knew how Mom felt about money. She always said everyone needed to find what they loved, then find a way to make that work for them. That everyone 'needed to carry their own water.'"

"Crazy when you think about how easy her life could have been."

"If you'd asked her, she'd have told you she had the best life in the world. She had Dad—well, sometimes she had Dad—she had me, she had the house she adored, and she had her shop. Those were the things that mattered to her. Need I remind you she was raised by hippies?"

"I wish I'd known her."

Cara got up and hugged her sister. "Oh, I wish you had, too."

Allie felt a surge of emotion. Sometimes Cara's loving, open nature seemed to sneak up on Allie and find her soft spot.

"So. Have you found what you loved and found a way to make it work for you?" Allie asked.

Cara nodded. "My yoga studio. If I decided to stay in Hidden Falls, I'll do the same here. Plus, I was thinking . . ." Cara hesitated.

"About . . . ?"

"About the fact that once the theater is finished, it's going to have to be reopened. I mean, why do all this work, spend a million dollars, only to close it up again?"

"I always thought we'd just sell it to someone else who'd open it."

"You can't be serious. Dad didn't make us go through all this to fix it up for someone else." Cara's expression was one of sheer disbelief. "He wanted it to stay in the family. I think that was the whole point of him buying it back from the guy he'd sold it to. I think he deeply regretted letting the theater out of the family. No, he did *not* intend for us to sell it."

"He didn't say we couldn't."

"No, but I believe he was hoping we'd respect it as part of the Hudson legacy."

"Well, who do you think is going to want to be responsible for it?"

"Be responsible for what?" Des came down the steps.

"The Sugarhouse," Allie said. "We were just discussing what we're going to do with it once it's finished."

"We'll reopen it, of course, and we'll run it." Des walked past her two sisters on her way to the kitchen. "Was there ever any doubt?"

Cara shrugged, gave Allie an *I told you so* look, and followed Des. "Don't finish the granola, Des. I promised Nikki I'd save it for her."

"Nikki already ate it. She went fishing with Seth and Mark at the butt crack of dawn," Allie called after them.

She stood alone in the great hall. She hadn't missed Des's use of *we*.

"We'll reopen it."

Allie assumed she meant Des and Cara and Barney. Allie assumed when she left, the others would as well. She hadn't counted on either of them finding reasons to stay.

She gathered her supplies for the theater and set out without bothering to say goodbye. The entire time she was at the Sugarhouse, the feeling of being odd man out stayed with her even as she worked, and it followed her back to the house when she'd finished for the day. She had just enough time to grab lunch, take a shower, and dress before Clint arrived.

He'd called Nikki last night and told her to expect him around three o'clock, that he'd be renting a car to drive from Wilkes-Barre/Scranton International Airport to Hidden Falls. As if Nikki weren't excited enough, he told her he'd be bringing her a surprise. Allie knew Nik missed her father and had been awake so late last night that Allie feared she'd not be able to wake up to go fishing with Mark in the morning. But she'd gotten up, and Seth and Mark had come for her at 5 a.m. A bleary-eyed Allie had meant to ask where Seth was taking them, but Nikki had bolted out of the door in shorts, a T-shirt covered by a sweatshirt to stave off the early-morning mountain chill, and sneakers, a hat she'd borrowed from Barney atop her head, and a bag carrying sunscreen, granola bars, a few bottles of water, and of course her phone.

It was so cute that Nik wanted to catch her father's dinner, Allie thought, certainly not something that your average L.A. teen girl would do. Then again, Nikki wasn't an average girl. All the Hudsons knew that. Allie hoped that if in fact the kids were lucky and caught a trout or two, Clint would express the proper amount of appreciation for the effort.

Sometimes he could be a jerk. Allie hoped today wouldn't be one of them.

Nikki blew into the house at 2:25, sweaty and smelling like fish.

"Smells as if you caught one," Allie remarked when Nikki ran past her.

"We did. We caught the limit! Out at the lake. Our lake." Nikki paused at the sink to pour a glass of water from the spigot and down it. "Compton Lake. We dropped them off at the café. Chef George was so excited. He said they were the most beautiful trout he'd seen all season. He's going to serve Compton Lake trout tonight. I'm so excited."

"You couldn't possibly have caught that many," Allie said.

"There's a limit on how much you can catch. It's five. Mark caught five and Seth caught five. And they're big! I couldn't believe it. And pretty! I almost felt sorry that we're going to eat them." She grabbed her bag from the chair onto which she'd dropped it and was gone in a flash.

Allie could hear Nikki's footsteps running up the stairs, fading as she went into her room.

"Was that Hurricane Nicole?" Barney asked as she came down the back stairwell into the kitchen.

Barney was, Allie noticed, dressed to intimidate, in a black linen sheath, and large South Sea pearls around her neck and on her ears. On the middle finger of her right hand she wore a ring with a huge blue stone solitaire.

"Barney, what's that ring?" Allie grabbed Barney's hand.

"Oh, this old thing?" Barney teased. "My mother's engagement ring."

"Is that a real—"

"Ceylon sapphire, yes. Indeed it is." Barney held it up to the light. "Flawless. It was in a brooch my grandmother wore, and when Dad decided he was going to ask Mother to be his bride, he wanted a family piece. He knew Mother didn't particularly care for colorless stones, so he took the brooch to a jeweler, had the stone taken out, and had the ring made. She never took it off her finger, and often said she was going to be buried with it, but when push came to shove, I couldn't let this baby go six feet under, never to see the light of day again."

"So you took it right off her hand?" Allie lifted an eyebrow.

"Don't be silly. Of course not." Barney dismissed her comment. "The mortician did."

Allie rolled her eyes.

Barney changed the subject. "How did our little fisherman do today? Did she actually catch anything?"

"She said *they* did, not necessarily that *she* did. She did say both Seth and Mark caught the limit, whatever that is."

"I believe it's still five fish." Barney went on to explain the fish and game laws in Pennsylvania. Allie's head was beginning to swim by the time Barney finished. She thought perhaps Barney might be a teensy bit nervous about Clint coming to see Nikki. Perhaps she was afraid Clint would spirit Nik away, or talk her into going back to California with him.

Allie knew neither of those things would happen.

"Anyway," Allie said when Barney had completed her monologue, "Nikki said they were big trout. I didn't see them. Before Seth brought Nik home, they dropped the fish off at the café. Nikki said George was really happy."

"My goodness, if you give a cook ten big Pocono trout—"

"Nikki called them Compton Lake trout."

"Oh, that's where they went? My dad used to take Fritz and me out there to fish. Of course, that's been many years. I'm not surprised the fish were large. We've never opened the lake up for public fishing, so I imagine those trout have had plenty of time to grow big and fat. Of course, I let the boys—Joe and Ben and Seth—use the lake whenever they want, to swim or canoe or fish, whatever. And I suppose the bears have caught and eaten quite a few trout over the years." Barney began to take lemons out of the refrigerator, then stopped. "Does your ex prefer lemonade or iced tea? I thought I'd have something cool to offer him when he gets here."

"He'd be happy with either, I'm sure, Barney. And that's very thoughtful of you."

"I'll do lemonade, then, because it's Nik's favorite. I'm thinking we should make it for the café on these hot nights."

Barney got out her old-fashioned glass juicer and a knife and lined up the lemons on the table.

"Want me to do that?" Allie offered.

"No, that's okay. I like to keep busy." Barney proceeded to halve and juice the lemons. "Besides, you're dressed for work and I'd hate to see that nice crisp white shirt spotted with lemon juice."

"I'm not sure what Nikki's agenda is for this afternoon, but I thought if Clint's late getting here and we chat for a few minutes, I wouldn't have time to change into my Goodbye uniform." Allie looked down at the shirt she'd ironed before putting it on. She wasn't accustomed to pressing her own clothes. For years she'd sent everything to the dry cleaners. Her first day or two as hostess, she hadn't bothered with the iron, but she'd decided yesterday that the slightly rumpled look she'd been sporting was not only unprofessional but so not her. However ambivalent she might feel about her hostessing duties didn't extend to her appearance.

"Mom, a car just pulled into the driveway!" Nikki called from the second floor just before she flew down the steps. "I think it might be Dad."

Barney and Allie went into the front hall, where Nikki was looking in the mirror.

"How do I look?" She'd changed into a cute white sundress

with red cherries on it, and white leather sandals that tied around her ankles. Her hair, still damp from the shower, hung straight down her back, much like her mother's, a waterfall of a perfect shade of blond. Barney once had called it Hudson blond, since it matched not only Allie's hair but Barney's as well.

"Like you've been fishing all morning," Allie said.

"Mom! That's so mean!" Nikki laughed despite her protest. "Aren't you going to wear shoes?"

"Oh damn. Be right back." Allie ran up the steps just as the doorbell rang.

She heard voices in the hall as she pulled on her black sandals and made her way back down the steps. She wasn't nervous about seeing her ex again—she was long past the point where she felt much of anything for him other than as Nikki's father—but she was slightly on edge for Nikki's sake, hoping that everything went the way she wanted. She needed time with her dad, and Allie prayed Clint didn't blow the conversation about his relationship with Courtney's mother.

Allie was halfway down the stairs when she realized she heard more than one new voice in the mix. She reached the first floor in time to hear Clint say, "Wow, this is quite a place you've got here, Miss Hudson."

"It's really gorgeous. There are no homes quite this grand in our town," a woman was saying.

Allie paused before continuing down and stopping on the bottom step, behind Cara, who half turned and whispered, "Did you know . . . ?"

"Uh-uh," Allie whispered back.

She peered over Cara to see a very pretty, petite, pleasant-looking woman, her short blond hair perfectly coiffed. She wore a light blue linen shirt over a matching tank and white ankle pants. Allie couldn't see her feet, but she'd bet she was wearing designer sandals. The woman had the demeanor of someone who was well-bred and wealthy. Of course. She was with Clint, and he had no time for anyone who wasn't.

"Clint," Allie said. "You're looking well."

"Hello, Allie." He stared at her for what seemed like a very long time. "You're looking—very well. I guess the mountain air agrees with you. Have you met Marlo Davenport?"

"I think so, at a school function last year. Marlo, it's good to see you. Did you have a pleasant trip?"

"We did, thank you. And Clint's right," Marlo said. "You do look wonderful."

"And . . . Courtney." Allie plastered a meaningful smile on her face. She knew it was fake and could tell by the way Courtney was staring that *she* knew it was fake, too.

"Hi, Miz Monroe." Courtney's voice barely rose to a whisper.

"Clint," Allie said pleasantly albeit pointedly. "You didn't tell me you were bringing Marlo and Courtney."

"I thought it would be a nice surprise for Nikki." His voice was just a shade or two more cheery than it needed to be.

"A nice surprise?" Barney went full-blown, no-filter diva. "Is this the same child that spread those horrid lies about Nikki?"

Barney peered at Courtney through her glasses, which she'd allowed to slip to the edge of her nose. Courtney seemed to shrink slightly under Barney's scrutiny.

"Well, about that . . ." Marlo's face flushed beet red. She poked her daughter in the back and said, "Courtney, I believe you have something you wanted to say to Nikki."

Courtney took a deep breath, and it was apparent to every adult in the hall that the forthcoming apology would be rehearsed and insincere. She stepped forward, her linen shorts and matching shirt wrinkled from the flight and the drive from the airport. Her hair was pulled back in a ponytail, and she wore her attitude as if it were a name tag: right out front and bold so as not to be missed.

"Nikki, I'm sorry I said those things about you. I texted everyone and told them it wasn't true." Her eyes were welling with tears but her voice was flat. "That I made it up."

It wasn't a good performance. Even her mother didn't appear to be buying it.

"Why would you do something like that? I thought you were my best friend, Courtney." Nikki was doing her best to not cry, but to Allie it was clear she was struggling. Even so, her voice was strong and her back was straight.

"I *was* your best friend." Courtney's eyes flashed and she appeared to forget about the adults in the hall. "Then you came here and all you talked about were your new friends and Mark and how cute he was and how smart and how funny. I got tired of hearing about him and all the stupid, dorky things you guys do. And those stories you tell were getting on my nerves, like you were living in your aunt's house, which was this beautiful old mansion—" Courtney stopped, apparently remembering where she was. "Okay, so that part's true, I guess. But that goofy story about a priceless emerald necklace that was given to your great-great-grandmother or something by a Spanish prince and was missing, and how you were looking for it because your aunt said whoever found it could keep it?" Courtney rolled her eyes. "Like I'd believe that."

"Is this the necklace you mean?" Barney's smile was solid ice as she stepped aside and pointed to the portrait of Althea Brookes Hudson wearing the emeralds.

Courtney's eyes widened. "It's real?"

Barney sniffed indignantly. "Obviously."

Courtney turned to Nikki. "And that fancy theater . . . ?"

". . . is right in the center of town. You know it's real. I sent you pictures. My mom and her sisters are still working on it. There was a big storm earlier in the summer before I got here and a part of the ceiling got damaged. My mom is painting it. We can walk over and I'll show you."

"Good idea, Nik. I was hoping to have some time to talk to you, alone, while I'm here." Clint had been watching the interchange between Courtney and Nikki. Allie hoped he was smart enough to second-guess his decision to bring Marlo and her daughter.

"Could I offer you something to drink?" Diva Barney could also be an incredibly gracious hostess.

"No, thank you, Miss Hudson. I think I'd like to go on over to the theater. Nikki seems eager to show it off," he replied. "And as I said, I've been wanting to speak with her alone for a few minutes."

Allie gave him points for being polite. He wasn't always.

"We can go into the projection room," Nikki said. "We'll have privacy there. Courtney and Mrs. Davenport can look around while we're upstairs. The theater is beautiful and there's a lot to see."

"And then I thought the four of us"—Clint motioned to Marlo, Nikki, and Courtney—"would drive back to Scranton and have dinner. I went online yesterday and found a suitable restaurant and made reservations. We have rooms at the best hotel in town, and I thought we'd stay over and tour the city tomorrow." He smiled as if proud of himself for thinking ahead.

Nikki's face went white. "No! No, Dad, we can't. We have to have dinner at the Goodbye!"

"The what?" Clint asked.

"The Green Brier Café. Everyone calls it the Goodbye. I told you about how Aunt Barney's friend had this great little café but she was selling it and moving across the country and how Aunt Barney's buying it. I'm going to work there as soon as I get my working papers. You have to have them if you're not seventeen yet."

"Nik, we already have reservations at Le Petit Chat. It's five stars, it's French, and the menu looks phenomenal. You're going to love it." Clint moved to grab the door handle, as if the discussion was over, because of course Nikki would rather eat at the restaurant he'd selected.

"No. We have to go to the Goodbye." Nikki looked at Allie, pleading. "Mom . . ."

"Clint, it was nice of you to include Nikki in your dinner and evening plans, and I know she appreciates it, but she has a very special surprise for you at the café here in town."

Clint glanced at Nikki. "A surprise? You do?"

Nikki, close to tears, nodded.

"What kind of surprise?" Clint asked.

Allie could have smacked him.

"Clint . . ." Allie knew he'd recognize the tone of her voice and realize it was time to take a step back. "If she told you, it wouldn't be a surprise."

"I'm sorry, Nik. I should have checked with you first. I thought maybe you'd want to go someplace different. But of course we'd love to go to your café, wouldn't we, Marlo? Courtney?"

Courtney was silent, but Marlo smiled graciously. "I think it's a great idea. I can't wait to see your café and the surprise you have in store for your dad."

"Well, I'll catch up with you all there later," Allie said as she stepped down from the bottom stair.

"Of course, you're welcome to join us," Clint said somewhat magnanimously. "You, too, Miss Hudson. Des. Cara."

"I'll be there," Allie told him, "but I'm working."

"You're what?" He raised an eyebrow.

"I handle the hostess duties from around four until we close or someone remembers to come and take her turn." She side-eyed Barney. "It's actually been fun. Sort of."

"I should warn you I'm having a goodbye party for the friend from whom I'm buying the restaurant," Barney said. "So I expect it to be quite busy."

"Cara and I are helping Barney," Des told him. "But thanks anyway."

"Well, in that case . . ." Clint gestured to the door. "Shall we go? Nik? You ready?"

Nikki nodded. "Mom, I'll see you at the Goodbye."

"See you all later." Allie watched the four of them leave, then closed the door behind them.

"Well, that was . . . interesting." Barney turned to Allie. "You did tell me he was a bit of an ass. However, he did seem to defer to Nikki, so that's a point in his favor."

"And Marlo actually seemed quite nice," Des said. "I admit to being surprised, since her daughter is such a brat."

"That happens sometimes when the parents are divorced," Allie replied. "Nik said Courtney's father gives her whatever she wants and lets her do whatever she feels like doing. I expect he'll give her a very expensive car when she turns sixteen this fall. He's a surfer dude—trust fund baby—who lives in a house on the beach in Malibu with his girlfriend du jour, who is something like twenty-two."

"Courtney's older than Nikki?" Barney asked. "I was under the impression they were in the same grade."

Allie nodded. "They are. She was held back at one point when she changed schools. I'm not sure why."

"Marlo impressed me as thoughtful and smart, and she's definitely attractive," Cara said. "Funny how a guy like Clint always seems to attract smart, beautiful women."

"I'll take that as a compliment to me as well as to Marlo."

"What did you think of Courtney's apology?" Des asked.

"I thought Courtney should have practiced looking sincere while she was memorizing her lines," Allie said.

"Yeah. Even her mother didn't appear convinced," Cara said. "I thought Marlo looked embarrassed."

"I find it hard to believe Nikki ever wanted to be friends with that little brat." Barney, as usual, pulled no punches. "Her apology was as phony as her friendship."

Allie searched her bag for her phone before she swung it over her shoulder. "Even though I personally never warmed to her, Nikki really liked her and they always seemed to have fun together. She was the first person Nik met when she moved from my house to Clint's so she could go to Woods Hall. Courtney introduced her to the other kids, and they did everything together. But you heard her in the hallway. Maybe she's feeling left out since Nik left for the summer and met new kids and made new friends. And another thing: Nik told me that Courtney prays every night that her father and mother would reconcile, so seeing her mother with Clint might be upsetting her. And maybe she sees Nik abandoning her the way her dad did."

"Wow, Al. That was deep," Des said.

"Yeah, well, still waters and all that." Allie opened the door and stepped out onto the porch.

"Girl, the water's never still when you're around." Des closed the door with a click.

Chapter Nine

Despite the evening's humidity, the sidewalk in front of the Goodbye was crowded with tables and stacks of chairs being unloaded from the back of a pickup parked illegally. As Allie drew closer, she recognized Tom as the man on the curb directing three strapping young men. Allie recognized Mark, but not the other two. Friends of his, she supposed.

"I see Barney's putting everyone to work tonight," Allie called to Tom.

"You know Bonnie." Tom greeted her with a wave, then walked toward her. He still refused to refer to Barney by her nickname, which he thought was unbecoming to her. "The more the merrier. Besides, I don't see her out here unloading the tables. Telling me where to put them, yes. Taking them off the truck, no."

Allie laughed. "Ah, you do know her well."

"I used to. I'm still getting to know this Bonnie. I guess she's still getting to know this Tom," he admitted. "It's been a long while since we last saw each other. Longer still since we had a chance to really talk. I like to think we're making up for lost time."

"Barney said you were good friends with Gil when you were in school," Allie said.

"Yeah, he was a great guy. You couldn't blame Bonnie for

falling for him. All the girls had a thing for him, even my sister, Emily. They were all crushed when it became apparent Gil only had eyes for Bonnie." Tom shook his head. "It was tragic, him dying so young. The man was full of life. It's still hard to believe he and Bonnie didn't get the chance to marry and live happily ever after with a houseful of kids. They were perfectly matched."

"It's difficult for her sometimes, I know." Probably not Allie's place to remind Tom of how long Barney had grieved for Gil, since he and she looked like they might have a thing going for them now. "But hey, I saw your high school pictures in one of Barney's yearbooks. You were a pretty good-looking guy yourself. I bet you had your pick of the ladies back then."

Tom shrugged. "Well, when you feel like there's only one girl for you, and she's only got eyes for someone else, it's not fair to expect someone else to play second fiddle."

Allie knew he was referring to Barney.

"I bet your wife was a great lady and your life together was wonderful," Allie said.

"She was, and it was, and I have no regrets."

"I'm glad." Allie watched two of the boys carry a stack of tables in her direction. "I guess I'd better get out of your way."

"Yeah, looks like I have a little more work to do. See you later on, Allie." Tom set off in the direction of the boys unloading the tables and chairs.

"Hi, Miz Monroe!" Mark jumped down off the back of the truck. He reminded Allie of a golden retriever pup, happy and cheerful and born to make you smile. "How're things going with Nikki's dad?"

"I think they're going well, thanks, Mark."

He started unfolding chairs and setting them where Tom designated.

"She did get a bit of a surprise, though." Allie stepped closer and lowered her voice. "Courtney and her mother came along on the trip."

"Yeah, she texted me." He paused, his hand on the back of the chair he'd been about to unfold.

"I guess Nik might have mentioned her."

"Yeah, she mentioned her." He seemed to think for a moment before saying, "I know Nik told you everything. About Courtney, I mean. The stuff she was spreading around. You know none of that's true, right, Miz Monroe? I really like Nikki a lot, but we never . . . she would never . . ."

"Of course I know that, Mark, but I appreciate you wanting to defend my daughter. What Courtney did was inexcusable, but she says she told the other girls that she'd made it up and that none of it was true, so hopefully by the time Nik goes back to school, all this will have been forgotten."

"I hope you're right, but I don't know if I'd trust her. I have a sister, and I see how girls act sometimes. I mean, Hayley's pretty straight up, but some of the girls in her class aren't. I hope Courtney's telling the truth now, for Nik's sake." Mark was so earnest Allie wanted to give him a hug. She didn't, but the impulse was there.

"Yeah, well, there's always that chance that she's saying what her mother wants to hear, I get that, Mark. We're going to hold her to it, though. Believe me, by the time I get back to L.A., there'd better not be a peep of any of this, or someone's going to be in deep . . . stuff."

Mark smiled. "I'm glad you're her mom. I know you'll stick up for her if she needs you to."

"You betcha.'"

Tables were being set up, and Allie was blocking the sidewalk, so she started toward the building. "Maybe we'll see you later on."

"Nik invited me to have dinner with them all here, but I told her I don't know how comfortable I'd be with Courtney there. I might say something I shouldn't."

"I'm sure Nik would like to have you meet her dad, but it's up to you."

"It's not that I wouldn't want to." He glanced down at his cutoff jeans. "Besides, I'm not really dressed for dinner. I was working on the farm till I came here with Uncle Seth."

"Is Seth here?" Allie looked around the group working on the sidewalk. There weren't so many of them that she would have missed Seth, tall and distinctive as he was with his clean-shaven head and tattoos.

"He walked over to your place to get Des."

"Oh, well, I'm sure I'll see them later. I should get inside and go to work."

"See you." Mark gave a half wave and went back to work opening chairs.

Ginger was looking out the window when Allie came into the Goodbye.

"It's going to look so cool out there," Ginger said. "All the tables and chairs set up on the sidewalk."

"Almost like a sidewalk café in Paris."

Hmmm. A sidewalk café. Could be sweet. Allie made a mental note to discuss the possibility with Barney.

"Have you been busy?" Allie glanced at the specials sheet on the desk. They really should have them written on a blackboard near the front so customers could have more time to mull over their choices.

"All the activity outside seems to have drawn attention to the café. We were really busy at lunch, and we've had several people come in for an early dinner, waiting for the party to begin, I guess." Ginger nodded in the direction of the dining area.

Was there any way of knowing if any of the partygoers would decide to come in for dinner? Allie didn't have a clue. "How many waitresses do we have on tonight?" she asked.

"Just Alice so far. Penny doesn't work on Saturdays, so Judy usually calls in a second person, usually Carolee, but I don't know if she called her," Ginger said. "Want me to call Judy and ask?"

"I'd appreciate it, yes. Thank you." While Ginger made that call, Allie made one of her own, to Barney, to ask if she had permission to bring in an extra waitress. Barney gave her the green light, telling her, "If you ever see the need for extra staff, don't bother wasting your time calling me. Find someone who can come in!"

Judy admitted she'd forgotten about the staffing for Saturday night, so Ginger lined up Susan, who filled in sometimes, and offered to extend her own hours as well if Allie thought they'd need an extra pair of hands. "I can call my mom and ask her to keep Ava for a few more hours."

Allie nodded. "I'd really appreciate that, Ginger. I have a feeling we're going to need all the extra hands we can get tonight."

It wasn't long before her intuition proved spot-on.

She sent a text to Nikki, asking what time they'd be there so she could save a table because they were filling up quickly. With Ginger's help, Allie pushed together two tables along the inner wall to reserve. There'd be four of them for dinner, but she wanted extra room in case Mark or Barney and Tom or any combination of the three decided to join them.

Through the window, Allie could see a crowd beginning to gather. Fifteen minutes later, Barney arrived with Judy in tow. Then two women carrying a huge flat box came into view and placed the box on a long table. Barney, Judy, and others oohed and aahed over the contents, which Allie assumed was the cake. It wasn't long before there was an influx of diners waiting for a table inside as well. It appeared the entire town had come out to say goodbye to Judy and thank her for all the years she kept the Goodbye open, and all of them seemed to want to have dinner while they were there.

Allie had very little time to watch the festivities, and she began to feel guilty about keeping those two tables off to the side unoccupied while the line of those waiting began to grow. She started taking names for a wait list and suggested that those near the back of the line go outside and have a slice of cake since it was being cut, whether they knew Judy or not: No one was going to ask. She promised she'd call for them in order when a table opened. Finally, she began to offer a glass of water or iced tea to those waiting in line. She'd have considered it a personal failure had anyone given up and gone home. From time to time she glanced out the window. Seth and Des were standing next to the cake table talking to several members of the town council. Joe and Cara and Joe's sister, Julie, his mother, and an older couple Allie didn't recognize were chatting off to one side. Allie thought both her sisters looked right at home in the crowd, which was good for them, since they'd be making Hidden Falls their home, and most likely marrying hometown guys. Allie pinched back a little stab of envy.

Good for them, but it's not for me. I'm an L.A. girl, born and bred. Small town East Coast isn't for me.

At first glance, it would seem somewhat ironic that Allie, who from all appearances was the one of the three sisters most likely to party, would be the one inside working while the other two were outside having a good time. And while she was working her butt off, it occurred to her that she wasn't minding it at all. There was something, oh, not exactly fun, but satisfying about feeling useful. She didn't have time to dwell on such thoughts, though, because Nikki and the others arrived. Allie seated them immediately, earning frowns from those still in line waiting.

"They just got here," the woman first in line complained loudly. "How do they rate a table?"

"They called earlier in the day to reserve a table," Allie said loudly enough to be heard down the line. "I'm sure you'll be seated soon. It looks like one of the tables in the back is opening up."

Allie tracked down Ginger. "That's my daughter and my ex, and his girlfriend," Allie confided. "Any chance you could take that table? I'll bring the menus over, but could you wait on them?"

"Of course," Ginger told her.

As Allie approached the table, she heard Courtney's voice, a sneer unmistakable. "This is the fabulous, great, cool restaurant your family bought?"

"It's the best place in Hidden Falls. Everyone comes here." If Nikki had picked up on Courtney's condescending tone, she gave no sign.

Way to go, Nik. Ignore the little brat.

"Best of two?" Courtney looked around the room pointedly. "It's kind of dingy and there's not much ambience. It's more like an old diner than a café."

Marlo interrupted her daughter. "Courtney, you're embarrassing me. You're being rude and obnoxious, and I don't care for it." She turned to Nikki. "I think it's really cute. Homey and old-fashioned in the best way."

"My mom has plans to redecorate. I know she'll come up with something great."

"If what I saw in the theater was any indication of your mother's talent, I'm sure this place will be perfect when she's finished. And it's certainly busy. The wait line is getting longer, so we know the food must be wonderful."

Courtney rolled her eyes. "Mom, Nikki's aunt said it was a special night."

"They wouldn't be here at all if the food wasn't good." Marlo turned back to Clint.

Allie was liking Marlo more and more, and Courtney less and less.

No time to let her mind wander now, though. The room was packed.

She was just about to hand out the menus when she heard Clint say, "So, Nikki, you said you had a surprise for me when we got to the restaurant."

Nikki turned her attention to her father, her face beaming.

"Well, you know how when we go out to dinner, you always order fish?"

"Yes," Clint said. "Usually salmon."

"And then you complain 'cause salmon's the only kind of fish they have," Nikki teased.

Clint nodded. "That's happened more than once."

"Well, tonight you're having Pocono trout." She made the pronouncement proudly.

"Pocono trout?"

Allie could see Clint trying to place this on his mental list of acceptable-for-consumption fish.

"Freshly caught—only this morning, by the way—Pocono Mountain, Compton Lake rainbow trout." She grinned and pointed her thumb toward her chest. "Caught by me."

Clint leaned toward her. "Caught by you? Really?"

"Well, me and my friend Mark and Aunt Des's boyfriend, Seth."

"You went *fishing*?" Courtney's nose turned up. "Did you have to, like, pick up worms?"

"No. We used lures. We were out on the lake by six this morning, and we fished until we'd reached the limit," Nikki said.

"You got up that early so I could have fish for my dinner?" Clint appeared almost dazed that his daughter would do something that he perceived to be out of character for the Nikki who lived with him in L.A.

Nikki nodded. "I hope you like lake trout, Dad."

"I know I'll love it. I bet it'll become my favorite fish," he said softly. "Nik, you amaze me. This might be, well, this is the best surprise I've ever had."

"We—that is, Mark and Seth and I—caught enough so that we could all have some. Chef George is going to put the rest on the menu tonight."

"When did you learn how to fish?" Clint asked.

"This morning, but Seth said I could come back anytime because I was good at it. I even learned how to cast my line. It was fun."

Allie signaled to Ginger that she could take their orders whenever she was ready, then turned her attention to the line of customers waiting for tables. She went to the window and looked out at the tables on the sidewalk. Was there any reason she couldn't seat diners out there? The crowd outdoors for Judy had thinned somewhat, and eight tables were sitting out there empty.

"Ginger, I'll be right back." Allie skirted the line and went outside, where she found Barney and Tom talking to Judy and a woman Allie didn't recognize. She excused herself and took Barney aside.

"We're so backed up." Allie pointed to the line. "Why can't we seat people out here?"

Barney never hesitated. "Great idea. The last thing I want to hear from that annoying Irene Pettibone is that service at the Goodbye has gone downhill since the Hudsons bought it."

"I recognized her from the town council meeting we went to with you," Allie whispered. "She looked old and bitter then, and she still looks old and bitter."

Allie went straight into the kitchen to search for a clean cloth to wipe down the outside tables. As she came back, she realized two tables inside had opened up and the people waiting in line were glaring at her impatiently. She tucked the cloth on the back of Nikki's chair and went straight to the first party.

"You've been so patient," Allie said as she led them to their seats. "Your appetizers are on the house tonight."

She seated the second party, then tried to remember where she'd left the cloth. Spying it on the back of Nikki's chair, she grabbed it and went outside. She'd wiped down two of the eight tables when Nikki appeared at her side.

"Mom, what's going on?"

Allie explained as she started on table number three.

Nikki took the cloth from her hand. "I'll do this, and I'll ask Mark to put the chairs around the tables. You go inside and do whatever else you need to do. When I come back in, you can start seating people."

"Thank you for being the most amazing child, but you have guests inside," Allie reminded her.

"I won't be long. Besides, Courtney's still trying to decide what she wants for dinner." Nikki rolled her eyes. "She's afraid the trout might be polluted, have too many bones, or won't be as good as the fish she had at some froufrou restaurant in Malibu when she was visiting her dad."

"Oh dear lord." Allie wasn't sure whether she should laugh or cry. She went back inside, where she paused for a moment to watch her daughter from the window. *I've never done anything in my life so good that I should have been given this gift.*

She watched for another few seconds, then was about to turn from the window when she saw Ben in the crowd. She wondered which of the sweet young things milling about was his date. He held his phone to his ear and walked toward the street.

A few moments later, Ginger tapped her on the shoulder. "Allie, I've been looking for you. Are we still taking reservations for tonight?"

"What?" Allie turned her back on the window and the gathering outside.

"Someone's on the phone asking about a reservation for later."

Allie started to shake her head no, then said, "I'll take it." She made her way through the wait line to the desk and picked up the phone. "Can I help you?"

"What time do you close tonight?"

It was so loud close to the line of people, all of whom seemed to be chatting away, she could barely hear.

"Usually nine, but tonight—" Allie couldn't even begin to imagine when they might empty out. "Who knows?"

The man on the phone said something else, but Allie couldn't hear clearly.

"I'm sorry, but could you repeat that, please?"

"I'd like to reserve a table for two for around ten. I'm assuming you'll still be open."

"Probably." *And if we're closed you'll know by the fact that the lights are turned off. But chances are we'll still be here, judging from the crowd.*

Allie walked to the window and absently looked out. She scanned the crowd, ignoring any thoughts that she might be searching for Ben even when she spotted him. He was still on the phone and seemed to be looking straight at her.

It's not like you have to look for him. The only person in the crowd taller is Seth.

"Fine. I'll just need your name . . . Hello?" The line went dead. "Oh, for crying out loud."

"What's wrong?" Penny asked as she walked by.

"Some guy just called to make reservations for later and didn't leave his name." Allie pulled the scrunchie from her ponytail. Her hair fell free, but she grabbed it with her right hand and forced it back into a tail. "Which means some clown is going to come in here and wonder why he has no table. In the meantime, we're going to seat people outside. We'll start taking customers from the front of the line, and . . ." She realized Ginger had stopped nearby and was staring at her. "What?"

"Allie, we don't have the staff to handle what we've got in here plus another"—Ginger looked out the window and counted—"eight more tables."

"Look, there are four of us. If we each took two tables, that wouldn't be too bad, would it?" Allie thought that might be reasonable.

"No offense, but have you ever waited tables before?" Ginger asked.

Allie shook her head. "I've eaten in a lot of restaurants, though." When she realized how absurd that was, she started laughing.

"I guess we'll see how funny you think it is in about an hour." Ginger flagged down Alice to tell her the news. "If you need help, just holler."

"How are George and his crew holding up?" Allie asked.

"He loves a challenge. I think he might have called in another line cook, though. Had he asked you about that?"

Allie shook her head. "No, but it's fine under the circumstances. He knows best what he needs back there, just as you know what we need out here."

Nikki came inside. "All ready, Mom." She held out the cloth.

"Put that back in the kitchen then go wash your hands," Allie said. "And, Nik, thanks again. You're the best."

"I know." She took a few steps toward the kitchen, then turned back. "And I know to wash my hands."

"Sorry, sweetie." Allie rolled her eyes. "I'm a little over-whelmed."

Allie asked along the line who might be interested in dining al fresco, and in no time all eight tables were filled. The crowd from the party was beginning to thin, and Barney was directing Seth and Joe to carry the remains of the cake into the kitchen.

"Free dessert for everyone tonight," Barney said as she passed by Allie. "If they want cake, that is."

The people at the table Allie had just seated craned their necks to see what was in the box.

"A cake for the previous owner's going-away and thanks-for-the-memories party," Allie explained. "You heard the owner. Free cake."

She passed out menus and relayed the specials to the diners at her tables, then realized she'd have to set the tables as well. She scribbled their orders on the back of one of the papers on which the specials had been typed and wondered how people who did this all the time remembered who at which table had ordered what. She all but ran back inside, put the orders into the new computer, and hoped she hadn't screwed things up. Then it was back out with flatware and glasses for each of her tables. When the orders for her table were up, she served them two at a time, noticing with no small amount of envy that Ginger, Alice, and Susan were carrying all their orders at once, two in each hand.

Once she'd served her tables, she was back at the desk, try-ing to keep the other table assignments straight. She stopped here and there to ask diners if they enjoyed their meals and made suitable small talk. She'd seen the hostesses in other res-taurants do this and thought it was expected of her. When she passed Nikki's table, she stopped to ask Clint how he'd found the trout.

"It was delicious. Seriously, Allie. Maybe the best fish I've ever had." He patted Nikki on the shoulder. "And to think my baby girl caught it for me."

Our baby girl, bucko, she was tempted to say, but held her tongue. Mostly because she was almost too tired at that point to get into it with him.

"We're just about to have dessert," Clint told her. "Why don't you join us?"

"I'm working." She had to bite her tongue from adding, *As any idiot with eyes could see.*

"Oh." He appeared confused.

"What did you think I was doing?" Allie would have laughed if he wasn't so clueless.

"You never worked in a restaurant," he blurted.

"None of us have, Dad, but Barney said it belonged to all of us," Nikki said. "We all have to work here."

"So what's your job?" Courtney asked.

"I'm baking brownies, but I'm not sure what else I'm going to be doing, since I don't have my work papers yet," Nikki explained in her usual matter-of-fact manner. "And right now while I'm waiting, I'm helping Aunt Des with the puppies. But when I'm able to work, I want to waitress. They get the bet tips, right, Mom?"

"So they tell me," Allie said as Barney joined them and took a seat. "Barney, can we get you something?"

"Ask George if there's any of that fish left. You know I love trout, and if it's from our lake, I know it will be delicious."

As Allie walked away, she heard Courtney ask, "What puppies? Who has puppies?"

"My Aunt Des rescues dogs. She got an entire litter of puppies last week. I'm helping to train them to walk on a leash. I'm really good at it."

Smiling, Allie went into the kitchen and found that George had put an entire fish aside for Barney, which in the end she shared with Tom, who came in later. Judy's outside crowd of well-wishers had dwindled to two or three small groups who were chatting on the periphery of the area where the diners were sitting. One by one, the inside diners began to leave, and even the tables outside were vacant. Allie was leaning on the desk, hoping to keep herself upright, when the door opened.

Oh God, not one more diner . . .

"I called earlier to reserve a table. Looks like there's plenty of room." Ben stood in the doorway, his hands in the pockets of his uniform pants, his shirt partially unbuttoned from the collar just far enough to show some dark chest hair.

"I should have known it would be you." Allie couldn't help herself. She had to laugh. "You could have left your name."

"I figured you recognized my voice."

"I could barely hear you," she said, "which is why I kept asking you to repeat yourself. It was really crowded and noisy in here."

"Well, it's not now. I guess I can sit anywhere?"

"Sure." She'd already told Alice she could leave, and Susan would be right behind her once her last two tables left. She held out a menu. "You might want to make a quick decision, though. I think the kitchen is starting to close up."

"Then you should probably take the 'Open' sign off the door." He walked to the table at the back where she'd seated him once before. "And I don't need a menu. I heard there's trout tonight."

"I doubt there's any left, but your waitress can check. In the meantime, I suggest you have a plan B in mind." Allie handed him a menu, then nodded to Ginger to take the table. "And hey, you reserved a table for two. Your date cut out early, *Benny*?" Allie turned the sign to the CLOSED side.

"No date." He didn't bother to look up from the menu but there was a smile in his voice. "I've been on duty."

Nikki and the others showed signs of getting ready to leave. Allie walked over to the table.

"I guess I'll see you all tomorrow before you leave," she said, her hands on the back of Barney's chair.

"We liked your restaurant so much we thought we'd have lunch here tomorrow before we head to the airport." Clint turned in his chair to face her.

"That's nice. You'll have a little more time to spend with Nik before you go."

"Well, yes, that, and we'll need to pick up Courtney," he said.

"Pick up Courtney from where?"

Nikki stood, her face unreadable. "Dad suggested that Courtney spend the night here, with us, instead of going back to their hotel in Scranton."

Before Allie could comment, Clint said, "We thought it would be nice for the girls to have a little more time to get reacquainted. You know, before Nik comes home to California and school starts in September."

Allie tried to gauge Nikki's feelings, but she was showing no emotion one way or the other.

"Did you ask Aunt Barney if it's all right?"

"I said it's up to Nikki." Barney's smile was bland. "My house is her house."

"Nikki's fine with it, right, Nik?" Clint patted her on the back.

"Of course. It's okay. Court and I have a lot to catch up on." Unlike Barney's, Nikki's smile held just a bit of flint.

I hope you give her a piece of your mind, was on the tip of Allie's tongue. Instead, she said merely, "Well, then. It's settled. Courtney spends the night at the Hudson house."

Courtney had been silent the entire time.

"Well, then." Clint was his usual self, unaware of the undercurrents from Nikki as well as Courtney. "How 'bout we drop you off at the house, and we'll be on our way."

Courtney finally spoke up. "I don't have anything to sleep in."

"You can borrow something of mine," Nikki assured her.

"And I don't have my toothbrush."

"Not to worry, dear. We always have extras." Barney turned to Nikki. "Tom and I will be along later. You have your house key, I'm assuming."

Nikki nodded.

"Then you two go on home. I'm not sure who's there tonight, but no matter. Don't forget to take Buttons out for a walk before you turn in." Barney extended a hand first to Marlo, then to Clint. "It's been nice meeting you. I'll see you both tomorrow. And, Allie? I assume you're staying here to close up?"

"I will." Allie watched the entire group go toward the door, followed by the last table of diners, who complimented Allie on the food. She thanked them and unlocked the door to let them out, then relocked it.

Ginger met Allie at the desk.

"Should I remind the chief that we're closed?" she asked Allie.

"No. I'll kick him out myself." She walked to Ben's table. As she drew near, he used a foot to push out the extra chair from under the table.

"Have a seat." He was just finishing a chicken salad sandwich but was apparently unwilling to leave just yet.

"Ginger, you can go. I'll close up. Tell George he and his guys can go when they've finished back there." Allie sat. She was too tired to argue, too tired to come up with a suitable quip. She just needed to sit.

"Chief," Ginger said. "Coffee?"

"That'd be great, thanks, Ginger." Ben smiled pleasantly.

Allie placed her right elbow on the table and leaned into the palm of her hand to rest her chin.

"Big night," Ben said.

Allie nodded.

"Worked your ass off, didn't you?"

"Yup," was all she could muster.

"To tell you the truth"—Ben leaned a little closer—"I was surprised. You really looked like you were enjoying yourself. Well, until you reached your present condition, which looks like maybe near collapse. But up until the last half hour or so, you were a demon. Even waited on tables. You ever do that before?"

Allie shook her head.

"Well, I have to admit, no one would have known."

"Thanks. That's the nicest thing you've ever said to me."

Ginger brought Ben's coffee and a cup for Allie, then removed Ben's plate.

"You saved my life, Ginger," Allie said. "I was dying for coffee but I was too tired to go into the kitchen to get it. Thank you. You were a rock star tonight. Now, go home to your daughter."

"Thanks, Allie. You were pretty damned good yourself. You really took care of business. Night, Chief," Ginger called over her shoulder as she left through the kitchen.

"I was and I did." Allie was having a hard time holding her eyes open. She was hoping the coffee would keep her on her feet until she got home.

Ben nodded. "You were."

"As evidenced by the fact that I can barely move. I'm actually too tired to engage in our usual banter."

"That's okay. It was starting to get old. I suggest we find another means of communicating."

Allie looked at him across the table to see if he was kidding. He didn't appear to be.

"Okay by me." She drank a few swallows of coffee. "Ugh. I don't drink it black. Pass over that thingy of sweeteners."

He handed her the container, then passed her the cream pitcher as well. She fixed her coffee to her satisfaction, then took another sip.

"Oh, so much better." She sipped for a moment, her eyes at half-mast. "You're right, you know."

"About burying the hatchet?"

"Well, that, yes. But you were right about me working my ass off and enjoying myself tonight." She shook her head. "What's happening to me? I'm accustomed to being the wait*ee*, not the wait*er*." She frowned and faked bewilderment. "It's almost as if the old Allie is fading away, and she's being replaced with someone entirely different. Someone I barely recognize."

"I hope not. The old Allie had a way of growing on you." Ben sat back in his chair watching her face.

Allie's lips curved into a sly smile. "Was I growing on you, Sheriff?"

Ben laughed out loud. "There she is. The old Allie. Apparently she just took a little time off tonight. Thank goodness."

"I'd think you'd appreciate a woman who didn't give you so much sass."

"A little sass is good for the soul."

"Sometimes. I know I have to watch my mouth. Things just come out without me thinking." She glanced at him over her coffee cup. "I guess you know all about that. Better than anyone in Hidden Falls, anyway."

Ben rested his cup in the saucer. "About that. I'm sorry I've been so rough on you. I should have just accepted your apology and moved on."

"I didn't mean to bring up your son, Ben," she said softly.

"I know. I knew as soon as you said it. It's just so hard for me sometimes to reconcile the fact that my beautiful little boy is gone." He swallowed hard. "There are times when it hurts so much I feel paralyzed by the thought of him. I miss my wife, don't think I don't. But somehow it seems a little easier to work through losing an adult than a child. Losing my son guts me every time I think about him. I can't move on from him. He was my only child, and I don't know if I'll ever have another."

"How old are you?"

"Forty-one."

Allie nodded. "Plenty of time. Especially if you keep going after that young stuff."

Ben looked up from his coffee, blinked, then laughed.

"Sorry. None of my business." She shook her head. "Go on. You were saying?"

"Nothing more to say. Just that I'm sorry."

For a long moment, they sipped their coffee, Allie contemplating this different, reconciliatory, no-hard-feelings Ben.

Finally, Ben looked over at her and said, "So that was the ex."

"Yeah. How'd you know?"

"I heard Nikki call him Dad." There was that half smile again. She was starting to get used to it, maybe even like it. "Dead giveaway."

"We had a little crisis with Nikki, and I asked him to come out and handle it in person."

"Nothing serious, I hope."

Allie shook her head, then told him the entire story.

"Just another reason why I'm glad I wasn't born female. I couldn't handle stuff like that. I'd be inclined to just swing until I landed a punch or two."

"I'm hoping it doesn't come to that. Somehow Clint managed to arrange for Courtney to stay overnight here with Nikki. I wasn't part of that conversation, but Barney apparently was and left it up to Nikki." Allie thought about the expression on Nikki's face. "Nik agreed, but I'm thinking she's probably given Courtney a piece of her mind by now. I know they had words on the phone, but there's nothing like being confronted by a former friend when you've been the bitch, you know?"

"Not really. Like I said, a punch or two, then it's over." Ben shrugged. "Move on."

"I'm hoping they do move past this. I don't want Nikki to have to deal with this when she goes back at the end of the summer. I don't think Clint knows how to handle this sort of thing."

"Sounds like he handled this okay."

"Because I told him what to do and what to say. Trust me, he's clueless." She tapped her fingers on the side of the cup. "I'm just going to have to keep close tabs on her—and him—until I can go back home and she's living with me during the week again."

"You're going to go back for good?"

"Sure. That's where . . ." She started to say *where my friends are*, but she knew that wasn't true. She wasn't sure she ever had any true friends there. "That's where my house is. Nikki's school. I always planned to go back."

"Your sisters—"

"Will both stay, I'm sure of it." Allie sighed, then stood. "I hate to toss out a customer, but I don't think I'll be able to stay awake too much longer."

"How are you getting home?" he asked.

Allie held out one foot. "Walking."

"You'll never make it. Come on. I'll give you a ride. My truck's right outside." He looked around the table. "Did Ginger leave my check with you?"

"Nope. But it's okay. We're trading your dinner for a ride to Hudson Street."

"Fair enough."

"Give me a minute to make sure the kitchen crew is gone." Allie checked into the darkened kitchen, where the dishwasher droned. Before returning to the dining room, she checked the back door and found it locked.

"All clear," she told Ben. She stuck her hand into her pocket for the key and began to walk to the front of the room. "Oh, wait. I have to get"—she went to the desk and opened the cash register—"tonight's receipts."

She could feel his eyes on her back while she removed all the cash from the register. She returned the amount they usually left for opening the next day, then stuffed the rest of it into her bag.

"Don't you need to count it?" he asked.

"Not capable right now." She tapped her head. "No math cells left. I'll count it tomorrow. Or Barney will." She turned off the light over the desk.

"You just put all that cash in your bag?"

Allie nodded.

"And you were going to walk home with it?"

"Uh-huh."

"Please tell me that isn't what you do every night."

Allie shrugged. "I don't know what else to do with it."

"You could get a safe, then take it to the bank in the morning."

"Barney has a safe at the house." She turned off the rest of the lights.

"That's not going to be of any use to you if you're mugged on the way home."

"I'm too tired to worry about that now." Her hand was on the door handle. The room was dark, the only light coming in from the streetlamp outside, and she was suddenly, acutely aware of Ben. He was so close behind her she thought for a moment he was going to turn her around and kiss her.

Instead, he reached over her shoulder and gave the door a push, and with one gentle hand on her back as if to guide her, he led the way outside.

"Come on," he said, his voice soft. "Let's get you home."

CHAPTER TEN

Allie stretched across her bed and felt the knots in her calves unwind and stiffness in her shoulders begin to ease. She hadn't been kidding when she'd said she'd never worked that hard. She wasn't even sure if she'd ever been on her feet for that length of time. She sat up and moaned as she kicked off her sandals and sighed as she stripped down to her underwear. She was too tired to wash off her makeup or change into a nightshirt. Within minutes she'd fallen into a deep, dreamless sleep. She slept so soundly she missed breakfast the following morning, and by the time she arrived downstairs, everyone else seemed to be somewhere else. The kitchen clock read eleven forty-five. Allie couldn't remember sleeping that late since college. Even when she was drinking alone back in her L.A. house after Nikki went to live with Clint, she'd never slept past ten that she could recall.

She threw together a minimal breakfast of coffee and a banana and opened the back door. Nikki and Courtney were facing each other in Adirondack chairs under the maple tree and laughing. Allie stepped outside, banana in hand, and joined them.

"Good morning, girls." Allie pulled a chair closer to them and sat. "How are we doing this morning?"

"Fine." Nikki nodded. "We're just wasting time before Dad gets here."

"We're doing great, Miz Monroe." Courtney began babbling about how she and Nikki had just decided to try out for the varsity field hockey team right before school begins.

"Is that what you want to do, Nik?" Allie asked.

"I guess," she replied.

"Oh, you have to. It'll be fun, especially when we have away games. All our friends are trying out. Peyton and Cassie and Devon and a couple others. And you'll make it for sure, since you're so good. You were the best forward on the freshman team last year. Probably the best player on the entire team." Courtney was acting so chummy Allie had to wonder how sincere she was.

"I'll think about it." Nikki turned in her seat to face Allie. "Mom, did you skip the theater this morning?"

"Baby, even moms run out of gas sometimes. After last night, I couldn't have gotten up at six or seven. I really needed the sleep. Besides, it's Sunday."

"Everybody needs to take a day off now and then. Aunt Barney always says that. And you're almost finished with the ceiling. Dad and I climbed up to the top of the scaffold last night so he could see close-up how good you're doing. I couldn't tell which ones you already did, but I showed him the ones that were missing and explained your process to him. He was really impressed." Nikki stared at her mother for a moment. "Did you ever think about being an artist? Like, a real artist? Where you paint all the time and sell your stuff?"

"I have thought about it, yes, but I'm realistic enough to know that I don't have that kind of talent. But thank you for thinking that I do."

"You totally should, Miz Monroe. The ceiling at the theater is beautiful. Nikki pointed out where you worked on it. You're really good."

Nikki slanted a look in Courtney's direction—*Great side-eye, Nik!*—but didn't comment.

"Thank you, Courtney." Allie finished the banana, then turned her attention back to Nikki. "What time is your dad expected?"

Nikki checked her phone. "In about thirty-five minutes."

"Just enough time for me to get a shower." Allie stood and stretched. God, she was still tired. "Oh crap."

"What's wrong?"

"I need to get down to the Goodbye to open. It should have been opened hours ago. What the hell was I thinking?" Allie ran to the house trying to figure out how long it would take her to look presentable.

"Mom, it's okay. Barney's there," Nikki called to her.

"She is?" Allie stopped on the top step.

Nikki nodded. "She was just leaving when I came downstairs for breakfast. She said she was going to do the first shift so you could sleep."

"God bless her. Now I can take a shower."

Allie got out of the shower feeling like a new person. She dried and even styled her hair for a change from the ponytail or the braid she'd been sporting all summer. But she just couldn't bring herself to put on the shirt and pants she'd dropped onto the floor as she'd shed them the night before. She decided on a sporty dress she hadn't worn since she arrived in Hidden Falls. It had a boatneck, short sleeves, and fell a few inches above her knees. It was a simple lightweight knit fabric in a glorious shade of blue. Darker than sky blue, lighter than navy, the color matched her eyes almost perfectly. Cinched at the waist with a pale green belt, it set off her figure quite nicely, she thought. Sandals and a row of beaded bracelets finished off her look for the day. She glanced in the mirror and admitted she felt happy with what she saw. The gaunt look she'd had when she first arrived in Hidden Falls was gone, and while she had gained a few pounds, she couldn't deny she'd needed them. If she'd filled out, it was all in the right places, and was due to her improved diet. And, she had to admit, the fact that she'd cut back—way back—on her consumption of alcohol. Not entirely by choice, but still. Whatever the reason, she was looking and feeling all the better for it.

Clint and Marlo had arrived while she was putting on makeup and she told the girls to go to the Goodbye and have lunch, and to tell Barney she'd be on her way soon. She walked to the café, so much on her mind she could barely keep up with where her thoughts were going: they ping-ponged all around her brain. Foremost in her mind was her suspicion that Courtney was not to be trusted. Should she talk to Nikki, warn her that Courtney wasn't what she appeared to be?

Tough call, Mama. The two girls had been inseparable for the past two years. It was a tricky situation for Nik to be in because Courtney was the center of the group of girls Nikki hung out with, and there was a good chance they might become stepsisters someday.

Ugh.

How would Clint handle things if the situation blew up once Nikki was back home? Would he ignore it? Would Nikki even discuss such problems with him? Allie doubted it. Nikki never had before.

Allie couldn't wait to get back to L.A. She wanted to be close enough to Nikki to protect her from . . . oh, everything, not the least of which were catty girls and horny boys.

The oak tree at the foot of the driveway was just starting to drop leaves, not a flurry, just a few now and then. She could feel a hint of crispness in the air last night when she got out of Ben's car. He'd walked her to the door saying, "I don't want to be responsible for you passing out on the lawn. I'd have a hell of a time explaining that to Barney."

She was glad Ben'd approached her to end the tension between them, and grateful that he'd accepted her apology. Not that it mattered for any reason other than the fact that her sisters were dating—*seriously* dating—his two best friends. They were bound to see each other frequently, so it was nice they could be cordial to each other.

Cordial? Friendly with a bit of a flirty edge tossed in was more like it. There'd always been a subtle undercurrent, and she couldn't make an argument to herself that she hadn't enjoyed it. She liked the fact that he'd made the first move to smooth things over, that when he'd reserved a table for two it had been with her in mind. Which was why he'd waited until almost the last minute to come inside. He'd been out in the crowd all night, and could have come in at any time, and could have brought any one of the local cuties with him. But he'd done neither. And he'd called ahead. Which meant he'd put some thought into it.

He'd even complimented her—had hell frozen over?—and he'd recognized how hard she'd been working. And he'd noticed that she'd seemed to be enjoying it.

Well, she had. She was only half kidding when she'd wondered what was happening to her. Other than her sporadic appearances on Des's TV show, and her job as assistant director on two others, she'd never really worked. She'd never known what it was like to sweat or to be on your feet until your back ached and your legs begged for mercy. She'd never had to be so organized, and she'd certainly never been in charge or had to make decisions like she'd had to yesterday. It had felt good, every bit of it. Maybe because she got to see herself in a different light, or because she'd felt she had to prove something to herself. Whatever, she found she liked the fast tempo and having to think on her feet. She'd even liked interacting with their customers and making the obligatory small talk. It had all mattered to her, which made her realize the Goodbye mattered to her as well.

Well, damn. Who'd have seen that coming?

She waved to someone passing by in a blue sedan and thought she recognized the driver but wasn't sure. When he called out, "Great party last night! Great dinner!" she called back, "Thank you! Come back again sometime."

"We definitely will!"

The friendliness made her smile, made her feel like she belonged. Oh, she knew it was only temporary, but still. It was nice.

She reached the café and noticed the tables and chairs had been folded and stacked curbside, waiting, she assumed, for someone to pick them up and return them to wherever Barney'd borrowed them. She'd have to remember to talk to Barney about buying some small tables to put out there in nice weather. It really could be cute, she thought as she went inside.

The café was filled with chatter, not loud, but consistent with a room where people were engaged in conversation. Allie looked around for Barney, who was talking with a small group at a table against the wall. She gave Allie a small wave of acknowledgment but went right on talking.

She spied Nikki's group and went over to their table.

"How was your night in Scranton?" she asked Clint.

"Great. Nice city." He touched his napkin to the corners of his mouth and nodded. "Very nice, right, Marlo?"

"It is. The scenery out here is amazing. The mountains and the farms, and oh, we passed some lovely lakes. They looked like postcards," Marlo said.

"You guys want to see a beautiful lake, next time you're here, I'll take you out to *our* lake," Nikki said. "Compton Lake."

"What's so special about your lake?" Courtney seemed to slip back into mean-girl Courtney after having been BFF Courtney all morning. Strange, Allie thought, and wondered what was behind the change.

"Well, for one thing, it's pristine. It's fed by fresh springs. Seth said it's one of the cleanest lakes around. It's got woods all around it, and Seth said it's filled with wildlife, deer and foxes and bears. The fishing is great because it's private and not open to the public to come in and catch all the fish or to shoot the deer. And it's clean because we don't let people camp there or anything."

"Why not? That's kind of selfish, don't you think?" Courtney made a face. "Other people should be allowed to enjoy the lake, too."

"There are plenty of lakes up here, and there are state parks with lakes. That lake is ours. Aunt Barney said our ancestor who settled out here won the lake and—I don't remember how many acres of ground, do you, Mom?" Nikki asked.

Allie shook her head.

"Anyway, he won it in a poker game and it's never been sold. So it's ours." Nikki's voice had a slight edge to it.

"Everything up here is yours," Courtney muttered.

Nikki shrugged. "It's Hudson country, what can I tell you? My grandpa's family settled out here, like, hundreds of years ago. They cleared the wilderness, right, Aunt Barney?" Nikki asked as Barney joined the group.

"All true, darling." Barney smiled, surely knowing, as even Allie did, that *hundreds* of years might be an overstatement, but Nikki was making a point.

The wilderness part was true, though, as was the part about the lake and all the land around it having been won in a poker game. Points to the kid for remembering that.

"So we should make plans for you to come back home, right?" Clint was saying.

Nikki turned her head quickly to look up at her mother. "Not yet. I don't have to go back yet, do I, Mom?"

"Of course not. There's still time before school starts in September."

"You do need to think about it, Allie." Clint directed the comment to her. "We need to make flight arrangements. I need to know when that flight lands, so my schedule is cleared to pick her up. And Courtney said something about coming back a week early for field hockey tryouts."

"I haven't made up my mind about that, Dad," Nikki said.

"Well, what else would you do? You know you need one major activity every semester," he reminded her.

"I don't know. Maybe drama. Maybe debate. I want to think about it." Nikki averted her eyes from both parents.

"Drama? Debate?" Courtney scoffed. "I thought we agreed on field hockey."

"I said I'd think about it," Nikki said.

"Okay, if you want to be a dork," Courtney said, an obvious attempt to demean anything Nikki might want to do other than what Courtney was doing.

"Nik, I think you should—" Clint began, but Allie cut him off.

"Clint, I think you should do as Nikki asks and allow her to weigh her options without anyone leaning on her." Allie mentally gave herself a high five for not only speaking calmly and rationally, but for not grabbing him by the throat and grunting, "Back off," in his face.

He nodded. "All right. You're right, Allie. Nik, you go ahead and see what's going to be available first semester and pick whatever you think you'll most enjoy."

"Thanks, Dad. I'll pull it up online." Nikki's gaze followed someone behind her mother. When Allie turned around, she saw Mark, along with his mother and sister, waiting at the desk.

"Excuse me," Allie said. She walked to the desk and greeted Roseanne and Hayley. Mark said good morning to Allie, then walked around her to say hello to Nikki, who'd motioned him over with a big smile.

"Dad, this is my friend Mark. Mark, I want you to meet my dad, Clint Monroe." Nikki's pride in both her father and her boyfriend were apparent. Allie couldn't hear what Mark and Clint were saying to each other, but they were both smiling, so she figured it was okay.

She seated Roseanne and Hayley and placed three menus on the table. She motioned for the Sunday morning waitress, Dolores, to bring Roseanne a cup of coffee. They made small talk for a few moments before Allie left them alone to study the menu and make their selections. From the desk, she had a clear view of Nikki's table, and a very clear view of Courtney's attempts to get Mark's attention as she stared at him, a rapt expression on her face.

The evil little brat was trying to flirt with Nikki's boyfriend. Mark, to his credit, barely paid any notice, engaged as he was with Clint. If his gaze strayed from Clint, it rested only on Nikki.

Oh, honey, you picked a good one. But you might want to think about looking for a new BFF.

Even Marlo picked up on it, saying, "Courtney, stop trying to interrupt."

Soon enough, the dining room filled up, with tables emptying and being immediately filled, and the level of chatter rose in proportion to the number of people talking.

"People come right after church, if they've gone early, then later in the morning, if they've attended one of the later services," Barney told her when they met up at the desk. "Then we have the folks who enjoy an early lunch. It's been like this on Sunday mornings for as long as I can recall."

"If it's always going to be like this, I guess you won't have to worry about a return on your investment," Allie said.

"I never did, dear. Oh look, there's the Mattlock family. I wonder why they didn't stop by to see Judy last night." And Barney was off to find out.

"Wow, we're really packed." Cara appeared at Allie's elbow.

"Oh hey. I didn't see you come in," Allie said.

"I just did. Joe likes to take his mom and sister for breakfast sometimes on Sundays. Can we sit anywhere?"

"There are four of you?" Allie glanced at her table chart.

"Five. Ben's joining us." Cara paused. "That won't make it uncomfortable for you, will it?"

"Why should it?"

"Well, you know, you two haven't been on the best of terms lately."

"No, we're fine now," Allie assured her, and turned to smile at a party of six who were leaving. "Grab that table before someone else comes in." She looked around as the others came in. She greeted Joe, his mother and sister. "I thought you said Ben was coming with you."

"He got a call about a possible burglary, but he'll be along." Joe looked around the room, spotted Nikki, and waved. "Is that her dad?" he asked.

Allie nodded. "That would be him. And his girlfriend. And the girlfriend's daughter, who used to be Nikki's best friend."

"Used to be?" Joe asked.

"Long story. I'll tell you later." Allie showed them to the table.

Ben came in just as Clint and company were getting ready to leave. The two men nodded at each other in a sort of wary greeting when they both apparently realized the other was staring at Allie.

"Looking good this morning, Miz Monroe," Ben whispered as he walked past to join Joe and Cara.

She smiled. She walked Clint and Marlo to the door, Courtney lagging behind. Had she just taken a photo of Mark with her phone? And had she taken a second before dropping her phone into her bag, or was she photographing the café?

Nikki hugged her father, and Marlo held her arms open to give her a hug, which Nikki stepped into tentatively. Allie's heart constricted, and she wanted to shout at Marlo to get her hands off her daughter, but her better angels intervened and she said nothing. Chances were good that Marlo would be her stepmother someday, and at the very least, she appeared to show genuine affection for Nikki, which in the long run could only be a good thing. But when she caught Courtney hugging Nikki, she couldn't help but send her best mom's stink eye in her direction.

That girl was trouble, Allie was sure of it. She couldn't help but feel sorry for Marlo, and by extension, Clint. Well, maybe not so sorry for him. Allie smiled to herself. *Maybe when he compares Courtney to Nikki—which he will inevitably do—he'll have to admit that I did one hell of a job with that kid of ours.* Allie wasn't modest about taking 90 percent of the credit.

Nikki walked her father out and waited on the sidewalk until the car pulled away from the curb. When she came back into the café, she gave Allie a hug.

"What was that for?" Allie asked.

"Just for being my mom."

"Do you feel sad about your dad leaving?" Allie said.

"I'd feel sadder if he'd come by himself." Nikki went over to Mark's family table and pulled out a chair.

The influx eased as the afternoon progressed. Barney finished her table hopping and came back to the desk.

"After watching you in action," Allie said, "I do believe you bought this place strictly for the opportunities to socialize for hours on end."

"Ah, she's on to me." Barney looked around the restaurant. "Do you think we should redo the interior with a vintage look? Something that might be compatible with the theater?"

"That's a thought." Allie shared her ideas about painting the room and reframing the old photos. Barney agreed to all Allie's ideas, and asked what Allie thought they could do about the floor.

As they exchanged ideas for the café's new look, the breakfast and brunch diners began to make way for the late-lunch crowd. Allie sent Barney home—it was clear the woman was exhausted— and later, when it came time to close for the night, Allie locked the front door behind the last diner, sent the staff home, and was on her way out when she remembered she'd wanted to check the waitress schedule for the coming week.

She went into the office, then sat at Judy's old desk and resisted the urge to put her head down and sleep. As uncomfortable as she usually found Judy's chair, it felt wonderful to sit anywhere after having been on her feet the entire day. Judy'd promised to clean off her desk before she left for New Mexico, but she hadn't done it. Allie didn't like riffling through someone else's correspondence, but she'd been told the schedule was on the desk. She found an unmarked folder and opened it, but the form she was looking for wasn't among the seemingly random papers. She was just about to close the folder when something she'd seen toward the back of the file caused her to pause. She flipped through a layer of bills to a note that was written on plain white paper.

J. ~

   *Just a heads-up that I'm going to be on vacation starting the
week after next, but I have someone who can cover for me if need
be. Give me a call.*

                                                              J.

Allie stared at the writing, at the form of the letter, at the signature at the bottom.
   "Oh my God . . ."

CHAPTER ELEVEN

"**B**arney, are you awake?" Allie stood outside Barney's bedroom door and knocked.

"Mom, what's going on?" Nikki stepped out from her room, which was across the hall from Barney's.

"I need to talk to Barney." Allie knocked again. "Barney, are you up?"

"I am now," Barney barked. "Stop banging on my door. Just come in."

Allie opened the door and found Barney half sitting, half lying on her bed.

"What is it?" Barney sat up to turn on the lamp on the bed-side table, then fell back against the pillow. "And it had better be good."

"It is." Allie stood at the foot of the bed, Nikki next to it. Des and Cara wandered in to see what was causing the commotion. "I know who J is."

"What?" Barney sat all the way up.

"It's Justine Kennedy."

"Justine?" A blatantly skeptical Barney frowned. "Why on earth would you think it's her?"

Allie took the note out of her bag and handed it to Barney. The others gathered around.

"I found this note on Judy's desk. I've seen Judy's handwriting, and this isn't it. But it's the same style, set up the same way J set up the note to Dad. The exact J signature." Allie was confident. "It's the same handwriting."

Allie held up the note J had written to Fritz all those years ago. She'd stopped in the sitting room to compare, just to make sure. There could be no mistake: the J's were identical.

"Justine Mitchell." Barney studied the note to Fritz, then scratched the back of her head. "I never saw that coming. This is really hard to believe."

Barney handed the two notes to Cara and pushed her pillow up behind her back as if holding court. Which, Allie mused, in a way she was.

"Why is it so hard to believe?" Cara asked. "Why not Justine?"

"Justine was just . . ." Barney paused as if searching for a word. "She was just *so* not Fritz's type. He always went for the girls who were petite and beautiful, you know. He liked long hair. Nora to a T. Justine was tall, lanky, and had a pixie haircut back then. She and her sister both had those cute little pixie cuts that looked so off on that tall body. I can't imagine what he'd have seen in her, to be blunt."

"There had to have been something," Cara said. "What else do you remember about her?"

Barney appeared to give it some thought.

"Back in the day, the Mitchell girls were considered too modern about things like women running for Congress and anchoring the TV news. Things we take for granted turned a lot of heads back then, especially in small towns like Hidden Falls. I remember Justine ran for student government against Fritz one year. He seemed amused by it."

"Why was Dad amused that she ran against him?" Des asked.

"Because Fritz knew she didn't have a snowball's chance in hell to win. He knew no one could beat him. Your father was the golden boy of Hidden Falls, remember. He won everything he'd ever gone after."

"Including Justine, apparently," Des said.

"She was very smart, I do seem to recall that. She might have gone to law school, which wasn't common for girls back then. I think I heard some talk about that." Barney's raised right knee supported her elbow that rested on it. "That could have been it, you know. My brother loved a beautiful girl, but he also was intrigued by intelligence. Nikki, would you mind running down to my sitting room? All the old yearbooks are on the second to the bottom shelf on the first bookcase. I think Justine would have graduated in . . . oh, just bring all the ones from the early 1960s."

Allie sat down on the edge of the mattress at the foot of the elaborately carved bed. Barney'd told her once that it had belonged to a great-great-aunt who'd never married but lived with her sister and her Hudson husband in this house. It was Eastlake in style, as were the dressers and the desk. The bedroom walls were papered—dark red roses on a sage green background—the drapes heavy green velvet. Not for the first time, Allie wanted to suggest a change in décor. The furniture was old enough to be considered not only vintage but extremely cool. The wallpaper and drapes, not so much. She was envisioning the lovely mahogany of the wood, with that tinge of dark red undertone, against walls painted cream or palest gray. The drapes had to go as well, maybe replaced with lacy curtains that would sway and billow in a gentle breeze. She knew Barney was attached to the furniture—understandable—but she didn't understand her reluctance to strip the walls or pitch the drapes.

"Allie, I'm still having a hard time believing it was Justine," Barney was saying. "Nora was absolutely his type. She was younger by about four years, as you know, and I'm sure you remember what a tiny little thing she was. She had such beautiful features and skin like porcelain. When Nora was around, Fritz couldn't keep his eyes off her. I think he found it hard to believe someone so ethereal looking could be real."

"She may have looked like an angel, but living with her was hell." Des sat opposite Allie.

Nikki came back into the room, a stack of gray yearbooks in her arms. "Here you go, Aunt Barney. Where would you like them?"

"Right here is fine." Barney patted the space next to her on the bed. She sorted through the pile until she found what she was looking for. "Ah. Here we go. I think this would have been Justine's junior year." She leafed through the book. "Here's her photo, girls, as a member of the newspaper staff."

Barney turned the book around. Allie had to stretch to see the black-and-white photo.

"Which one is Justine?" Allie asked. "Oh, right. The tall girl with the—duh—pixie cut standing behind the guy seated at the desk?"

Allie leaned closer and tried to see the angry woman from the café in the teenage face. "She's not so bad looking. She's actually kind of cute. Though I agree her hair being so short pulls her out of proportion a bit. She sure has changed, though. And she looks a hell of a lot nicer when she's not pissed off."

"We'd be able to see her face better had the photo been taken closer, but I get the idea." Des looked at Barney over the top of the yearbook. "She's cute, and if she was really smart, I could see Dad being interested. Though since she wrote that note well after high school, they probably didn't get together back then."

"Maybe. We'll never know unless Justine decides to tell us, and I'm not going to be the one to ask." Barney closed the yearbook and put it back on the stack.

"Which brings up the question, are you going to say something to her?" Allie asked.

"Something like what?" Barney repositioned the pillow behind her head.

"I think it's pretty obvious that she holds a grudge against the family because Dad played around with her—or whatever it was he did—and then left her to go to California with Nora. Maybe if you talked to her about it, she'd realize the whole family wasn't to blame," Allie said.

"So what do you propose I do? Ring her doorbell and say, *Justine, I'm sorry my brother dumped you. Can't we all be friends?*"

"Yeah, I guess that wouldn't be a good idea," Allie conceded.

"So we just let her off the hook from baking for us because Dad jerked her around?" Des was clearly annoyed.

"I checked the café's freezer yesterday, and it looks like we might have another week or maybe two of Justine's goodies," Barney said. "I'm thinking of putting ice cream sundaes on the menu, at least for the rest of the summer. Once everyone's back in town from their vacations, I'll start asking around to see if anyone we know has some hidden talent, or at the least some suggestions. I'd like to keep things in town if possible. But now that the mystery's been solved, is there any reason why I shouldn't be going back to sleep?"

They all shook their heads and got off the bed.

"Nikki, love, please put these yearbooks on the desk over there. And then you may all leave." Barney snuggled back into her pillow and pulled her light blanket up to her chin. She didn't wait until the foursome left before turning off the light. Nikki slipped out of Barney's room and across the hall into hers.

"Okay, so now we know who J is and why Justine hates us so much she won't bake for us." Cara was the last out the door, and she closed it quietly behind her. "Good work on your part, Al."

"With all the discussion going on in there, I forgot to thank you. Good job." Des patted Allie on the back as they headed down the hall.

"I just wish we could have gotten the whole story, though, you know?" Allie paused at her bedroom door. "I bet it's a whopper."

"Maybe so, but like Barney said, you really can't say anything to Justine without bringing up something in her past that obviously still bothers her a lot." Des stood opposite Allie's door. "We just have to let it go and be glad you were able to figure out who wrote the note. Anything beyond that would be prying into someone's private life, and we're not going there, right?"

"Right," Allie and Cara both agreed.

"Okay. Well, I'll see you all in the morning." Des went into her room and closed the door.

"Night, Al." Cara did the same.

"Night, guys." Allie pushed her door open, but before she could close it, she heard Nikki call to her from the end of the hall.

"Mom, I wanted to ask you if my friend Wendy could come over tomorrow." Nikki caught up with Allie in her bedroom doorway.

"Who's Wendy again?" The name rang a bell but Allie couldn't put a face with it. Had she met this girl?

"She's staying in her grandma's house next door to Hayley and Mark. That's how I met her. She and her mom visit every summer, so Hayley's known her forever. Mark and Hayley leave early tomorrow morning for sports camp for the week. Wendy's really nice and I'd like to get to know her better."

"Sure, as long as it's okay with her mother. What are you planning on doing?"

"Just stuff. We'll probably go down to the theater 'cause she's never seen it. Maybe have lunch at the Goodbye. Maybe walk out to Seth's farm. Wendy's mom's teaching a summer class at the high school, so she's not home during the day, and her grandmother's still on vacation."

"It's fine with me. Just mention it to Barney in the morning as a consideration of the fact that it's her house." Allie stepped toward the door and kissed her daughter's cheek. "Night, sweetie."

"Night, Mom, and thanks." Nikki twirled around and danced quietly down the hall to her room in the front of the house.

Allie changed and dragged her tired self to her bed. It was barely midnight, but to her, it felt like the wee hours of the morning. She'd been on the go since Barney took over the Goodbye, so it seemed she always felt on the verge of sleep. She closed her eyes and tried to recall the last time she remembered a dream, but she was out before she could tap into her memory bank.

She hit the snooze alarm three times in the morning before she could force herself to move.

"Rise, I can do. Shining, however, is probably too much to ask," she murmured as she made her way to the bathroom.

Allie was midway through the first stencil when she heard voices in the lobby. She put the lids back onto the jars of paint and rested her brushes on an old wooden cutting board Barney had given her for the purpose. As she swung her legs over the side of the scaffold, she recognized Des's and Cara's voices along with two others.

By the time she reached the bottom, Des, Cara, and the two Werner sisters were at the base of the platform. Allie introduced herself, and Rita Werner, who appeared to be the elder of the two upholsterers, greeted her politely, then wasted no time in turning to the business at hand.

"We've brought our sample. If you ladies approve, we'll order what we'll need to re-cover the seats."

As she spoke, her sister removed a folded piece of rose-colored velvet from a bag. "Let's head down into the audience and see if this will do the trick," Elsa said.

"Great. Let's do it." Allie gestured for Elsa to lead the way.

They went into the audience section and Cara turned on the overhead lights. Elsa stopped at the first seat in the back row and placed the fabric over the seat, so it lay directly next to the chair to the left.

"It's not a perfect match," Des said.

"But it's awfully close." Cara knelt to get a better look. "I don't know how noticeable the difference would be if the lights aren't real bright." She glanced over her shoulder at Allie. "What do you think?"

Allie stood three rows below. "Cara, turn the lights down just a bit." She watched the lights dim slightly. "In lower light, it's really hard to tell there's a difference. Honestly, I don't know if we'd ever get an exact match, unless we tracked down the original manufacturer of the chairs and they just happened to have some of the fabric left over from the 1920s and in good enough shape to use. Let's face it, guys, in a few more years, this place will be one hundred years old. I don't see how we'll do better than this, the colors are so close. I say we go with it."

"If the artist in residence is okay with it, who am I to argue?" Cara stood. "I'm fine with this."

"Me, too," Des agreed.

"So we have a yes on the seats. Now the stage curtains." Allie walked down the aisle in the direction of the stage. "You said you thought you could repair them?"

Rita caught up with her. "Absolutely. They're not in bad condition, considering their age. The few tears can be fixed. And since they are original to the building, we should make every effort to restore them."

Allie turned to Cara. "Any idea when Joe can get these taken down?"

"I'll remind him," Cara assured her. "He's been really jammed with work these past few weeks, but he should get a break soon."

"Would you mind texting him now? Maybe we can nail down when he'd be available to take them down and get them to Scranton." Allie thought maybe they'd speed up the entire process if the curtains could be delivered to the Werners' by the weekend.

Cara walked away to send her text while Elsa and Des went row by row, marking the chairs where new seat covers were needed with strips of bright blue duct tape. The previous count had been sixty-two, which when you considered the size of the audience, wasn't so bad.

"Joe said if he could get someone to help him, he'd come in on Friday night after work and take the curtains down, then drive them to the shop on Saturday morning." Cara turned to the upholsterers. "Does that work for you?"

"That would be fine, yes." Elsa nodded. "We can repair, clean, and press them for you and have them back in . . . oh, probably a week."

"That would be great, thank you." Allie was pleased to mentally draw a line through the curtains on her mental checklist. "And the seats . . . ?"

"About two weeks, maybe three, Elsa?" Rita asked.

"Probably. We'll do the cutting at the shop, but we'll have to fit them onto the seats here." Elsa looked around the audience and appeared satisfied with her estimate.

"Works for me." Allie stood with her hands on her hips, wondering which project to tackle next.

The carpets, she thought. She'd found a few rips under several of the seats, but other than that, the carpets were mostly just faded from wear.

They walked Elsa and Rita out of the theater, then Allie called Des and Cara back inside.

"I'm thinking about the carpets next," she told them.

"I think the floor sanding should be done next," Des said. "The stage and the entire backstage area need to be sanded and stained. We don't want to pay to clean the carpets, then get sawdust all over them."

"Good point. That means in addition to dropping off the curtains, the guys are going to have to do all the sanding. Which come to think of it they should do before the curtains are hung and the seats are re-covered."

"And the walls need to be painted," Des reminded her.

"Are we still paying Joe to be the construction manager?" Allie asked.

Cara nodded. "Yes, but not as much, since we're down to one crew—the one in the basement—and they're supposed to be finished in another week or so."

"Then we should be able to get him to find a painter for the interior." Allie's head was starting to swim. She wanted it all done *now now now*. The sooner the better.

"I'll talk to him about that tonight." Cara's hands were on her hips as she surveyed the lobby. "This place is shaping up really nicely. In fact, it's coming together better than I'd ever have dreamed back in March when we first saw it."

"We've come a long way, babies," Des said.

"All true, but we have a way to go yet," Allie reminded them. "I need to pull the bathrooms into shape. The tile in there still needs to be replaced, which means I'll have to find something else we can use. The plumbers had to take two walls down to get the old pipes out, so much of the original tile work has been destroyed. I'm sure we can find reproductions that are compatible with the rest of the theater. Joe said there are tile companies that special-ize in vintage designs. I'll look online tonight if I get home in time from the Goodbye."

"About that," Cara said. "Would you want me to share the hostess duties with you? It seems like Barney's working you pretty hard these days."

"Thanks, Cara. But I think she's just trying to get her pound of flesh while I'm still here. Once I'm back in L.A., I'm sure she's going to be working the two of you the way she's working me." Allie laughed. "And I don't mind putting the time in now. I want to do my share while I can."

"Well, if you ever feel you need a break, let me know." Des sat on the steps leading up to the balcony. "I'm glad to help."

"Stay there. I have an idea." Allie disappeared around the cor-ner, then returned five minutes later, her arms filled.

She passed out bottles of water and held out boxes of fresh popcorn.

"I thought I smelled butter. Yay you." Des reached for a box. "One of my favorite things."

"And just what I need this morning. Thanks, Allie." Cara was already taking the cap off her water.

"Thank Seth for giving Des that wonderful, quick, efficient popcorn maker for her birthday," Allie said. "I remembered we'd had some bottles of water left over from the birthday party. Barney put them in the cooler behind the candy counter."

"I can't wait to see that baby loaded up with sugary goodness," Cara said. "Just think of that glass candy case all filled up with tasty snacks."

"Could this really be our all-organic-all-the-time sister Cara lusting after movie theater candy?" Allie raised an eyebrow.

Cara laughed. "Come on, who doesn't like movie theater candy?"

"What's your favorite?" Des asked.

"Milky Ways, definitely," Cara replied without hesitation.

"Milky Ways? We're talking *movie* candy here, girl. Like Milk Duds." Allie sat down next to Des.

"Raisinets. Best movie candy ever," Des said. "Followed by Twizzlers."

"Uh-uh. Junior Mints. Hands down," Allie said.

"Oh, Sno-Caps," Cara said.

"That's better." Allie nodded. "Now, who's going to be in charge of stocking the candy counter?"

"Me." Cara and Des answered at the same time.

"You're in charge of the popcorn machine," Cara reminded Des. "I'll do the candy ordering."

"Done." Allie stood. "See how easy it is to keep this project moving forward? Just a little consultation and *bam*. On to the next."

"Which would be . . . ?" Cara asked.

"Well, so far we're knocking out the seats, the curtains, the wood floors, the tile in the bathroom, and the candy counter. How much more could there be?" Des asked.

"I'll check my list when I get back to the house," Allie told her.

"You really can't wait to get back to California, can you?" Cara asked softly.

"Nothing personal, but Nikki goes home really soon. I've sort of been in denial, because we've had her here all summer, but she's going to have to go back to start school. It'll kill me to put her on that plane." Allie started to chew on a fingernail and Des swiped her hand away.

"It's been a different sort of summer, that's for sure," Cara said.

"Yeah, but for you, it isn't really going to come to an end. You're staying, and you'll establish a business here and probably marry Joe and live happily ever after." Allie turned to Des. "And I can totally see you marrying Seth and raising a bunch of little grape-stomping, wine-making, apple-picking puppy lovers." Allie could sense they were all starting to feel just a little sentimental, bordering on possibly weepy, so she added, "Cara, you think Des's kids'll come out bald with tiny Harley-Davidson tattoos on their shoulders?"

"Aww, that could be cute," Cara said.

"Oh my God, I almost forgot to tell you! Seth said the most amazing thing!" Des stood, obviously excited to share.

"Let me think." Allie pretended to ponder. "He said he loved the way your curly hair frizzes in all this humidity."

"Stop. No, he was playing around with labels for the wines he's going to make, and guess what he's naming his first wine?" Des's eyes filled with tears, she was so obviously moved. "Guys, this is the most romantic thing ever. You're going to die when I tell you."

"I'm really not ready to die, but this is easy. He's going to name it Desdemona, after you," Allie said. "Will it be white or red?"

"Desdemona, *My Love*," Cara corrected her. "And of course it will be red." She grabbed a strand of Des's red hair and added, "Duh."

"You two. No. He's calling it Rescue Me." Des looked from Allie to Cara and back again. When neither reacted, she said, "Get it? *Rescue?* Because I rescue dogs?"

"Right. Got it. That's so cool, Des. And yeah, romantic as all get-out," Cara agreed.

"Yeah, 'cause he could have named it something else with you in mind. Montana Babe. Short and Sweet," Allie quipped. "Or he could have gone retro and called it Des Does It All after your old TV show."

"Okay, that's it. I'm taking my popcorn and going home." Des laughed despite her efforts to pretend to be offended.

"Seriously, I love it," Allie said. "I know Seth won't be ready to make wine for another few years, but I intend to sample the maiden batch on one of my trips back east."

"You'll come back to visit?" Cara asked.

"Of course." Allie felt dismayed. "Do you really think I could just go back and never see you again? Guys, you're my sisters." She looked at Des. "And for the first time in a very long time, I can say with all honesty that I'm so happy that you are."

"Aw." Des reached an arm toward each sister and embraced them. "Group hug."

"And there's Barney," Allie added. "Now that I know her, I'm going to want to visit her, too. And growing up, Nikki has to know you guys."

"We're going to miss you, too." Cara broke the circle and reached for her bag. "And we want to watch Nikki grow up."

"Of course we do." Des tossed her bag over her shoulder. "We adore her."

"We'll both come back for the weddings," Allie said as she walked to the lobby. "If you guys can wait a minute, I have to go up for my stuff."

"We'll wait," Cara said.

"You'll all be in my wedding," Des said.

"Did you and Seth already talk about getting married?" Cara asked.

Allie listened as she climbed, not missing a word.

"Sort of. Nothing definite, but you know how you do. How something comes up in conversation and one of you sort of tosses out a comment, and that leads to more conversation."

From the top of the scaffold, Allie called down, "So who did the tossing, Des?"

"Actually, Seth did. But it's still in the tossed category. I'll let you know if anything comes of it."

"I'll bet you'll be married before your first year in Hidden Falls is over." Allie took her time packing her tools, making sure the paint jar lids were secure and the brushes wrapped in foil to be cleaned as soon as she got back to the house.

"We'll see. I'm not ruling out anything," Des said. "But I will say sooner has a lot more appeal than later."

Allie finished getting her things together and climbed all the way down without pausing to think about how high she'd been. All she could think about was Des dressed in frothy white with flowers in her hair.

They chatted companionably all the way back to the house, and anyone eavesdropping on the happy chatter would be hard-pressed to believe that a mere nine months ago they'd not been loving sisters who laughed and cried and teased, but strangers, wary of each other and the task that had been set for them.

CHAPTER TWELVE

Allie was cleaning her paintbrushes at the utility sink in the laundry room off the kitchen and singing along with the radio—Journey—when she heard Nikki calling her.

"In here, Nik."

Two pairs of feet could be heard coming toward her, starting in the hall and echoing through the kitchen.

"Mom, this is my friend Wendy Dunham. Wendy, my mom, Allie Monroe." Nikki started to make the introductions before she reached her mother.

Allie turned down the radio's volume. "Hello, Wendy. I understand you're another summer visitor to Hidden Falls."

Wendy nodded. "We come every summer 'cause my mom teaches summer school here at the high school. Then we house-sit while my grandmother is on vacation."

"Do you miss your friends at home?" Allie dried off a brush and turned to get a good look at her daughter's new friend. She was the same height as Nikki, with pale strawberry blond hair not quite as long nor as straight as Nikki's, and very blue eyes behind dark blue-framed glasses. Wendy was pretty in the way you knew would become beautiful in a few years.

"Sometimes. I always spend a lot of time here with Hayley and

Mark, though. This year I went to sleepover camp in Massachusetts for a month, so I only got here a few weeks ago."

"Did you enjoy camp?" Allie asked.

"Not so much. I mean, it's okay, we do a lot of different stuff there, but I really have more fun here," Wendy said.

"Why is that?" Allie cleaned another brush, wiping the excess water on a paper towel.

"I think it's because we're in school all year long, and it's very structured. Camp is very structured, too. You swim at a certain time, you play volleyball at a certain time, you eat at a certain time, you know?"

Allie nodded. She knew.

"But when I'm here, I can hang out with my friends or swim in my grandmother's pool or go to school with my mom. She's teaching a graphic design class, so sometimes I sit in. Sometimes I just hang out in the library or go to the park. You know how some days you just want to sit somewhere quiet and read a book?"

Allie looked over her shoulder at Wendy, whose expression was so earnest she had to smile.

"Yes, I do. And I agree. Sometimes you should be allowed to just sit and read if that's what you feel like doing."

"Yeah." Wendy's head bobbed up and down in agreement. "I read a lot. It's one of my favorite things."

"Wendy and I have read all the same books. How cool is that? Right now we're both reading *The Guernsey Literary and Potato Peel Pie Society*," Nikki said. "Next will be *The Lost Queen*. Hayley read it and said it was the best book ever. Aunt Barney has a ton of books and she reads every day."

"And after *The Lost Queen*, we're both going to read *The Nightingale*. My mom said it was okay for me to read it," Wendy said. "She said it was an important book about an important time in history, so she let me borrow her copy."

Nikki nodded. "Aunt Barney has the book and she said I could take her copy back home with me if I haven't finished it by the time I have to leave." She turned to Wendy and added, "We can talk about the book on Skype if we go home before we finish it."

Wendy nodded. "You, Hayley, and I could even have our own book club even after you go back to California and I go back to Kingston." She turned to Allie and said, "That's near Wilkes-Barre. It's famous because the first public school in Pennsylvania was in Kingston."

"That's certainly something to be proud of," Allie said. Then, before she could ask what they had planned for the day, Nikki said, "Can we go to the Goodbye and have lunch? Then I want to take Wendy out to Seth's so we can play with the puppies and she can help me teach them how to walk on a leash. It takes a while for them to learn," she told Wendy, "because they're really young. But they're really cute and fun."

"Sure. Ginger's probably there if Aunt Barney isn't. Just tell her I said it was okay so she doesn't hand you a bill on the way out."

"Yay. Come on, Wendy. Let's go. See you, Mom." Nikki blew a kiss from the doorway. "Thanks!"

The excited chatter grew faint as the girls moved closer to the front door. Allie stepped out of the room to try to hear more of the conversation. She knew Nikki was bright, knew she was inquisitive, but in the past, she'd only heard her daughter and her friends, particularly Courtney, talk about clothes and boys and what happened at school. Not that there's anything wrong with kids in junior high or high school freshmen talking about their social life, but it seemed shallow to never talk about anything else. Hearing Nik talk about books—and such good books at that—gave Allie pause. Wendy seemed really smart and mature, certainly more like Nikki than Courtney—or, Allie had to admit, more like the way she saw Nikki.

I guess we're all different things to different people, Allie conceded. It was nice to see this different side of Nikki, though, and nice for her that she's found a friend she feels comfortable discussing books with. Allie recalled that in the past, Nikki'd said that both Hayley and Mark were readers, too.

Oh well. Different environment, different influences. In any event, Nikki seemed to like her new friend, so that was a good thing. Allie'd run out of time to think about it. She had to get ready to work the afternoon and evening shift at the Goodbye, and the morning was moving swiftly.

The girls had just finished lunch when Allie came into the café. Nikki was showing Wendy the photos on the wall of old Hidden Falls.

"This is the Sugarhouse," Allie overheard Nikki tell Wendy. "My great-great-grandfather built it like a hundred years ago. My mom and my aunts are restoring it. It's the coolest place in the world. I'm going to talk my mom and my aunts into doing summer stage so when I come back next year, I can be in a play. My grandad met my grandmother there. She was a famous actress . . ."

Albeit a poor excuse for a mother. Allie smiled and gave her attention to the couple arriving for lunch. She seated them, then returned to the desk. The girls had moved on to other photos, Nikki explaining the who and the what in each before deciding to start the two-mile walk to Seth's farm.

"You could stop home and see if Aunt Des or Aunt Cara can drive you," Allie said. "It's a long walk."

"It's okay. It's not hot today." Nikki leaned across the desk and kissed her mother on the cheek. "Thanks for lunch."

"Thanks for lunch, Miz Monroe," Wendy echoed.

The girls started to leave, but one last photo caught Nikki's eye and they stopped to take a closer look.

Interesting that Nikki had made up her mind that not only would she and Allie spend next summer in Hidden Falls, Allie mused, but she'd be acting in a play at the Sugarhouse. Because, of course, Nikki couldn't imagine she wouldn't be able to talk her mother and her aunts into holding summer stage. And of course, there was a good chance she could talk them into pretty much anything.

Allie wondered where she'd be this time next year, what she'd be doing. Would she and Nikki be back in Hidden Falls, or would the pull to family fade over time as the draw to other as of now unknown things grew stronger? It made her sad to think things could change between her and her sisters, her and Barney, Nikki and the aunts she loved so dearly. There was no sense in denying that her time in Hidden Falls was growing short, Nikki's time even shorter. Funny, but she hadn't wanted to come east, hadn't wanted to disrupt her life in L.A.—such as it was—and now that she'd become comfortable, it would soon be time to leave.

If not for Nikki, would she stay?

But her daughter was the priority, and she had to go back to school, so soon Allie would have to focus on her plans. She'd call Mary Pat, the Realtor who handled the rental of her house, and have her ask the current occupants if they'd like to purchase it. The renters' lease didn't expire until March, but Allie had no intention of living there again. She'd also ask Mary Pat to begin to look for a place she could buy close to Nikki's school now. Or should she consider a rental while she searched for something to buy?

Too much to think about on a busy afternoon when there were customers to seat.

Out of the corner of her eye, she saw Des and Barney pass by the desk. Barney waved as she strode with apparent purpose through the café until she noticed Nikki and her friend on their way out. Barney stopped and stared, an unreadable expression on her face. Nikki waved to Barney as she and Wendy left, then Barney continued toward the back of the café where the office was located.

Allie flagged down Des. "Hey, what's going on?"

"Barney arranged a sit-down with Chef George about ordering whatever he needs for next week's menus," Des said. "Judy went over it with us at one of the meetings we had before she left, but Barney's decided she's too busy right now to 'get involved with all that.'"

"So she's delegated that to you."

Des nodded.

188 • MARIAH STEWART

"Does this feel like part of a plan to keep at least one of us in Hidden Falls even after the theater is ready to go?"

"That's exactly what it is." Des laughed. "She doesn't know that I've already decided to stick around, so I think I'll just let her have her fun."

"You're a good sport," Allie said.

"I know."

"You better get in there. I just saw Chef George go in." Allie nodded in the direction of the office.

"Does that guy live here?" Des asked as she started to walk away. "Doesn't it seem he's always here?"

"From lunch through dinner, it's all Chef George," Allie told her. "Earlier, it's Henry, who you probably haven't met because you're never here for breakfast."

"Neither are you," Des reminded her.

"No, but I've been here for the changing of the guard," Allie said, "when Henry leaves and George is reporting in. Now, scoot before Barney comes looking for you."

Des made her way around the tables and headed for the office. The lunch crowd was building, and Allie had tables to tend to. Alice had called in sick a half hour before she was scheduled to arrive, so Allie'd told Ginger she'd pinch-hit.

"Well, I guess you'll do," Ginger had teased Allie. "You didn't do all that badly last time."

"Adequate at best, I admit it." Allie had no delusions about her waitressing, but she had maintained her sense of humor. "And I did exceed Penny's standards. At least I didn't spill soup in any-one's lap."

Barney and Des emerged about forty minutes after they'd sequestered themselves with the chef to figure out how to plan future menus (with George's input) and where to buy what they needed (a food supply service and local farms in season) and how to figure out how much they'd need. Des confessed to Allie she expected she'd make some mistakes, over- or underestimating for a while, but they'd get it right eventually.

"Allie, who was the girl with Nikki?" Barney asked before leaving.

"Nikki's friend Wendy. She's another summer transplant, like Nik," Allie told her.

"What's her last name?"

"Ummm, I don't remember. I think it started with a D. She seems like a nice kid. She didn't mention her father, but she said her mother teaches in Kingston and she's teaching summer school locally."

Barney didn't comment further before leaving to go to the bank. "I'm picking up additional signature cards for the operating and payroll accounts, in case for whatever reason I'm not around when a check needs to be written, any one of the three of you can sign."

Nikki called around four thirty and asked if she could spend the night at Wendy's.

"Her mom is going to take us to the movies," Nikki told Allie.

"What's playing?"

"That new film about a girl who finds out she has dragon blood and has to save the world."

"Well, that should be exciting." Allie hesitated. While Wendy had made a good impression on her, she'd not met the girl's mother and had no idea where they lived.

"Mom?"

"I'd feel better if I knew her mother," Allie admitted. "I've never even spoken to her."

"I can give you her number and you can call and speak to her," Nikki said. "Please?"

"Give me the number and I'll call." Allie wrote the number on the back of one of the specials menus.

"Thanks, Mom."

"Okay." Allie sighed. "Stay tuned."

It was still early for the dinner crowd, so Allie made the call while she had a few minutes to chat.

"Hello, is this Wendy's mother?" Allie said when the call was answered, wishing she'd thought to ask Nikki for the woman's name.

"Yes, this is Tess Dunham." She hesitated. "Has something happened to—"

"No, no," Allie hastened to say. "Sorry. This is Nikki Monroe's mom, Allie. I should have asked Nik for your name, but I didn't think of it. I'm sorry to have alarmed you."

"Oh, yes. Allie. So nice to speak with you. I guess Nikki called about going to the movies tonight and sleeping over."

"Yes. I just wanted to touch base with you."

"Of course. Wendy's hoping you'll say yes. She adores Nikki and they seem to have so much in common, not the least of which is that they're both more or less outsiders in town. And both here visiting relatives for the summer."

"And they both like the same books." Allie repeated the conversation from this morning.

"Wendy's always been a reader, and I'm so glad. My late husband read every minute he wasn't doing something else. Wendy always says that her favorite memory of her dad was of him reading to her when she was little."

"Oh, I didn't know. I'm sorry."

"Me, too." Tess sounded wistful. "He was a great guy and a super dad."

"How long ago . . . ?" Allie didn't want to pry, but she didn't want to change the subject as if the man's passing was immaterial.

"It's been six years. Wendy was nine. It was hard for her to accept that he was gone. Still is sometimes, I guess, for both of us."

Allie was curious to know more but wouldn't ask. Instead, she merely said, "I'm very sorry for your loss, Tess."

"Thank you. So. Back to the kids. As soon as Wendy and Nikki started hanging around together, nothing would do but that we invite your daughter along for the movie. I'll have dinner for them when we get back, and I can bring Nikki home in the morning."

"That would be fine. I know Nikki really wants to go."

"Then I'll pick the girls up now . . . Oh, Wendy said they were at a farm somewhere playing with puppies and painting a trellis? I'm not sure I know what that's all about," Tess said.

Allie explained about her sister's start-up rescue shelter and Seth's vineyard.

"Ah, I see. Could you give me directions?"

Minutes later, Allie was on the phone to Nikki, giving her the green light for the evening.

"Ask Wendy's mom to stop off at Hudson Street to pick up your things, since you're staying over," Allie told her. "And if you're a mess after playing with the pups, clean up a bit, please."

"I will. Promise. Mom, you really are the best mom ever. Thank you, thank you, thank you! I'm dying to see the movie."

"So I guess I'll see you in the morning," Allie said. "Oh, wait. Nikki. Money."

"Dad gave me some cash before he left, so I'm good. See you tomorrow, Mom."

Des came in around eight with Seth and she claimed a table before coming up to the desk for menus.

"We worked later than we planned in the vineyard, so I suggested we take a quick shower and come down here for dinner."

"How quick was the shower?" Allie teased.

"Not all that quick, actually." Des smirked. "I guess it's safe to say it was no quicker than it needed to be."

Des grabbed menus and started to walk away.

"Oh, hey." Des turned back to Allie. "I met Wendy's mother when she came out to the farm to pick up the girls. There's something familiar about her, but I can't put my finger on it. Seth said he's seen her around this summer, so maybe I have, too. Anyway, she seems really nice, and Wendy is a doll. She and Nikki had the best time with the puppies, and then when the dogs all collapsed from exhaustion, they came into the barn to help us paint the new trellises Seth built. Honestly, that man has more energy."

"Good for him. He'll need it with all he's got going on." Allie lowered her voice. "And may I say, good for you."

"I don't kiss and tell," Des whispered as she walked away. "But I can confirm that the man has incredible stamina."

Allie grinned as her sister walked away to join her guy at the table. Between waiting on the few diners who remained, Allie stopped to chat with Des and Seth. It never failed to amuse her that her preppy sister, who'd always dressed in tweeds and silks, now wore T-shirts sporting Harley-Davidson or Metallica logos. And that the girl who'd admitted that in the past she'd only dated tweedy, buttoned-down guys who played tennis and golf had fallen in love with a man whose clean-shaven head towered well above her own, who favored colorful tattoos, and was teaching Des to drive that Harley he kept in his barn.

He was also one of the most gentle, sincere, kind men Allie had ever met, and that he was crazy in love with Des was as apparent as the reflection of the overhead lights on his bald head.

The café began to thin out around nine, though Des and Seth were still chatting over coffee and dessert. Some of the kitchen crew began to leave and Allie gave Ginger the green light to go home a little early. She grabbed coffee for herself and carried it to her sister's table.

"Mind if I join you?"

"Pull up a chair," Des told her, and Seth slid one out for her.

"Long day?" Seth asked.

Allie nodded. "They've all been long since Barney decided to buy this place and take over right away."

Seth laughed. "That's the Barney I've known pretty much my entire life. She's always been one to jump right in and learn as she went along."

"There's been a learning curve for all of us," Allie agreed. "Especially you, Des. How're you doing with all the bookkeeping that's been dumped in your lap?"

"The bookkeeping is pretty straightforward with the accounting system Judy was using. It's actually been easier to learn than it was to keep track of the theater expenses, since I had to make up my own system as we went along. From day one, I had to figure things out. It's a snap when there's a real system already in place."

"The theater project should be wrapping up soon. I'm guessing six weeks or less," Allie said.

"If that. The last items are pretty much in line." Des's fork mushed a bit of peach pie that remained on her plate. "How much longer before you're finished with the ceiling?"

"A week. Maybe less. I do want to go back and repaint the outlines on several of the diamond shapes. The color isn't quite what I'd hoped for. I think a second coat will match up better with the original."

"You sure can't tell from the floor. It looks perfect." Des turned to Seth. "It seems my sister has a boatload of artistic talent she's kept to herself all these years."

Seth looked across the table, one eyebrow raised. "Maybe you could come up with something for the logo of the vineyard and labels for the wine bottles."

"That's a whole different area of design," Allie told him. "But since there's probably two years or more between now and the time you'll need a logo and some labels, I'll see what I can work up. You call the farm . . . willow something?"

"Willow Lane," he replied.

"Right. Because of all the willow trees that line that long drive-way of yours." Allie paused, a vision of those graceful trees in her head. "I could see a label with a tree with long fronds just skim-ming the ground. Yeah, maybe. I'll keep it in mind. Something to work on when I get home."

The door opened and closed, and Seth waved at the new-comer. Allie turned to see Ben grab a menu from the desk and head toward the table.

"Is this a private party or is it open to anyone?"

"It's open to anyone who comes through the door between now and the time I lock it." Allie rose and did exactly that, then turned the sign from OPEN to CLOSED. "But you won't need that menu.

I'm pretty sure the kitchen is mostly closed. There might still be something available, though. Were you looking for dinner?"

"I'm looking for anything that's hot," he replied. He walked back to the desk and left the menu, then took the remaining seat at the table. "On second thought, it doesn't even have to be hot."

"You look beat, buddy," Seth said.

Ben nodded. "Five-car accident out on the highway. One tractor trailer, a sedan, two SUVs, and a VW Beetle."

"Any serious injuries?" Des asked.

"Yeah. The driver of the sedan was DOA." Ben sat back in the chair, his eyes hollow, his face's summer tan somehow paler than it had been just days earlier. "Elderly guy from Harrisburg. The couple in one of the SUVs have serious injuries, the family in the other, bumps and bruises. The truck driver walked away without a scratch, as did—oddly enough—the driver of the Beetle, which was the car that caused the accident."

It must have been a nightmare for Ben to handle a traffic accident death and the resulting notification of the family, Allie thought. How many times had he had to do that since losing his wife and son?

"Let me go see what we still have." Allie stood. "Anything you don't like?"

"Not tonight," he said. "Tonight I'd eat anything. A cold sandwich is fine."

"I'll be back."

The remainder of the beef stew Chef George had made as one of the dinner specials and that he'd added to the next day's lunch menu had yet to be put away.

"Could I heat up some of that?" Allie asked.

"Didn't I tell you, if you eat too early, you're gonna be hungry again by nine?" George said.

"It's not for me. Chief Haldeman just came in and he—"

"I'll take care of him. Danielle, grab one of those salads out of the cooler. And the homemade ranch dressing. That's what he likes. And, Allie, take a few of those rolls I made this morning, they're still fresh. Here's a plate . . ." George barked out his orders in his gravelly voice, and Allie and Danielle, one of his kitchen staff, responded without question.

"George will have something ready for you in a few minutes," Allie told Ben when she brought out his salad and the plate with the rolls. She grabbed a place setting of flatware and brought them to the table.

"Thanks." Ben forced a weary smile. "I might have to take back all those things I said about you, Allie."

"Now, now, you don't want to say anything you might regret." She gave him a friendly pat on the back.

"I'm too tired for a comeback, but thanks for the salad." Ben looked at the salad like a man who hadn't eaten in days. "I should go wash up . . ."

Allie's gaze followed him as he walked to the men's room. Even his gait looked exhausted.

"That is one tired man," Seth said. "I bet he hasn't slept in two nights."

Allie made a face. "He's not the only cop in town."

"No, but when there's something serious going down, Ben is there, whether he's on duty or not. I know he was out on Campbelltown Road most of yesterday and all last night," Seth told her, "because of that truck they found smuggling drugs and explosives up from Georgia. He made the arrests, but he had to wait for the FBI and the ATF people to get here."

Ben came out of the men's room, the front of his shirt spotted with water after he'd apparently tried to wash his face.

"Think I could get something to drink?" he asked.

"What would you like?" Allie asked.

"Just water, please."

"Sure." Allie went back into the kitchen and grabbed a glass and a pitcher, which she filled with water. She tossed in a few ice cubes, then added some lemon slices from a bowl near the iced tea stand. She brought the pitcher back to the table and poured him a glass. He took a long drink.

"Thank you." He held up the clear glass pitcher. "The lemon's a nice touch. Thanks."

"You're welcome." Allie turned to her sister. "So what are you doing with all the dogs you've been taking in?"

She sat back and listened while Des outlined her plans for finding homes for the dogs she'd been caring for at Seth's farm.

"Of course, there will always be a few we can't find homes for, but—" Des shrugged.

"—we'll keep those," Seth said, finishing Des's sentence. The look that passed between them was sheer love, and for a moment, Allie felt a wave of sadness. Not that she coveted her sister's guy, but because it had been so long since anyone had looked at her like that.

"You could end up with a barnful of dogs, Seth," Ben said as he finished his salad.

"We'll manage." Seth draped an arm over the back of Des's chair, and the smile she gave him held her heart.

"Chief, sorry it took so long to get something out to you." George burst through the kitchen door.

"Hey, I'm the one who came in at closing time, so don't apologize," Ben told him.

George placed a bowl heaped high with beef stew in front of Ben and added a small plate of several more rolls.

"It smells amazing," Ben said.

"Just the way my mother made it for me," the chef told him. "Can I get you something else?"

"No, this is more than I'd expected. Thank you, George."

"Gotta keep Hidden Falls's finest well fed. You want anything else, you let Allie know and we'll take care of you. I'll be in back for a while yet."

George returned to the kitchen, and Des looked at Allie. "Where did Judy find that man?"

"I don't know, but I'm so glad he stayed even after she left. He treats this place and the customers like family," Allie said. "We could replace everyone else—the waitstaff, the kitchen crew—but if we lost George?" She threw her hands up. "Bye-bye, Goodbye."

"I'm glad Barney's taking care of him," Des said. "You know she gave everyone a raise when she bought Judy out, just to make sure they all stayed on until we could decide if we wanted everyone."

"Good move on her part," Allie said.

"I think we should be on our way." Seth glanced at the clock over the door. "Someone has some pups to walk before we turn in for the night."

"I thought all the dogs were in that kennel you have out back," Allie said.

"All the rescues are. But we still have Ripley and Belle. They're the official house dogs." Des stood and stretched. "I guess I'll see you tomorrow."

Seth put his hand into his back pocket. "Got our bill?" he asked Allie.

She waved him away. "Family and friends discount."

"Thanks." Seth slapped Ben lightly on the back as he passed behind Ben's chair.

Allie followed them to the door, then locked it behind them.

George stuck his head out of the kitchen. "How you doin' there, Chief?"

"I'm doing great, thanks. Just finished. It was great."

"What else can I get you?"

"Not a thing, Chef. I couldn't eat another bite, but thank you. You might have saved my life."

George nodded and disappeared back into the kitchen.

Ben sat back in the chair. "That was the best meal I've had since . . . well, since the last time I ate here."

"That was Saturday," Allie reminded him.

"Was it?" He frowned as if trying to remember. "Oh yeah. Your ex was here."

Allie stood and picked up Ben's plate.

"He still hanging around? The ex?"

"Nope. He left right after breakfast yesterday, taking the probable future Mrs. Monroe and her devil spawn with him."

"He's marrying the woman he was with?"

"That would be my guess. Maybe not right away, but yeah. I think he will."

"Does that bother you?"

"Oh, hell no." Allie laughed at the thought. "I do feel sorry for her, though. She's nice and seems to have her feet on the ground. Sure you don't want anything else?"

He shook his head. "But thanks."

She went into the kitchen, where George took the plate from her hands. "Danielle," he said to the last of the kitchen helpers, "go out and clear the table after the chief leaves." To Allie he said, "You go on home. I'll close up."

"Thanks, George." She turned in the doorway. "You know, you really are a treasure. We're so lucky to have you."

George nodded his thanks and pointed to the door for her to leave.

When Allie went back into the dining room, Ben was standing at the desk, wallet in hand.

"Put it away," she told him. "Like I told Seth, family and friends."

"Thanks, Al, but this place is going to go bankrupt if you keep comping everyone's meals."

"Family and friends," she repeated.

"Well, thanks. You have to hang around?"

"George said he'd close up." Allie walked behind the desk and reached for her bag, then took the day's receipts from the cash register and stuffed them into a large envelope.

"Come on, then. I'll take you home."

She turned off all but the one light Danielle would need to clean up the table and replace the tablecloth. She locked the door behind them and walked out into a chilly night damp with fog.

"I'm parked in the lot," Ben told her.

They walked through hazy pockets of fog that seemed to follow them across the parking lot behind the Hudson Diner.

"Odd that the town only has two eateries and they're so close to each other," Allie remarked.

"Odder still that people who are loyal to one wouldn't be caught dead stepping inside the other. I did see a few folks stop over to say goodbye to Judy the other night, but they all went back to the diner."

"Why's that?"

"The sister of the owner of the one place ran off with the husband of the sister who owned the other. People took sides."

"Barney's eaten at the diner," Allie told him. "Sometimes she's had breakfast there with the ladies she walks with early in the morning. Actually, I think one of the ladies she walks with works there."

"Yeah, that would be Kim. I see them when I pull the morning shift. But that's Barney. When she worked for the bank, she was careful never to take sides. Knowing Barney, even now that she owns the Goodbye, I bet she still walks with Kim and her other old buddies."

The police car was one of the few vehicles remaining in the lot, and it sat between two pickups, one white, the other black. Ben steered her to the passenger side.

"Are you going to make me sit in the back seat behind that screen?" Allie asked.

Ben paused. "I don't know. Have you been bad?"

"Who has time to be bad? I'm too tired to be bad."

"Then you're in luck. I won't have to write you up, and you get to sit up front with me." He opened the front passenger door and she slid in.

Ben walked around the car and got behind the wheel, stifling a yawn.

"Don't tell anyone I let you sit there. I think it's a violation."

"You're the chief. You get to make the rules." She leaned back against the seat, noticed it had a rip here, a tear there, as did the remnant of carpet under her feet. Ben's seat didn't look any better. "It's not a violation unless you say it is."

"Good point." Ben started the car and drove out onto Main Street, then turned right onto Hudson.

"No lights on," Allie noted as the car drove up the dark driveway. "I guess Barney's out, too."

"Cara's at Joe's," Ben told her.

"Surprise, surprise."

He parked in front of the carriage house and turned off the engine.

"Come on. I'll go in with you, just in case."

"Just in case what?" She got out of the car and walked toward the house, Ben a step behind her.

"Just in case there's someone there you don't expect or don't want to see." He took her elbow, then paused. "Front door or back?"

"Back, since we're here." She led the way down the path.

"Good thing you have the key."

"What key?" Allie frowned. "Barney never locks the back door."

"I hope you're kidding." Ben followed Allie up the back steps.

"Nope. She leaves it open for the last person in to lock. It usually isn't her." Allie paused, her hand on the doorknob. "Well, until lately, it wasn't. These days, she's been known to come in carrying her shoes like a teenager."

"Ah, yes. Tom Brookes."

"You know Tom?" Allie went inside and turned on the back porch lights as well as those in the kitchen.

"Sure. He went to school with my dad."

Allie shook her head. "Everyone in this town went to school with everyone else. It's almost incestuous."

Ben yawned.

"Well, as you can see, there's no one here. But thanks for putting the thought into my head that there might have been."

"Don't mention it." He yawned again. "Sorry."

"Look, why don't you let me make you some coffee before you fall over. I'd hate to be responsible for you running some poor fool off the road at midnight. Especially in that fine department-issued ride of yours."

"Fewer and fewer fools on the road at midnight these days. Wait till everyone's back from vacation and school starts up again.

Then you'll see the parade of fools. This time of year, last few weeks of summer, things are slow. Except for accidents out on the highway. They're always a problem this time of year."

"Why this time of year?"

"People coming back from or going to their vacation place around the lakes. Wallenpaupack. Arrowhead. Beltzville. Harmony. There are a bunch of them east of here."

"The Hudsons have a lake, Barney said."

"Compton Lake. Best lake in the Poconos." He paused. "You've seen it, right?"

She shook her head.

"What is wrong with you, woman? Compton Lake is . . . Well, it's one of the most beautiful places around. What have you been doing for fun this summer?"

Allie had to think long and hard. Finally, she said, "Not much. I've been busy working on the theater ceiling. I guess the summer's just about over and I haven't even had one yet."

"That's just wrong, Allie."

"You're probably right." She opened the cupboard. "Any coffee preference?"

"Nope. I'll drink just about anything that's caffeinated enough to keep me awake between here and my place. It's only a few blocks, but still. It'll be a challenge."

She selected a pod of one of her favorites and turned on the coffeemaker.

"Let's go into the sitting room. It's a lot more comfortable. I'll bring your coffee in when it's done."

"It's been a long time since I've been in this house," he told her as they walked down the hall to the front room. "I always thought it was the best house in town. Not just because it's so big and looks so grand, but because you always felt welcomed here. And Barney always had the best candy on Halloween."

"Did you used to come here, besides Halloween?" She switched on the overhead light in the hall, then went into the sitting room and turned on the lamp on the table next to the love seat.

"My grandmother and Barney are friends. They—"

"Yeah, yeah, I know. They went to school together."

Ben laughed and sat on one end of the love seat, his long legs out in front of him. He looked out of place, Allie thought, in this feminine room of Barney's.

Allie looked around for a place to sit. There were two chairs, one opposite the love seat, another next to the fireplace. The love seat itself was small and seemed too intimate somehow.

"Think that coffee's ready?" he asked.

"I'll get it. How do you take it?"

"Black is fine." He settled back into the cushions, his eyes closed.

"I'll be right back."

Her footsteps echoed down the long hall. In the kitchen, she poured Ben's coffee, and having been spooked by him earlier, she locked the back door and turned off the lights.

"Here you—" She paused in the doorway. Ben was draped across the love seat, his legs half on the floor, one of the toss pillows propped under his head, and he appeared to be dead to the world.

Allie set the mug on the table and picked up the crocheted throw from the back of the chair. She stood over the love seat, the throw in her hands, and watched the rise and fall of his chest. The tension she usually saw in his face was gone, as if everything he'd had to witness over the past forty-eight hours— over the past several years—had temporarily been forgotten. In sleep, his hair tumbled over his forehead, his mouth slightly parted, Ben looked like a younger, sweeter version of the man she'd come to know.

With one hand, she brushed back the hair from his face, covered him with the throw, and whispered, "Good night, Sleeping Beauty," as she turned off the lamp.

"Allie."

He spoke her name so softly she wasn't sure that he'd spoken at all.

"If I kissed you . . . would you kiss me back?"

Allie paused in the darkened room, the only bit of light coming from the hall. There was just a hint of mischief in her voice when she leaned over him and whispered, "Why don't you kiss me and find out?"

He reached up and pulled her down, one hand on the back of her neck, the other at her waist. She hadn't expected much more than a mild little peck. His lips on hers were gentle as a caress at first, almost teasing. But then both hands were on the sides of her face, pulling her in, and the kiss was anything but a tease. She was surprised at the flash of heat that rose between them, and at how quickly the kiss deepened. Mostly, she was surprised by how much she enjoyed it. When she finally pulled back, she gazed down, and for a moment tried to think of something flippant to say.

Ben's eyes had closed when he'd kissed her—and stayed closed. He'd fallen fast asleep, a smile on his face.

Allie laughed softly in spite of herself. Had anyone ever fallen asleep immediately after kissing her? She'd cut Ben some slack this time. After all, hadn't the poor guy been fighting sleep for the past hour? And at least he was smiling, so he must have enjoyed it.

Yes, but it had better not happen again.

Again?

Again implied there'd be another time, another kiss.

Oh, there would be, she nodded to herself as she climbed the steps to her room. And next time, there'd be no falling asleep on the job.

CHAPTER THIRTEEN

Ben was gone by the time Allie got downstairs in the morning. No surprise there, she thought as she made coffee. The mug she'd prepared for him the night before was on the counter where she'd left it, but it was empty. Had he really gulped down cold coffee before he left the house at whatever time he had?

She wondered how long he'd stayed. Surely not too long, given the cramped position he'd been in. A smile touched her lips when she thought about kissing him the night before—and it wasn't the first time since it happened that she'd thought about it. He'd surprised her, no denying that. For one thing, who asks a woman if he could kiss her? Well, that wasn't exactly what he'd said, but still. For another . . . who knew Ben Haldeman could kiss like that? If she'd known, Allie thought, she'd have kissed him sooner, and she wouldn't have waited for him to ask.

The chief had been full of surprises last night.

But this morning she had work to do, so time to put away all that and take care of business. She was determined to finish the theater ceiling before the end of the week. She'd see if Ginger could take over for her at the café from seven until closing. Allie needed to spend some time looking for tile to replace the original in the bathrooms. She was hoping to locate a dealer close enough to drive so she could see the selections in person. She made a mental note to remember to ask Cara if she could use her car.

She looked out the kitchen window, drinking her coffee, thinking about the falls and the lake, the two things she wanted to see before she left Hidden Falls. The house was so quiet, with Nikki at her friend Wendy's and Barney possibly at Tom's, though she could have come in late. She knew where Des and Cara were, and for a moment, she envied them both for having found their place. Allie knew she was still looking.

The sound of the front door opening brought her to the hallway.

"Good morning, Barney," she called to her aunt, who was doing a really good impression of an older woman trying to sneak into the house after a wanton night of sin.

"Oh, good morning. I was just . . . oh hell." Barney sighed deeply. "I suppose you're never too old for the walk of shame."

Allie laughed. "Barney, no one cares if you spent the night with Tom."

"Shhhh. I don't want Nikki to hear you."

"Nikki's not here. She spent the night with her friend Wendy." Allie turned back to the kitchen as Barney came down the hall. "Her last name is Dunham, by the way."

Barney frowned. "I don't know that name."

"She's from Kingston, so you probably wouldn't know. Her mother's name is Tess and her father is deceased, though I've yet to get that story. I spoke with the mother yesterday. She seems really nice. She took Nik and Wendy to the movies last night and the girls stayed at her house. Well, Wendy's grandmother's house."

"Where?"

"Where what?"

"Where's the grandmother's house?" Barney proceeded to make a cup of tea for herself.

Allie shrugged. "I don't know. Oh, wait. Next door to Mark's family."

It seemed to Allie that Barney'd gone still. "Which side of Mark's house?"

Allie shrugged. "I have no idea. Why? Does it make a difference?"

"Just wondering. I think I'll take my tea upstairs while I get ready for the day."

"What's on your agenda today?"

"I'm meeting with a few people who are going to back my run for town council. And I'll be at the Goodbye by ten to take over for Ann. She opened for Judy often, so I've asked her to open for us. I can't get there at six in the morning these days. I just can't seem to get up that early anymore. I can't even get up to go on my walks with the girls, and I haven't skipped walking since we started."

"Guess that wouldn't have anything to do with the handsome widower across the street," Allie said innocently.

Barney ignored her, which was probably for the best.

By the time Allie finished up at the theater and arrived at the Goodbye, it was almost noon. Barney was going over the specials with a group of older men who'd pushed several tables together, and the room was lively with chatter and laughter. It almost seemed as if there was a party going on.

"Oh, it's a party all right," Barney had agreed. "The guys at the long table along the wall are from the new golf course out past Seth's farm. They've decided to hold their monthly lunches here. The ladies at the front table are from the library board." She fussed with a button on her white shirt that had popped open. "I missed the meeting this morning, so they brought it to me this afternoon."

Barney smiled and handed the list of specials to Allie. "Now, look these over before you seat the folks just coming in. I'm going to sit with my library board friends and enjoy some of that delicious beet salad Chef George makes. Did you know we're getting our goat cheese from a farm right here in Hidden Falls?"

The rhythm of the café had become familiar, and Allie coasted through the rest of the day. When she approached Ginger to ask if she could take over the desk that evening, she learned that Barney had already arranged it. Earlier, Nikki sent a text to let her know that she and Wendy were on their way back to the house to spend the afternoon, so Allie was able to leave the café by seven and bring home a quiche to share with whomever might be home.

"Hello," Allie called out as she opened the front door. "Anyone here?"

Barney responded from the office, so Allie made a stop there first.

"I brought dinner," Allie said, holding up the bag she'd carried the quiche in.

"Go ahead and heat it up. I'll be in when I finish this." Barney didn't glance up from whatever she was working on.

"What're you doing?" Allie stepped closer to the desk.

"Oh, just some paperwork Pete sent me about the estate."

"What estate?" Allie set the bag on the desk.

"Your father's. Pete just had a few questions. Nothing important, but I did want to get it out of the way while I was thinking about it." Barney raised her head, her glasses sliding down to the end of her nose.

"I see you found them." Allie pointed to the gold-rimmed glasses.

"Right where I left them. Imagine that," Barney said dryly.

"How's Uncle Pete?"

Barney shrugged. "Same old Pete. But you can ask him soon, since he's planning a trip here once the work on the theater is finished. He wants to see the theater and all the wonderful changes you three have been able to make." She smiled. "And I guess I did mention to him that Tom was back, and I suppose he'd like to see him as well, since Tom was Gil's best friend back in the day."

"It'll be nice to see Uncle Pete again. Even nicer to show off what we've done. I know he wasn't expecting much from the lot of us. Of course, he'd only seen us together in his office when he brought us together to read Dad's will." Allie paused, remembering. "What a day that was. Poor Uncle Pete had to explain to us not only that Dad's will came with some really long strings attached, but who Cara was and why she was there."

"You've adjusted well to each other. Better than Pete expected, certainly."

"And you? How did you think this would all work out, Barney?"

Barney took off her glasses but held them in both hands. "I had every faith in the three of you. Yes, you were all the offspring of my unpredictable brother, but you were also my nieces. Hudson women. I knew you'd rise to the task and I knew you'd open your hearts."

"Hudson women," Allie repeated.

Barney nodded. "Not one of you has let me down since the day you showed up on my doorstep. I couldn't be more proud of you. All of you. And as crazy as it may have seemed to have set things up the way your father did, more than anything, he wanted you to be sisters, and you are. He wanted us to be a family, and we are."

"All true, Barney. I didn't have your faith, not in the beginning, but somehow it's all working out." Allie picked up the bag and took a few steps toward the door. She'd felt her throat begin to tighten. "I just want you to know I wouldn't have missed a minute, Barney. Next to Nikki, this has been the best thing that's ever happened to me."

She left the room when she felt tears begin to back up in her eyes.

Allie turned on the oven and opened the back door to let in some fresh air, surprised to see Nikki sitting alone on the bottom step.

"Hey, tootsie." Allie went out onto the landing. "What's doin'? Why so glum?"

Nikki shrugged.

"Did you have dinner?"

Nikki shook her head.

Allie frowned. Nikki's silence was so rare. She always had something to say.

"Is Wendy still here?"

"She went home." Nikki's voice was barely above a whisper.

"Sweetie, did something happen?" Allie joined her at the bottom of the stairs. "Did you and Wendy have a falling-out?"

"Oh, no." Nikki shook her head again. "She had to go home because there's something on TV that she and her mom watch together every week."

Nikki fell silent again.

"Scooch over to make room." Allie sat next to her daughter. "So what did you guys do this afternoon?"

"I took Wendy up to the attic to show her all the old fancy clothes and the paintings. I told her about the old books Barney said her grandmother had put up there, so we looked through some boxes for them."

Nikki raised her face, and Allie could see her eyes were rimmed with red. *Oh, poor baby. What now?*

"I'm guessing since you're so blue you didn't find the emerald necklace."

"No." Nikki broke into sobs. "Wendy did."

"Wendy did what?"

"Wendy found the emerald necklace." She sobbed louder. "It was inside a handbag we found in a box with a bunch of old letters."

"Wonderful! Barney will be thrilled. Where is it now?"

"Well, remember Barney said . . . Barney said . . ." Nikki could barely get the words out, and suddenly, Allie knew exactly where the necklace was.

"Barney said what, sweet pea?" Barney came down the steps, obviously concerned that Nikki was so distressed. "What's wrong, love?"

Allie held her breath.

"You said . . ." Nikki turned around to look Barney in the eye. "You said finders, keepers."

"What are we talking about?" Not having heard any of the conversation that had preceded *"Barney said,"* Barney was confused.

"You're going to have to help me out here," Barney said to Allie. "What is going on? Why is she so upset?"

"Nikki and Wendy were in the attic today. Nikki told her friend about the necklace, and that—"

"And that you said finders, keepers." Nikki wiped her face with the back of her hand and tried to clear her throat.

"And . . ." Barney lowered herself to the step, motioning for Nikki to continue.

"Well, Wendy found it." Nikki stared at the ground. "I'm sorry, Aunt Barney. I didn't know what to do. I didn't want her to take it, but you'd said . . . So I told her it was all right, she could have it to keep, 'cause that had been the deal."

"When Barney said that, she meant whoever in the family found it could keep it," Allie said softly. "I'm pretty sure she didn't mean a stranger."

"Wendy's not a stranger," Nikki protested. "But she's not family, either."

Barney and Allie looked at each other in horror.

"It had been the deal, you're right," Barney said gently. "And having told your friend that, you couldn't very well have demanded she hand it back over once she'd found it. I understand exactly how that played out, sweet pea. I do."

"But . . ." Allie said, and Barney nodded.

"But we are going to have to appeal to Wendy, and possibly her mother, to return it." Barney smoothed Nikki's hair. "I understand she is your friend and you don't want to do anything to damage your new friendship or embarrass your friend, but at the same time, the necklace needs to be returned to us. I will offer her a reward for its return, just as if it had been lost, but we need to get it back."

"Barney's right, sweetie," Allie said. "I'm sure once she understands how important that piece is to the family, she'll be fine giving it back. Wendy strikes me as a very smart girl. I'm sure she'll do the right thing."

"She will. At least, I hope she will. When should I call her?" Nikki asked. "What should I say?"

"Oh, Nik, we're not going to make you call your friend. We're going to go over to see her, you, your mom, and I. We'll explain and I'm sure there isn't going to be a problem. No hard feelings, I guarantee."

"When are we going to go?" Nikki asked.

"There's no time like the present." Barney tapped Allie on top of the head, then stood and went up the steps.

"I agree. Come on, Nik." Allie waited for Nikki.

"Okay." Nikki followed Barney, and Allie brought up the rear. "Aunt Barney, I'm so, so, so sorry."

"I know you are, Nikki. And it's fine. We'll get the necklace back and all will be well. Not to worry."

"Why not take a minute and wash your face, Nik? It's obvious you've been crying, sweetie."

"Okay, Mom. I should probably change my shirt, too. It's got cobwebs all over it." Nikki went up the back steps.

"Dear lord, how did that happen?" Barney leaned on the back of a chair.

Allie relayed Nikki's version of how the necklace had been discovered in an old black purse.

"It must have been one of Mother's. She had a zillion purses, all black. I thought I'd looked in every one of them. Apparently not."

"Well, at least we know where it is," Allie said as she turned off the oven.

For a moment, Barney looked uncertain. "What if she won't give it back? What if her mother stands on that 'finders, keepers' thing? We can't claim it was stolen, since Nikki gave it to her."

"I'd be surprised if she didn't just hand it over once we explain. Really, Barney, she's a good kid."

"You sound very sure of yourself after having met the child, what, once? Twice perhaps? And the mother . . . how many times?"

"Actually, I haven't met the mother. We've only spoken on the phone. But she seemed to be a very reasonable person."

Barney rolled her eyes. "Everyone's reasonable until there's a fortune in emeralds involved." She grabbed her car keys off the wall hook near the back door. "Well, I suppose I should go back Lucille out of the garage. Time I took her for a spin anyway."

Allie waited for Nikki, then the two of them went out to the driveway and got into the waiting car. Nikki climbed into the back seat, for once not asking Barney to put Lucille's top down.

"What street does your friend live on?" Barney asked as she exited the driveway.

"I don't know the name, but I know how to get there. Turn left here, then go to the stop sign and go right," Nikki told her.

From there, Nikki navigated, and when they reached Third Street, she said, "Aunt Barney, it's the fourth house on the right. The stone house with the big porch."

Barney slowed in front of the house. "This house? Nikki, are you sure?"

"I'm sure, Aunt Barney."

"Are you positive?" Barney parked in the middle of the street and turned around to face Nikki.

"Yes, Aunt Barney. It's her grandmother's house."

Barney pulled to the curb, muttering under her breath.

"What did you say?" Allie asked.

"I said, this is not going to go well." Barney put the car in park and turned off the engine. "Not going to go well at all."

"Why so negative all of a sudden?" Allie asked.

"Because that"—Barney pointed to the stone house—"is Justine Kennedy's house."

Allie bit back the string of expletives that were dancing on the tip of her tongue. She tried hard to keep all that to a minimum around Nikki. Instead, she said, "Oh crap."

"Exactly." Barney nodded. "Nikki, why didn't you tell us Wendy's grandmother was Justine Kennedy? I know you've heard us talk about her."

"I didn't know that was her name. Wendy always just called her Nana." Nikki looked annoyed. "Besides, I already told you, Wendy and her mom are staying at her house while her grandmother's on a cruise."

"So she's not here?" Allie asked. "Are you sure?"

"I'm sure." Nikki was clearly exasperated.

"Thank God," Barney said. "If I had to deal with that battle-ax tonight, it would not be pretty."

"Can we just do this and get it over?" Nikki tried to push the seat up with Allie still in it. "And please don't call Wendy's grandmother a battle-ax. Wendy loves her."

Allie opened the passenger door and got out, with Nikki close behind. Barney joined them on the sidewalk.

"I think it might be best if you let me do the talking," Barney said.

"Why don't we play it by ear?" Allie suggested.

"Why can't I just tell Wendy the truth?" Nikki started to the door, well ahead of her mother and great-aunt.

They were almost to the porch when the front door opened, and Wendy and the woman Allie assumed was her mother stepped outside. The woman was every inch of Allie's height, though a little rounder here and there. Her blond hair was cropped short but feathered around her pretty face, and her bold blue eyes scanned Allie and Barney in less than a blink.

"We were just on our way to your house," the woman said.

"You're Tess?" Allie asked, and when the woman nodded, Allie introduced herself and Barney.

"I just tried to call you," Wendy told Nikki, "but you didn't pick up."

Nikki felt her pockets. "We were in such a hurry to come here, I forgot my phone."

Tess drew a box from her bag and held it out. Barney reached for it.

"It's in there. The necklace," Tess explained. "Wendy had no idea what she was bringing home. She said Nikki told her it was real, but

Wendy thought she was just pretending. She said her aunt"—Tess turned to Barney—"said whoever found it could keep it."

"I didn't understand that she meant someone in our family," Nikki said apologetically. "Like one of my aunts or my mom or me."

"I was pretty sure that's what was intended," Tess said. "We were just on our way over to return it."

Allie realized Barney hadn't said a word since Tess and Wendy came out of the house. In fact, she realized, the only movement Barney'd made was to reach for the box, her body still while her eyes darted between Tess and Wendy.

"Really, she didn't know this was real. When she showed me, I almost had a heart attack." Tess placed her hand on her chest. "It was obvious to me this wasn't a piece of costume jewelry, but to Wendy . . ."

"Honest, Miz Monroe, I'm really sorry. I really didn't mean to take something so valuable." Wendy offered her apology.

"Of course you didn't know," Allie said gently. "I don't think even Nikki knows how valuable the piece is, not just from a monetary standpoint, but as a piece of family history. This was a total misunderstanding all the way around. Thank you so much for being so good about it."

"There's no way we could have kept such a thing," Tess said.

"Tess." Barney finally spoke. "We're very grateful to you for your understanding. Would you and Wendy join us for dinner tomorrow night at the café? We'd love to have you as our guests to show our appreciation. A thank-you."

"Oh, please, Miss Hudson, you don't have to . . ." Tess began.

"It's Barney, and it would be our pleasure. Please." Barney reached out her hand, and Tess took it.

"Well . . . all right," Tess said. "Thank you. We'd love to."

"Excellent. We'll meet you at the Goodbye at seven. Is that too late?" It appeared to Allie that Barney squeezed Tess's hand before dropping it.

"It's perfect. Tomorrow's my tutoring day," Tess was saying. "I don't get home until six, and it's always a scramble for dinner."

"Oh yay. Maybe we can ask Chef George to make crab cakes. They're so good. They don't taste like the ones in California." The crisis resolved, Nikki came back to life.

"Different kind of crab, I bet," Wendy said.

"Totally. I think we use Chesapeake Bay crabs," Nikki told her. "I saw that on the menu."

"We'll see you then." Barney turned to Allie. "Ready?"

Allie nodded and said good night to Tess after thanking her and Wendy again. Wendy made the universal *call me* gesture to Nikki as Allie ushered her daughter from the porch.

"Oh, Tess." Barney turned back before Tess closed the front door. "Give your mother my best when you speak with her."

"I'll be sure to do that. Thanks again." Tess and Wendy disappeared into the house.

Nikki chattered all the way back to Hudson Street.

"I knew Wendy'd be cool about it. At least, I hoped she would. I'm glad because I want her to still be my friend. I wish she lived in California and went to my school. I'd hang out with her all the time." Nikki continued until Barney stopped the car in front of the carriage house to let Nik and Allie out.

"Take a breath, Nikki," Barney said as Nikki got ready to jump out of the car. When Nikki inhaled deeply, Barney said, "That's better, dear."

Allie got out and closed the car door after Nikki, who raced ahead, presumably to find her phone and call Wendy. Allie waited for Barney, then helped her to close the garage door.

"That went very well," Allie said.

"It did."

"So we're having dinner with Tess and Wendy tomorrow night as a thank-you." Allie fell in step with Barney on the path that led to the back steps.

"Please ask Des and Cara to be there," was the extent of Barney's reply. She went past Allie to climb the steps. She opened the back door and went inside, not bothering to hold the door for her niece. She went straight to her sitting room, and without another word, closed the door behind her, leaving Allie in the hall, wondering what *that* was all about.

Allie shrugged, went into the kitchen, made herself a cup of coffee, and turned the oven back on to heat up the quiche. She and Nikki would need dinner sooner or later, and Barney was welcome to join them.

Barney should be in a good mood, Allie thought as she locked the back door. A valuable piece of jewelry—an important piece of family history, indeed—that had been missing for years had been found. At the very least, Barney could have let Allie peek into the box. Despite the evening's drama, it had been returned, so all was well.

So what's with Barney closing herself in her sitting room alone when she should be out here, draped in emeralds and having a glass of wine to celebrate that the search for the gift from a long-forgotten Spanish prince is over?

Chapter Fourteen

"**O**h my God, that's crazy!" Des exclaimed after hearing the necklace had been found, almost lost, then recovered after a quick trip across town. The sisters ran into each other in the front hall early the next morning, Des on the way in, Allie on the way out.

"Where is it now?" Des knelt to unsnap the leash from Buttons's collar after her early walk and the little dog danced around Allie's feet begging for attention.

"Barney has it. I'm assuming she's going to put it in the safe in the office or the safe-deposit box at the bank." Allie had been heading to the theater but she let her bag drop onto the bottom step of the staircase while she scratched behind the dog's ears. "Honestly, she was acting so weird when we came back last night. I heated up dinner for Nik and myself and went upstairs to bed, as it was the first night I got to turn in before midnight. Since we've been involved with the Goodbye, it's been all work and no play—and not a whole lot of sleep. I went out like a light. I guess Barney did, too, because I haven't seen or heard her yet this morning."

"And oh my God, to think that Wendy is the granddaughter of Justine, the dessert Nazi." Des went down the hall to the kitchen, where she hung the leash on its hook, then went back to the front hall, where Allie was looking out the door. "So is it gorgeous beyond words? The necklace?"

"I wouldn't know. Tess handed it to Barney in a box, which Barney didn't open while we were standing there, maybe to be polite? I'm not really sure why she didn't open it, frankly. Maybe she didn't want to look like she was checking to see if it was really in there? Anyway, I figured we'd open the box when we got home so we could ooh and ahh over it, maybe take turns trying it on. But nope. Barney went straight into the sitting room and closed the door."

Des's jaw dropped. "You mean you didn't even see it?"

"No. That was what was so weird. After all this time, she just takes it into the other room and closes the door."

"Bummer. What a letdown." Des appeared to think it over. "I bet she's going to show us all at once, you know, when the three of us and Nikki are together. Make a big deal out of it. Then we'll pass it around and we'll all try it on. Then she'll lock it up somewhere."

"Maybe. But it almost seemed like . . ."

"Like what?"

"Like she'd almost forgotten she had it. As if she wasn't even thinking about the necklace, like it didn't matter. In all the time we've been here, I've never seen Barney act that strangely."

"There's an explanation, I'm sure."

"I guess. So what are you doing back here so early? Seth kick you out of bed?"

Des laughed good-naturedly. "Hey, farmers get up before the sun. Like, at five in the morning. It's a lot of work. I thought since I was already awake I'd come home and see my girl." She leaned over to give Buttons a scratch under her chin, but the little dog had other ideas. She rolled over on her back in full *rub my tummy* mode, and Des accommodated her by sitting on the hall floor. "Seth let me drive his truck home. I want to get some bills paid for the theater while I'm here. Then I'm taking a nap." Des looked up. "I guess you're off to the theater."

Allie nodded. "But in case I don't see you later, Barney invited Tess Dunham and Wendy to have dinner with us tonight at the

Goodbye. She told me to let you and Cara know, so you might want to tell Seth if he's expecting to have dinner with you." Allie picked up her bag and hoisted it over her shoulder. "And tell Cara if you see her."

"If she's not here when I leave, I'll send her a text."

"See you at dinner." Allie opened the front door. "And in case it comes up, you better not see that necklace before I do."

"So if Barney waves the box under my nose, I should close my eyes?"

"Absolutely. Since I didn't get to see it, I think there should be an official unveiling for all of us at the same time."

The theater was quiet for most of the morning. Allie wondered if the guy with the radio had taken a sick day or was on vacation. Every sound seemed to echo through the lobby. She worked without pause for over an hour before her neck pleaded with her to take a break. She opened her second bottle of water and took a long drink before turning on her iPad. Grateful that Des had insisted on installing Wi-Fi right from the beginning, Allie continued her search for vendors for the ceramic tile she wanted for the theater bathrooms. One close by looked promising, so she scanned the gallery of photos until she found something that very well might work. She tucked the iPad into the front of her shorts and climbed down the scaffold.

Allie held up the tablet to the original tile in the ladies' room. Not bad, she thought. Not a match, but complementary. She'd continue to look, but if nothing better caught her eye, this one was it. She stepped back to assess the space. The fixtures looked great, but the room definitely needed furniture. A settee, a couple of pretty chairs. Things that would go with the era. Good antiques were pricey, but maybe there was something in Barney's attic. She always said neither her mother nor her grandmother ever parted with a thing.

She'd seen vintage mirrors in the attic, and they'd go nicely over the row of sinks along the one wall. A few of those paintings and prints she'd seen would pretty up the wall behind the settee.

In her mind's eye Allie could see where she'd place every piece—assuming she could find the pieces she had in mind. But that left one wall totally blank. Maybe a mural, she thought. Some scene from Hidden Falls.

She went into the men's room and found there, too, the fixtures had been installed but the space was a blank page. Leather chairs here, she thought, maybe in brown or dark green rather than the more expected black. A mural in here as well, a hunt scene or something rustic from the area surrounding the town. She'd have to make an effort to spend time looking for something suitable. Where had she gone besides Barney's house on Hudson Street, the theater, and the café?

Well, there was the park on the Fourth of July. The gun club Barney'd dragged them to to hear bluegrass music one night. Add to that the liquor store and the paint shop in that little shopping center outside of town, and that would be just about it. Oh, and of course there was that night they'd all gone to Althea College for a fund-raiser where Barney had made a point of showing off the larger-than-life statue of their ancestor for whom the college had been named.

It was amusing to imagine how a man might react to being greeted by a life-size rendering of Althea Hudson gracing the wall when they walked into the restroom.

She climbed the scaffold to the top and went back to work, pushing out thoughts of emeralds yet to be unveiled and what natural wonders she might find once she started exploring the area. Her focus had to be on the work overhead. The more time she spent in the theater, the more important it became that what she did here, the part of her she would leave here, could stand the test of time.

When the alarm on her phone signaled it was time to stop for the day, Allie packed her bag and set off for the house. Routine though her schedule may be, she hadn't felt bored. On the contrary, she felt more alive these days than she had for a long time. Certainly more alive than she'd been before she'd gotten the call from Fritz's lawyer that her presence was required in his office for the reading of her father's will. Those days when she'd kept herself in a bit of an alcoholic haze seemed so far behind her now.

Allie arrived at the Goodbye dressed for dinner in ankle-length pants and a pretty top, knowing they were fully staffed, which meant she could have dinner with her family and Tess and Wendy without jumping up every five minutes to seat someone. Barney left as soon as Allie got there, but returned at six fifteen to supervise pushing tables together and chilling wine she'd driven to the state-owned liquor store to pick up.

"It would have been nice to have flowers," Allie heard Barney mutter.

"Flowers for the table?" Allie frowned. "We could probably do that. A single flower on each table, maybe with an interesting leaf stuck in the vase for texture. Some small vintagey-looking vases would be perfect. You know, there's a new thrift shop up at the end of Main Street. I wonder if they have anything like that."

"I meant for our table. Tonight," Barney told her. "Though something small on every table would be a nice touch."

"You have those beautiful zinnias in your garden, Barney. The gold ones make me think of the color of sunshine. And those cherry red ones are so bright and lively. We just need vases."

"We have a cupboard full of vases—maybe two cupboards full—at home. All different sizes. Help yourself."

"Flowers would be pretty on the desk, too. Why didn't we think of this sooner?"

"Because we haven't had a family dinner here, all of us together," Barney told her.

"Well, it's not exactly a family dinner, Barney," Allie pointed out. "Since Tess and Wendy aren't family. But I think it will be fun. I know Des and Cara are looking forward to meeting Wendy, since Nikki spends so much time with her."

"Yes. Of course. Wendy," Barney replied somewhat absently.

"Nice that you dressed for dinner, Allie. I hope your sisters are appropriately dressed as well."

Allie glanced at Barney, who was dressed in a linen sheath and wore her big real pearl earrings and necklace. A bit formal for a dinner at the Goodbye, she couldn't help but think.

"Barney, are you all right?" Allie asked.

"Certainly," Barney snapped. "Why wouldn't I be?"

"You're just acting . . ." A glare from Barney cautioned Allie to tread carefully. "Different."

"Well, I'm not." And with that Barney disappeared into the kitchen.

Allie rolled her eyes and went back to the desk to await the arrival of her sisters. She didn't have to wait long. Des and Cara came in together, both dressed in navy ankle pants and white shirts, which while different in style, emphasized their similarities. *They do look like sisters, with their curly hair,* Allie thought. *I don't look like either of them. Our eyes, and maybe our cheekbones, but that's about it.*

"We're early," Cara announced after looking around the dining area. "No one else is here."

"Thank you, Captain Obvious." Des poked her.

"Actually, Barney's here. She went into the kitchen a minute or so ago. But I have to warn you, she's acting a little strangely."

"How strange?" Des asked as her eyes were drawn to the door. "Oh, hi, Ben. What are the flowers for?"

"Hey, Des. The flowers are for Allie." Ben turned to the desk and handed over a beautiful bouquet of summer blooms.

"Oh." Allie stared at the flowers in her arms. "They're gorgeous. But what . . . why . . . ?"

"I just wanted to thank you for the other night," he said.

Behind him, Des's and Cara's eyes flew wide open. Allie tried to ignore the fact that they'd turned to each other and were mouthing the words *Thank you for the other night?*

"You didn't have to . . ." Allie tried her best not to laugh at her sisters' shock, but she couldn't not smile.

"Well, I just wanted you to know I'm sorry for leaving in the middle of the night like that," Ben was saying. She suspected he was playing it up just a little for Des and Cara's benefit. "And we'll have to do it again sometime soon."

"I'd like that. Thank you. But really, you didn't have to." She held the flowers to her chest, adding a bit of drama because she knew it must be driving her sisters crazy. "But I'm glad you did. They're beautiful."

"My pleasure. See you later." He turned to Des and Cara, who immediately tried to pretend they hadn't been eavesdropping and weren't dying to know what *that* was all about.

"What's going on, ladies?" he asked.

"Ah, we're just here for dinner," Cara said.

"Right. Dinner. With Barney. And some other people. Long story," Des told him.

"Tell Barney hi for me. Allie, I'll talk to you later."

"Aren't you staying for dinner?" Allie walked him to the door, the flowers still in her arms.

"I'm on duty till eleven. I just wanted to drop those off. But I'll probably be in tomorrow at some point."

"I'll see you then." She stood aside while he opened the door, then watched him walk to his cruiser, which was double-parked out in front of the café, before turning toward the kitchen. "I hope we have something to put these in."

"Whoa, girl. Not so fast." Des grabbed her by the arm.

"Don't even try to slip away without an explanation." Cara blocked Allie's way.

"Nothing to explain," Allie said innocently. "Ben was tired after pulling a double shift the night before last. He fell asleep on the love seat in the sitting room, so I tossed a throw over him—ha-ha, see what I did there? Tossed a throw?—and let him sleep."

"That doesn't explain why he was in the sitting room on the love seat in the first place." Cara stood her ground.

"Oh, that. Well, he stopped into the Goodbye, as you know, Des, because you and Seth were here. He stayed for a while after you left while I closed up, then he offered me a ride so I wouldn't have to walk home alone in the dark, carrying the receipts." Allie smiled. "That's all. So if you'll excuse me . . ."

"Nope. Not yet. So he drove you home. Why was he in the house?"

"Look, the poor guy was exhausted. I made him a cup of coffee. Honestly, he was bleary-eyed. I didn't think he'd make it to his apartment. So I invited him in. I left him in the sitting room while I made coffee. When I came back, he was out cold. Covered him. Turned out the light. Left him there. Went to bed." Allie shrugged. "That's pretty much it."

Des narrowed her eyes. "Why do I feel there's more to the story?"

Cara nodded. "What did you leave out?"

"Nothing. Now, I have to find a vase for these beautiful flowers. Excuse me." Allie, still smiling, walked around her sisters, took three steps, then stopped and turned around. "Oh. He kissed me. Or, I kissed him. I guess we kind of kissed each other. Then he passed out." She turned on her heel and continued to the kitchen.

"I knew it," Allie heard Des say. "I knew she was holding out on us."

Allie was still laughing when she emerged from the kitchen carrying the huge bouquet in a soup pot filled with water.

"I couldn't find anything else. I'll have to bring something from home," she told her sisters when she returned to the front desk, where they both stood, their arms crossed over their chests. "You look like those guys in the paintings of the Inquisition."

"We're not done," Des said.

"Oh, come on, it's not such a big deal," Allie said.

"You've spent months sniping at each other. The last I heard you were just beginning to be cordial. How did you guys go from verbal smackdowns to kissy face?"

"The short answer is I don't know." Allie'd been wondering the same thing. "The long answer is I don't know."

The door opened and several diners came in, and Allie moved to greet them, menus in hand.

"Hi, come on in. Welcome to the Goodbye Café. I'm Allie," she said as she led them to a table.

Ginger arrived promptly at seven to relieve Allie, who stepped away from the desk just as Tess and Wendy walked in.

"Right on time. We're glad you could make it." Allie took Tess's arm lightly. "Come meet my sisters."

As promised, Barney had reserved the table in front of the windows overlooking Main Street. She'd plucked a few stems from Allie's bouquet and placed them in a vase she found in the office closet.

"Cara, Des, meet Tess Dunham and her daughter, Wendy." Allie made the introductions. "Tess, Wendy, my sisters, Des Hudson and Cara McCann."

"Good to meet you, Tess," Des said. "But Wendy and I are old friends."

Wendy nodded and turned to her mother. "Des has the dogs I told you about. The puppies. She rescued them after they were abandoned and she's going to try to find homes for them."

"I know that look, and the answer is no. Not now, anyway," Tess said good-naturedly. "Between school and sports once we get back to Kingston, there'll be no time for puppy training this year, but you get points for subtlety."

Wendy grinned as if having anticipated her mother's reaction. She brightened when she saw Nikki come in from the kitchen.

"Hi, Miz Dunham. Aunt Barney will be out in a minute. She's looking for wineglasses," Nikki said.

Des and Cara exchanged a look, then glanced at Allie, who returned their *Wineglasses? We don't sell wine* look and shrugged almost imperceptibly.

"Ah, wonderful, you're all here. Hello, Tess. Hello, Wendy." Barney buzzed out of the kitchen, wineglasses in hand. She passed out the glasses to Tess and her nieces, saying, "I don't know where anyone is sitting, so just take these with you and find a place. I did pick up some nice red and a lovely white, not know-ing what our guest prefers."

"Oh, you needn't have gone to any trouble," Tess said.

"No trouble at all, dear. Shall we take seats and look at the menu?" Barney sat at the head of the table. "Allie, any specials we should know about tonight?"

You should know, since you were the one who told Chef George what to put on the menu, Allie could have said. Instead, she got up and grabbed several of the specials menus from the desk and passed them around the table.

"Everything here is really good, if I do say so," Allie told Tess. "We source our vegetables and fruits mostly from local farms. The chicken is from a place outside of Clarks Summit, and the beef is all from downstate in Chester County. The previous owner had started to turn the café into a place that served as much locally produced food as she could, and we've been follow-ing her lead."

"Listen to you, a regular walking, talking promo ad. But I would like to add that starting next year, some of that local sourc-ing will be from Willow Lane Farm," Des said. "And a few years after that, you might be able to buy the wine from Seth's vine-yard."

"Is this the same farm Wendy's been talking about?" Tess looked up from her menu to address Des. "She's been having such a good time there."

Des explained how after Seth returned from his deployment in Afghanistan, he bought the farm from an old man he'd helped, how he'd been renovating the farmhouse, and his plans for the future.

"And that's where you're starting your rescue shelter," Tess said. "I think that's wonderful. If we're ever in a position to have a dog—and that's a big if—we'd definitely look for a shelter pup."

"When," Wendy said adamantly. "*When*, not *if*."

"We'll see." Tess rolled her eyes. It was obviously a conversation they'd had many times, and one they would have many more. But if Allie were to guess, she'd put her money on Wendy to win out eventually.

"Tess, did you grow up here in Hidden Falls?" Barney asked.

"No, I grew up in Kingston," Tess replied. "My parents both grew up here, but my dad took a job with an insurance company in Kingston and moved there. Then he and my mom got married and she joined him. I've lived in Kingston all my life, but we visited my grandparents in Hidden Falls frequently and I always spent some time here in the summer."

"Where did you go to school, dear?" Barney asked.

They were interrupted by the waitress, who took their orders, after which Barney opened the bottles of wine. "We don't have a license to sell alcohol," Barney explained, "but you can bring your own."

"Really?" Allie frowned. This was the first she'd heard that.

"Yes." Barney began to fill the adults' glasses, then proposed a toast. "To Tess and Wendy, our new friends. We're looking forward to getting to know you both."

Allie glanced across the table at Des and Cara, both of whom seemed as slightly puzzled as Allie was. Barney was always gracious, always polite, but tonight she seemed solicitous, even overly attentive and almost too interested. It seemed as if Barney hung on every word Tess uttered. What was with that?

"You were saying, Tess," Barney said after she'd made her toast and everyone had taken a sip and touched the rims of their glasses with each other's. "You were about to tell us where you went to school," Barney reminded her.

"Oh. Yes, well, all through public schools in Kingston, then I went to West Chester University. I'd wanted to go to Althea, actually, but my mother thought West Chester would be a better fit." Tess sipped her wine. "I don't know if West Chester was better, but it was a great school. And the wine is delicious, Barney."

"What did you major in?" Barney asked.

"Art. Well, art education, with a minor in drama," Tess said.

"I majored in art as well," Allie said. "Small world."

"Did you teach?" Tess asked.

"No. Actually, I never did anything with it," Allie admitted.

"That's not true, Mom," Nikki jumped into the conversation. "You painted that awesome mural on my bedroom wall when I was little, remember?"

"I do. But that was when you were two. I've done precious little since." Allie thought of the mural with the faces of all the animals from the books Nikki'd loved best. If she sold the house, what would happen to that bit of Nikki's history? She tucked the thought away for another time.

"And you're painting the ceiling in the theater," Nikki said as if Allie'd forgotten.

"You're painting a ceiling?" Tess turned to Allie. "I'd like to hear about that."

Allie paused while their meals were served, then explained about the task their father had left them to bring the Sugarhouse back to life, and how they'd gotten close to finishing when the roof leak had damaged the ceiling.

"My mom is repainting it. You can't even tell when you're standing in the lobby that it's not all original." Nikki dug into her turkey club, which had become one of her favorites at the cafe.

"I'd love to see it sometime," Tess said. "When is it open?"

"Oh, it's not open to the public at all yet, but we're happy to give you a tour." Vegetarian Cara had been looking to add more vegetarian entrées to the menu. Tonight she'd ordered a vegetable stir-fry. She speared a strip of red pepper with her fork and held it for a moment. "We still have a little more to do before we can open it to the public, and we're not even sure what form that will take."

"Will you be showing films?" Tess nibbled on a piece of chicken that had been cooked in orange sauce. "This is delicious, by the way."

"We won't be showing movies on a regular basis," Des told Tess, "but we could do occasional movie nights."

"Live theater?" Tess took another bite. "Seriously delicious."

Nikki didn't wait for anyone else to respond. "Summer stage. For sure. Next year. I can hardly wait."

"Don't get your hopes up, Nikki," Allie cautioned. "No decisions have been made. We really haven't even had that conversation yet."

"But we will be having one soon," Des assured Nikki, "and we'll certainly take that into consideration, I promise."

"Yes!" Nikki pumped her fist.

"Perhaps if we do go in that direction, you'll want to get involved in some way." Barney lifted a piece of fish onto her fork and turned to Tess. "You did say you minored in drama."

"If we're here, I'd love to. I started a drama club for our middle schoolers, and that's gone very well. I did it all in college. Costumes, sets, and I did my fair share onstage."

"Dad always said you should have been a star," Wendy, who'd followed Nikki's lead and ordered a club sandwich, interjected.

"Your father was a tad prejudiced." Tess smiled. "I wasn't that good, but I like to think what I lacked in talent, I made up for in effort and enthusiasm."

"So you teach art—at what level?" Des cut a piece of her steak.

"Elementary through middle school," Tess replied.

"I thought you were teaching at the high school this summer." Allie picked an olive from her plate and turned to Nik. "Did you tell me that?" Allie'd ordered the salade Niçoise. Not a vegetarian herself, she sometimes felt odd eating meat when Cara was munching vegetables.

Nikki nodded.

"I did get my certification to teach high school, so I could teach here during the summer. But during the regular school year, I teach lower grades and I love it."

"You'll want to see the Sugarhouse," Barney told her. "Perhaps one day this week."

"Just say the word."

"Let's plan on Friday around noon, shall we? We can all have lunch together afterward." She paused and looked thoughtful for a moment, as if suddenly remembering something. "Oh, actually, I'll be here in the morning. Allie, would you give Tess a tour of the theater, since you'll be there anyway?"

"I'm afraid lunch is out, since I teach until two, but thank you for the offer." Tess smiled at Allie. "But I'd love to see the theater on Saturday morning, if that's convenient for you."

"I'd be happy to show you around," Allie said.

All through dinner, Barney's focus was on Tess, asking her questions, encouraging her to elaborate on her remarks. Tess related how she'd lost her husband to a rapidly growing and deadly cancer six years earlier, and how she and Wendy have made a life for themselves in Kingston.

"Have you ever thought about moving to Hidden Falls?" Barney asked.

"I have," Tess admitted. "My mother wants us to live with her in my grandparents' house. It belongs to my mom now, and she said it will pass to me someday, so I should get used to living in Hidden Falls. But my in-laws—Tim's parents and his sisters—all live in Oregon, and they'd like me to move out there so they could see more of Wendy."

"Oregon is so far." Barney put down her fork.

"It is. And don't think my mother hasn't pointed that out to me about two hundred times. I'd love for Wendy to know her West Coast family, but I'm an East Coast girl."

"I visit my other grandmother and my granddad when I have vacations. I went there right after school got out, and I spent my spring break there, too," Wendy added. "I have two cousins there, but they're way older. There's really no one for me to hang out with and nothing for me to do there. I'd rather be here."

"True. One of Tim's sisters is eight years older than he, and she married right out of high school. The other graduated from college two years ago. His parents live on the outskirts of a small town and there's no one for Wendy. She can't even go to the library without someone giving her a ride into town, since it's too far to walk, so visits there aren't the most fun for her."

"I love my dad's mom and dad, but I like to keep my visits short," Wendy said.

"Still, I understand how they feel. Tim was their only son, and Wendy looks very much like him as a child," Tess said.

"It's always interesting to see what's passed on from one generation to the next." Barney glanced around the table at her nieces. "Physical resemblances, certainly, but there are other things as well. Mannerisms, for example."

"True enough," Des said. "But we're still trying to figure out where Nikki got her gift of gab."

Nikki wrinkled her nose, then laughed.

"Oh, that was Fritz," Barney said. "He could charm the birds out of the trees, and when he got worked up over something, there was no slowing him down."

Cara began to laugh. "I remember one time we were walking toward the beach after the bird migrations had begun. Birds were everywhere, and the horseshoe crabs were coming onto the beach to lay their eggs. The birds—mostly red knots, but also ruddy turnstones—were swooping in to eat the eggs and there were horseshoe crabs crawling all over each other. Dad was beside himself. He'd never seen anything like it, and he was almost tripping over himself with excitement. It was all I could do to keep him at a safe distance, close enough to watch, but not too close to deter the birds." She looked to the end of the table where Nikki sat. "Much like someone else we know and love who talks extra fast when she's excited."

"What are red knots?" Wendy pushed her glasses up on her nose.

"They're shorebirds," Cara said. "They start out at the tip of South America and have to fly ten thousand miles to the Arctic to lay their eggs. The Delaware Bay is just about the halfway point, so they have to stop and refuel so they can continue their journey north. As you can imagine, they are exhausted by the time they get as far as Delaware and New Jersey. They get the energy they need to complete their journey from the horseshoe crab eggs."

"That would be fun to see," Wendy said, and Nikki nodded her agreement.

"Maybe some spring we'll drive down and watch. We'd have to stay in the car or watch from a blind so we don't scare the birds, but it's still fun," Cara told them. "There aren't as many birds as there used to be, though. They're endangered. Mostly because there aren't as many horseshoe crabs."

"Why not?" Nikki's interest had been sparked. "What happened to them?"

"That sounds like something you girls might want to look up, find out for yourselves," the teacher in Tess emerged to interject.

Both girls immediately pulled out their phones and began to type, but Tess reminded Wendy about the no-phones-at-the-table rule. The phones disappeared. "Tomorrow," Nikki told Wendy. "Let's research this tomorrow."

They'd finished their entrées and their places were cleared so dessert could be served.

"Yay! Brownie sundaes," Nikki enthused. "I love brownie sundaes."

"Me, too." Wendy dug into hers with gusto. After a few bites, she said, "These taste just like the brownies my nana makes, don't they, Mom?"

"I was just thinking the same thing," Tess agreed.

Allie glanced around the table, wondering who would speak up. Finally, she did.

"Actually, Wendy, these *are* brownies your grandmother made. She used to bake for the woman who owned the café before Barney bought it. Judy—the previous owner—left some in the freezer for us to use."

"She can make more when she returns home." Wendy turned her attention back to her dessert.

"No, she won't. She doesn't want to bake for us," Nikki announced. Barney, Cara, Des, and Allie practically froze, their eyes all shifting to Nikki.

"Why not?" Wendy's spoon was paused halfway to her mouth.

Nikki shrugged. "She just doesn't."

"Mom, why doesn't Nana . . ." Wendy began.

Tess apparently sensed a shift in the atmosphere at the table. "We can talk about it when Nana gets back from her vacation. I'm sure there's an explanation."

Wendy turned to Barney. "Oh, I know. I bet she said she wasn't going to bake for you guys because she was going on vacation and she wasn't going to be here. I bet she will when she gets back."

"We'll see, dear." Barney plastered on a smile that anyone who knew her could tell was fake.

The wine, coffee, and desserts having been consumed, the women spent the next several moments making mostly casual getting-to-know-you talk. When Tess announced they needed to be leaving, everyone else at the table pushed back their chairs and stood when she did.

"Barney, I can't thank you enough." Tess gave Barney a quick hug. "This has been so much fun, and such a nice change for Wendy and me from our usual thrown-together dinner of reheated takeout from the night before."

Barney smiled and returned the hug. "We're so glad you could join us tonight. Now, talk to Allie and figure out a time for you to visit the theater. It's a Hidden Falls landmark, you know."

"I do. I've driven past hundreds of times and wondered what it was like inside. I'm excited to finally get to see for myself." Tess turned to Allie. "What time works best for you?"

"I'm usually there from around six thirty or seven in the morning till eleven or so. Anytime within that frame is fine."

"Let's make it nine. I teach a class at ten fifteen, so that gives me time to take the tour and get to the high school for my class." Tess held out her hand. "Thank you so much for letting Nikki spend the night the other night, and for allowing Wendy to spend so much time at your house. I haven't seen my daughter

234 • MARIAH STEWART

this happy in a long time. It's as if she's found a kindred spirit in Nikki."

"I'm delighted that Nik's made another friend here. She's mostly been hanging around with Mark and Hayley, who seem great, and Mark and Nikki share a special relationship, as you've probably heard. But it's nice to meet other kids, too."

"I agree." Tess whispered, "And I have heard that Mark and Nikki are a bit sweet on each other."

Allie sighed and lowered her voice. "Her first boyfriend that I know about."

"She couldn't have found a nicer guy. I'll see you on Friday morning at nine."

"The door will be unlocked, so just come in and find the lobby. You can't miss it," Allie said. "There's a scaffold that goes to the ceiling. I'll be at the top of it, so just give a shout when you come in."

"I'll do that. Thanks." Tess turned her attention to Cara and Des to say goodbye, then she and Wendy left, Wendy waving as she went through the door.

"Well, that was lovely, wasn't it?" Barney sat again, her fingers tapping on the sides of her wineglass.

"It was, yes." Allie leaned over the back of the chair in which she'd been sitting. "But I don't think I'm the only one who's wondering what was at the root of this dinner."

"Whatever do you mean?" Barney checked the bottle of red to see if there was anything left. When it turned up empty, she tried the white, and got a little more than a trickle for her trouble. She watched it drip into her glass, then drank it.

"You don't usually invite strangers to a family dinner, Barney. We've met lots of people since we've been here," Des said. "I don't remember inviting any of them to dinner."

"Her daughter is a good friend of Nikki's." Barney glanced from one to the next of her nieces, clearly annoyed. "Her daughter, if I might remind you, found a necklace worth a fortune in our attic and willingly returned it. She was on her way to our house to bring it back when we arrived at their place. I felt we should reward such honesty. There are many who would have refused to return such a valuable piece. Such a windfall would surely come in handy for a single mother with a teenage child, don't you think?"

"Well, when you put it that way . . ." Cara nodded.

"There's no other way to put it. Now, if you'll flag down Ginger for another cup of coffee for me, I'm going into the office to do a little work." Barney rose somewhat imperiously; that streak of diva they all knew was there but seldom saw was alive and well.

Allie arranged for Barney's coffee, then offered to finish the night for Ginger, who waved her off. "Go on home with your daughter and your sisters. You could use the rest, and I could use the hours."

"In that case, I'll see you tomorrow." Allie scooped up the flowers Ben had brought her, and with her sisters and her daughter, headed out into the night to make the walk to Hudson Street.

Nikki lagged behind a little, talking on her phone, and Cara stepped between Allie and Des, looping her arms with theirs.

"So do you think that's all there was to it? That Barney appreciates that Tess handed over the necklace willingly?" she asked.

"I don't know what other reason there could be," Des replied.

"Unless it's simply wanting to be a pain in Justine Kennedy's ass," Allie said. "I still think that's a big part of it, like Barney's way of getting the last word. I think she's tweaking the woman's nose behind her back, and she knows there will be some sort of explosion when Justine gets back from her trip."

"Which will be when?" Cara asked.

Allie shrugged. "I don't know for sure, but I think it's soon. And I bet we'll know when it happens. I have a feeling something big is in the works." She grinned mischievously. "I just hope I'm still here to see it when it blows. I think it's going to be epic."

CHAPTER FIFTEEN

Allie, Des, and Cara were all standing in the kitchen, arms folded over their chests, when Barney came in through the back door. Allie'd heard Lucille's tires crunching acorns in the driveway and called her sisters to come downstairs quickly.

"We need to present a united front," she'd told them, and they'd both agreed.

"What's going on, girls?" Barney looked them over suspiciously, then hung Lucille's keys on the hook.

"We're waiting," Des said.

"Waiting for what?" Barney frowned.

"We're waiting for you to show us the necklace." Allie rolled her eyes. "You've been holding out on us. We want to see it. Touch it."

"Take turns trying it on," Cara added.

"Oh, for heaven's sake, you three." Barney laughed, then waved for them to follow her into the office. She dropped her purse onto the desk before going straight to the wall safe. She swung aside the photograph of the first Reynolds Hudson and exposed the safe. She entered the combination on the lock, and the door swung open. The box was as she left it, wrapped in cloth.

"Barney, didn't you open that to see if it was really in there?" Des asked.

"No. Why should I?"

"What if Tess hadn't really put it in the box? What if she'd put in some cheap costumey thing and left town with the real one?" Cara sat on one end of the desk.

"Don't be ridiculous. How far do you think she'd have gotten? It isn't as if we don't know who she is and where to find her." Barney carried the box to the desk and opened it. "There. You see? That's the necklace."

"Oh, man, did you ever see stones so green?" Des peered into the box as Barney lifted the necklace.

"No. Never." Allie shook her head. "And they're so big. They don't look this big in the portrait in the front hall."

"Perhaps the artist scaled them down to conserve space." Barney's eyes twinkled as she held the necklace up to the light. "Actually, I'd forgotten how big the stones are. And yes, how green."

"Look at all the beautiful gold filigree around the stones." Allie reached out a hand to touch it and Barney handed her the necklace, saying, "Go ahead. Try it on. You know you're dying to."

"God, yes." Allie raised the necklace and fastened it in the back. "It's heavy. I need a mirror."

She went into the front hallway and looked at her reflection in the mirror. "Ahhhh, it's magnificent. Guys, look."

Des and Cara were right behind her.

"Oh wow."

"My turn." Des held her hands out.

"In a minute." Allie turned this way and that, admiring the way the stones caught and played with the light from the chandelier overhead.

"Come on, Allie." An eager Des poked Allie in the back, and reluctantly, Allie removed it.

"It's exquisite," Des declared as she put it on. "I've never seen anything like it."

She, too, preened in the mirror until Cara said, "Time's up. Pass it on."

Des took one last look, then took off the necklace and handed it over.

"Oh. Just . . . oh." Cara sighed. "It's just glorious."

"Who gets to keep it?" While the sisters had been oohing and aahing over the necklace, Nikki had come down the steps to see what the commotion was about. "Wendy found it, but she had to give it back." She looked from her mother to her aunts. "So who keeps it?"

"Well . . ." Barney thought it over. "I suppose we all do."

"We should each wear it on our wedding day," Cara proposed.

"Which means I won't get to wear it at all," Allie said, "but you two have fun. Wear it in good health."

"It might look a little out of place on the farm, since that's where I'd want to get married, but that's fine with me." Des grinned. "Nothing like a little bling amid the grapevines."

"Come here, Nikki." Barney stood behind Cara and unhooked the clasp, then held up the necklace. "Your turn."

Grinning broadly, Nikki stood motionless while Barney placed the necklace on her. She looked in the mirror, her eyes wide as she admired the sight.

"Oh, it's so pretty! Look how it sparkles! Do I look sophisticated?" She turned, watching her reflection. "Do you think it would be a bit much to wear to, like, you know, a prom or something?"

"A bit much for a prom, yeah," Allie said. "And you're a million years away from getting married, so you'll have to wear it only in the house here."

"It's the sort of thing people would go to great lengths to steal," Barney told her.

"Miz Dunham could have, but she didn't," Nikki reminded them.

"True. And we're grateful," Barney said. "But everyone isn't as honest as Tess and Wendy. And aren't we lucky that they are?"

"Barney, you need to try it on, too. We haven't seen it on you yet," Cara pointed out.

"Yes, of course, it's my turn." Barney waited for Nikki to take off the necklace and hand it to her. "I have worn it before, though.

I had this on when I had my engagement photos taken. Gil's mother was livid. She thought it was ostentatious and way over the top. But my mother had insisted. She didn't care whose nose got out of joint. Frankly, neither did I." Barney put on the necklace and turned around to show her nieces.

"It looks gorgeous." Cara sighed.

"Fabulous. The neckline of that dress is just right," Allie said.

"Barney, you look like a princess." Des stood behind Barney and adjusted the necklace so the stones lay flat against her skin.

"Well, remember this did once belong to Spanish royalty. I imagine any number of princesses wore it at one time or another."

The ringing of the doorbell startled them all, they'd been so engrossed in the necklace.

"Oh, it's Joe." Cara put her hand over her heart, then opened the door to let him in. "You scared the bejesus out of us."

"Why are you all huddled around in the hall?" he asked. "Not that it's any of my business."

"We were all taking turns trying on the—" Cara began.

"Oh, the infamous necklace. Wow, that's something else. Those are some stones you've got there, Barney." Joe stood with his hands on his hips, admiring the emeralds.

"They are lovely, aren't they? And now that we've all tried it on, the necklace is going back into the safe, where it belongs. Unless you'd like to try it on, too?"

"Thanks, Barney, but I don't think it goes with this flannel shirt I'm wearing," Joe said. "Maybe some other time."

"Anytime, dear." Barney patted Joe on the arm as she passed him on her way to the office.

"Well, that was fun." Allie started toward the steps, but Joe called her back.

"I just wanted to touch base with you about the theater. The painters we called in to do the walls are going to start next week," he said. "Assuming you're finished with the ceiling, so the scaffold can come down. Right now, it's in their way. Not to rush you. I can put them off another week if we have to."

Allie thought about what she had yet to do to finish her work. "I can finish the ceiling in about another week, so you can call the roofers to come for their scaffold after that. I'm sure they'll be delighted to get it back. I doubt they expected us to have it for so long."

"They understand, but yeah, they'll be happy to have it. It was good of them to loan it to us." Joe turned to Cara. "You ready to go?"

"I just have to run upstairs and get my things together. I'll only be a minute." She disappeared up the stairs in a flash.

"I'll have the guys meet me at the theater next Monday to sand the stage floor and that entire backstage area," Joe said. "We can stain the floor on Tuesday, and by Wednesday it should be dry."

"What if it's not?" Allie asked. "Isn't that cutting it close?"

"It is, and if it's not dry, the painters will start on Wednesday or Thursday." He leaned back against the newel post.

"So how are things going at your place? Cara says you're doing some renovation there as well." Allie sat on one of the steps.

"It's slow going. It's tough to work all day on someone else's place, then go home and work on your own. But we're getting there. We painted the dining room—Cara's looking for a nicer chandelier for in there—and we did over the living room, so we've made some progress. The kitchen needs the most work, but Cara's got a great plan for in there. We're taking that step by step."

Cara bounded down the steps.

"Allie and I were just hashing out plans for the rest of the stuff we need to do at the theater," Joe told her.

"Oh good." Cara turned to Allie. "We should think about making plans for our big reveal to the community."

"We can talk about that anytime. Right now, I'm headed off to bed. See you guys later." Allie started up the steps, then turned back. "Oh, Joe. Do you know anyone who sets tile?"

"Sure. What do you need?"

"We're going to have to replace tile in the two restrooms. So much of it was destroyed when the new plumbing was installed."

"Just let me know when you need someone. If I can't line up a contractor for you, I'll do it myself," Joe assured her.

"Great. Oh, and could you ask the painters to include the restroom walls when they work up their price?"

"Consider it done. Anything else?" Joe asked.

"Nope. That about covers it for today. Thanks." Allie continued up the steps to her room. She heard the front door close as she shut the door to her own room.

She'd promised herself all day that tonight she'd treat herself to a nightcap and maybe a little reading, but she barely had the strength to change her clothes before she crashed.

Allie awoke in the middle of the night from a dream so distressing it tossed her out of a deep sleep. Her heart pounding, she lay alone in the dark, reminding herself it was just a dream. But it had seemed so real—Nikki being chased around an endless track by Barney, Courtney, and Tess Dunham, Justine Kennedy chasing them all. Des sat on the sidelines in a blue plastic chair filming it, her hair up on top of her head in a tall do à la Marge Simpson, telling Allie, "I told you something wasn't right," over and over and over again.

She wiped the sweat from her face, the fear of something threatening her daughter still alive in her chest. From previous nightmares, she knew to take deep breaths until her breathing was normal, then to get a glass of water and drink it slowly.

"Forget water."

Tossing back her blanket, she went into the bathroom and came back to bed with the half-full bottle of vodka in her hand. She started to open it, then stopped, leaned back against the headboard and exhaled deeply. Therapy had taught her to examine her fears and sort them out, to not allow fear to make her choices for her. She didn't want to fall back on the dependency she'd developed last year when Nikki first moved to Clint's and soon after she'd lost her job. If she was going to move back to L.A. and have Nikki living with her full time, she was going to have to change the way she handled things.

She twisted the cap back onto the bottle. Next time, maybe . . . but not tonight.

Logic told her the dream reflected her fear of Nikki returning to California and facing God only knew what from Courtney. Allie knew in her gut the girl was up to no good, and Nikki, while she obviously didn't look upon her onetime BFF as anything but a former friend—at the least, someone not to be trusted—may not be fully aware of how sneaky Courtney could be. Allie knew, too, that Nikki was too nice a kid to keep as much distance from Courtney as she should. Why Barney and Tess were in the chase—Allie shrugged. Probably because they were all together earlier, but why Justine would be chasing Barney and Tess was a no-brainer. Justine was sure to be annoyed—*understatement!*—when she returned from her vacation and discovered Tess's new friends were all Hudsons. It was sure to hit the fan then.

Allie returned the unopened bottle to the bathroom closet, then got back into bed. She closed her eyes, then sat straight up. She'd left the flowers Ben had brought her on the kitchen counter.

She turned on the hall light and crept down the stairs, trying not to awaken the others as she made her way to the kitchen. The flowers were right where she left them, thankfully no worse for having been out of water for several hours. She went into the pantry to search for a vase, and as Barney had promised, found shelves full of containers of all shapes and sizes. She found one perfect for the bouquet—a large pale green pottery vase with an Art Deco design—and several smaller ones for the tables in the café. Those she left on the counter as she filled the large vase with water and arranged the flowers. She paused, debating whether to leave them downstairs where they could all enjoy them, or take them to her room. Her room tonight, the kitchen table in the morning, she decided, and made her way back upstairs.

She smiled as she set the vase on the table next to her bed, recalling the stunned expressions on Des's and Cara's faces when Ben came into the café bearing flowers and thanking Allie "for the other night." She knew he'd said it intentionally, loud enough for them to hear, just to be a devil. She turned off the light and slipped under the covers. It really had been sweet of him to bring her flowers, though.

Wait. Did I just call Ben Haldeman sweet? I think that nightmare rattled my brain.

But it had been a sweet gesture, no denying that. And sooner or later she was going to have to give some serious thought to why Ben caused her heart to beat just a little faster, and why, these days, he never failed to bring a smile to her face.

Allie was halfway up the scaffold the following morning when she remembered something else that needed to be done. When she reached the top, she texted Nikki and asked her to call when she got up. Ten minutes later, just as Allie started painting one of the two remaining geometric shapes, her phone rang.

"What's up, Mom?" a sleepy Nikki asked.

"After you wake up and you've had breakfast, could you come down to the theater for about a half hour? I'd like you to go through the pile of old movie posters we found and pull out about a dozen for us to frame and hang in the theater."

"I'm on it." Nikki came to life. "I'll be there in five minutes."

"No, you will not. You'll eat breakfast at a normal pace first. The posters have been around for many years, sweetie. They're not going anywhere. Take your time, get dressed, walk on down here. I expect it should take closer to a half hour."

"Okay. See you in a while."

Allie smiled as she ended the call. She loved Nikki's enthusiasm for everything. Had she ever felt that much joy at having a task to perform? Allie couldn't recall. But she was grateful that her child found life so exciting that even the smallest things inspired her.

Nikki was there in less than twenty minutes.

"Where are the posters, Mom?" Nikki called from the lobby floor.

"That was fast." Allie turned around and looked down. "In the cabinet in the projection room. I'd like to frame posters from the big movies—you know, *Gone with the Wind*, *The Wizard of Oz*, *The Philadelphia Story*, films like that. Want to see what else you can find? It shouldn't take you too long."

"I'm on my way, Mom." Nikki disappeared in a blur of blond hair.

An hour later, Nikki was back. "Mom, can you take a break and come see?"

"Good timing. My neck is killing me." Allie set her paintbrush aside and swung down to the floor, one level at a time. "Let's take a look."

She followed her daughter through the balcony to the projection room, where Nikki'd made several stacks of posters.

"Here are the ones you asked for," Nikki said, "the oldies but goodies, right? The ones you named, and some others—like, here's one with Grandma Hudson on it. Then over here"—she pointed to the second pile—"are ones I thought would be fun for October, for Halloween?"

Allie went through the stack. Nikki had pulled out posters from a bunch of classic horror and sci-fi movies from the 1950s: *The Blob*; *The Creature from the Black Lagoon*; *The Tingler*; *The Curse of Frankenstein*; *The House on Haunted Hill*; *The Horror of Dracula*.

"Oh, Nikki, these are perfect. Just perfect. As soon as I finish up with the ceiling, we'll go to the art shop near Althea College and have them framed."

"I haven't seen any of these films, but I know who Dracula and Frankenstein are. And the others . . . the titles and the posters give them away."

"You did a great job. Oh, Lord. *The Invasion of the Body Snatchers*. We'll have finished the renovations by next month and can include these in the décor for the grand reopening." She paused. "We still have to figure out what that's going to entail."

"Will you tell Dad to let me come back for that?" Nikki's fear of being left out was evident.

"Of course. We couldn't have such a big-deal event without you," Allie assured her.

"What if he says no?"

"Why would you think he would do that?" Allie leaned on the table.

Nikki shrugged.

"Did he say something to you about not coming back here?"

"No." Nikki's face creased with anxiety. "I don't want to go back," she blurted. "Why do I have to go back there? Why can't I stay here?"

"Sweetie, your father lives—"

"Dad's going to marry Courtney's mother and I'm going to have to live with *her*. She's supposed to be my *sister*," Nikki wailed. "Mom, do you know what it's like to have to live with a sister you don't like?"

"Actually, yes, I do." Allie pulled the projectionist's stool over to the table and sat, resting her forearms in front of her. "For a long time, Aunt Des and I didn't get along very well. And Aunt Cara—I didn't even know about her, and when I found out, I didn't want to get to know her. Yet here we are, after being forced to all live together, and now we're the very closest of friends. Sisters for real."

"Mom, Aunt Des and Aunt Cara are nice people. Courtney's not nice. She's gotten mean. She didn't used to be, but she is now." Tears were in Nikki's eyes.

"Oh, sweetie, I'm sorry." Allie held out her arms and gathered Nikki to her.

"She's saying all this mean stuff to me, and I just know when I get back to California she's going to be really mean at school. And if you say anything to Dad or her mom, she just acts sorry, but then she does it behind their backs and it's even worse."

"Who does she think she is?" Allie wondered aloud, her mama bear instincts coming to life. "Why does she think she can give you a hard time? And why isn't she your friend anymore?"

"She's best friends with Savannah now."

"Why can't you have more than one best friend?"

Nikki shrugged.

"I guess you're just going to have to make other friends at school, honey, because in two weeks you'll be back there and—"

"No, Mom. I have to go back *next* week," Nikki corrected her.

Confused—she'd been so sure—Allie pulled her phone from her pocket and checked the calendar. Nikki was right. "Oh, for crying out loud." She blew out a long breath. "Sorry, sweetie. I lost track of time. I kept thinking it was two weeks."

"A week ago, it *was* two weeks." Nikki tried to crack a joke, then burst into tears.

Allie held her weeping child while holding back her own tears. She knew that her girl was feeling as if everything in her life was beyond her control. Where she lived. Where she went to school. Whom she lived with. Who her friends were. Allie had never experienced what Nik was going through, and she wasn't sure how to react. She hadn't had friends turn on her—well, not as a child, anyway. If anything, *she'd* been the mean girl.

Karma, Allie told herself. What goes around comes around. The sins of the father—in her case, the mother—being visited on the child, and all that.

"Look, I'll tell you what. I'm going to talk to your dad about you living with me during the week and spending the weekends with him when I get back to California."

"Why can't I live with just you all the time? Why do I have to go to his house ever?"

"Nik, you know the answer to that. Your father loves you."

"I love Dad, but I don't want to live with him as long as *she's* around. And, Mom, *she's* around all the time." Nikki hiccuped. "Courtney and her mom stay at our house sometimes on the weekend, and she *stays in my room.*"

"Well, that's going to stop. I'll call your dad and we'll work something out."

"I wish you were coming home with me."

"I know, sweetie. I wish I could, too." Allie smoothed back Nikki's hair from her face where it had caught in her tears.

"Why can't you?"

"Because if I leave before the theater is ready to open, I will not get my inheritance, and I need that to buy a house in your dad's neighborhood so we can live closer to your school and I can have you live with me during the week again like you used to." Allie paused. "Actually, if any one of us sisters leaves before the job is done, no one gets their share of our dad's estate. So even if I were willing to give up my part, Aunt Des and Aunt Cara would lose out, too."

"That's a stupid will. Why did your father do that?"

"Because he wanted your aunts and me to get to know each other and learn to live together and maybe even learn to love each other."

"You live together okay." Nikki leaned back and looked into her mother's face. "Do you love them? Aunt Cara and Aunt Des?"

"And Aunt Barney, too." Allie nodded, a lump beginning to grow in her throat. "Yes, I do. But it didn't happen right away."

Her tears all spent, Nikki rested her head against her mother's forehead. "Well, maybe it was worth it, then."

Nikki's situation had Allie in knots, and she'd already put in one call to Clint that morning. She'd gotten his voicemail and had to leave a message, which only served to keep her nerves on edge.

She was at the hostess desk arranging a few flower stems in a tall thin vase she'd found in Barney's pantry when Clint called back. Allie gestured for Ginger to keep an eye on the desk while she went outside to take the call.

"What's up, Allie? You sound upset," he said in his usual blasé manner.

"We need to talk about Nikki."

"Don't even think about trying to change her flight. It's booked and paid for."

"This has nothing to do with her flight arrangements." Allie was momentarily sorry she hadn't waited to call him, to think through exactly how she wanted to present the facts, but she'd been impulsive, and now she had to deal with it. "Look, Nikki's unhappy about coming back, and she—"

"She's coming back, Allie. Just because you let her run wild and go out with a boy two years older than her—"

"Whoa, buddy. No one's running wild, and Mark—I'm assuming that's who you're referring to—is a great kid. An honor student. He's . . ." Allie exhaled and forced herself to slow down. "He and his sister have been good friends to Nikki. Trust her on this if you don't trust me. Actually, either of them has been a better friend to her than Courtney has."

"Don't start that again." His voice rose. "Why bring it up when it's behind them?"

"Behind who? It's not behind Nikki, because Courtney is still being a little bitch. She may be denying it to you and Marlo, but she's still at it, and Nik's afraid she's going to make life hell for her once she gets back to school."

Clint sighed. "I'll talk to Marlo again."

"And Courtney is not to stay in Nikki's room. As a matter of fact, Courtney is not allowed *in* Nik's room. Period."

"What's wrong with her staying there if Nikki's not there?"

"Because she goes through Nikki's things, that's why," Allie snapped. Okay, Nikki hadn't said that, but Allie knew that a girl like Courtney would never pass up the chance to look through someone else's private things. Allie herself had never hesitated back in the day.

"All right. Courtney doesn't stay over if Nikki's not here."

"Courtney doesn't stay over unless Nikki *invites* her. Not you, not Marlo. *Nikki* has to want her there, or she isn't there at all. Got it?"

"Got it. Anything else?" He sounded royally pissed off—at her or at Courtney, Allie wasn't sure—but he hadn't argued with her. Yet.

"Well, now that you ask, there is something you should know. Once we've finished what we have to do here, I'll be looking for a house in your area. Probably in your neighborhood."

There was silence on the phone. Allie knew Clint was trying to weigh what that might mean to him.

Finally, he said, "Well, that will be convenient for you to go to Nikki's games and other things at school." He paused. "Which reminds me, she should have agreed to come back on Sunday, so she could go to field hockey practice."

"She doesn't want to play field hockey. I thought we already discussed this."

"She didn't sound definite."

"She's definite. She doesn't want to play."

"All right. If that's her choice."

"That's her choice." Allie took a deep breath. "One other thing. When I come back, Nikki wants to live with me during the week again."

"Uh, no. That's not going to happen."

"Uh, yeah, it is. That's per the court order, Clint, an order that's still in effect."

"I'll go to court and tell the judge about how you abandoned your daughter and moved to Pennsylvania."

"And I'll tell the judge how you moved thirty miles away and enrolled Nikki in a school just a few blocks from you but an impossible commute for me, so I had to agree to let her stay with you during the week, while I got her on the weekends."

Clint went silent.

"You've had her all year, Clint, and I appreciate that you've given her a good home. But she's convinced you and Marlo are going to get married and she's going to have to live with Courtney." When he said nothing, she asked, "Clint? Can you convince her otherwise?"

"It's a possibility," he admitted. "A strong possibility."

"Then congratulations if that happens. Marlo is a very lovely woman, a lovely person. You are a very lucky man." *What she sees in you, I will never know. Then again, I saw something in you once, so there's that. You don't deserve her any more than you deserved me, but that's for another day.* "But it doesn't change the fact that her daughter is a vicious little brat and I won't stand by and see her hurt Nikki."

"That's mine to deal with, I suppose. And I will. Look, I'm on my way out to a meeting. We'll discuss the custody arrangement when you get back. Give Nik my love." And with that, Clint hung up.

"I'm trying really hard not to hate you," she muttered as she went back into the café. "I'm trying really, really hard . . ."

She remained rattled for the rest of the afternoon and into the evening. It wasn't until Ben came in a little after eight that she had any reason to smile.

"Way to get my sisters riled up last night," she said when he walked up to the desk.

"I know. Fun, wasn't it?" He smiled that smile that was getting to her, and she laughed.

"Actually, it was kinda fun, seeing their mouths drop open and their eyes get really big." Allie grinned. "But you didn't have to bring me flowers."

"I wanted to." Ben leaned across the desk, just a little closer to her. "Get used to it. I'll probably do it again sometime."

"Why?"

"Because the times, they are a-changin', Allie Monroe. And the next time I kiss you, you're going to kiss me back."

"Ben, I did kiss you back," she said flatly. "You fell asleep."

"I did?" He frowned. "Well, that won't happen again."

She leaned forward so her face was inches from his.

"Count on it, Sheriff."

CHAPTER SIXTEEN

Allie and Nikki sat next to each other on the sitting room floor, shopping for school clothes online, when Allie's phone rang. She didn't recognize the number, but she took the call tentatively.

"What are the chances you could take off tomorrow afternoon?" a man's voice asked.

"Who is this?" she asked, though she knew.

After a pause, he said, "It's Sheriff Haldeman."

Allie laughed. "I thought it was you. What's up?"

"Well, I got to thinking about how you're going to be leaving soon, and you haven't even been out to the lake yet. I thought maybe you should go."

"With you."

"Of course with me." When she didn't respond right away, he said, "It'll be fun. You'll like it. Prettiest lake in the Poconos. And don't worry, I won't push you in. We've turned over a new leaf."

"Whatcha got in mind?"

"Little spin around the lake. Little stroll in the woods. All that flora and fauna." When she didn't immediately respond, he added, "Here's your chance to see what you've been missing all those years you spent in L.A."

His heavy emphasis on L.A. made her laugh.

"Come on, city girl. Expand your horizons. Honor your Hudson heritage."

"Enough." She laughed. "Actually, you had me at 'It'll be fun.' But I'll have to see if Ginger or Barney will cover for me, and I will have to be back in time for the dinner hour."

"Fair enough. Let me know when you've worked it out."

"Will do, and thanks for—" Allie sighed. He'd already hung up.

"Who was that?" Nikki asked.

"Ben. Chief Haldeman."

"What did he want? And why do you call him Sheriff most of the time?" Nikki asked.

"He said he thinks I need to see the lake—I guess he means Hudson Lake—before I leave Hidden Falls, and he suggested he take me out there tomorrow afternoon. And I call him Sheriff because it annoys him."

"You mean Compton Lake—it's not Hudson Lake—and he's right. You should go there. That's where Mark and Seth took me to fish for Dad's dinner, remember?"

"I do remember."

"And why do you like to annoy him?"

"I don't anymore. But I used to." Before Nikki could ask—because of course Nikki would—Allie said, "Because he seemed to go out of his way to annoy me."

"Why?"

"I don't remember."

Allie did, of course, remember how she'd gotten onto his list in the first place. He'd been tipped off by the bartender in the Bullfrog—the local watering hole—that a woman was tossing back shots and she was leaving the bar with car keys in her hand. That woman had been Allie, and when she got into her car and drove away, Ben followed her in his cruiser all the way to Barney's house. When she pulled into the driveway, he parked and got out of his car, asked for her license and registration, and told her in no uncertain terms that *"no one drives drunk in my town."* Allie'd been offended because she wasn't drunk, but from that moment on, they'd placed targets on each other's backs. Targets that were just beginning to slip away.

Did Allie want to spend a day out on the lake with Ben? She thought it over while Nikki chatted away about what she was putting in her cart at the J. Crew website.

"Mom, I love this short chambray dress." Nikki pointed to her iPad screen.

"See if they have your size."

"They do."

Allie reached in front of Nikki to click on "add to bag." "What else?"

I wonder what exactly he has planned. Nikki said they fish out there. I don't fish. Don't know how to fish. Don't really want to learn.

"This short dress with the ruffles! I could wear that for a dance at school."

"Go for it." *Good. She's thinking about having a social life when she gets back, Courtney be damned. That's good, right?*

"This denim skirt?"

"Too short, kiddo. Way too short." *And what would we do for a couple of hours out there? He had that city girl thing right. Hiking in the woods does not sound like my idea of a good time.*

"How 'bout this one?"

"Better." *Still, what if I didn't get another chance to spend some time alone with him? Would I regret it?*

Allie pointed to a cute black dress. "Check that out, Nik."

Yes. I would. I'd be kicking myself. Besides, he still owes me a kiss. One he'll remember.

Nik finished her shopping with some T-shirts, three sweaters, a couple of pairs of shoes and sneakers from another website, a backpack, and a great leather bag from a third.

"You're all set," Allie told her. "And here I was feeling bad about not going back with you to take you shopping."

"I wish you were coming back with me, Mom." Nikki looked solemn. "And it has nothing to do with shopping."

"I know, sweetie." Allie put her arm around her daughter. "But you do understand why I can't."

"I do. I just wish your dad hadn't put that goofy stuff in his will."

"Well, that was Fritz, and we all have to live with it. It seems our dad was goofier than any of us ever suspected. But it won't be much longer, I promise. Joe's getting a lot of the remaining things done at the theater over the next couple of weeks, and you know Joe's as good as his word."

"Is he going to marry Aunt Cara?"

"Probably."

"Cool. I like him. And Seth is going to marry Aunt Des?"

"I'd put money on that." There was no question in Allie's mind that Des was headed to the altar wearing a long white dress and draped in emeralds.

"Excellent. He's the best."

"He's certainly the best for your aunt Des."

"Maybe someday you'll meet someone, too."

"Unlikely, but who knows. I'm not looking, kiddo."

"Aren't you afraid of being lonely?"

"Nope. I've got you."

"I'll be in college in, like, three years, Mom."

"Then I guess we'll just have to make sure you go to a college close enough to home so you can still live with me," Allie deadpanned. "Wouldn't that be great?"

"Mom! Not funny!" Nikki made a face and got up to leave. She stopped in the doorway, looked back, and blew her mother a kiss. "Thanks for shopping with me, Mom."

Allie nodded and listened to her daughter's footsteps as they danced up the stairs, then turned off her iPad and sighed. Time to get ready for her shift at the café.

Nikki's words were still ringing in her ears as she walked toward the center of town. *Aren't you afraid of being lonely?*

When she was in California, she'd lived by herself after her divorce and had precious little to do after she'd lost her job. But she'd been a loner for much of her life, so she would have said no, no fear of being lonely. She'd been lonely and survived. But after having lived with her two sisters and her aunt for the past six months, she wasn't so sure. She'd have sworn the last thing she'd ever do would be to live with Des again, yet here she was. She'd never had any desire to visit the East Coast—outside of New York City, of course—but she'd come to feel at home in Hidden Falls. And way, way down at the bottom of her bucket list would have been *work in a restaurant*.

She smiled as she pulled open the door to the Goodbye, greeted the other waitresses, and waved to Barney. She said hello to a few of their regular customers, the smile still on her face. Who'd have thought that the things she'd have deplored less than a year ago would become so important to her in so short a period?

"Life is funny sometimes," she overheard a woman at a nearby table tell her companion.

Lady, you have no idea . . .

Ginger was more than happy to work for Allie the next afternoon—and Barney was mighty interested in the fact that Allie had agreed to spend the day with Ben.

"Not the day," Allie corrected her. "Not the entire day. Just the afternoon. I'll be back in time for the dinner shift."

"Take your time, dear. I'll fill in if you run late."

When she realized Barney was wearing her smug little smile, Allie felt inclined to add, "Don't read too much into this. It's just a few hours, sightseeing."

"Of course. Now, while you're out there, would you check the cabin, make sure it hasn't been broken into? I know the police include the lake on their evening rounds, but we also know kids go out there to party and such."

"Sure. Oh, and FYI, Nikki tells me that Wendy's grandmother will be back this weekend."

"Good to know. I'll be prepared." A shadow crossed Barney's face. "I suppose that means Wendy and Tess will be leaving soon."

"I got the impression from Nik they'd only stay another few days after Justine gets back."

Barney nodded. "I think I'll go on back to the house, now that you're here. I'll see you later at home." She gathered her purse, and without saying goodbye to any of the staff, she walked out the door.

"Is she okay?" Penny asked Allie.

"I think she's just tired." But even as Allie spoke, she knew there was more to it. She just didn't know what.

"Barney asked that we check on the cabin. Could we do that?" Allie climbed into the cab of Ben's pickup truck and snapped on the seat belt.

"Sure. It's been a while since I was there, but I remember how to find it." Ben slammed the passenger door after she was seated and strapped in.

"This is pretty snazzy for a pickup truck," she said when Ben got behind the wheel. She pointed to the instrument panel. "Nice wood-grain look."

"Are you being sarcastic?" His hand paused over the gearshift.

"No. I like the look."

He backed out of Barney's driveway silently.

He turned onto Hudson Street and headed north. "What kind of car do you drive, back in California?"

"Well, I was driving a Mercedes," she said.

"Figures."

"Until it was repossessed." She slanted her eyes across the cab to see how he reacted. A year ago, she'd have endured torture before she'd have admitted such a thing to anyone, especially to a guy she was . . . what was she doing with Ben Haldeman anyway? She still hadn't decided.

He stopped at the stop sign and turned to her as if trying to decide if she was kidding. "Seriously?"

"Totally."

"You say that so casually."

Allie shrugged. "It's the truth. I lost my job and I couldn't keep up with the payments. It was just another one of life's little disappointments. But that was last year."

"And this year?"

"This year I'm here, and my life is very different."

"Better or worse?"

"Oh, better." She laughed. "Oh, so much better."

"Well, to toss my two cents in, even though you haven't asked—you seem like a different person than the one I met back in March."

"I am a different person."

"And when you go back to California, will you take the different person you are now back with you? Which Allie will you be?"

"Are you implying that I put on and take off personalities as it suits me? It doesn't work that way."

"So how does it work?"

"Are you trying to be annoying? Are you making a special effort to get under my skin? I thought we'd called a truce on snark." She stared at him so hard she was certain she'd bored a hole from one side of his head to the other, but he kept his eyes on the road.

"No snark intended. Why would I ask you to spend the afternoon with me if I was going to start out by annoying you?"

"It seems that's what you do best. It's like you just can't help yourself sometimes." She folded her arms over her chest and looked out the window. "I knew this was a bad idea."

Ben reached across the seat to take her hand, and she smacked it away—and then he laughed.

"Allie, I'm not trying to annoy you. I'm glad to hear you're happy enough in Hidden Falls to relax and just be yourself." He pulled over to the side of the road and put the truck in park. "I didn't like the Allie I first met—yeah, I know you're shocked. She was brittle and self-centered, and she didn't care how she made other people feel. And she drank too much. Let's call her West Coast Allie. Now you've been here for what, six months? Seven?"

"Yes," she said, but she still didn't look at him.

"How many of your friends back in California did you tell when your car was repossessed?"

"None."

"And yet you just told me straight out with no hesitation whatsoever. Why did you do that?"

"Because I knew you wouldn't judge me. You wouldn't think less of me."

"But you didn't tell your friends because they would have judged you? They would have thought less of you?"

She nodded. She'd never put it into words before, but yeah. They would have had a field day talking behind her back.

"That's pretty sad, don't you think?" His fingers touched a strand of her hair, and he slipped it back behind her ear. "So when I asked you which Allie'd you be once you went back to L.A., I was asking if you were going to take the Allie who is honest enough to meet things head-on—the Allie who isn't above working in a restaurant and gives all appearances of liking it."

"I told you before, I do like it." She swiveled in her seat to face him. "And there's nothing wrong with working in a restaurant."

"When you lost your job, did you apply for a hostess position out there?"

She shook her head.

"Would you now?"

"I won't have to now. When I go back, I'll have an inheritance from my dad."

"Suppose you didn't. What if there was nothing left in your father's estate? What if everything he had, he'd had you three put into the Sugarhouse?"

She stared at him for a long time. The possibility had never occurred to her. "Do you know something I don't know?"

Ben laughed. "No, I'm just trying to make a point."

"You've made it. You want to know if I'm going to revert to being Allie the L.A. snob when I go home. And the answer is no. I've learned to look at things—and people—differently now. I even gained eight pounds and I'm okay with it."

"I'm always afraid to comment on a woman's appearance, especially her weight. But for the record, I think you look terrific. Way better than you did when you got here. You looked too thin and not healthy." He paused. "Was that okay to say?"

"Under other circumstances, I'd probably say no, I wouldn't appreciate you or anyone commenting on my weight. But this is a different sort of conversation, so I'm letting it ride."

"Thanks. I think."

"And to answer your other question, if I had to get a job, and I could work in a restaurant, I'd take it and I wouldn't lie about it to my friends." She paused. "If I still have any friends." She thought about the women she'd hung out with when she was working at the TV studio, and the friends she'd made at her spin class. "They'd probably drop me anyway, so it doesn't matter."

"It would be their very big loss." Ben leaned over the console and touched her face, then drew her closer and kissed her lightly on the lips. "I really like East Coast Allie. A lot."

He sat back behind the wheel and checked the rearview mirror before pulling back onto the road.

"I find you very confusing sometimes, Sheriff." She watched as his smile spread slowly, and waited for him to reply, but he said nothing.

He drove down a long lane lined with signs that read NO TRESPASSING, KEEP OUT, and PREMISES PATROLLED. The narrow roadway ended in a parking lot with broken concrete scattered amid clumps of grass knee high in places.

"Oh, this looks promising," she said. "Like the parking lot at that creepy hospital where the guy in the hockey mask goes around killing his friends."

"Michael Myers," he said.

"Who?"

"The guy in the mask. Michael Myers. He's after Jamie Lee Curtis."

"It's somewhat disturbing you would know that." She looked

out the window, then peered over the dashboard. "Where's the lake?"

"Behind the trees."

"You sure about that?"

"Been coming here all my life, and I drive out several times a week just to check on things. I know Barney doesn't like people coming here, but it's hard to keep kids away, you know? They drink beer and smoke and make out at night."

"How do you know what they do?"

"Because I or one of my guys patrol out here late at night and we're always chasing kids away. Compton Lake is on the regular route. And because I used to do some of the same stuff when I was in high school."

"Ha. Figures. When was the last time you came out here for, you know, 'stuff'?"

"The night before I deployed. Me and Eva Langroth. Hot little devil, that Eva."

"Did I know about that? I don't think you told me before."

"Why would I have told you about Eva Langroth?" he deadpanned.

"You know what I meant. The part about being deployed." Allie laughed, pleased they were back to where they started, with humor and the easy way that had only recently begun to develop between them.

"The short version is Seth, Joe, and I all enlisted in the army when we got out of college. The recruiter gave us every assurance we'd be kept together. That man's nose must have grown like Pinocchio's, because we were sent every place but together. Seth was wounded in Afghanistan and was sent back after about a year and a half. Joe trained as a medic. He was in Afghanistan for a while, too."

"And you? What did you do?"

"Military police. I found I liked police work, applied for a job locally when I got back. End of story."

Allie knew there was way more to his story, but she already

knew some of it. The important parts anyway. He'd fallen in love and married a woman named Sarah and they'd had a son named Finn and they both died in a horrible car accident caused by Joe's drunken father. It never failed to amaze Allie that even after all that, Ben's friendship with Joe had never wavered.

"Come on. Let's head down to the water." Ben hopped out of the cab and walked around to open the passenger door, but Allie was already out of her seat belt and had opened the door herself.

"I'm wondering if this is some kind of a ruse. I don't see a lake. Are you sure it's still here? Maybe you're the guy in the hockey mask."

Ben laughed. "This way." He took her hand and led her through a stand of ancient pines.

On the other side of the trees, as promised, the vista opened up to a wide lake where the water was dappled with sunlight and tiny waves slowly tumbled to the shore on a gentle breeze. Tall trees circled the water all around as if forming a barrier, and the trees and the sky were reflected on the surface of the lake.

"Oh, it's beautiful," Allie exclaimed. "It's like a picture in a magazine."

"It's even more spectacular in the fall, when the leaves all turn colors. It's hard to describe it, the blue water and the reds and yellows and oranges of the trees." He pointed across the lake. "The maples change, and it's something to see. Maybe you'll still be here when that happens. It's quite a show. People come from all over to see the hills and the mountains in all that pretty foliage."

"Maybe." It did sound glorious, she thought. She'd seen pictures but had never experienced autumn in the mountains. For a moment she hoped her remaining time in Hidden Falls would stretch a little longer, then she thought of Nikki, and how she wanted her mother to come home with her.

They walked to the shoreline, the grass giving way to something that was not quite dirt, not quite sand, but pebbles of different sizes, shapes, and colors. To their right, a dock extended twenty feet into the lake, and a little farther, nestled back between trees, a structure appeared to have sprouted up in the forest.

"Is that the cabin?" She pointed to the shedlike building.

"No. That's the old boathouse. There's a rowboat in there."

She stared out across the lake. "When everyone said 'lake,' I was thinking something small." She held her arms out in the shape of an O.

"That would be a pond."

"How does something this big belong to one person?"

"The land all around the lake—the forest, and all the way to the highway—has belonged to the Hudson family for almost two hundred years. Barney's told me that there have been many opportunities to sell it all, but she doesn't want the forest chopped down and she doesn't want to see a bunch of houses or cottages up. She's been offered millions of dollars by developers, but she doesn't want to sell," he explained.

"Millions of dollars?" Allie raised an eyebrow. "And she turned it down?"

"Some things are more important than money. And if you're Barney, and you've always had a comfortable life, the money doesn't mean that much to you." He tugged on her hand and started to walk toward the boathouse, then stopped and pointed around the lake. "You see how beautiful this is now? Picture most of the trees gone, and little cottages built on the lake and on roads that circle around it. Picture the water with dozens of boats on it. Picture the—"

"Okay, okay, I get it. Barney's right to hold on to it, but I wonder how long she'll be able to keep it out of the hands of developers. I mean, what happens to it when she . . . you know." Allie couldn't bring herself to say *when she dies*.

Ben shrugged. "You'll have to ask her. I don't know what she has planned. Maybe she'll give it to the state, or . . . who knows? Maybe it'll be your problem someday. Yours and your sisters."

They resumed walking and Allie fell silent. Would Barney do that? Pass along the lake and the woods? She'd never bothered to think about what would happen to all the Hudson properties and the house, and now, the Goodbye. Allie had no idea of the extent of Barney's holdings. Who knew what she was thinking?

The shed had a padlock that could have withstood just about any onslaught. It was made of iron and must have weighed twenty pounds.

"Boy, Barney isn't messing around when she decides to keep people out," Allie noted.

"I'm sure you saw the 'No Trespassing' signs on the way in and down at the dock, but you can see by the trash that no one heeds them." He pointed to some fast-food containers near the water's edge. "I should come back with a bag and pick up that stuff."

"Why would you do that? It's not your responsibility."

"No, it would be Barney's. And by extension, yours. But I don't expect her to come out here with a plastic bag to pick up trash. Now, if you and your sisters want to . . . be my guest."

"No, you're right. And thank you. It's nice of you to do that for her." She didn't want to address the issue of whether the responsibility might be partially hers. To do so would be to make a commitment she wasn't sure she could keep.

"Go back to the part about me being right." His mouth curved into a smile. "That might be the nicest thing you've ever said to me."

"Yeah, well, don't get too used to it." She suppressed her own smile but gave his hand a little squeeze.

Ben dropped her hand and worked the combination on the lock, which fell open. He pulled the door open and peered inside. "Give me a hand, will you?"

Ben stepped up into the small building, then held out a hand to Allie. When she hesitated to take it, he said, "What's the matter? You don't have to come all the way in. Just stand here where I am and take the bow when I tell you to. We'll walk it out and slip it into the water."

"How long has that thing been in there? It looks pretty old. How do you know it doesn't have holes in it?" She poked her head into the boathouse only far enough for her eyes to scan the dark interior. "I'll bet there are spiders in there. Snakes, maybe, too. Ugh. I hate . . ."

Ben had been about to push the boat toward her, but he stopped for a moment. "It's been in here for about two weeks, which was the last time I took her out. If it had holes in it, I would have sunk then." He paused. "I have no control over spiders. If they're in here, we'll flick them out. Snakes . . . no snakes in the boat. Are you done?"

She nodded slowly. "I think so."

"Good. Then grab the front of the boat and just pull it toward you. It's fiberglass. It's not all that heavy."

She pulled—he was right, it wasn't so heavy that she couldn't hold on to it—and he pushed the back of the boat.

"Okay, let your end drop to the ground—slowly, please. There you go." He brushed his hands off on his jeans. "See, that wasn't so hard, was it?"

"No." She inspected the interior of the rowboat. No spiders, no snakes.

Ben ducked back into the boathouse and returned with two oars.

"Better take off those sandals and roll up your pants legs," he told her. "Unless you want them to get wet."

She gave him a questioning look.

"We're going to have to walk the boat out into the lake a ways before we get in it. The water's too shallow here." He took off his sneakers and left them on the shore.

"What's on the bottom?" She pointed to the lake.

"Stones, mostly. There are a few places where there might be grass growing. Maybe some mud." He stopped, then said, "Are you going to go all diva on me and refuse to walk ten steps into the lake where—God forbid—you might step on something you can't see or a fish might swim by and touch your leg?"

"I was thinking about it," she admitted as she leaned over to take off her sandals. "But when you put it that way, I guess not. Let's get this done, okay?"

Ben smiled and stepped into the water, then walked out until it hit the bottom of his khaki shorts. "And before you ask, it's not cold on this side of the lake. It's actually pretty warm."

She left her sandals on the shore next to his sneakers, then rolled up her pants—*Why in the name of all that's holy did I wear linen?*—then stepped into the water at the edge. Ben was right. It was pleasantly warm. She walked out behind the boat until the water was almost to her knees. She tried to hike her pants up a little more, but they'd gone as far as they could go.

"You could have told me to wear shorts," she said.

"Sorry. Those were nice pants."

"Yeah, they were," she muttered.

"Now hoist yourself over the side and get into the boat."

"Okay." She made it on her third try. "Not as easy as it looks."

"You did fine." He pushed the boat out a little farther into the lake, then hopped on board.

Allie held up an oar. "What do we do now?"

"Now," he said, "I slide the oars into the oarlocks."

Allie watched him place one oar into a fixed metal pivot on the side of the boat. Then he said, "Hand me the other oar, please."

The second oar went into the pivot on the other side of the boat. Ben rolled up the sleeves of his shirt until they encircled his biceps. Allie'd never been attracted to guys with big muscles, but she couldn't help but stare.

"Ready?" he asked as he adjusted the oars.

"I thought I was going to row, too," she said.

"You're thinking of a canoe, maybe. In a rowboat, only one person rows, and today that person would be me, unless you feel you need the workout."

"Nope. Tried the rowing machine at the gym once. Didn't care for it. I'm going to just sit here and admire the scenery." She smiled and relaxed on her seat and gazed around the lake as the boat began to glide through the water. Canada geese drifted down to land close to the shoreline, and several pairs of ducks swam ahead of the boat as if guiding it across the water.

"There's no wind today, or this would be a little harder than it might look. As it is, the water's calm and we can go in any direction you like. So which way?"

Allie pointed to an area directly across the lake.

"Good choice, since the cabin is there and Barney wanted us to check it out." He rowed at a steady pace and Allie put her face up to the sun, her eyes closed, and she stayed that way until they were almost to the other side.

"My daughter was right, and so were you," she told him, opening her eyes and looking to the shore. "I definitely needed to see this place. It's beautiful and it's peaceful. I understand why Barney wouldn't want to see it developed. Thanks for bringing me."

"My pleasure." He rowed up to a low dock that had steps leading up and posts onto which he tied up the boat with a length of rope that was on the floor behind him. He held out a hand to her and said, "Come on. I'll hold the boat steady so you can climb up the ladder."

She climbed onto the short dock and watched Ben tie up the boat. "Why doesn't that dock on the other side of the lake have steps?"

"I think it did at one time, but the rails rotted out." He climbed up behind her. "This way."

They walked through a worn path in the woods where wildflowers grew in clumps—blue cornflowers and Queen Anne's lace and clover in spots where the shade wasn't deep. They passed a grove of white birch, hickory, and maple trees. There were stones and sticks hidden beneath the layers of pine needles that defined the path, and Allie was pretty sure she'd stepped on every one of them. She silently gave herself points for not complaining.

"When I was a boy, we used to come out here and tap the sugar maples in these woods for syrup," Ben said. "I haven't done that in a long time."

They came to a clearing where the cabin stood tucked back among the trees and surrounded by azalea and mountain laurel, the blooms all faded but the leaves still dark green. The cabin itself was two stories and built of logs with a porch that stretched across the entire front of the modest-size building.

"Your grandfather had this built years ago. Barney told me once that he'd always fancied having a log cabin and he wanted it built with native logs. She said he always used to say he had the heart of a pioneer," Ben said, apparently anticipating Allie's question.

"I wonder if he came out here often or if he ever actually stayed here."

Ben shrugged. "Maybe he invited his buddies to come along for fishing, hunting, poker—who knows? Could have been the precursor of the hunting club."

"It's beautiful, though. It looks just the way I'd imagine a log cabin would look," Allie said as they drew closer to the building.

"Right. Just the way an early settler would have built it. With a generator for electricity and heat, and a brass doorknob," Ben pointed out. "Now, for the key."

He counted the shrubs from the right of the steps, and when he reached the fourth one, he knelt and picked up a rock. "I hope this is the right one."

Seconds later, he said, "Yup." He smiled up at Allie, who watched from the front steps. "Memory like an elephant."

"She left the key under a rock?"

"Fake rock. It's hollow inside, see?" He held it up, then brought it to her. "But it's heavy like a real one would be. Would you think it was fake?"

She took the rock and turned it upside down to see the opening. "No. That's so clever."

"That's our Barney." He took the steps two at a time. "Come on. Let's check it out."

Ben unlocked the door and pushed it open, then waited for Allie to enter. It was dark inside because the shades were all drawn, but even in the dim light, she could make out the big open space and the large stone fireplace. The furniture was covered with sheets, but it looked like there was a sofa and several chairs set around the fireplace. The kitchen was off to the right and was open to the large room, and steps led up to the second floor.

"I'd say old Reynolds was way before his time. Open concept is big these days. He'd have done well on HGTV," Allie said as she wandered around the first floor.

Ben shrugged. "I have no idea what that means."

"Obviously you don't watch enough television."

"Hardly any," he admitted. "Unless, you know, football."

She went up the steps and found a large loft area with more sheets draped over the furniture—a bed, chair, and two dressers— and a bathroom with a window that overlooked the woods. "It's quite a romantic place, you know?"

"You think? I think it's kind of rustic."

"Rustic can be very romantic. Look at that gorgeous fireplace and imagine a beautiful fire there. And the beams overhead." Allie went to the loft railing and leaned on it. "This looks more like a getaway than a place for guys to come and drink and play poker, or fish and hunt."

"I'd come out here with my buddies to drink and play poker." Ben walked down the hall to the right of the fireplace. Allie heard him open, then close several doors.

"What's down there?" a curious Allie asked as she came down the steps.

"A couple of bedrooms and a bathroom."

"There's a bath upstairs, too. Boy, whatever he used this for, it seems he spared no expense." Allie went into the kitchen and opened and closed the cupboards. "Dishes, glasses, flatware, and enough pots to cook a meal in. This place is fully equipped."

Ben stood near the front door, the key in his hand. "Are you finished exploring?"

"Pretty much."

Allie looked across the room to where he stood, one hand on the doorknob. She narrowed her eyes and walked toward him slowly.

"What?" he asked suspiciously.

"This." She wrapped her arms around him and kissed him, a soft, slow burn of a kiss that had him dropping the key. He pulled her closer, his hands on her hips, his tongue meeting hers in a dance that gave every indication it could heat up fast.

"What was that for?" he asked, his breath slightly ragged, when she began to pull away.

"Just collecting what you owed me," she said smugly. She'd caught him off guard, and that tickled her. The fact that she'd been caught off guard, too—she'd liked it way too much—was irrelevant. The man could kiss.

"There could be interest on that debt. Maybe you should check it out."

"Oh, I imagine I will. But right now, we need to get moving. I promised Barney I'd be at the cafe by five." Allie bent down to pick up the key and handed it to Ben, saying, "I'd like to come back here sometime. There's just something about this place."

"Rustic yet romantic," he deadpanned.

"Like I said."

"Beats poker and fishing."

Allie laughed and took one last look over her shoulder. She'd definitely be back, once the spiders had been moved out. Ben walked out onto the porch and Allie followed. He turned the key in the lock, then tested the door.

"Ready to go?" he asked.

"I am." She watched him return the rock to its hiding place. "Does it seem a little dark here?"

"That's because the sun's on the other side of the lake this time of day." Ben took her hand and led her back along the path. "And the woods are denser here."

He stopped in the path and pointed off to their right. "There're caves back there. One time when I was a kid, I ran away from home and hid in one of them."

"You must have been really angry about something to come all the way out here to hide."

"Yeah, back then I was angry about a lot of things."

"You say that as if you're still angry." She stepped around a large rock in her path.

"Nah, I'm over it now."

When she looked up at him with one eyebrow raised, he said, "Short version? My mom left when I was eight, took my little brother and sister with her, left me with my dad. Never heard from her again. My dad died when I was in my teens."

"What did you do? You couldn't have lived alone."

"I lived with Joe and his family until I started college."

Allie stopped walking. "What about your siblings?"

He tugged on her hand to start walking again. "No idea where they are."

"I'm so sorry, Ben." *And I thought I had a bad mother. Oh, wait. I did.*

He didn't respond, and they continued walking until they emerged from the woods. Once at the dock, Ben got into the boat first to help Allie. He untied the boat, then sat, grabbed the oars and said, "All set?"

Allie nodded. He began to row back toward the opposite shore.

"This place is just magical," she said. "It's so pretty and peaceful, and— *Oh my God!* Bear! Bear, Ben! Bear!"

She jumped up and started to lunge toward him, the small boat rocking wildly.

"No! Allie, sit down! You're going to turn the boat over!" He moved frantically to try to steady the boat, attempting to balance the craft by using his legs. Water sloshed over both sides, and he almost dropped an oar while grabbing for her arm to keep her from going overboard. "For the love of God, woman, sit down!"

Allie sat. "But the bear . . ." She pointed to the shore where the beast stood on its hind legs.

"Yes, I see her. And if she didn't know we were here before, she knows now." He repositioned the oar.

"How do you know it's a she?" Allie whispered, her voice trembling. They were less than fifty feet from the large black animal.

"Because she has cubs with her." Ben rowed very slowly, his strokes hard but not fast.

"Where?"

"Look behind her." Ben rested the oars for a moment.

Allie craned her neck. "Oh." She watched for several minutes as the three cubs played, rolling in the grass behind their mother, who seemed more focused on the water in front of her. "Oh, they play like puppies." She glanced up at him. "Not that I ever had puppies, but I've seen them playing at other people's houses and once in a pet shop in the mall." She continued to watch, a broad smile on her face. "They're so roly-poly."

Then a minute later—"Uh-oh. She sees us! Mama's waving her arms! Why aren't you rowing? Why are you just sitting there? Row!"

"She's checking the air for scent, and there's nothing to worry about. The wind is blowing away from us. Black bears—which is what we have here—aren't generally aggressive."

"'Not generally aggressive' isn't all that reassuring. 'Cause they can swim, right?" Allie watched the huge animal, which was still standing, looking out across the lake. "Ben, she's watching us. *Why aren't you rowing?*"

"Shhhh. She's just looking around. Making sure there's no danger to her cubs."

"Could she sink this boat if she swam out here? I bet she could sink this boat." Allie held on to the sides warily. "We have no life jackets."

"She has no reason to swim after us, and we were in more danger of *you* sinking the boat. Calm down. Look." He motioned in the bear's direction.

The bear had gone back to fishing, swatting at something in the water. Cautiously, Allie removed her phone from her pocket and took a few pictures of the bear and her cavorting cubs. She and Ben sat in the boat, watching the animals frolic, until Mama gave up on fishing and herded her babies back into the woods.

Ben began to row again.

"Are you mad at me?" she asked.

"Nope. But I think you'd have been pretty pissed off if you'd gotten dumped into the water and had to swim all the way back to the other side of the lake. I thought everyone knew that you don't stand up in a rowboat."

"I'm sorry. I've never been in one that I can remember, and I've never been that close to a bear." She tried to look contrite, adding, "And it was unexpected. Scary. What if we'd run into her in the woods?"

"We didn't. And I never heard of anyone being attacked out here."

"Joe was attacked. Cara said he has scars."

"Yeah, but he was attacked up near the falls behind your house."

"Oh God, Cara did tell us that. Thanks for reminding me."

"That was the last bear sighting anywhere near town. Everyone thinks it got disoriented when it came out of its den, it was cranky and hungry, and Joe just happened to get directly in the way of it and its cubs. You're more likely to meet up with a rattlesnake than you are a bear."

"Now I know you're just trying to scare me. Everyone knows rattlesnakes live in the desert. Like Texas and Arizona. Places like that."

"Uh-huh."

He let the boat glide toward shore, and when they hit the shallow water, he removed the oars from their rests, placed one into the water perpendicular to hold the boat in place. "This is as close to shore as we can get."

She tugged her wet rolled-up pants a little higher and eased out of the boat.

Ben hopped out and started to push the boat out of the water and onto the pebbled beach. Together they carried it to the boathouse and returned it to its place, the oars inside. He closed the double doors and reset the lock. Allie sat on a big rock and put her sandals on.

"So there you have it." Ben sat on the end of the dock and tied his sneakers. "You've had your tour of Compton Lake, the cabin, geese, ducks, bears . . . did I leave anything out?"

"Rattlesnakes." She rolled her eyes. "As if."

Ben laughed, his hand on the small of her back as they walked back to the truck. "The thing you should know is, that was no joke. Rattlesnakes are common around here. You don't often see them, but they're here. You know that old saying about them being more scared of you than you are of them?"

"Yes, and it's a freaking lie! There is no snake on the planet more afraid of me than I am of it."

He laughed again. "You just have to be careful, know where to look, or in your case, where *not* to look. For example, would you look under a log? No. Under a rock? No. They're reptiles, remember, so they like to sun themselves on rocks in the summer."

"Oh, like the rock I just sat on to put my sandals on?"

"Yeah. Like that one. Smart of you not to look under it."

"Maybe next time I should just sit on the ground." Allie stopped at the edge of the pines that separated the lake from the parking lot and looked back. "I wish I'd come out here sooner. It really is one of the prettiest places I've ever seen. And I wish I could see it in the fall, with the foliage all pretty colors and the sky really blue."

Ben looped an arm around her waist and pulled her closer.

"You don't have to stay away. There are planes, right? You could come back whenever you wanted."

"Will the trees still be colorful in November? Nik and I will be back for Thanksgiving. I've already decided that."

"Maybe some, but by then, most of the leaves will have dropped."

"Oh. Well, maybe you could take some pictures and text them to me."

"I could do that. I'd rather you were here to take them yourself, though."

"Don't. It is what it is."

"You don't sound happy about it, though."

"I don't have to be happy about it. I just have to make the most of it. However, Nikki did remind me she'd be away at college in about three more years, so maybe I could spend more time here then."

Ben didn't respond, but she knew what he was thinking, because she was thinking the same thing: Three years is a long time.

Chapter Seventeen

Allie was on her back, staring up at the ceiling of the Sugar-house, paintbrush in hand, trying to push away the memory of kissing Ben at the cabin, then making out in his pickup truck the afternoon before. While as a rule she'd never compare one man to another, after kissing Ben, she couldn't help herself. Clint had never kissed that way. If he had, they might still be married.

"Eva Langroth teach you to kiss like that?" she'd asked.

To which Ben had wisely replied, "Eva who?"

Allie sighed. The more time she spent with Ben, the more she regretted the time they'd wasted sniping at each other all those months. "Hindsight is twenty-twenty," a friend used to say.

"So true."

It was an effort to focus on the last diamond shape she'd stenciled, and one of the last elements she'd have to paint. She was so close to completing this project she could see the finish line and couldn't get there fast enough, but she was having a hard time not thinking about the shape and feel of Ben's smooth biceps. She'd run her hands over them, telling herself she'd just wanted to see what biceps like that felt like in real life.

"Boy, what a mistake that was," she muttered.

The paint on her brush was beginning to dry, and she cursed softly even as she laughed at herself.

"Listen to me, Allie Monroe. You're too old to be drooling over some guy and his muscles. Too freaking old."

She cleaned the brush and began again, painstakingly adding color to those missing places on the design above her head.

"Hello? Allie?" A voice from down below called her.

Allie turned and looked over the side of the plank. She'd forgotten Tess Dunham was to tour the theater that morning. *Crap.* She didn't need another distraction.

"Hey, Tess," she said as pleasantly as she could. It wasn't the fault of the other woman that Allie's mind kept going where it hadn't gone in a long time.

"Am I too early?" Tess called.

"I have no idea of the time, so no, you're not early. I'll be down in a minute." Allie capped the open paint jar and pulled herself up to a sitting position.

"Could I come up there? Nikki's been telling me about how the ceiling was damaged by water and how you devised this incredibly clever way of repairing it. I'd love to see, if you don't mind."

"I don't mind. Just be careful climbing up. And try not to land too hard when you reach the top. Paint jars." Allie held one up.

Tess climbed easily, hand over hand, and in a minute, she was next to Allie on the uppermost plank.

"It's really far up." Tess looked down through the scaffold. "It doesn't seem so high when you're standing down there."

"I've always had a problem with heights, so this has been a challenge for me. I don't always think about it anymore, I've climbed up so many times. But the first week was a little scary for me, I'm not going to lie."

"The theater is so beautiful I hardly know where to look first. This ceiling . . . incredible. From an artistic point of view, it's glorious. When you're standing in the lobby and looking up, it takes your breath away. But up close, the colors are so rich. You're so lucky to be part of such an amazing work. And so talented to be able to blend the colors so perfectly." Tess glanced over at Allie.

"Even this close, I can barely tell where you filled in what was missing."

"Well, thank you," Allie said, somewhat embarrassed by the praise. "We really had no choice but to try something out of the box. The 'professional' artists were priced so far out of our range we'd never have been able to afford to have someone else come in to do the work." She smiled wryly. "That is, if we still wanted to repair the seats and build new bathrooms, that sort of thing."

"I don't think anyone else could have done better. I mean that."

"Thank you again, Tess. That's nice of you to say." She looked upward. "It's been gratifying. As I mentioned the other night at dinner, I majored in art back in the day and always fancied I'd become an artist someday. Not that this qualifies me as an artist—I mean, I traced the designs to make a stencil."

Tess interrupted her. "How do you think the original artist was able to make every single design the same size and shape as the others? Don't you suppose he might have had a template of sorts he used?"

"I've never thought about it, to be honest. Alistair Cooper was the artist, and I've seen quite a bit of his work. He was local and there's a family connection. His work is wonderful, and his use of color bordered on genius."

"I know his work. My grandparents had several of his paintings. My mom still has them hanging in her dining room. Yes, I agree, his use of color was unique."

"Cooper was married to a great-aunt of ours. He did a mural in Barney's dining room as a way of proving to his beloved's parents that he was a great artist and worthy to marry their daughter. He painted the falls in the mural," Allie told her. "The falls the town is named for. And yes, he won the girl."

"That's amazing. I'd love to see that mural sometime. And I knew there really were waterfalls, but I never saw them."

"Neither have I. And it's almost embarrassing to admit, since they're on Hudson property and right up the hill behind my aunt's house. I'm determined to go, though, once before I leave. Everyone says they're beautiful."

"I'd love to see them, too. I've been thinking about painting some scenes from around Hidden Falls when I have time to paint again."

"I've been thinking the same thing. When I get back to L.A., I thought I'd set up a studio and paint some of what I've seen here."

"Well, they do say great minds think alike," Tess said.

"How 'bout we take that tour I promised you?" Allie asked.

"I don't want to take up too much of your time. I know you have work to do."

Tess started down the scaffold and Allie followed, a full two levels behind. When they got to the bottom, Allie gestured for Tess to follow her into the audience.

"The stage, where my father met my mother," Allie told her.

"Nikki mentioned your mother was a famous actress, that she made movies a long time ago and your father was her agent."

"Right. He met her here. He was an actor, too. They used to do summer stage, and the theater also offered performances during the year. As I understand it, my dad was expected to take his place at the local bank and become president when his father stepped down. But Dad had other ideas." Allie walked toward the stage and Tess fell in step with her. "My mother was a beautiful woman, there's no denying that. But back when she and my dad were young, they fell in love here, on this stage, and since she wanted to go to Hollywood, he took her."

"And she became a star."

Allie nodded. "She did."

"And you and your sister Des also acted?"

"Well, mostly Des." Allie laughed, then realized it was the first time she'd ever talked about those days without feeling animosity or bitterness toward her sister, and it was liberating. She found she could honestly say, without hesitation and without envy, "Des was really good. She had her own TV show because she was naturally talented. Me, not so much. I had a little recurring role because my mother insisted on it. She'd become the ultimate stage mama by then." She smiled remembering. "I'm sure she was a terror for the crew and the director."

"And your sister Cara—did she act as well?" Tess asked.

Allie turned toward the lobby and gestured for Tess to come along. "We didn't know Cara back then when we were kids. We—Des and I—just met her in January at the reading of our father's will."

"Oh. Well, that's very different." Tess looked chagrined, as if afraid she'd stuck her foot in her mouth.

"It's fine." Allie told Tess the entire story as they walked to the lobby.

"So you didn't even know your aunt, but you all had to come here, live together, and bring this wonderful place back to life?" Tess had obviously followed the story in detail.

"In a nutshell, yes."

"How did that feel, as an adult, meeting a sister you never knew you had?"

Allie laughed again. "It was strange. I didn't want anything to do with her. But it's been one of the best experiences of my life."

"So he did you a favor by forcing you together," Tess observed.

"Yes, he did. It was a crazy way to go about making that happen, and in the beginning we all thought he'd lost his mind, but as our old housekeeper used to say, it all comes out in the wash."

Allie showed Tess the balcony and the projector room, pointing out the old movie posters she was going to have framed.

"This is my mother." Allie pulled out the poster Nikki had selected of one of Nora's films.

"Wow, she really was gorgeous."

"All her beauty was on the outside, unfortunately." Allie replaced the poster. "All Des and I can think is that Dad was dazzled by her beauty, and by the time he saw her for who she really was, it was too late for him to turn back."

Allie realized she was talking to Justine's daughter—the brokenhearted, angry, unforgiving J of the letters Cara had found in the carriage house. Surely Tess wasn't aware that her mother had at one time been involved with Fritz.

Not my place to tell her what she doesn't know, Allie thought.

"I'm sorry you and Des didn't have a better relationship with your mother. I can't imagine . . . Well, let's just say my mom has been wonderful on every level. She's always supported me, always been there for me no matter what. Looking back, I can honestly say I had a perfect childhood. My mom was always there when I got home from school to help me with my homework or make sure I had a snack before I went out to play. We had great vacations every summer, and—" Tess stopped, her face turning red. "I'm sorry. I should be more sensitive."

"No, no, don't apologize. I'm happy for you that you had a great mom. Cara did, too. It sounds as if you had similar childhood experiences."

Allie closed the door behind them when they'd exited the room. "I don't mean to make my dad sound like he was always flakey or a jerk. He was a great guy. He was smart and funny, and when the three of us looked back, we could see where he always tried to make us happy. We each have great memories of him. Cara spent the most time with him growing up, because he was busy building his career when Des and I were little. God knows he had his quirks, but he wasn't a bad guy. And when he was around, he was a good dad."

"I'm glad you added that. I had a great father, too, a wonderful father, and I'll always be thankful we had him as long as we did. There was nothing he wouldn't do for my mom and me. I think about him every day. I miss him every day."

"Sounds like you had an ideal childhood."

"Pretty much, I did. I would have loved to have had siblings, though. I always wanted a sister."

"Growing up, I'd have gladly given you mine."

They went back down the stairs to the area off the lobby where the refreshment stand had been located.

"For Des's birthday, her boyfriend, Seth, bought her the new popcorn machine. Does that say true love or does that say true love?"

"Definitely," Tess agreed.

"We were trying to remember all the movie candies we used to buy," Allie was telling her as she pointed out the candy counter. "If the theater is ever opened for business, we'll have to restock."

"Heavy on the Milky Ways, please—my personal favorite. Oh, and Sno-Caps," Tess said.

"Cara said the same thing: Milky Ways and Sno-Caps. But, uh, no. Milk Duds and Junior Mints. But the candy case is big enough for all those and many others."

They'd wandered back into the lobby, where Tess admired the decorative painting on the walls, the painted garlands of roses that wound over the arched doorways, the crystal chandeliers overhead.

"It's a magnificent place," Tess said, moving toward the front of the theater and the door. "Just magnificent. I hope I can come back when it's finished."

"Of course. And when it's reopened, we'll be sure to put you on the VIP guest list," Allie told her.

"May I ask just one question, though?"

"Sure."

"Why go to all this trouble and expense to renovate this wonderful place if you don't reopen it? I mean, what would be the point?"

"I'm not sure what Dad had in mind." Allie shrugged. "I guess we'd have had to ask Fritz, if he'd given us the chance."

It was a conversation she and the others should have soon, though, Allie thought as she walked Tess to the door.

"This has been wonderful. I can't thank you enough." Tess gave Allie a quick hug, and to Allie's surprise, she hugged her back.

"Anytime," Allie told her. "And we'll definitely put your name on the VIP list for the theater's grand opening."

"Do that. I'll come back for it. I know Wendy will want to as well. She's going to miss Nikki."

"Nikki's going to miss her, too. I'm thinking about coming back for Thanksgiving, so maybe we'll see you then."

"Deal." Tess smiled and walked through the door Allie had opened for her.

"What do you want to do for your birthday, Nik?" Allie asked when she'd arrived back at the house that evening. Nikki was sitting alone in what they referred to as the big living room in the front of the house. It was furnished with period pieces, which were formal and elegant, but not necessarily comfortable, which explained why it was rarely used.

"Nothing. I don't want a party this year."

"Why not?"

"Because I don't know who my friends are going to be when I get back home, that's why," she snapped. A moment passed, and she apologized. "Sorry, Mom. It's not your fault."

"You're worried about Courtney and what she might be saying about you?"

"I know what she's saying about me. I've seen some of her texts."

"Do I want to know what she's saying?"

"She's telling people I'm not going out for field hockey because I've turned into a total nerd and a country bumpkin." Nikki pulled out her phone and showed Allie a picture someone had sent her. Courtney had put Nik's face on a body dressed in overalls and a straw hat, and she'd photoshopped a piece of straw sticking out of her mouth.

"Oh, for the love of . . ."

"Are you going to tell Dad?"

"Did the sun come up this morning?"

"It's not going to stop. Court's mom will ground her for a weekend—she'll make her stay in on Friday night, but by Saturday she'll give in and that'll be the end of it. It won't change a thing." Nikki looked up at her mother with red-rimmed eyes. "I don't want to deal with planning a party and having no one show up, okay? Or they'll show up and make it clear they don't want to be there. Court already gave her mother the guest list. She only invited her friends."

"I thought they were your friends, too."

"Not anymore." Nikki leaned back, holding a throw pillow to her chest. "It's okay, Mom. I don't want to hang around with them anyway."

"All right. We'll tell Dad no party." Allie sat next to Nikki on the big Eastlake sofa and draped her arm over the curved wooden back, trying to find the right words while keeping her temper under control.

"I wouldn't mind having a party here, though," Nikki said softly. "With you and my family and my friends. I feel like my friends here are my real friends. Wendy and Hayley and Mark. They'd never do stuff like what Courtney did."

"Then a party here it will be. We don't have much time to plan it, though." Allie thought of the logistics. They really were out of time. "We could have it the night before you leave."

"I was just thinking that. It'll make me sad, but I'm going to be sad anyway, so we might as well have a party. Cake makes everything better."

Allie laughed despite being angry and upset for her daughter. "I'll talk to Barney about having it here. I'm sure she won't mind." She paused. "Would you rather have it someplace else? The café or the theater or the farm?"

"Nope. This is our home. Barney said." Nikki's chin rose. "I want to have it in our house."

"Perfect. We'll do it."

"Thanks, Mom. And thanks for . . ." Nikki paused. "Well, you know. Everything."

"Come here and hug me before you get too old." Nikki did as she was bidden. Allie inhaled the lemony scent of her daughter's shampoo and felt the tears well up. "When do you suppose that might be?"

"Sixteen might be the cutoff for parental hugging, but I can check that on Google." Nik gave her one last squeeze and left the room looking a little cheerier than she had when Allie'd walked in.

Allie tapped her foot in agitation, trying to get her thoughts together before she called Clint. He needed to keep a closer eye on what was going on. Okay, that might be tough, since his interactions with Courtney were limited, given the fact she didn't live with him. But he needed to have a serious talk with Marlo. Again.

One thing Clint was going to have to understand: There would be hell to pay if their daughter walked into a viper's pit when she returned to California.

CHAPTER EIGHTEEN

The following afternoon, Allie heard the doorbell ring, then seconds later, there was pounding on the front door. From the top of the stairwell, she saw Barney open the door. Peering over the upstairs newel post, Allie saw Justine Kennedy rush into the hallway.

"What do you think you're doing?" Justine yelled. "You stay away from my girl! I don't want anything to do with you and I don't want them to have anything to do with you or anyone in your family. Hear me? You. Stay. Away. And you tell that girl to stay away from Wendy."

"Perhaps you should let Tess make that decision."

The vitriol Justine spewed had riveted Allie to the floor. The woman had blown in like a cold November wind and created as much energy. But to Allie's ear, Barney sounded almost unreasonably calm, as if she'd been expecting the tirade and had prepared for it.

"No. It's not her decision. It's mine. Stay out of our lives, Barney."

"Or what, Justine?"

"Or . . ." Justine huffed for a moment. "You don't know. You just don't know."

"Actually, I believe I do." Barney's calm was a stark contrast to Justine's ire.

Allie came down several steps, close enough to see Justine blink.

"You couldn't possibly." Justine stepped up into Barney's face again.

"Trust me, Justine. I do know." Barney never hesitated, nor did she back up. "I found the letters between you and Fritz."

Justine struggled unsuccessfully for words, then burst into tears.

"Why didn't you come to us? Why didn't you tell us?" Barney's voice was all kindness, while Justine looked deflated, much like a sail deserted by the wind. "Come in. Please. Let me make you a cup of tea, and we'll talk." Barney took Justine by the elbow and led the sobbing woman into the kitchen.

Barney saw Allie coming slowly down the steps. "Have a good day at the café, dear. I'm here if you need me."

A wide-eyed Allie nodded and watched the two women move down the hall. Barney was saying something softly to Justine, but Allie couldn't make out the words.

Wow. Justine must still be angry over having been dumped by Fritz back in the day. Way to hold a grudge.

Allie wasn't sure where Cara and Des were, but as she walked to the Goodbye, she sent them both a text:

Justine just set off fireworks at the house, Barney defusing. Come to Goodbye ASAP!

ASAP turned out to be almost an hour later, but Des and Cara came into the café together.

"What's going on?" Des went straight to the desk, where Allie was answering the house phone.

When she finished the call, Allie said, "I don't know what's going on. I was getting ready to go downstairs to leave for work when the doorbell rang and there was this manic pounding on the door. Barney answered, and Justine came flying in, yelling about how Barney needed to stay away from Tess, and how Nikki had to stay away from Wendy. It was rough. I was afraid for Barney for a minute."

"What did Barney say?" Des asked.

"She calmly told Justine to come into the kitchen and she'd make her a cup of tea."

"What? No." Cara laughed.

"I'm not kidding. That's exactly what happened," Allie said.

"They didn't say anything else?" Des asked.

"The only other thing was Justine said something like, Barney didn't know, and Barney said she did. And no, I have no idea what any of that meant. It was really strange, guys. And Justine was crying. Like, buckets."

"Crying over Fritz? Why?" Cara pulled a chair from a nearby table closer to the desk and sat.

"After all this time, why would she still be crying over Dad?" Des wondered. "That thing between them had to have been, what, over forty years ago? Man, that is a long time to carry a torch."

"I was dumped by my husband and I stopped crying months ago," Cara said. "That must have been some affair. Dad must have been hot stuff."

Allie and Des both turned to look at Cara. There was silence for a long moment.

"Cara, when I think about Dad, the words 'hot stuff' don't normally come to mind." Allie made a face.

"Yeah, it's kind of creepy, actually," Des added.

"I'm just thinking about how Justine might have looked at him. Not how I saw him. What's creepy about that?" Cara looked from one to the other. "Besides, can you think of another reason why she'd still be crying over him?"

"No," they both replied.

"Unless it's not Dad she's crying over. It could be something else," Allie said.

"Like what else?" Des asked.

"I don't know." Allie shrugged. "But I bet Barney does. I think we need to have this conversation with her when I get home."

But hours later when Allie returned home, Nikki was watching

TV in the sitting room with Barney. She jumped up when she saw her mother, her eyes sparkling.

"Aunt Barney said I could have my party here and I can invite anyone I want. We're going to string up colored lights all around the backyard so we can be out there. And she's going to ask Chef George to make food for us and we're going to set up tables outside."

"Breathe," Allie told her.

Nikki laughed. "You always say that."

"I'm always afraid you're going to turn blue and pass out from lack of oxygen." Allie dropped her bag onto the floor and sank into the nearest chair.

"Busy night, dear?" Barney looked up from the notepad in her hands.

Allie nodded. "It's always busy. Were you aware when you bought it how busy a place it is?"

"Of course." Barney smiled. "Did you remember to bring home tonight's receipts?"

"You're kidding, right?" Allie opened her bag and handed Barney a fat white padded envelope.

"Thank you." Barney rose and left the room, the envelope in her hand. "Be back in a minute. Just want to tuck this away in the safe until the morning."

"So who are you planning on inviting?" Allie asked.

"All of you guys, and my friends. And Mr. Brookes. And Chief Haldeman and Seth and Joe. That's all." She made a sad face. "I don't think Wendy will be able to come, though. She said her mom wanted to leave on Wednesday after dinner. It's her mom's last day teaching here. I really wanted her to be there."

"Well, maybe we should have the party on Tuesday night," Allie suggested. "Your flight on Thursday is very early in the morning. Maybe we should spend Wednesday packing and—"

"And maybe go out to the farm to say goodbye to the puppies. I'll bet by the time I come back, all the puppies will have been adopted. I won't even get to be there when they leave for their new homes and I'll never see them again."

"I'm sure Aunt Des will know exactly where each of the dogs go to live, and you could probably go visit them when you come back."

"Yeah, she'd know for sure. She'd never give a dog to someone without knowing where they live. Did you know she even goes to the people's houses and makes sure there's enough room for the dog and there's a fenced yard? That makes me feel a little better."

"Good. Now maybe we should make an invitation and email them out tonight, since it's already the weekend."

"Right. I'll run up and get your iPad." Nikki flew out of the room and barely avoided running into Barney.

"Where's the fire?" Barney laughed.

"I need to run up to get Mom's iPad." Nikki's voice trailed up the steps.

"What's she up to?" Barney came in and sat on the love seat.

"She's going to send out online invitations for her birthday party. She's decided to have it on Tuesday night," Allie told her.

"What shall we give her for presents?" Barney asked.

"Maybe some little thing. I know she's become quite the reader this summer. Maybe a book. Or maybe send something to her in L.A. for her to open on her birthday," Allie suggested.

"I'll have to think about it." Barney picked up the remote control. "I think I'll watch the news. I have no idea what went on in the world today."

"You're probably better off."

Barney switched channels until she found her favorite evening news program. "Oh good. The weekend weather."

"Barney, what's going on?" Allie leaned forward to ask.

"The weather, dear."

"You know that's not what I mean." When Barney didn't respond, Allie said, "I'm talking about Justine."

"Hush. I want to know if it's going to rain next week. Nikki wants her party outside."

Allie grabbed the remote and turned off the television. "What is going on with Justine? Why was she so upset?"

"I'm not ready to talk about it yet." Barney snatched the remote out of Allie's hand and turned the TV back on.

"Why not?"

"Here you go, Mom." Nikki came into the room and handed Allie her iPad.

"That's why," Barney told Allie, her eyes on Nikki.

Allie frowned. What could Nikki possibly have to do with Justine being upset?

"Nikki," Barney was saying, "the weather forecast says we'll have perfect weather for your party. Now, show me what you're sending out to your friends. I'm not sure I've ever seen an online invitation."

Barney had conveniently used Nikki's presence to keep mum on Justine, and feigning exhaustion, had taken herself upstairs to bed while Nikki was still working through her invitations on Allie's tablet.

Leave it to Barney to slip away when she doesn't want to discuss something. Allie watched her aunt kiss Nikki good night and head off upstairs.

"So, Nik, do you want me to give you my present while you're here, or would you rather have me send it to you at your dad's to arrive on your birthday?"

"I'd rather get it on my birthday, please. You always give me my present on my birthday."

Allie made a mental note to order Nikki's iPad tonight and have it sent to Clint's house.

Before Allie turned in, Nikki had invited all her guests, made a list of food she'd like to have and decorations she'd like—balloons and fairy lights ("Nothing crazy, Mom. No funny hats or those things you blow into that make a stupid noise. I'm not a five-year-old"), and a handy list of things she'd like. "Mostly books, if anyone asks."

When Allie went upstairs, she tapped lightly on Barney's door, but though she thought she'd seen a sliver of light under the door as she walked down the hall, Barney didn't answer, and when Allie peeked in, she appeared to be sound asleep under her covers.

"You know Barney," Des said after Allie told her in the morning about Barney's elusiveness. "All in her own time. If she doesn't think it's any of your business, the time is—"

"Yeah, never. I know." Allie picked up her bag of paints and left for the theater. She had one last element to paint, and the ceiling would be finished.

She took her time, trying to make that last design as perfect as she possibly could. When she finished painting, she took a break and rested until the paint dried so she could add the last touch, the gold outline. She photographed her work, then gathered her things and went down to the next level, where she stopped and took another photo looking up. At each level, she took another photo, so that by the time she reached the bottom, she had the entire ceiling in the shot. She stood and stared upward, amazed at what she'd accomplished, so pleased that she'd put her idea out there and the others had accepted it. So proud she'd been able to deliver exactly what she'd promised.

She sat on the bottom plank and sent a text to Joe.

Tell the roofers they can come get their scaffold.

Her phone rang minutes later.

"Hey, congratulations! We knew you could do it," Joe said.

"Thanks. I think I surprised myself," she replied.

"You didn't surprise your sisters," he told her. "Cara and Des said all along you'd do a bang-up job. And you have."

"Thank you for telling me that." Allie bit her bottom lip, touched by the knowledge of their faith in her.

"I was going to text you later. I just got word from the painters they can't start until Wednesday."

"That's soon enough." Allie mentally crossed off another item from her list.

"Can you take a little more?"

"Always. There's no such thing as too much good news," she said.

"Seth is, as we speak, picking up the floor sander. Then he, Ben, and I are going to start working on the stage and the backstage area this afternoon."

"OMG, as Nik would say! That's fabulous!"

"We'll still have to put a finish on it, but we'll get that done before the painters come in."

"Thank you, Joe. I don't know where we'd be if not for you. Best decision we made was to hire you as our general contractor."

"Just doin' my job, ma'am." He paused. "But thanks. It's been my pleasure since day one. I'm proud to have been involved with the theater. It's a landmark in town, part of our heritage, and it's been a once-in-a-lifetime opportunity to work on something this important."

"Before I forget, did you get Nikki's invitation for her birthday party?"

"I did, and I already responded as a yes. I wouldn't miss it," he said.

"She'll be happy to have you there. So I guess I'll see you then."

"You will."

Allie ended the call and tossed the phone into her bag. She couldn't wait to get back to the house and tell the others she'd finished the ceiling. That weight lifted from her shoulders made her want to dance.

Nikki would, she thought as she left the theater and locked the door behind her. Then again, Nikki was fourteen and had yet to shed all her inhibitions.

Almost fifteen, she reminded herself. Thinking about the reasons Nikki'd rejected a party in California took some of the shine off Allie's mood. It infuriated her to know that one girl could turn all of Nikki's friends against her. Courtney clearly had a problem. Of course, Allie had to admit, she was acting much as Allie herself had, once upon a time. It was only recently that she'd not only acknowledged her behavior as bullying but admitted the reason for it: She was jealous of her sister's success as an actress, jealous of the fact that Des had her own TV show.

What was Courtney's excuse? That was something Marlo would have to deal with.

She'd crossed Main Street and was nearing the house when a police cruiser pulled up to the curb.

Ben rolled down the window and leaned across the front seat. "Hey, mom of an almost fifteen-year-old."

"Oh God, that makes me sound so old." Allie stepped to the curb and knelt next to the passenger door. "So I'm guessing you got Nikki's invitation."

"I did, and I sent in my RSVP."

"Yea or nay?"

"I sent back a maybe. I usually put myself on night duty, so my officers can spend the time with their families. But I'm going to see if someone will switch with me for Tuesday night. I'd like to be there for her." He paused. "And I'd like to be there for you. I know she's leaving soon and it's hard on you. So you'll have a great party for her, and she'll know how much she's loved here."

"She knows," Allie said. "So why are you working? Joe said you're supposed to be helping sand the stage floor today."

"My shift ends at three, and I'll be down there doing my part. We'll get 'er done, don't you worry."

"Thank you. We all appreciate it. *I* appreciate it."

He gave her one of those half smiles that turned her insides to mush and appeared about to say something when his phone beeped.

Ben looked at the screen. "Gotta go. See you at the party."

Allie nodded and stood, watched the cruiser disappear around the corner, then sighed. How could this have happened, she asked herself as she walked up to the house? How could it be that the first man she wanted since her divorce had to be the one man who'd driven her crazy since she set foot in Hidden Falls?

"The universe doesn't owe you an explanation for everything," as Mandy, Allie's across-the-street neighbor back in L.A., used to say. Then again, she reminded herself, Mandy set traps for unicorns in the hills behind her house and sprinkled visitors with glitter before they walked through her front door. Only two of the many reasons Allie never expended much energy cultivating a friendship with her.

Buttons barked when she came into the house, but she dropped her fierce guard dog stance when she realized it was Allie.

"You should look embarrassed," Allie told the dog, whose tail wagged slowly, apologetically. "Oh, come here and let me rub that tummy." She leaned over and gave the dog a few minutes of her attention, then stood. "That's it for today. Gotta run. Things to do. Places to go."

"Wait, are you talking to the dog?" Des grinned broadly as she came downstairs. "You, who used to mock me for talking to Buttons?"

"Guilty. I never thought I'd see the day, but here we are. Is Cara around?" Allie left her bag of paints and brushes near the bottom step. "She said she'd drive me to check out a tile store on the highway."

"She mentioned she had an errand, but she'd be back by noon. Aren't you working at the Goodbye?"

Allie shook her head. "I arranged with Ginger to work today, and earlier I sent her a text and asked if she'd work again tomorrow. Yay me! I have an entire two days off in a row."

"How's it feel?"

"I haven't gotten far enough into my day to know, but I can get back to you on that. Where are you off to?" Allie noticed Des was wearing her old jeans and a plaid shirt that had seen better days. "And I don't recognize that shirt."

"It's Barney's. She loaned it to me. I was lamenting I hadn't brought any of my old clothes with me and she said she had planned on tossing this one. It's a bit faded, and one of the sleeves has a tear in it."

"So is this the look you think will make Seth go so crazy with lust he'll fall on his knees and beg you to marry him?"

"I've tried just about everything else." Des laughed. "I told him I'd work to tie up the vines that are starting to branch out. But I'm irresistible to flying insects, apparently. Had the same problem in Montana. Mosquitoes, no-see-ums, gnats, and don't start me on the yellow jackets. I've been stung three times in four days. Hence the long sleeves and the long pants."

"I hope it does the trick."

"If it doesn't, Seth is going to have to find a new helper." Des turned and called up the steps. "Nik? Ready?"

Nikki responded by running down the steps.

"I thought you were doing something with Wendy today," Allie said.

"Her grandma's back from her vacation and she wanted to take Wendy school shopping, so she can't come over," Nikki explained.

"I see. Is she coming to your birthday party?"

"She didn't say," Nikki told her, apparently unaware of the drama that recently engaged both families. "I sent her a text, but I didn't hear back from her yet." She turned to Des. "Ready, Aunt Des?"

Des held up the keys to Seth's pickup and shook them. "Just waiting for you, kiddo."

"See you, Mom." Nikki went out the front door in a flash.

"Have a good time," Allie told them.

Allie had just finished a quick lunch of leftover chicken salad when Cara arrived.

"Where'd you go?" she asked when Cara came into the kitchen, a bag in her arms.

"Grocery store." Cara opened the refrigerator door and tucked a few items inside.

"Out of organic catsup for your organic faux burger?"

Cara laughed. "Out of organic faux burgers. You still want to go look at tile?"

"I do if you still want to take me," Allie said.

"Of course." Cara looked over the apples in the fruit bowl, selected one, and took a bite. "Get your stuff and let's go. I'll be out in the car."

Allie was outside, her shoulder bag in her hand, by the time Cara had turned the car around.

"That was quick," Cara noted. "I barely got through the second verse." She turned the radio up loud and began to sing along. "'It's my life . . .'"

"Bon Jovi? Really?"

"Ah, Jersey girl here." Cara eased the car down the driveway. "What says hello, Jersey, more than Bon Jovi? Unless, you know, Springsteen."

Cara continued to sing along until the song ended.

"What?" she said, glancing across at Allie in the passenger seat.

"That was quite the lusty rendition."

Cara laughed. "Don't tell me you were too cool to sing along with the radio when you were in high school."

"Of course not. But my taste in music was a little more refined. I mean, what was cooler than the Spice Girls?"

"You didn't just say that."

Allie pointed a finger at her and said, "'Say You'll Be There.' A classic. And the video with all those wild kung fu moves? Please. Perfection."

Allie sang the song in its entirety.

"So who was your favorite Spice Girl?" Cara was trying unsuccessfully not to laugh.

"Beckham, of course. Her name wasn't Beckham then, but her."

Cara stopped for the light at the top of Main Street where it intersected with the highway.

"Left or right here?" she asked.

"Left, then take a left at the next right." She looked at the handwritten directions she'd jotted down while talking to a salesperson at the tile shop. When she looked up, she realized she knew exactly where they were. Straight ahead as they drove into the shopping center was the paint store where she'd had the chips from the ceiling matched. And off to the right was the liquor store she'd frequented on more than one occasion.

"What are we looking for?" Cara asked.

"Sherman's Designer Tile and Flooring. There. Way down on the right."

Cara parked out front, and they went into the shop and asked for Steve. He was waiting for Allie near the back of the store, the tiles she'd asked about already set out on the counter. After the introductions, Steve pointed to the tiles.

"Do these work?" he asked.

Allie pulled up the photos of the original tiles that remained in the theater restrooms. "These are the ones I tried to match."

Steve leaned over her shoulder, then looked at the tiles he'd laid out for her. "They're not a match, but they could work."

"That's what I thought. They complement nicely."

"How many would you need?" he asked.

"I had our contractor work it out." Allie took Joe's worksheet from her pocket and handed it to Steve.

"Let me see if I have enough on hand." He checked their computer and their warehouse, and five minutes later, Steve was ordering the tiles from the manufacturer, since they didn't have quite enough in the store.

"You don't want two different lots," he cautioned. "The colors could be off, and you don't want that."

On the way home, Allie said, "Well, that's one more thing I can cross off my list." She took a small notebook from her bag and did exactly that.

"You have an actual list," Cara said.

"I do, and it gives me great pleasure to draw that little line right through each item on it."

"What else do we still need to do?" Cara asked.

"Well, the floor's being worked on today, so that's a big one. The guys working downstairs have to finish up the wall, but I

stopped down there a few days ago and they said by Tuesday."
Allie referred to her list. "Paint the walls, but Joe has that lined up
for Wednesday. The carpets need to be cleaned."

"The grocery store rents out carpet-cleaning machines. Maybe
we could do that ourselves," Cara suggested.

"I think we should go the professional route. You have all those
rows to go through and all those seats to go under. Maybe the
Werner sisters could recommend someone. I can call them on
Monday and see when they'll be bringing back the curtains and
begin working on the seats. I keep forgetting to thank Joe for taking the curtains down and driving them over."

"He's been thanked. Next."

"Not much else. The guy who bought the theater from Fritz
had the marquee completely restored, so all we have to do is take
the boards off."

"You left off something important."

"What's that?" Allie looked back at the list of items. They'd
discussed them all.

"Restocking the candy counter."

"Well, if we were reopening the theater, that would be high on
the list," Allie said.

"Des and I think we should invite the entire community for
our big opening day. We could get the popcorn machine going,
stock some movie candy in the case, maybe get a soda machine.
Maybe even run an old film if any of them are still good. We were
going to discuss it with you and Barney after Nikki left. We know
she has to get back to school, and she'd be totally bummed if she
knew we were planning something she'd miss out on."

"We'll come back for it, whenever it is. I'd love for us to spend
Thanksgiving here."

"Does Barney know that?"

"Not yet."

"Wonderful. It wouldn't be a holiday without you guys." They'd
arrived back in Hidden Falls and were turning into the driveway at
the Hudson house.

Allie nodded. She'd been thinking the same thing. Holidays were for families, and she was sure Nikki would agree. While Clint was in California, he was on his way to starting a new family. But for Nikki and Allie, family was in Hidden Falls, and that's where they'd be come Thanksgiving.

CHAPTER NINETEEN

❖◆❖

"Nikki, are you dressed?" Allie tapped lightly on her daughter's bedroom door. "People will be arriving very soon."

"I'm coming."

Allie heard a drawer close and something hit the floor, but seconds later Nikki opened the door and came into the hall.

"How do I look?" she asked anxiously.

"Adorable." Allie realized such a term might not fill a fifteen-year-old's heart with confidence, so she added, "Beautiful."

Nikki moved her hair back to show off her dangly earrings. They were made of gold wire and looked like figure eights that twisted around and around themselves.

"Aunt Cara gave me these. She said her mother made them. Aren't they amazing? See how the light moves around on them when I turn my head?"

"I do. They're perfect. And they're you. Always changing, always moving."

"That's what Aunt Cara said." Nikki beamed. "But she said these weren't my birthday present. She gave me these just because she wanted me to have them. How great is she?"

"Pretty great. And I love that dress on you. It's adorable and the belt is just right," Allie said, approving Nikki's outfit. The dress was denim, sleeveless, collared, and buttoned down the front with

a frayed hem, and the perfect shade of blue. A half dozen bracelets made of colored stones wrapped around her left wrist, and
silver bangles swung on her right.

Barney announced when Nikki came downstairs, "The dress is
a perfect match to your Hudson blue eyes. Well, all of ours, actually. I might not have chosen a wide brown belt, but it's just right.
Nice job on the length, too. Not too short to make the adults
gasp, short enough to be young and hip." Barney appeared to
think about that for a moment. "Does anyone say *hip* anymore?"

"Not so much, Aunt Barney," Nikki said gently. "But you could
say *cool* and it would mean the same thing."

"Right. Cool. I knew that." Barney smiled. "Would you like
your present now, or would you rather open them all at the same
time?"

Nikki looked out the kitchen window. Seth and Des were
chatting as they hung up the last strand of fairy lights Nikki had
wanted in the trees around the patio, while Joe hung small speakers from low branches so the music from Nikki's hand-picked
playlist could be heard throughout the backyard. Cara had gone to
Rose Hill to pick up the birthday cake Barney had ordered from
the bakery there.

"I think maybe now," Nikki said.

"Wait here. I'll be right back." Barney went off to wherever
she'd stashed Nik's present.

"What do you suppose she got me?" Nikki whispered.

"I don't have a clue. But you know Barney. It could be anything, but whatever it is, I bet it will be just right."

Nikki nodded as Barney came back into the room, carrying a
package wrapped in white paper. Red ribbon wound around it and
ended in a big bow.

"Here you go, dear." Barney handed Nikki the gift.

"Oh, it's so pretty, Aunt Barney. I almost don't want to open
it." Nikki untied the bow and looked up, grinning. "I said almost."
The wrapping fell away and slid to the floor. "Oh, Aunt Barney. I
love this. It's beautiful."

She held up a leather-bound book with NIKKI'S JOURNAL and the year lettered in gold on the front.

"I never had a journal, but ever since you showed me the ones your grandmother kept, I've been thinking about it. Thank you so much." Nikki wrapped her arms around Barney and gave her a long hug. "I didn't even realize how much I wanted one until just now. I love it, and I love you. And look, Mom, it has my name on it."

"It's beautiful, Barney," Allie said.

"Look inside, Nikki." Barney gestured for her to open the book. Inside was a white envelope.

Nikki studied the two pieces of paper for a moment, then whooped. "Thank you! Thank you! You don't know how much I wanted this!"

"What is it?" Allie held out her hand and Nikki handed her the envelope. "Plane tickets for November. Oh, Thanksgiving week." She and her daughter exchanged a long look. Allie hadn't discussed coming back for the holiday with her daughter or her aunt. "Did you tell Aunt Barney you wanted to come back for that weekend?"

"No, but I wanted to so, so much! This is the best present I could have!" Nikki hugged Barney again. "Thank you for these and for my journal. This is the best birthday ever."

"Well, I hope you write all your best thoughts in that book, and if you do, I will give you another one next year," Barney told her.

Nikki nodded. "I will use it. It might be important someday."

"Important how?" Allie asked.

"I'm going to be an investigative journalist. I'm going to go all over the world and investigate things no one else wants to talk about. Like, a whistle-blower. I'm going to be famous." Nikki delivered her life plan in a matter-of-fact, straightforward way without hesitation or doubt. "Haley's going to be a photographer and she's going to come with me. Then when we come back, we're going to write a book together with her photos and my stories about what we found. Doesn't that sound like the best?"

"The absolute best. There's no question in my mind you will do whatever you set your mind to," Allie told her.

"Thumbs-up from me as well," Barney assured her. "That book will be a winner for sure. The two of you will do a bang-up job."

"Thanks."

"So what's Mark going to be doing while you and his sister are traveling the world?" Allie asked.

"Oh, he's going to law school." A sound from outside drew Nikki's attention. "Oh, Mark's here! And Hayley."

"Go on and greet them," Allie said. Nikki left the journal on the window seat and ran out the back door.

Allie heard Hayley exclaim, "Oh, I love your sandals," as Nikki went down the steps.

"How did you know I'd decided to come back for Thanksgiving?" Allie asked.

"I didn't. I wanted you to, and I thought if I purchased the tickets, you'd come."

Barney looked out the window. "How on earth did the universe decide to bless one child with so many gifts?" she asked. "She is remarkable, Allie. Smart and fearless and so much heart. I applaud the job you and Clint have done raising her. Well, having met Clint, I suppose the accolades should go mostly to you."

"Thanks, Barney. She's been a delight since the day she was born." Allie had to swallow back tears. She couldn't help but think about Nikki leaving in two days. It was like a knife to her heart. "It's interesting to see how much she's changed over the summer. She's a totally different girl than she was back in California. I haven't heard her mention the name of one shoe designer since she got here, and she's even talking about going to Haiti next year with Mark and Hayley's church group to build houses. I suppose I can thank them for having awakened her inner social conscience."

"She'd have come to it on her own, but the O'Hearn kids were raised right. Roseanne has been a single mother these past few years, and she runs a tight ship. Seth, as Roseanne's cousin, has been a wonderful influence as well. Now that little snit Courtney . . ."

"It's such a shame. All that negativity surrounds her like a dark cloud and she takes it wherever she goes. If I were Marlo, I'd have her talking to a therapist to find out what's at the bottom of it. She's a very unhappy girl, in my not-at-all-professional opinion."

"Don't try to make me feel sympathetic toward her. It's not going to work. She's still a little brat, regardless of what caused it," Barney said. "Now, let's go out and join the others. I see Ginger just pulled up with the goodies from the Goodbye." She started out the door. "Hmmm. Goodies from the Goodbye. Must do something with that. Maybe use that on the menus in place of simply saying *desserts*."

Allie stood at the back door and watched her daughter and Mark. They were standing apart from the others, and Nikki was chatting away, her usual animated self, Mark's hand slowly closing around hers. She held on to his hand, and Allie wondered how heartbroken Nikki would be if things were different when she returned in November.

She went out to help Barney arrange the food table with Nikki's requests: barbecued chicken, potato salad, corn on the cob, and a big tossed salad. For dessert, there would be the cake. That was all the birthday girl wanted, and Barney followed Nikki's wishes to the letter. Joe was hanging balloons from the trees, and the atmosphere was festive. Allie couldn't help but compare this one to the birthday parties Nikki's friends back home had, where it seemed each mother felt compelled to outdo the last party the kids had attended. This was relaxed and happy, with all the people Nikki loved best—well, except for her father, but Allie had sent him a text reminding him that Nikki's birthday was the following weekend, she was adamant about not wanting a party out there, and he should take her out to dinner—just her, not plus Marlo and Courtney—on the actual day, and ask her what she wanted. He'd texted back okay.

Tess and Wendy arrived, and Wendy joined the small group of friends that stood apart from the adults. She hugged Nikki and handed her a gayly wrapped gift, which Nikki added to the small but growing pile on a nearby chair. Tess came directly to the table where Barney and Allie had just finished placing platters of food. She greeted them both with smiles and commented on how pretty the yard looked.

"Your mother has returned from her trip?" Barney asked, though Allie knew that Barney knew darned well Justine was back. Why pretend not to know? Why pretend she hadn't come barging into the house, yelling at Barney and crying?

"She has. She had a great time with her cousins on the cruise."

"You should have brought her along," Barney said.

"Oh. Well, actually, she seemed to not want Wendy and me to come," Tess confided.

"Oh? Did she say why?" If Barney had thoughts on that, they didn't show on her face.

"Not really. I thought she was being silly. I told her Wendy wanted to be here, that Nikki had become one of her best friends, and it was going to be hard enough to go back to Kingston tomorrow knowing they wouldn't see each other until next year. I remembered how hard it was for me when I was a kid and we'd come to Hidden Falls for weeks at a time in summer and I knew no one. I was always an outsider. I was never here long enough to make friends. I'm sure you can understand how happy I was when Wendy and Nikki became friends."

"Well, you can let Wendy know we'll be here for Thanksgiving. They can get together over that weekend," Allie said.

"Oh, that would be wonderful," Tess said. "I'll tell her tonight when we get home. I know she'll be sad about leaving, so a little bit of good news might make it better."

Nikki turned up the music she'd chosen—a strange mixture of hip-hop, rock, country, classical, pop, and show tunes, but it seemed there was something for everyone to like. They ate dinner before the sun went down, then had cake, an extravagant-looking three layers with a marzipan dog on top that looked a lot like Buttons, much to Nikki's delight. She blew out all the candles and stood before the cake, her eyes closed solemnly, as she appeared to make her wish.

"Where's the cake from?" Allie asked Barney, who'd arranged for it.

"The bakery in Rose Hill. I've had to promise to order from them for the café for the next month, but it was the only way I could get them to take the order on such short notice."

The party began winding down when the sun set, but the fairy lights twinkled, and Joe went to his car to retrieve some tiki torches he'd brought from home. He returned to the yard accompanied by Ben, who carried an arrangement of flowers in a hot pink vase. Allie watched him present the flowers to Nikki, who jumped up from her seat to hug him. Nik set the vase on the table next to the remains of her cake, then pulled her phone from her pocket and took a picture, which she then showed to Ben, who nodded his approval.

Allie was disposing of the paper cake plates when Ben approached her. "Smooth move," she said.

"I have no idea what a fifteen-year-old girl likes or wants, and it was kind of short notice. But I haven't met a girl yet who didn't like flowers."

"She loved them. Thank you, Ben. I'm pretty sure she's going to try to find a way to fit at least some of those into her suitcase."

"So it's this week, definitely?" Ben asked.

Allie nodded. "Clint bought the tickets online a while ago and emailed them to her. It's going to be hard to put her on that plane. She really doesn't want to leave. Not that I blame her. She loves her friends here and she loves living with all of us. Barney, Des, Cara—it's like we've formed this very tight group."

"That's called a family." He looked behind her. "Is that beer I see in that cooler?"

"Joe brought it. And there's wine there as well."

"Nothing takes the place of a good cold beer. Can I get something for you?" She held up the glass of sparkling water in her hand, so Ben grabbed a beer for himself from the cooler and took off the lid. "So how would you feel about dinner on Thursday night?"

"I don't think I'd be very good company, but thanks. Maybe could we make it another time?"

"How 'bout Friday? If you're still blue, I promise I'll do everything I can to make you smile. Card tricks, magic tricks, tossing pizza dough, juggling. Stand-up comedy. Whatever it takes."

"Do you know how to do all that stuff?"

"No, but I figure between now and then, I'm good. I mean, how hard can any of that stuff be?"

"I admit I'm tempted to see you try your hand at juggling. And stand-up comedy? I never thought you were that funny, actually."

"I'm a man of many talents. So far, you only know me as the tough defender of the people of Hidden Falls. Believe me, that doesn't even scratch the surface of this guy."

"How can you say that with a straight face?"

"It was a challenge." He took a long drink from the bottle. "So what do you say? Dinner on Friday night?"

"Okay. As long as we're not talking the Goodbye."

He leaned forward and whispered, "Something wrong with the food there? You can tell me. I can keep a secret."

"No. The food is actually great for a small-town restaurant, as you very well know. But I spend all my waking hours between there and the theater. Which reminds me. You guys did a fabulous job on the floor! It's perfect."

"Thank you. It was our pleasure. Don't change the subject. Dinner on Friday will be at my place."

"Your place?" She raised an eyebrow.

He nodded. "Yup. I'm going to be your chef for the night."

"Don't take offense, but do you even know how to cook?"

"No offense taken. Yes, and I'm pretty damned good, if I do say so myself."

"Well, then, we're on. What time?"

"Seven thirty work for you?"

"Perfect. I'll be there."

"Great." He nodded again, his eyes still on her face.

Allie knew if they were alone in the backyard he'd be kissing her silly, and that would have been fine with her.

Bowing to the demands of the group, Nikki sat in a lawn chair and opened her presents. She was delighted to find that most of the packages contained books: Mary Stewart's *The Crystal Cave*, *The Hollow Hills*, and *The Last Enchantment* from Mark, who couldn't believe she hadn't read them; *The Night My Sister Went Missing*, by Carol Plum-Ucci from Hayley ("It's one of my favorites—I love a good mystery, don't you?"); from Wendy, Leigh Bardugo's *Six of Crows* duology ("I have them, too. We can read them together and Skype!"); and several books about inspiring real women from Cara and Joe—P. O'Connell Pearson's *Fly Girls*, and *Code Girls*, by Liza Mundy. Des and Seth gave her framed pictures of Buttons, Belle, and Ripley, and the litter of puppies Nikki had helped train. Proving the theory that great ideas do circle the universe, Tess had enlarged and framed a picture Des had taken on Wendy's phone of Nikki and Wendy playing with the puppies. All in all, Nikki had declared she'd never in her whole entire life had more fun at a party or received more perfect gifts.

"Mom, Nikki will be back over Thanksgiving. Is that the best news or what? Would you ask Nana if we can come for Thanksgiving?" Wendy said as she and Tess were getting ready to leave.

"Nikki's mom told me. I was going to save the news for when you got home tonight, but I'm glad Nikki told you. And yes, of course, I'm sure we can have Thanksgiving at Nana's." Tess put her arm around Wendy. "Allie, Barney, thank you so much for including us tonight. It was a great party."

"Nik, I'm going to miss you." Wendy hugged Nikki, and the two girls wept just a little, but not as much as they might have had they not known they'd see each other in November.

"She's really, like, my best friend," Nikki told Allie as Wendy and Tess disappeared down the dark driveway.

"I should get some lights along there all the way to the sidewalk," Barney said. "Oh, there's Tom. I wonder where he'd gotten to."

"Sorry to miss the party," he said as he joined them. "Something came up and I had some phone calls to make."

"Nothing serious, I hope?" Barney asked.

"Just some back-and-forth among the kids. Sometimes you have to play referee even when they're adults." He placed a loosely wrapped package on the end of the table. "That's for Nikki. Now, where can a guy get a piece of birthday cake?"

Barney tended to Tom and Allie watched Nikki walk down the darkened driveway with Mark to say goodbye in private. She was pretty sure Nikki would be kissing him goodbye, because Nikki was kissing everyone goodbye. Mark's mother and Hayley had left a few minutes before, and Allie assumed Mark would be walking home. She gathered up all the discarded paper plates and tossed them into the trash. Barney had insisted on using real flatware, so Allie took those inside, stopping to pick up the package Tom had left for Nikki. She placed it on the counter and rinsed the flatware, watching out the window where Ben, Joe, and Seth stood under the fairy lights talking. Occasional laughter drifted through the open kitchen window, making Allie smile even though she had no idea what had been said. It was a beautiful night, made more beautiful by the friends and the family who'd come together for her daughter's birthday. She had to agree with Nikki. It was the best birthday party ever.

Des and Seth started to take down the fairy lights from the trees, but Barney stopped them. "Nikki might want them tomorrow night. We'll take them down at the end of the week."

Soon everyone was getting ready to leave, Des and Seth on his Harley—it still killed Allie to see her oh-so-preppy little sister wrapped in a black leather jacket, a helmet over her unruly hair—and Cara and Joe in the pickup. Ben had left his police car at the station, which was across the street from the theater and an easy walk from the Hudsons' house.

"I'll see you at seven thirty on Friday," he told Allie when he came into the house to find her. He startled her as she was rinsing out bowls and washing the platters they'd served the food on. "But I just have to ask—is washing dishes your idea of a good time?"

310 • MARIAH STEWART

"No. In the past, if I threw a party, I wouldn't lift a finger. If I attended someone else's, I expected to be treated like a guest and be waited on. But tonight I have to keep myself busy. There are a lot of emotions at work right now, and I need to get them under control or I'll fall apart."

"You can fall apart on Friday. I promise to help pick up the pieces." He kissed her then, long and slow and perfectly.

Allie tilted her head back and looked into his face. "You're probably the best kisser I ever kissed. Please don't tell me where you learned to do that. I don't think I want to know."

He laughed and kissed her again.

"To be continued," he said. "Unless, of course, you do fall apart and the whole putting-back-together thing takes up the whole night."

"I will try to avoid having that happen."

They heard Barney and Tom coming up the steps. Ben said good night to everyone, then left by the front door. Nikki came in carrying her vase of flowers, her eyes a little red from what Allie suspected was a bout of tears. She took a deep breath, feeling bad for Nikki but understanding how her daughter felt. Allie was pretty sure she'd be crying when it was her turn to leave, too.

"I think I'm going to go upstairs and read for a while." Nikki stood in the doorway, the pile of books in her arms. "Did you see my books? They all look so wonderful I don't know what to read first. Thanks again, Mom. I had so much fun tonight. I'll see you in the morning."

Allie nodded and watched her daughter disappear into the back stairwell, her sandals tapping on the worn wooden steps. She finished straightening the kitchen before noticing Tom's package on the counter. She should take it up to Nikki, she thought, and she picked it up. The contents slid out of the poorly wrapped package, but she managed to catch it before it hit the floor. It was yet another photo, this one in an elaborate silver frame.

Allie turned the frame over—and stared at the black-and-white photo.

"Thank you so much for cleaning up, Allie, but really, I could have done it in the morning. I do appreciate not having to lug all those platters in, though. I thought maybe we'd—" Barney stopped dead in her tracks when Allie held up the photo.

"Why did Tom have this picture of Tess, and why would he give it to Nikki?" she asked.

Barney stared at the photograph for a very long moment, then said, "I suppose you'll have to ask Tom," right before she left the room.

With Allie's help the following evening, Nikki managed to fit all her clothes in the one suitcase she'd brought with her, but the books were another story.

"I have a nice leather tote that should hold them all." Barney left Nikki's room and went downstairs, returning a few minutes later with a bag that held all Nikki's books with room to spare. She gave Nikki a good-night kiss and went to her own room to turn in.

"Which book did you read last night?" Allie asked.

"I decided to read them in the order in which I opened them," Nikki told her. "Which meant I'd start with Mark's. But I just didn't feel like reading. Mom . . ."

"What, sweetie?"

"What if Mark decides he likes someone else more than he likes me while I'm in California?"

"What if you decide you like another boy more than you like Mark?"

"I never thought of that." Nikki frowned. "But that won't happen. Mark is special."

"Well, I bet Mark feels the same way about you. And if he doesn't—if you aren't as special to him—he's not the guy for you."

Nikki seemed to digest that for a moment. "You're right. But I think he does think I'm special."

"Then there's no point in worrying about it. Besides, the time is going to pass very quickly, you'll see. You'll be really busy when school starts, and the next thing you know, we'll be on a plane back here for Thanksgiving."

"I'm going to miss everyone so much." Nikki sat on the edge of the bed and pulled her legs up to her chest. "I never felt as much at home anywhere as I do here. Maybe when you and me and Dad lived together, but not since. Dad's house doesn't feel like my home. I feel like I just eat and sleep there. Especially when Courtney and her mom are there."

"How often is that?"

"A pretty lot, but it's okay. Court's mom is nice, much nicer than she is. But I love my aunts so much, I just want to be with them. Just think, before you came here, I didn't even know them. Now they're my family. They're like best friends, only better, because we're related, you know?"

"I do know," Allie said softly. "I think we both should get some sleep now. We're going to have to get up at a crazy-early time to get you to the airport on time."

"Gee, wouldn't it be a shame if I missed my plane?" Nikki slid under the covers.

"That's not going to happen." Allie laughed.

"I feel like if I stay awake, tomorrow won't come, and I won't have to leave." Nikki yawned.

"That's something you would have said when you were maybe five or six. Are you regressing?"

It was Nikki's turn to laugh. "I know it doesn't work like that. It was just a thought that popped into my head."

"Good night, sweetie. See you in the morning." Allie kissed her daughter on the cheek, turned off the light, and left the room.

Allie went downstairs in search of a bottle of sparkling water left over from the party and found Cara in the kitchen.

"I thought you were going to Joe's," Allie said as she went through the fridge.

"I need to stay here if I'm going to get you to the airport on time tomorrow."

"Nikki's kind of hoping you won't."

"I don't want her to get on that plane any more than anyone else does. But you won't be far behind her. And you can cross off the carpets, since the cleaners finished around one today."

"I didn't realize it took so long."

"Well, the point is that it's finished. So we're looking at maybe two more weeks and you can go. Actually, we can all go."

"Not that you will," Allie pointed out.

"Not that I will," Cara agreed.

"And Des, too. She'll stay. You'll both get married and settle down here and raise pretty families. More Hudsons for Hudsonville."

The back door opened and closed, and Des came in.

"We were just discussing the fact that with you guys staying there will be two more Hudsons living in town," Allie said.

"Allie referred to it as Hudsonville," Cara said.

"Cute." Des nodded. "Anyone join me in a glass of wine?"

Cara raised her hand, but Allie declined.

"Why aren't you staying at Seth's tonight?" Cara asked.

"No way is that kid leaving town without me here to say goodbye to her." Des moved things around in the fridge, searching for an open bottle. "I know there's one in here. Oh, here we go." She stood up, a bottle of merlot in her hand. "And I know I'm going to bawl my eyes out tomorrow."

"That'll make five of us." Allie knew they'd all be weepy in the morning.

"You know she belongs here with us, right?" Des stated the obvious. She uncorked the bottle while Cara grabbed two wineglasses from the cupboard.

"She knows it, too. Nothing we can do about it right now. Her father has visitation rights. I can't take her out of the state to live unless he agrees to it." Allie stepped back as the scent from the bottle reached her nostrils.

"What are the chances that could happen?" Cara brought the glasses to the table and Des filled them.

"What do you think?" Allie made a face. She drained her glass

314 • MARIAH STEWART

of sparkling water, then immediately refilled it. She was deter-mined she was not going to have a glass of wine regardless of how good it smelled. She was afraid in her current state of mind she'd drink the entire thing.

Des pressed her. "So there's nothing that can be done about that?"

"Nope."

The three fell silent.

Finally, Des asked, "So what's with you and Ben?"

Allie shrugged. "If I knew, I'd tell you, but I don't. With me leaving, apparently even sooner than I realized, there just isn't time to . . . you know."

"We don't know." Cara gestured for her to keep going.

"It's occurred to me that if Ben and I hadn't been trying to out-snark each other all these months, we might have had something worth thinking about. Now . . ." She shrugged. "Too late. The clock's run out."

"It's never too late," Cara and Des said at the same time, then toasted each other.

"Cara, you said yourself, the theater will be done in a few more weeks and I'll be outta here."

"You don't sound as happy about that as you used to," Des said.

Allie shrugged. "Something else I can't do anything about."

"This stinks."

"Let's talk about something fun." Allie needed to change the subject. "When are we going to have the open house for the the-ater? You know, where the community is invited, and the local papers come, and the TV stations send cameras?"

"Not till you and Nikki are here," Des said adamantly. "We're not rolling out the red carpet for anyone without you two."

"Just give me a date," Allie told them, "and we'll be here." She looked from one sister to the other, wondering what they were thinking about the future of the theater. "And then what?"

"We'll have to talk about that. The three of us. And Barney.

She's going to want to throw her two cents in," Cara reminded them.

"But what do you want to do?" Allie persisted.

"I want to reopen it as a theater." Des's glass was empty, so she poured herself a little more wine. "Otherwise, what was the point of the past six months?"

"Almost seven, but who's counting?" Cara smiled. "Do you realize what we accomplished in less than a year?"

Des nodded. "We're awesome."

"We are," Allie said.

"Nikki asked me if we could do summer stage next year." Des grinned. "Then she asked if she could pick the play."

"That's my girl," Allie said, right before she burst into tears. "Pride and sadness, sisters, that's all. It'll pass."

"You have no idea how much we are going to miss you," Des said quietly. "Nikki, yes, our hearts are bleeding because she's going home. But we're going to miss you like crazy." Des tilted her head, then asked Cara, "Did I really just say that?"

"You did." Cara poured the little remaining wine into her glass. "And what Des said."

"I'll miss you, too. I'll miss everything about Hudsonville. I'm even going to miss working at the Goodbye."

Des set her glass quietly on the table. "Who are you, and what have you done with my snarky diva of a sister?"

"It must be something in the water here," Allie said. "I'm sure I'll be myself again once I get back to California."

"It's been a great summer," Cara said. "Could be the best summer of my life. But it's coming to an end, the way summer always does. And that's more than I can think about right now, and since I have to get up early tomorrow and actually drive to the airport, I'm going to bed."

"Me, too." Des rinsed her wineglass at the sink, then followed Cara into the hall.

"I'm right behind you." Allie locked the back door, then turned off the lights and headed upstairs.

CHAPTER TWENTY

"Nikki, are you sure you have everything?" Allie stood at the back of Cara's car, the trunk open, Nikki's suitcase inside.

"Pretty sure. If I left anything, you can mail it to me. Or bring it when you come ho— Back to California."

"I'll be back out there sooner than you think."

Nikki turned to Barney, who clutched an old-fashioned handkerchief with a fancy crocheted edge in her hands.

"Thanks for loaning me *The Nightingale*, Aunt Barney. I'll bring it back when I come for Thanksgiving. I'll take good care of it."

"I know you will, dear girl." Barney cleared her throat. "Buttons is going to miss you."

"I love you, Barney." Nikki hugged Barney, then picked up the little dog, who sensed somehow that something important was happening. She licked Nikki's face as if they'd just been reunited after a long separation. "I love you, too, Buttons. You're my first dog."

Nikki kept the dog in her arms as she hugged Des. "I love you, Aunt Des. Thanks for letting me work with your dogs and showing me how to teach them things. And for letting me and my friends hang out with you this summer at Seth's farm."

"You were such a big help with the dogs. I don't know what I'll do without you."

"Mark said he'd help."

"Yes, he did. I'll be sure to call on him and Hayley from time to time." Des embraced her niece. "Love you, child."

"Love you back." Nikki turned to Allie. "I think we need to go now."

"We do." To Barney and Des, Allie said, "We'll be back in a few hours."

Nikki had asked to sit in the back alone so she could play music and text her friends, so Allie got into the front passenger seat. Cara slid behind the wheel and started the car.

"All right, kiddies. We're on our way. Allie, you have the directions, right?"

"I forgot you don't have GPS. I'll do a search on my phone."

Allie opened her bag, but Nikki piped up from the back seat, "I have the GPS app. I'll look up the address for the airport and I'll type it in so I can tell you when to turn and stuff."

"Great. Thanks."

Nikki began to type a text to someone, and after driving in silence, Cara turned on the radio. After several miles, Cara said, "So, Nik. Aunt Des told me you want to help pick out the play for next year's summer stage."

"OMG, you're going to do it? You're going to reopen the theater? That's the best news ever!" Nikki almost bounced out of her seat belt. "I'll think about it. We did a lot of plays at school, so I know a bunch of them. I like *Our Town*, but I think everyone does it. Oh! I know! Let's do *Spoon River Anthology*! I love that. Mom, do you know it? It's like, all these dead people talking . . ."

And so it went, all the way to the Wilkes-Barre/Scranton Airport.

When it came time to say goodbye, Allie held it together quite remarkably, as did Nikki. Oddly, it was Cara who lost it.

"Sorry, sweetie. It's just that I spent my whole life without your sisters, and finding them and Barney has been the greatest blessing of my life. But you, my sweet girl, you are the icing on the cake. Best niece ever."

"Same here, Aunt Cara. You guys are the best aunts in the world, and I'm the luckiest girl I know."

Nikki turned to Allie. "Talk to you soon, Mom. I love you."

"Love you more, sweetie."

And with one little wave of her hand, Nikki passed through to security, and she was gone.

Allie stood mutely for a moment, as if she'd been caught off guard rather than having been fully aware that Nik was going to proceed to board her plane alone.

Cara touched her arm and said, "Allie, time to go."

They walked back to the short-term parking lot and found the car. On the way out of the airport, Cara said, "You know that seat reclines. I don't expect you got too much sleep last night."

"I didn't." Allie found the lever and let the seat drop back. "Thanks, Cara, for driving us."

"You're welcome."

Allie closed her eyes, not to sleep, but to be alone with her thoughts. There was very little conversation on the way home except when Cara asked Allie if she recognized this landmark or that. On their way into Hidden Falls, Allie sat up.

"Would you drop me off at the theater?" she asked.

"Sure, but I thought you finished the ceiling. It looked finished the other day when I stopped over there to see how the guys were doing with the floor sanding."

"I am finished. I just want to check something."

"Okay." Cara turned into the library parking lot to turn around, then stopped in front of the theater. "Here you go."

"Thanks. I'll see you back at the house."

Allie got out of the car and went straight into the theater. Music drifted up from the basement as it did every day. She walked into the lobby and found the scaffold had been removed. Looking up at the ceiling, she felt a flush of pride. Everyone was right. You couldn't tell where the repairs were made. From the lobby, she walked through the audience to the very back of the theater and up the stairs to the stage. The newly refinished floor was beautiful. She knelt and ran her hand over the wood. It was smooth and shiny, the splintered areas gone. The three guys had done a wonderful job.

She went back into the audience and took a seat in the first row, imagining Nikki performing in a play on the stage where Nora's very big dreams were born, and where her parents had fallen in love. Nikki would have her way, and the theater would be open for summer stage next year, Allie had no doubt.

Allie went back to the house and took a long nap. When she woke up late in the afternoon, she found the house was too quiet and the silence too stark. Her phone alerted her to an incoming text from Nikki.

Back at Dad's safe and sound. xxoo.

Already? Unpacked? Everything OK? Did Dad take you to lunch? xxox, Mom

Haven't unpacked. Will later. Leaving now to pick up Courtney and her mom for lunch.

Allie counted to ten. When she found that ten wasn't long enough, she started over and counted to twenty-five before speed-dialing Clint.

"You couldn't even spend your daughter's first few hours at home with just Nikki?"

"Marlo thought it would be a nice welcome home." Clint sounded confused.

"Well, it's not." Allie proceeded to tell Clint all the ways in which Courtney had been making Nikki's life miserable, even from across the country. "And I hope you remembered to tell Marlo that Nik doesn't want a birthday party."

"Why wouldn't she want a party?" Again, confusion seemed to reign. "I'm pretty sure Marlo and Courtney have been planning—"

"I don't care. I told you before, she had her party here and she doesn't want one out there. Tell them no."

Clint sighed. "I'll try to call it off."

"No. You *will* call it off. Grow a pair, will you?"

"Fine. The party's off. Anything else?"

"Yes. On her birthday, take Nikki out to dinner. Just you and Nik. Not you and Nik and Marlo and Courtney."

"Fine."

"Clint, you need to understand that child is toxic and she's being really horrible to Nikki. Keep them separated and stop planning things that throw them together."

"Are you finished?"

"For now."

"Good." Clint hung up.

Allie covered her face with her hands. Was he really that dense? Or was he just so in love with Marlo that when she said Courtney was being nice to Nikki he believed her? Allie knew she was going to have to keep a close eye on the situation.

It was so quiet in the house with everyone gone, Allie changed into her white shirt and black pants and walked to the Goodbye. Whoever was covering for her could leave. She wasn't going to sit in the house and feel sorry for herself for the rest of the night. When she got to the café, she was surprised to find Barney, rather than Ginger, on the front desk.

"What are you doing here?" Barney asked.

"It was too quiet at the house. Cara's out in the carriage house telling Joe what she wants done in there, and Des is out at the farm. Why are you here?"

"Same reason."

"What did you do all those years you lived alone, Barney?"

"That was different. I was used to it. Now that I'm used to a little hustle and bustle, everyone leaves. You don't have to be here. I can cover for the rest of the night."

"Thanks, Barney, I appreciate it. But I feel like I need to keep moving tonight."

"All right. The desk is yours. I think I'll go home and read for a while."

"Where's Tom these days?"

"Still refereeing his children. Apparently for years, no one wanted anything from Tom's parents' home. Now everyone wants everything."

Barney stopped at several tables on her way to the door, and Allie picked up where her aunt had left off, chatting with the regular customers, making small talk with the first-timers.

Ben came through the door and asked, "You okay?"

Allie forced a smile. "Just skippy."

"We still on for tomorrow night?"

She nodded. "Seven thirty. Your place."

"See you then." Ben left and hopped into the cruiser he'd left running next to the curb.

Just as Allie was closing, Cara walked in.

"Why aren't you at Joe's?" Allie asked.

"I thought I'd walk home with you."

Allie's first inclination was to say something like, "That's all right. You don't have to." But instead, she thanked Cara, surprised at how comforted she felt by her presence on the way home. They walked mostly in silence, but the quiet support on such an emotional day was soothing.

Barney was walking into the sitting room just as Allie and Cara came through the front door.

Allie remembered what she'd wanted to ask Barney.

"Barney, why did Tom have a picture of Tess, and why did he give it to Nikki?"

Instead of responding, Barney picked up her book and pretended not to have heard.

"Barney, come on. What's going on?"

"What are you talking about?" Cara asked.

"Show her," Allie said to Barney. "Show her the photo."

The front door opened and closed, and Des called out, "Anyone home?"

"We're all in here," Allie called back. "Come in."

Des walked in with Buttons on the leash. She knelt to remove the dog's harness, looked up, and asked, "What's everyone doing?"

"Barney's just about to show us a photograph that Tom had framed for Nikki," Allie told her.

"Allie, sometimes it's wisest to leave things alone." Barney glared at her.

"I don't understand what the big deal is."

Barney got up and left the room, her footsteps pounding on the stairs as she went to the second floor, obviously displeased. She returned in a minute with the photo in her hand.

She held it up so all three of her nieces could see it.

Allie took a closer look at the photo, then sighed. She should have seen it right away.

"It's not Tess." Allie looked directly at Barney. "It's you."

Barney nodded. "Tom took that picture when I was a sophomore in high school. I was at their house doing a homework project with his sister, Emily. We went out to the backyard, and that's where Tom took the picture. He thought Nikki would get a kick out of having a photo of me at her age. I'd just turned fifteen."

Des moved closer to the photo, then took it from Barney's hands. "It really does look like Tess."

She held it out to Cara, who said, "Wow, there really is a strong resemblance. That's so odd."

"Not so very odd"—Barney's voice was heavy with resignation—"when you consider Tess is my niece."

The silence that followed was palpable.

"Wait . . . you mean Tess isn't Stephen Kennedy's daughter?" Cara asked.

"She's . . ." Des couldn't get the words out.

"Dad's," Allie said. "She's Dad's daughter with Justine, am I right?"

Barney nodded. "She is."

"Did you know?" Cara asked.

"Of course not." Barney shook her head adamantly.

"That's why Justine was so angry when she found out you bought the Goodbye. Why she didn't want to bake for us," Des said.

"I couldn't understand her attitude. I went to her house think-ing we could come to an agreement, but you remember how that worked out. It made no sense to me. Until I saw Tess. One look at her, and I knew. It was like looking at myself at her age. I could hardly believe it, but I couldn't deny it, either."

"That's why you wanted Justine to confront you," Allie said.

"I couldn't very well go to her house and say, *'Look, I know you had this child with my brother.'* I had to wait for her to come to me. When she got back from her vacation and Tess told her how Wendy had found the necklace and how they'd returned it, and how we'd taken them to dinner as a thank-you, Justine just about had a heart attack. When she came here that day and I told her I knew, she fell apart. She was afraid I'd tell Tess, you see. I assured her I never would."

"So she admitted it?" Des asked.

"She couldn't very well have denied it. The proof is in her daughter's face."

"Did Dad know? Did she tell you what happened?" Allie asked.

"She said she realized she was pregnant after Fritz left town with Nora and she had no way of contacting him, so no, she never told him."

"She could have told you," Cara pointed out.

"She said she came to the house one day and spoke to Mother, but that Mother seemed very vague and didn't seem to understand. I told her my mother had Alzheimer's and was vague about a lot of things back then. Anyway, Justine had just finished her first year of law school. She and Stephen had been dating, but they'd broken up because he took a job in Kingston and she began to go out with Fritz on the sly because everyone knew he was with Nora. Justine didn't realize she was pregnant until about six weeks later. Well, about that time, Stephen de-cided he couldn't live without her and he begged her to marry him. Justine told him the truth, that she was carrying another man's child, and it had been a horrible mistake on her part, but there it was. Stephen didn't care. He loved her and promised to raise the baby as his own, and from all accounts, he did exactly that. No one—not even Justine's parents—knew about her brief fling with Fritz. Eventually her sister did figure it out—she knew about Justine and Fritz, as you may recall from reading the letters."

Allie nodded. "Her sister warned her about Dad."

"Yes, and remember I went all through school with her sister. As Tess grew older and looked more and more like me, and less and less like Justine or Stephen, her sister put two and two together. But they agreed no one would be the wiser, since Tess didn't live in Hidden Falls." Barney sighed deeply. "Justine's guarded that secret carefully because Stephen was such a wonderful father to Tess. She never wanted Tess to know."

"And then Nikki arrived in town and she and Wendy met and became the best of friends," Cara said. "Talk about life being stranger than fiction."

"Nik and Wendy becoming friends put this whole thing in motion," Barney agreed. "We might never have crossed paths with Tess, and we'd be none the wiser."

"Nik and Wendy are cousins, and we can't even tell them," Allie noted. "Is Justine going to tell Tess?"

"She's trying to figure out what to do. But it's her decision to make, hers and only hers. I gave her my word not to interfere, and not to tell anyone, and yet here I am, telling the three of you."

"You didn't have a choice. Once we saw the photo, there were questions," Allie said.

"Which is why I didn't want Nikki to see it. Why I hid Tom's present," Barney admitted.

"Nikki isn't aware Tom brought her a present. You did the right thing," Allie assured her.

"So what do we do now?" Cara asked.

"Nothing. It's all in Justine's hands. I imagine she'll let me know once she makes a decision, but I wouldn't be surprised if she did nothing," Barney said.

Allie, Des, and Cara exchanged a long look.

Finally, Allie said, "And then there were four . . ."

After they all retired to their rooms, the subject of Tess having been exhausted, Allie got ready for bed and opened the window, and cool night air drifted in. She felt her brain was at the breaking point, between Nikki leaving and Clint being so damned clueless and finding out that Tess was her half sister. She went into the bathroom and came back with her half-filled bottle of vodka. She never drank it straight, but she was tempted. She'd been avoiding alcohol in any form because of Nikki, but now Nikki was gone. She held the closed bottle in her hands. All she had to do was go downstairs and get something to mix it with—there was still lemonade in the fridge, wasn't there? In five minutes she could be enjoying a cocktail, and God knew she needed one. She deserved one after the week she'd had, and how hard she'd been working. Just holding the bottle reminded her how much she enjoyed a little bit of a buzz. What was the big deal about having just one drink?

It was a big deal, she admitted, because she'd never had just one drink. She was able to ease off it when Nikki was around, but now Nikki was gone.

She swung the bottle gently between her fingers, watching the clear liquid splash softly against the sides of the bottle. It would be so easy to open it and let the vodka soothe her ragged nerves. All she had to do was open the bottle and take a sip.

Allie got up and walked into the bathroom and put the bottle back on the shelf. She got into bed and turned out the light and reminded herself she needed to keep her eye on the prize and finish the work at the theater so she could go back to her daughter. Nikki was going to need her to be there for her if her love-struck father wasn't going to stand up for her. If ever Allie needed to be responsible, it was now. Besides, if Nikki found out she'd been secretly drinking, she'd be so disappointed.

Allie got up and went back into the bathroom and turned on the overhead light. She grabbed the bottle and opened it. She stared at it for a moment, then turned it over and poured its contents down the drain without regret. She went back to her bed and slept deeply.

When Allie arrived at the theater the next day, she headed straight to the basement to check on the status of the concrete wall.

"How much longer?" she asked the job foreman.

"Two, three days," he told her. "No more than the beginning of next week."

"Thanks." Allie smiled and went into the office in the basement. They had one, they might as well use it. She rearranged the furniture, asking one of the guys in the hall to give her a hand with the desk. She borrowed the shop vacuum from the contractor and cleaned up the floor, the desk, and the underside of the chair to make sure there were no critters lying in wait. Next, she washed down the desktop and the chair. Once both dried, she sat at the desk and opened her notebook.

Her first call was to the Werner sisters to see what their schedule looked like. Rita told her they were planning on coming on Tuesday and they'd work through the weekend. If necessary, one of them would be back to finish before the end of the week. They'd bring back the stage curtains and start on the chairs.

Her second call was to the tile salesman to check on the delivery of the tile.

"I was just going to call you," he said. "The tiles will be here on Wednesday morning and you can pick them up anytime after noon."

"Thanks. We'll have someone there at noon on the dot." She hung up and sent a text to Joe, asking if he could pick up the tiles on Wednesday.

Joe called her minutes later. "Sorry, Allie," he said. "I'll be tied up on a job. But if you can get them, I'll start setting them over the following weekend."

"Thanks. Let me see what I can do."

Allie thought for a moment. She didn't want to ask Seth to drop what he was doing, but she knew the boxes of tile were going to be heavy. She sent texts to Cara and Des, and they both agreed to meet her at the theater when she got back to help her carry the tiles from the car into the building. She called the tile store back and confirmed they'd have someone there to load the boxes into the car for her, then crossed another item off her list. She was feeling so efficient her head was spinning.

Feeling in control felt so much better than being hungover, she realized. She was glad she'd opted to give it a try.

She heard a commotion upstairs, and when she went into the lobby, found the painters Joe had hired setting up to start working on the first-floor walls. She showed them the areas they wanted painted, including the walls in the two restrooms, then she headed for the house. She needed to check out something on the third floor.

Barney had said that her mother and her grandmother moved things up to the third floor when they no longer wanted them, but they never got rid of a thing. Allie'd been in the attic several times and knew there was a room up there filled with furniture that had been replaced as styles and trends changed. She was hoping to find some special pieces for the ladies' room.

The house was quiet, but today the silence didn't bother her. She marched up to the third floor and went directly to the room where the furniture was stored. She moved things around, pulling out a piece here and a piece there. In the end, she'd selected an Eastlake love seat and a pair of matching chairs. She moved them onto the landing, closed the door, then went into the attic. There were stacks of paintings and mirrors of every size and shape. She spent the next two hours looking over mirrors and rejecting some—too big, too small, the frame wasn't right—and eventually finding several that she thought would be perfect. Next, she sorted through the artwork, through paintings and prints, until she found exactly what she'd had in mind. She lugged all her findings onto the landing with the furniture. When she heard the front door slam, she leaned over the balcony.

"Barney, if that's you, could you please come up?"

"Now? Must I?" Barney called back. "I've been on my feet all morning."

"I need to show you something."

"Oh, all right." Barney reluctantly made her way up the stairs. When she got to the landing, she looked around at everything Allie'd pulled out. "What's all this?"

"This is what I'd like to put in the ladies' room in the theater once the tile is completed. This love seat and these chairs are perfect."

Barney looked them over. "The upholstery looks like it's in good condition. And I'll bet it's the original horsehair. And these prints—perfect for the vintage look of the theater."

"I was hoping to use the mirrors in there as well."

"Absolutely. Take whatever you want. What about the men's room?"

"I thought maybe a few cushy leather chairs. I'll see if Des and Cara agree, then I'll look online for something reasonably priced. I saw a few prints in the attic that I think would go perfectly with the leather seating."

"Well, then, it sounds like you have everything under control. May I please go take a shower now?" Barney asked.

"Go." Allie sat on the love seat while she ran an online search on her phone for leather chairs. When she found something she liked, she sent the picture in a group message to Des and Cara, explaining what she wanted them for. Both replied almost immediately.

Love it. Go for it—D.

Agreed. Order—C.

What about the ladies' room?—D.

Will show you when you get home—A.

Allie looked at the time on her phone and realized she needed to get to the Goodbye. She felt she'd taken advantage of the staff enough this week, even though no one had protested, and everyone had seemed happy to have the extra hours. Ginger was going to come in to take over for her at six thirty, so she'd have time to get ready to go to Ben's and get there by seven thirty.

She went down to her room, cleaned up, changed, and set off for Main Street. She was feeling pretty good about herself. Last night she'd beaten back a demon and today she'd taken control of the theater situation with both hands. She'd be seeing Ben later for dinner and she was looking forward to it.

She enjoyed this little bit of walk into the center of town every day. Back in California, there'd been spin classes and Pilates, but walking had never been her thing. Here it seemed natural. Mark drove by in Seth's truck and beeped the horn. She waved and wondered how many times he and Nikki had messaged each other in the past twenty-four hours. She thought again how Nikki's friendship with Mark and Hayley had led to her getting to know Wendy, and that had led to Tess, and that had led to . . .

Whew.

She went into the café and after greeting that day's waitstaff, made the rounds of several tables. There were regulars who came in every day, people who were lonely or who needed a quick stop in their busy schedule. Barney had been right when she'd said the Goodbye was important in the framework of the town. She'd been right to buy it rather than see it boarded up until another buyer could be found.

The lunch hour was busy even by the Goodbye's standards, and by the time Ginger arrived, Allie was ready to bolt. When she returned to the house, she found Des and Cara waiting. The minute they heard her come up the stairs, they opened their bedroom doors and came into the hall.

"You're home early," Cara said.

"I . . . uh . . ." Allie stammered.

"You're having dinner with Ben. At his place. Just the two of you." Des leaned back against her doorjamb.

330 • MARIAH STEWART

"How'd you find out?" Allie opened her bedroom door and went inside. Her attempts to close her sisters out were useless.

"Duh. Seth." Des came in and sat on Allie's bed. "What are you going to wear?"

"What are we, sixteen?" Allie dropped her bag on the chair.

"So. What are you going to wear?" Cara joined Des on the bed.

"Oh my God, are you two going to interrogate me?"

"This is nothing compared to what it's going to be like tomorrow," Des told her with a straight face. "You know. The morning after."

Allie covered her face with her hands. "I'll be back tonight. I promise there will be no morning after."

"So she says now." Des wiggled her eyebrows, and Allie laughed in spite of herself.

"Look. This is just dinner."

"If you say so." Cara smiled sweetly. "So what are you wearing?"

"Seriously? I have to answer this?"

Des and Cara both nodded.

"Okay, so it's been a little cooler at night, so I thought just a pair of pants and a top."

"Which top?" Cara asked.

Allie opened her closet door and searched for the shirt she had in mind. When she found the white silk top with the white embroidery on the sleeves, she held it up. "This one."

"Oh, pretty." Cara leaned forward to touch it. "Nice."

"Des, does this have your approval?" Allie asked.

Des nodded. "It's beautiful. I never saw that one before."

"Because I haven't worn it before. Now, both of you leave so I can get out of here on time."

They got up to leave, Des already out the door, but Cara stopped in the doorway. "How are you getting there?"

"I'm walking, why?"

"I could drive you if you want."

"What, like you're my mother driving me to the movies where I'm going to meet all my little friends?"

"Something like that, yeah." Cara grinned.

"Thanks, but I'll walk." Allie started to close the door, then paused. "Guys. Thanks."

"Anytime. And talk to me before you leave"—Cara grinned—"so we can discuss your curfew."

CHAPTER TWENTY-ONE

◆◆◆

It was only a ten-minute walk to Ben's apartment, but Allie spent most of it trying to calm the butterflies that had taken up residence in her stomach. The only other time she'd been to Ben's apartment, he'd not only kicked her out, he'd blocked her out of his life completely until the recent night they'd called a truce. She stopped to read a text from Nikki—the sidewalk was too uneven to walk and read at the same time, and she was carrying a package in one hand—then resumed walking while she tried to decide how to respond. Clint had suggested they all—all meaning he, Nik, Marlo, and Courtney—spend the weekend in San Francisco before school started on Monday, but Nikki didn't want to go, for the obvious reasons. Allie stopped in front of Ben's apartment and texted back that she'd talk to Nik's father in the morning.

What part of *keep Courtney away from Nikki* did that man not understand?

"Penny for your thoughts." Ben had opened the door and stood on the top step.

"Oh. Sorry. I just had to reply to a text from Nikki." She put her phone into her bag, then looked up. "'You may kiss the cook'? You're wearing an apron that says, 'You may kiss the cook'?"

Ben laughed. "Joe's mother gave it to me for Christmas last year along with a couple of cookbooks. She thought it would be helpful."

"Has it been?"

"More or less." Ben stepped aside so she could enter, then closed the door behind her.

"Well, then." Allie leaned in and kissed him lightly. "Have you used the cookbooks?"

"Using one of them tonight."

"Wow. It smells great." She followed Ben into the kitchen, where she leaned over a pan on the stove. "Ummm. That looks like chicken in some sort of sauce."

"That's what it's called. Chicken in some sort of sauce."

She handed him the package she'd been carrying. He opened it and slid out a six-pack of beer. "I thought you were bringing a bottle of wine." Ben took one beer and put the rest into the refrigerator.

"I had second thoughts," she told him. "I decided I liked it too much." She met his eyes for a moment, took a deep breath, and said, "You were right about me that first night. I had been drinking shots at the Frog. And the night we were all there when they were playing all that country music and Joe's sister was crying over some guy who'd been cheating on her—you were right about me that night, too. I do have a drinking problem. It's been a problem for more than a year. I have it under control, but I know it wouldn't take much to push me over the edge. I've decided I need to be more cognizant of my tendency to go there when I'm upset or depressed."

He stared at her as if not knowing what to say.

"I haven't been drinking much this summer," she told him. "Not while Nikki was here. I had a bottle of vodka in my bathroom, which was my emergency stash."

"*Was?* Did you polish it off?"

She shook her head. "I wanted to. Boy, did I want to. Last night, as a matter of fact. I came really close. But I poured it down the drain. The temptation was too great to keep it around. I need to . . ."

Ben gestured for her to finish her sentence.

"I need to be more responsible. Nikki's in a lousy situation and she needs me to be the kind of mom who takes care of her."

"You do take care of her. You're a great mom, Allie. You don't have to worry about that. But you're smart to worry about your drinking. Good for you to recognize it for what it is. Have you thought about joining AA?"

Allie nodded. "I have. Right now, I'm in control and I intend to stay in control. But if I ever thought I was careening off course, I hope I'd have the presence of mind to recognize it and I'd join. I know people who weren't alcoholics but who knew they had that predilection who joined, and they said it helped to avoid falling back into dependency. I may have told you my mother was an alcoholic. I need to be aware that I could go down that path if I'm not careful."

"AA's not a magic bullet, but it has helped a lot of people." He stirred something on the stove with a wooden spoon, then turned back to her. "If you ever wanted to go, the Episcopal church over on Walnut Street has meetings on Tuesday night."

"I'm not planning on being here that much longer, but thanks anyway." She swallowed hard. "I just wanted you to know. That, you know, you were right. And I should have listened."

He rested the spoon on the side of the pan and put his arms around her. "Thank you. Not just for admitting I was right—though I know that must have been hard for you—but for owning up to yourself."

"Nikki—"

"Forget Nikki for a moment. Nikki's not always going to be a kid, but you're always going to have to live with yourself."

She nodded. She knew he was right. "We—Nik and I—were talking the other night about how she would be going away to college in three years, and it's really made me think. I've poured so much of myself into being this perfect mother . . ."

"Hot tip, girl. No one's mother is perfect. It's not going to happen. That doesn't mean you shouldn't want to be the best Allie, the best mom. Just don't expect yourself to be able to walk on water."

Allie smiled. Everything he said was true. "You're smarter than

I'd been giving you credit for. Actually, I thought you were pretty boneheaded and I figured you for a—"

He cut her off with a kiss. Allie wound her arms around his neck and melted into him, kissing him back with everything that had been building inside her.

"Whoa." He leaned back and looked into her eyes. "Are you trying to seduce me, Mrs. Monroe?"

"Ha. Nice play on *The Graduate*, Sheriff."

"Thank you. Now answer the question."

"It's a possibility. So, maybe."

"Maybe, but not tonight. We're going to take this thing really slow."

"How slow?" She narrowed her eyes. "Just so I know."

"How long have we been sniping at each other? Six months? Seven?"

She counted on her fingers from March to September. "Something like that."

"It took us a long time to decide not to hate each other. Let's take a little longer to figure out how much we like each other."

"But I already figured out that I like you. And I thought you liked me." Was he just not as attracted to her as she was to him? Had she totally misread him?

"I do like you. More than I thought I could. But here's the thing. I'm not in the market for a fling."

"What makes you think I'm into flings? Whatever that means, exactly."

"Let's just say that's all I've been doing for the past year. I don't think I want temporary with you. I think I might want something a little more solid, see if we can spend a few hours in each other's exclusive company without resorting to picking at each other. Tonight's the first step. Let's see how it goes, okay?"

"Okay. I guess." Did she want something more solid with Ben? By solid, she was pretty sure he meant lasting. Is that what she wanted? "You know I'm moving back to California when the theater is finished, right?"

"Right. By my calculations, that should be maybe two more weeks."

Allie nodded. "That's about right."

"So then you go back. You've never pretended you were planning on staying."

"So how do you figure we're going to be able to build something solid—by that you mean lasting, right?" she added just to confirm.

"That's exactly what I meant."

"How do you figure that's going to happen with you on one side of the country and me on the other?"

"You'll be coming back. I can't see you staying away from your sisters and Barney for too long at a time."

"Of course I'll be coming back."

"Holidays and school breaks, summer vacations?"

"Yeah, Nikki's already talked Des and Cara into doing summer stage next year."

"So you'll be here for most of the summer."

"If I can talk Clint into it." She told Ben about her plan to revert to their original custody agreement, then added, "He's going to want some time in the summer."

"Then you'll work that out. My point is that you and I have plenty of time. Maybe I could come out there and visit you. I've never been to Los Angeles."

"You're really serious."

"I don't say things I don't mean, Allie. After all these months of giving each other our worst, can we see if there's something better we can offer each other?"

She nodded slowly. "I like that idea. I'm pretty sure there is something better in each of us."

"My point."

"But just so you know. The earliest I could move back here—if that's what I decide to do—would be three years." She smiled and whispered in his ear, "Are you saying you want to wait three years before we sleep together?"

"I think you're reading a little too much into the part where I said let's take a little longer."

Her smile spread slowly. "Just so we understand each other."

"I think we do."

"Good. Oh, Ben, whatever is in the pot on the back of the stove is burning. Like, it's black."

"Oh crap." He turned and grabbed a mitt and picked up the pot. "That was our rice."

"Ah, I think the chicken is done, Ben. The sauce looks like it's—"

"Yeah. That, too." He turned off all the burners, looking deflated. "I should have saved my little talk till after dinner."

"Well, maybe it was good to recognize the elephant in the room right off the bat. Takes the pressure off. *Is he going to make a move on me? Should I make a move on him? Now or after dessert?*"

Ben laughed despite his embarrassment.

"The more immediate issue is, can this chicken be saved?" She tried to make light of the situation. He was obviously upset he'd blown dinner.

"Doesn't look too good, does it?" Ben grimaced as they stood side by side looking into the pan.

"Well . . ." She tried to think of some way of salvaging the dinner he'd obviously put some thought into.

"Let's pitch it." He lifted the pan and scraped the contents into the trash. He sighed and asked, "How do you feel about pizza?"

"I love pizza."

"Pepperoni? Extra cheese?" The spark was coming back to his eyes.

"My favorite."

He took off his apron. "There's a place in High Bridge, near the college. I've been going there for years. It's been family owned since the 1960s. They make their own mozzarella, and I guarantee it's the best you ever tasted."

"Sounds perfect."

He took off his apron and tossed it onto the back of a chair at the kitchen table. "Let's go."

They went out through the back door to the alley behind the duplex to Ben's pickup. As she was getting into the cab, Allie said, "I really love that you went to so much trouble to make dinner for me tonight, Ben. I absolutely love your thoughtfulness."

"Well, that's a start." He leaned in and kissed her. "I'll take it."

"So how's the yoga studio preparations going?" The next morning, Allie'd looked through her bedroom window as she finished dressing for work and saw Cara in the backyard soaking up what could be the last bit of summer on a particularly warm September morning and decided to join her before she left for the Goodbye.

"Is that all you have to say to me on the morning after your big date?" Cara opened her eyes and sat up.

"Yes." Allie nodded in the direction of the carriage house. "How's it going?"

"I'll tell you after you tell me about your date with Ben. Did you get along? Or did you bicker for a couple of hours, after which he dumped your bloody body on the steps out front and went home to bandage up his wounds?"

Allie laughed. "None of the above. It was great. Maybe one of the best dates I've ever had."

"Ooh, do tell." Cara moved her legs and gestured for Allie to sit at the end of the lounge.

"Calm down. Nothing like that. He made dinner, but it burned, so we went out for pizza." Allie shrugged. "That's pretty much it."

Cara slid her sunglasses to the end of her nose and stared at Allie. "That's it? That's one of the best dates ever? Burned dinner and substitute pizza? Damn, even my first dates with Joe were more exciting than that."

Allie laughed, and pushing Cara's legs a little farther to the right, sat.

"It wasn't as boring as it sounds," Allie said somewhat defensively.

"I hope not."

"Look, we spent a lot of time talking. As you may have noticed, Ben and I haven't gotten along very well since that very first night."

Cara rolled her eyes. "Duh."

"Right. So we buried the hatchet, so to speak . . ."

"A poor choice of words, given the way you'd been treating each other, but go on."

"We'd decided to start over. We both admitted we're attracted to each other, and I was ready to either fight or give in to some major moves last night—I hadn't decided which. Then when I got there, he started talking about how he wanted to take things slowly and figure out if we had something that could be built on that might be worth . . . you know. I'm not phrasing it well, but that's pretty much it."

"All this from Ben, who if Joe is correct majored in one-night stands in college and has regressed to that stage since his wife died?"

"I know. It was the last thing I was expecting, but we started talking and I realized there was so much we don't know about each other. All this time I've been thinking he was the biggest jerk I'd ever met, and it turns out he's probably the most interesting man I know. And you know what, he was right. By taking sex right off the table—well, for now, anyway—he took the pressure off and we just relaxed and had the best time just talking."

"You're scaring me."

Allie laughed again. "I'm scaring myself. But the truth is that maybe we started off scratching at each other because we both recognized there was a pull, me to him, him to me, and neither of us wanted to recognize it. Chemistry, whatever you want to call whatever it is that calls to you from another person. You understand?"

"I do. I felt that about Joe. We didn't like each other all that much when we first met. Okay, he liked me, but I wasn't interested."

"And then there was Des. Determined to like a guy who she felt fit the right template. She tried so hard to like Greg," Allie reminded her. "Greg, who turned out to be totally wrong for her. And the guy she thought was the last person she could love— the one she'd put solidly into the friend zone and tried to keep there—turned out to be the love of her life."

"She'll be the first of us to get married. Which means she'll be the first to wear the emerald necklace."

"I like that we get to share it. It feels right. If one of us had it—like if I'd found it and taken it back to L.A.—it would be a piece of family history gone from here."

"You'd have brought it back."

"Yeah, probably." Allie slapped her hands on her thighs and stood up. "I need to be on my way. Barney's probably waiting for me so she can come home."

"Well, once the theater's finished and Dad's estate is divided up, you probably will never have to work in a restaurant again."

"True. But I know I could if I wanted to." Allie started into the house to grab her bag. "Oh, you never answered the question. How's the carriage house coming along?"

"By the time you come back for Thanksgiving, I expect to be teaching three days a week. If you're nice to me, I'll let you take classes for free while you're here."

"I'll take you up on that. I'll even bring my own mat."

By the end of the following week, the painting was well on the way to completion, the Werner sisters had replaced the damaged seat covers, and the newly cleaned and repaired curtains hung above the stage.

"It's almost there," Allie said, her eyes shining as she walked around the refurbished theater. Des had asked her to stop in on her way to the café because there was something she wanted Allie to see. "Everything is starting to look fresh and clean without detracting from the original décor." She sighed. "It's beautiful."

Des draped an arm around her shoulders. "No small thanks to you. Look up."

"I don't know if I can. I think my neck has a permanent crick in it." Allie rubbed the back of her neck.

"So bite the bullet and look up anyway. Before the roofers took the scaffold down, our guys cleaned the crystal drops on the chandelier. Watch." Des disappeared, and seconds later, the chandelier lit up and sparkled like sunlight on a mountain lake, every facet giving off a radiant beam.

"Oh my—oh, Des, it's glorious. It's almost blinding," Allie exclaimed. "I never saw it lit."

"I turned it on last week after you'd finished the ceiling, and it looked nothing like that. So I climbed up to the top and I could see how dusty the crystal drops were. I told Seth, and he and Ben and Joe decided to clean it before the roofers came for the scaffold. They were hoping they could do it justice without having to take the whole thing down."

"Thank you. It's beautiful."

"You're welcome. I figured after all your hard work, you should at least see the ceiling with the chandelier all cleaned up and pretty."

"It's spectacular."

"I know. I still can't believe how far this place has come. I can't believe it's ours. We own this place, Allie." Des, who never missed an opportunity to watch a penny where the theater was concerned, added, "And now we have to make it pay for itself."

"There are only two ways I can think of to do that," Allie said. "Sell it or put it to work."

"If I have anything to say about it, it will never leave this family again. The Sugarhouse is ours. But it's going to have to earn its keep. Maybe we could sit down together when you get home from the Goodbye tonight and talk about ways we can do that. We've tossed around ideas in the past, but we never really made a plan.

We can't avoid that any longer, and we should work it out before you leave."

"I'm up for that. I should be back around ten."

"I'll tell Cara and Barney. The office?"

"See you there at ten."

But Ben stopped in for a late dinner, and he and Allie continued their conversation from Friday night. It was closer to ten thirty when he dropped Allie off at the house.

"Sorry, sorry," she said when she realized everyone was waiting for her in the office. "We had a late customer and—okay, it was Ben, and he'd just gotten back from chasing down a guy who was trying to sell drugs to a couple of thirteen-year-olds."

"That's one of only several acceptable excuses," Barney said. "Now, take a seat. We're brainstorming."

There was a bottle of wine and one glass left on the desk.

"Allie?" Des picked up the bottle and was ready to pour it into the glass.

"Ah, no, thanks. I think I'd like a glass of water, though."

"I'll get it for you," Cara said, "while Barney brings you up to date on what we've been talking about."

"Thanks, Cara." Allie took a chair and pulled it closer to the desk where Barney sat.

"First, we've decided that none of us will be responsible to bail out the theater if it runs into financial problems the first few years. We've agreed it's one for all and all for one. Equal amounts. That way, no one of us will be running through whatever your father left you to keep the Sugarhouse afloat."

"That's fair, Barney. I agree with that." Allie nodded. "What else?"

"We will be doing summer stage next year. Des suggested offering subscriptions to whatever plays we do. Granted, there may only be a few the first year, but we have to start somewhere," Barney told her.

"Has anyone thought about the mechanics of putting on a play? We're going to need someone to direct, someone to work on scenery, costumes," Allie pointed out. "And there will need to be auditions. Who's going to do all that?"

"I'm going to run it," Des said. "I know how to direct, but only one of us has actually worked as a director. That would be you, so you can take the lead. We'll audition at the very end of the school year, when you're here, so kids can try out if they want, and we three will be the panel. Barney has declined to be a fourth voice because she thinks there should be an uneven number so there's a tiebreaker. You can be in charge of the sets as well, since you're the artist in the family, and Cara will take charge of the costumes." Des raised an eyebrow. "Who knew she could sew?"

"Another of the many gifts from my mother." Cara returned and handed Allie a glass of water. "I used to make all my dolls' clothes. It's been a while, but I still remember how to thread a sewing machine. Plus, for any period dramas we do, there's a wealth of clothes in the attic Barney said we could use."

"We'll need playbills and advertising and, oh, this could get complicated." The enormity of what they were talking about hit Allie all at once. "We're taking over what Dad used to do when he was young, running the theater, putting on productions—"

"We will do everything we can to involve the community as much as possible," Des said. "We'll give it five years. If we can't break even in five years, we'll have to look for other means of revenue. But I don't want to get to that point. So that's the plan. Do you have any other ideas?"

Allie thought for a moment. "How 'bout renting out the building for things like ballet recitals, school productions—"

"School graduations," Barney interjected. "The last few years, the high school rented space in Clarks Summit for their graduation because their auditorium is too small."

"You can be the contact person for all the local groups, Barney. You know everyone," Des said, and Barney nodded.

"I'll start making some phone calls this week. It's going to take time, but I do believe we can make the Sugarhouse the place to have events. Weddings, even," Barney added. "Eventually."

"Oh, good one, Barney. I'd get married in the theater," Cara said.

"And maybe someday soon you will." Allie poked her, and Cara laughed. "Des first."

"Maybe sooner than you think." Des smiled slyly.

Three pairs of eyes turned on her at the same second.

"What are you saying?" Allie's eyes narrowed.

"Well, Seth and I have been talking. You know I spend almost all my time out at the farm these days, between the dogs and trying to find homes for them, and helping Seth. He's taking on so much between fixing up the farmhouse and planting the grapevines and the produce garden. We were thinking we should just go ahead and get married. Something small, we're thinking. At the farm." Des's voice caught. "Down at the pond."

"With all that talking and thinking, did you guys come up with a date?" Allie asked.

"Christmas Eve," Des blurted out, then dissolved into tears.

Everyone descended upon her with hugs as Des continued to cry. "I've never been this happy in my entire life. I never thought I'd find someone . . . especially someone as wonderful as Seth. He's the most incredible man I ever knew."

Through her own happy tears, Allie said, "If you say *he completes me*, I will gag."

"And just that quickly, the old Allie is back." Cara poked her in the back, and Allie laughed.

"You're both going to be in the wedding," Des told her sisters. "And Nikki, too."

"Who's going to give you away?" Cara asked.

"Why, Barney, of course." Des turned to their aunt. "Will you, Barney?"

Barney nodded. "Nothing would make me happier."

"Wait a minute." Cara stared at Barney. "Why don't you look surprised, like Allie and me?"

"Seth came to me last week and asked for my blessing, and of course, I was delighted to give it to him."

"That's so sweet." Cara's eyes filled all over again.

"You'd better tell Joe, Seth's set the bar really high. He's going to have to follow precedent," Allie said.

"I'll warn him."

"Thanks, guys, for being my sisters, and for loving me, and for being here with me from the start of this journey."

"Aw, Des, that was beautiful. Have you ever thought of writing sentimental greeting cards?"

"Oh, Allie . . ." Des was laughing through her tears.

"So we need to plan." Allie pulled her notebook out of her bag. "Guest list. Food. Flowers. Music."

"Since when have you become the great organizer?" Des took a tissue from her bag and wiped the tears from her face.

"Since I've been living with you all. I admit I've been a bit—well, slapdash in the past. But working on all the different elements at the theater has made me organize things better. I had to follow up on things, so I had to keep track. But don't try to distract me. We've got a wedding to plan."

CHAPTER TWENTY-TWO

For the following two weeks, it seemed that every day brought something new. The theater seats were finished and the painting completed. Everything was crossed off Allie's list except for the tile work, but Joe was working on that.

"I can't believe the fabulous job our upholstery ladies did on the seats. They're pretty darned near perfect." Allie showed off the Werner sisters' handiwork to Des, who'd stopped in to check on the progress of the final renovation projects.

"I know," Des agreed. "We need to pick a date for our big reveal."

"What do you have in mind?" Allie led the way toward the restrooms, eager to check on Joe's progress.

"I'm thinking a Saturday afternoon in October. You'll come back for that, won't you? We can't have it without you and Nikki there."

"Of course. We wouldn't miss that for anything. Pick a Saturday and let's go with it."

They went into the ladies' room, where Joe was on his knees, swiping adhesive onto the wall with a trowel.

"That's going to look so fabulous I'm not going to be able to stand it," Allie announced. "I love the way it looks there, where you've already got the tile placed."

"Thanks. I like setting tile. It's relaxing. Not like some of the other jobs I do. Like putting down new floors in an old carriage house where the walls aren't straight." Joe nodded. "Yeah. Like that."

"You're a good sport to do that for Cara, Joe."

"What can I say? The woman wants a yoga studio, she gets a yoga studio." Joe set another tile while they talked.

"Ah, true love," Allie teased.

"Don't knock it till you've tried it," he quipped.

"Well, I did once. Didn't turn out the way I planned."

Joe looked back over his shoulder at her. "Sorry. Didn't mean to bring up the past."

"It's not a problem. The past is always with me." When he raised an eyebrow, Allie explained by simply saying, "Nikki."

"How's she doing in California?" he asked.

"Not well," Allie told him.

What she didn't tell Joe was that she had knots in her stomach most nights because Nikki called or texted to reiterate how much she hated being there. She had no friends, everyone was mean to her, Dad wasn't listening.

"Sorry to hear that," Joe said.

"Yeah, me, too." She paused for a moment, her hands on her hips. "So when do you think you'll have the tile work done? Not trying to rush you. I just need to make some arrangements. Plane tickets, reserve a car to lease for a while, find a place to live, that sort of thing."

"I thought you owned a house out there?" Des asked.

"It's been rented since I came east and the lease is good through March. I never thought we'd finish in six months, so while it's good we're ahead of schedule, it just means I have to make some arrangements before I get back there."

"Call a Realtor and see if the lease can be broken," Des suggested. "People do it all the time."

"I have a call into one." Allie thought she should probably follow up with Mary Pat and find out if her renters wanted to buy the house, and if she'd located anything for Allie to look at when she got out there.

She'd already made her reservations for the same flight as Nikki's for Thanksgiving. Barney'd promised a feast, and the thought of all of them cooking together in that big kitchen of Barney's and sharing the holiday meal with everyone she loved gave Allie a reason to smile, hopefully enough to get her through till October.

When Allie came into the house a little after ten, she followed voices into the office, where she found her sisters and her aunt in a planning session for the theater's grand opening.

"In the meantime, we'll need to start working on the promotion and advertising stuff. Posters, flyers, letters to the local TV stations and newspapers," Des was saying.

"I can do that." Allie came in and dumped her bag unceremoniously onto the floor. "It'll give me something to do when I get back to L.A., and it will make me feel like I'm still a part of it."

"Of course you're part of it," Cara said. "Why wouldn't you be?"

"It won't be the same as being here, so let's not kid ourselves. But we can Skype and FaceTime and message and I can send my ideas back to you." Allie tried to sound upbeat and positive, even if she felt anything but. "It'll be fine. I'll pretend I'm away at camp."

"Oh, Allie." Cara sighed. "I'm going to miss you so much. I can't believe you're actually leaving us."

"All good things come to an end, and all that." Allie tried to brush off Cara's comment. She didn't want to cry. She still had another few days before she left. If she broke down now, she'd probably cry right until the time her plane landed at LAX.

"You're just such a big part of this," Cara went on. "It just makes me so sad to think about you not being here."

"Then don't think about it. And don't make me think about it, okay?"

"Sorry," Cara said softly. "It's just that . . . okay, I'll shut up."

"Anyway, I suggested the weekend of October 28," Des said.

"That's just a little more than a month from now," Allie observed.

"I know." Des grinned. "It means less time for us to be without you and Nikki, and then it's only another month until Thanksgiving, and you'll be back then."

"And another month until Christmas. Well, aren't you the clever little minx." Allie returned her sister's grin.

"I am. Anyone object to October 28 as our day for our opening?"

"No objection from me," Cara said.

"Anything that brings our girls back home gets a definite thumbs-up from me," Barney added.

"Well, there you go, Allie. Better make another set of plane reservations," Des told her, "because the two of you are coming back a whole lot sooner than you planned."

"Back in March, when we first arrived here, did you ever think you'd see this day?" Allie unlocked the front door of the old theater, with its unique and beautiful stained glass portrayals of tragedy and comedy, and led her sisters and her aunt inside.

"No. The first time we walked in here, I thought we'd be here for the rest of our lives." Cara looked around in wonder at all they'd accomplished.

"And yet here we are." Allie nodded. "With a little help from our friends, of course."

"And now look at it." Des's gaze swept from floor to ceiling. "The Sugarhouse is ready to open for business. Again."

"Except that it probably won't until next summer," Allie said.

"I don't know. I've been thinking about maybe running some holiday movies. Just maybe one or two, in December. The films are still upstairs. Seth is going to do a trial run on that old projector he repaired," Des reminded them. "And since the films have been kept in those metal canisters, they should be good."

"That would be wonderful. Imagine watching *White Christmas* or *It's a Wonderful Life* or *Miracle on 34th Street* here." Cara looked around as if imagining the crowd.

350 • MARIAH STEWART

"We'll work on that," Barney said. "But for now, let's take care of business."

The four Hudson women filed down the aisle through the audience until they stood in the orchestra section. Barney opened the tote she carried and took out a bottle of champagne.

"Who has the glasses?" she asked.

"Here." Cara opened her bag and unwrapped the four delicate crystal flutes Barney had taken from her china cupboard and insisted they use for the occasion.

Barney popped the cork. "That's for you, Fritz, you old rascal you," she said as she watched it sail across the stage. "Glasses up, girls."

She poured the bubbly liquid into each of the glasses, then into her own. She held it up to them in a toast and said, "Here's to the Hudsons. To those who came before us, and those who will carry the family forward into the future. We've a proud heritage, girls, and I'm proud to see you each living up to it. To the Sugarhouse, her glorious past. May she be equally glorious in the years to come."

And with that, Barney tossed back her champagne and her nieces followed suit. Barney'd poured little more than a splash in Allie's glass, as per her request, but a sip was enough to join in the toast.

"We need photos," Des declared, and took out her phone.

"We do." Cara and Allie did likewise. Barney had brought a camera with her and they took turns posing and taking pictures all over the theater, from the stage to the balcony, the lobby to the refreshment area, and of course, in the newly tiled restrooms.

"Did anyone think to take pictures before we did all this work?" Cara asked.

"I did," Des replied. "We'll need them for the promotional materials we're going to make up." She turned to Allie. "I'll forward everything I have to you so you can incorporate whatever you like into the booklet you're going to do."

"I'm thinking we want to send it out to the media outlets well before the event so we can contact them ahead of time to see if we can line up some coverage," Allie said. "We should know who's interested and who's not."

They chatted and took photographs for another hour and asked a passerby to take a picture of the four of them in front of the theater as they were leaving. By the time they'd walked back to the house on Hudson Street, they were almost talked out. Des and Cara retreated to their rooms, while Allie took the champagne glasses into the kitchen to rinse them before she, too, headed upstairs. But as she prepared to climb the steps, she caught a glimpse of light under the sitting room door. Curious—the door was rarely closed—she opened it and found Barney on the love seat, a box on her lap.

"Am I interrupting?" Allie asked from the doorway.

"What? Oh, no," Barney said. "I was just looking at some old photos."

Allie came in and sat beside her aunt. "Who's that?" She pointed to the picture in Barney's hand.

"That's my grandfather Reynolds. He was quite distinguished looking, wasn't he?"

"He was. Dad looked a little like him."

"Yes. And we all have those brilliant blue eyes," Barney added. "Which was the first thing I noticed about Tess and Wendy. Dead giveaways." Barney put the photo atop a stack on the cushion next to her.

"What's that little photo album there?" Allie pointed into the box at the snapshot-size book with a pink quilted cover.

"Oh. Take a look." Barney handed the album to Allie.

The photos inside were of a small girl. In several of the shots, she wore a pink snowsuit with white fur trim around the hood, green mittens, and bright red boots.

"She didn't have much fashion sense, did she?" Allie remarked.

"Perhaps not then, but she grew up to be a beauty with a style all her own." Barney touched the photo gently. "Look closely, Allie."

Allie flipped the pages of photos until she found one where the child's face was totally visible. "Is that . . . is that me?"

"It most certainly is. Oh, how you loved those red boots. You wanted to wear them every single day." Barney stared at the photo and it seemed to take her back in time for a moment. "Remember me telling you that your father brought you here and left you with me for several months right after Des was born?"

Allie nodded. "I do. You said Dad told you that Mom was overwhelmed having both a new baby and a toddler, and he asked if I could stay with you until Mom was coping better."

"That's right."

Allie started from the beginning of the album again, carefully looking at each picture for the story it told. Her and Barney building a snowman that towered over the toddler. Her and Barney making cookies in the kitchen, flour everywhere, a broken eggshell on the table, chubby fingers covered with cookie dough. Walking on the sidewalk out front, Allie dressed in a pale blue dress with a bunny on the front, holding on to Barney's hand.

"I must have stayed for more than a few months," Allie said. "Des was born in July, and in some I'm wearing a snowsuit."

"From July until early December. Nora wanted you back for the photos for her Christmas cards." Barney's expression hardened just enough for Allie to realize how much her aunt resented Nora, who'd pushed off her inconvenient child to her sister-in-law and left her there until it was time for a photo shoot.

"It looks like we had a lot of fun together while I was here, though."

"One of the best times in my life." Barney's smile as she looked through the photos was bittersweet.

Through the photos, two things were clear: that Barney would have made a great mom had she had the chance, and that she'd loved the child Allie had been very much. It was written on her face in every picture.

"It wasn't easy, letting your father take you back." Barney apparently had read Allie's mind. "We both knew Nora wasn't going to be a good mother, though Fritz had promised to keep her in line. When you were young, he was able to do that, to a certain extent. Nora did love to dress up her pretty little girls and show them off. It used to kill me to see pictures in magazines or in the newspaper of the three of you. I think it was later, when you were a little older, when Nora's star was falling and Des's began to rise, that your mother's true nature became more obvious. The drinking, the way she ignored you unless she could use you to put her back in front of the camera—any camera—well, I couldn't blame your father for falling in love with another woman. I wanted him to own up to what she was, to walk away from her and take you and Des with him. Susa would have taken you in, I've no doubt about that. But Fritz was afraid that exposing Nora publicly as an alcoholic and a poor excuse for a mother would have been more harmful for you both in the long run. So we were at an impasse, my brother and I. I wanted him to man up, to tell Nora he wanted a divorce and to come clean to Susa about Nora. I thought Susa deserved to know he was still married to another woman. We both dug our heels in, and we didn't see each other for years, until right before he died."

"That's why we didn't know you while we were growing up."

"I told him he wasn't to set foot in this town until he did the right thing. He thought if he held back on letting you come to see me, that I'd give in. I thought he'd give in if I told him he wasn't welcome here." Barney closed the little album and put it back into the box. "We both lost so much. We were both fools. If I had to do it over . . ." Barney shook her head. "Unfortunately, we don't get do-overs." She patted Allie on the hand. "Something for you to keep in mind, my love."

"I will," Allie whispered. "I promise . . ."

There wasn't a dry eye in the house when the time came for Allie to leave Hidden Falls. She'd packed her things the night before, waiting until the last minute to give herself something to do beside lying awake all night and thinking about everything she was leaving behind, and how much she'd changed. When she'd first arrived, she'd been a sarcastic, bitchy divorcée distressed at having had to leave her life—and her daughter—behind for an indefinite amount of time to move across the country for what she thought was a sure sign that her father had lost his mind. After seven months living with her sisters and Barney, that woman no longer existed. Except for the occasional smart remark that still managed to shoot out of her mouth before she could push it back, she'd become someone else. Someone with greater compassion and more love than she'd ever thought possible. The woman Ben had referred to as West Coast Allie was taking East Coast Allie back with her.

Cara, Des, and Barney had accompanied Allie to the airport, though Allie had offered to rent a car and drive herself.

"Absolutely not," Barney had declared, adding that she'd offered to drive Lucille in honor of the occasion, but Cara had insisted on driving her car. Why take a chance on that classic beauty possibly breaking down on the road between Hidden Falls and the airport?

The ride had been all too short, and before she knew it, Allie was hugging her sisters and her aunt. There were tears all around, even though they all knew Allie'd be returning at the end of next month. It was the end of the time they'd spent living and working together for a common cause, and they all felt the loss acutely.

On the plane, Allie tried to watch a movie, then tried to read a book, but her mind was a jumble. They'd had a goodbye dinner for her at the Goodbye the night before, and Allie'd been touched by the number of customers who'd stopped by to wish her well. She'd walked back to the house with Ben, and it had all but broken her heart to say goodbye to him. They'd both come to understand where their relationship was headed, and they understood how hard the next few years would be. The fact that Ben fully supported Allie's need to be there for her daughter endeared him to her even more.

The car she'd reserved was waiting for her at the rental desk when she landed at LAX, and she drove the familiar roads away from the airport. She'd plugged the address into the GPS in the new SUV she'd asked for and headed for the Airbnb she'd rented sight unseen. Her Realtor assured her it was perfect for her, so she'd signed a three-month agreement with a clause allowing her to rent for three more months at the end of that period.

She arrived at the quiet townhouse and parked out front. Lugging her suitcases inside, she closed the door behind her and looked around. The living room was just off the entry, and the dining room opened to the kitchen and a small family room. The spaces were small, not particularly bright, and lacked character in both design and furnishings, a fact that Nikki didn't hesitate to point out.

"Boy, this is nothing like Aunt Barney's house," she declared after Allie'd picked her up at school, as she'd arranged with Clint.

"I know, sweetie, but it's only a roof over my head until I find a house I want to buy for us. I'm not even getting any of my good things out of storage until I find something permanent."

Allie'd watched Nikki go from one room to the next, her usual buoyancy noticeably gone along with a few pounds. That she'd lost weight was as sure a sign of her unhappiness as the lack of sparkle in her eyes. Clint had agreed that Nikki should spend Allie's first night home with her mother, but the minute Allie dropped Nik off at school the next morning, she parked her car and dialed his number.

"Did you have a nice reunion with Nikki?" As usual, Clint dispensed with a greeting.

"We did. Thanks for letting her stay with me."

"You're welcome. It's the least I could do."

Gag. He was such a self-righteous idiot.

Nikki was delighted with the change, but balked at going to Clint's on Friday night.

"Why can't I stay here?"

"Because in order for you to stay with me during the week,

you have to spend weekends with your father. Besides, you have a history project due on Monday. Just focus on getting that done."

"Okay, but I don't have to like it."

Nikki was subdued when Allie picked her up on Sunday night, but when she asked how the weekend had gone, she just said, "It was okay."

"Did you finish your project?" Allie asked, and Nikki nodded.

While Nikki was in school, Allie worked on the promotional materials for the theater, sending her designs and ideas back to Hidden Falls via email and discussing them with her sisters. Every night, Nikki messaged with Mark, Hayley, and Wendy, and it seemed to Allie that the only time she really laughed out loud was when she was on the phone with one of them or with her aunts.

"Is Courtney still giving you a hard time?" Allie asked one night after dinner.

"Did the sun come up this morning?"

"I'm sorry, sweetie. I wish I could fix it for you."

"It's okay, Mom. I hang out with other kids at school. They're not as cool as my old friends, but they're nicer." Nikki smiled. "I've found that cool can be overrated."

"You're pretty smart, you know that, right?"

"Straight A's in every subject, as always." Nikki took a bow.

"I'm so proud that you haven't let the situation with Courtney affect your grades."

"What do you mean?"

"Sometimes when you're unhappy"—Allie tried to choose her words carefully—"that can flow into other areas of your life."

"Mom, that little weasel is not going to get in my way. She can talk behind my back—and some of the stuff she says is so stupid I can't believe anyone pays any attention to her—but she can't make me not study," Nikki said. "I've been spending more time on my schoolwork because I'm not on the phone with everyone every night. Besides, it's driving her crazy that I'm tied for first place in our class with Lola Stevens, who has an IQ of about a thousand."

"You are? And you didn't tell me?"

"I thought I'd wait until the rankings came out officially, but yeah."

"We should celebrate," Allie said, so filled with love for her child, who'd figured out how to rise above.

"I'd rather celebrate when we're back in Hidden Falls. You know, with everyone."

"It's going to be a busy weekend," Allie reminded her, "with the theater being opened to the public for the first time in many years."

"I can't wait. It's going to be great."

"It will be, but we can celebrate just a little tonight. Put your shoes on, toots. We're going for pizza."

CHAPTER TWENTY-THREE

‐‐‐◆‐‐‐

Allie wasn't sure who was more excited, Nikki, Barney, her sisters, or Buttons, when Nikki burst through the front door of the old family home.

"I missed everyone so much!" Nikki tried to hug everyone at the same time. "Oh, it's so good to be back. I can't wait to see the theater all finished. And my friends are all coming tomorrow! I texted Wendy and her mom promised to bring her. Did you guys get candy for the candy counter? And popcorn? Is there a soda machine?"

"Yes, yes, and yes," Des said, laughing. "And we did hear from Tess that she and Wendy will be coming. We asked her to stop over here early so she can go with us." Des paused. "So Wendy can go with you."

"Mark and Hayley are coming over early, too. I'm so excited to see them all again. I missed them. Can I take my stuff up to my room? Mark said he'd stop over on his way home from his football game. I wish I'd gotten back early enough to go watch him play." Nikki started up the steps, then turned back and blew a half dozen kisses.

"Well, I'd say she's perked up a bit." Barney looked around at the others. "We weren't really sure what to expect."

"She's obviously happier living with me than she was living

THE GOODBYE CAFÉ • 359

with Clint. It's really sad, you know? He does love her, and when it comes to most things he's a good father," Allie said. "But he has this blind spot where Marlo is concerned. Courtney lies to her, Marlo believes her, and Clint's in the middle. As long as Marlo sticks up for her daughter, Clint is going to remain a blind man. I don't know what it's going to take to shake her faith in Courtney."

"Sooner or later, she's going to do something so outrageous that even Marlo will see the truth," Barney said. "Mark my words. It's only a matter of time."

"Nikki's made a few other friends, though they don't seem to socialize much. But for now, we're doing okay."

"Have you found a house yet?" Des asked as they walked to the kitchen.

"Still looking. I've identified an area I like, but there's nothing for sale there. It's near the school, so it's a popular neighborhood. The house we're in now is no great shakes, but it's okay. We're happy there."

They'd come into the kitchen and Allie headed for her favorite spot on the window seat.

"Oh, how I've missed this place. This view out the window. This kitchen. Remember how it looked when we first got here?" She turned to Barney. "No offense."

Barney laughed. "None taken. The room's much the better for all the work you girls did in here. The painting has made a world of difference."

The doorbell rang, and the sisters exchanged a look.

"Gotta be Mark," Allie said. "I'll get it."

But when she opened the front door, it wasn't a teenage boy, but a man in a police uniform.

"Allegra Monroe?" he asked, touching the brim of his police cap.

"Yes." It all but killed her not to laugh, he was trying so hard to be serious, so official.

"I'm afraid you're going to have to come with me."

"Oh? Am I being charged with something, Sheriff?"

"Disturbing the peace." He reached for her and pulled her close. "Leaving the scene. Hit and run." Ben paused. "Those are the only ones I can think of right now. There could be others."

Allie stepped outside, laughing softly, and kissed him, so happy to be in his arms again, so overjoyed to feel his lips on hers.

"Oh, Mom," Nikki said from the doorway. "Could you take it off the front porch?"

Saturday morning brought quintessential October weather in Pennsylvania. The sky was the perfect shade of blue and the trees were still dressed in their autumn glory. People gathered along Main Street awaiting the well-publicized first public showing of the totally renovated legendary Sugarhouse Theater. Announcements had been mailed out and flyers had been put under the wipers of every parked car in town for the past two weeks. Reporters from several television stations congregated in front of the theater with their camera crew, interviewing older members of the community who'd been to films, plays, and concerts at the Sugarhouse over the years. Some of the most senior residents of Hidden Falls remembered the days when their parents and adult neighbors would dress up in their best to attend a film showing, compliments of the Hudson family. There was an excitement in the town that Barney swore she hadn't seen since she was a child.

The Goodbye had been jammed for breakfast, and there was a long waiting line at lunch, especially when it had gotten around to the press that the Hudson family owned the café as well. They flocked there, hoping for an interview with one of the sisters or with Barney, all of whom had been lying low for most of the morning and the early afternoon. Invited friends gathered on their front porch for champagne and snacks. When Pete Wheeler arrived, he was engulfed by Hudson women, who were delighted to see him.

"Uncle Pete, we weren't sure you'd be here," Cara exclaimed as she hugged him.

"You're kidding, right? Like I'd miss this? This is a great day for the Hudson family, and a great day for Hidden Falls. I'm so proud of the three of you, and I know Fritz would be delighted that you were able to pull this together." He handed them each a sealed envelope. "Here's a breakdown of the distribution of your father's estate. I think it's self-explanatory, but if you have any questions after you review it, call me and we'll go over it. In the meantime, congratulations." He gave them each a last hug, then started to walk toward Barney. He stopped and turned around. "Oh. One more thing. First thing Monday morning, I'll be wiring the payments due each of you directly into your bank accounts. The amounts are clearly spelled out in the documents I just gave you. But again—any questions, you know where to find me."

"Are you going to open that and look?" Des elbowed Allie.

"Why don't you look?" Allie returned the poke.

"What if we drained the account with the renovations?" Cara asked.

"Would it matter if we had?" Allie tapped the envelope in the palm of her hand.

"Good question." Des thought it over. "Well, not to sound mercenary, but I'd be really bummed out if that were the case. I was counting on an influx of cash to finish the renovations in the farmhouse and help Seth buy the equipment he needs to start up his vineyard and the winery."

"I was hoping to put a new kitchen in at Joe's house before I move in." Cara turned to Allie. "Your plans for Dad's money?"

"All along I'd been hoping to be able to buy a house near Nik's school and just pretty much go back to my old life."

Des said, "I heard a 'but' in there."

"I don't know if I want to make that much of a commitment to living there, and my old life . . . it just doesn't seem as cool as I used to think it was."

"Well, how about your friends there? I'm sure they were happy to see you."

Allie laughed. "I did have lunch with a couple of my old girlfriends a few weeks ago. They about died when I told them I'd been working in a café and painting on the ceiling at the top of a mile-high scaffold. Oh, and that I've got a thing going with a cop. They all really loved that part. They thought I made it all up just to have a funny story to tell." She smiled. "Honestly, I thoroughly enjoyed the look on their faces when I told them it was all true and that I'd loved every minute of it. Haven't heard from any of them since."

"Aw, I'm sorry," Cara said. "You still have us."

"And that's all I need," Allie replied. "You two, Nikki, Barney . . ."

"Ben," Des whispered.

"Yeah, him, too," Allie agreed.

"Okay, then, shall we, or shall we not?" Des held up her envelope.

Cara nodded. "I say we shall."

"Who am I to hold out? Let's do it," Allie said.

The three women ripped open the envelopes, their eyes scanning the documents, looking for the bottom line. There was no doubt when each of them reached it.

"Holy . . ." Des's eyes widened.

Cara coughed.

"Wow. I knew Dad had a lot of money, but holy crap." Allie stared at the figure.

Cara coughed again.

"Well, I'd say all our hard work this past year was worth it." Allie folded the papers and returned them to the envelope.

"Dad's given us an incredible gift," Des said.

Looking at her sisters, Allie held up the envelope. "And not just what's going into our bank accounts."

Cara finally found her voice. "I know we all thought Dad was crazy when Uncle Pete called us into his office that first day and played that recording Dad made, but I'm starting to think he was a genius. He set this up in such a way that we had no choice but to get to know each other."

"And despite our rocky start and the ridiculous way Fritz

wanted us to be introduced to each other," added Allie, "we've accomplished everything he wanted. We finished the theater, and we've come to love each other as sisters."

"And once again," Des said, "Dad got the last word."

When it came time for the grand reveal, they walked as a group, accompanied by close family friends, to the theater, and made their way to the front.

Earlier in the week, Joe and Seth had removed the plywood that had been used to board up the marquee by the man who'd bought the theater from Fritz, and one of the first things he'd done was to repair the marquee. When the boards had been removed, they'd used the letters they'd found in the basement to place a new message there: WELCOME TO THE SUGARHOUSE!

It had been agreed that Barney, as a lifelong resident of the community and the matriarch of the family, would address the crowd. True to form, Barney'd dressed the part: calf-length camel skirt belted in brown leather, high brown leather boots, camel cashmere sweater, pearls, silk scarf, her blond hair tucked neatly behind her ears, her sunglasses giving her the appearance of a star in her own right.

"She does know how to draw a crowd, doesn't she?" Des whispered to Allie.

"I think she and Mom had more in common than she'd ever admit."

Barney began by telling the story of the Sugarhouse, from her ancestor who owned the coal mines to her nieces who'd brought it back to life with a little intervention from their father. She talked about what the theater had meant to the miners who, with their families, had been invited to every event held there, and who never had to pay for a performance. How her grandfather had carried on that tradition, showing films and plays even through the Depression. She told the crowd how much the building had meant to her family, and how much it meant to the town.

When she finished, the doors were opened, and the crowd was invited in. The orderly group dispersed once inside, some to the audience, some to the balcony, some staying in the lobby to admire the elaborate crystal chandelier overhead and the exquisite painting that spread out in all directions from the light. The sisters were all interviewed several times, as was Barney, though they spent most of the day talking to residents and listening to the stories of old Hidden Falls. Some had relatives who'd worked in the Hudson mines and had their own stories to tell. Allie wrote down as many names as she could, with a request to interview them at a later time. While so many who remembered the old days were still alive, Allie thought, this was the time to preserve their stories. She wasn't sure what she'd do with them, but she wanted them written down. Perhaps someday she'd turn them into a book about a coal mining town headed by an owner who'd done it right, and the legacy he'd left behind.

Eventually there would be a book of photos and a book about the theater's history. The movie posters would be available for purchase—in reproduction form—and there'd been inquiries about booking the venue for future events.

"Girls, this is remarkable," Pete told them when he came across the three of them in the lobby. "Beyond anything I imagined. I'll bet what you've done is even beyond what Fritz had imagined. It looks just the way it used to look when we were kids, only maybe even a little better. I'll tell you what your dad would say if he were here: You girls rock!"

"We've said that ourselves so many times," Allie told him.

When the last of the visitors had left the building and the front door was locked, the sisters gathered with their aunt in the lobby.

"Tired, Barney?" Des asked.

"Not in the least. I found the entire day invigorating. Let's go up to the Goodbye and grab a bite."

Chef George had apparently anticipated their arrival and had prepared several of their favorite dishes and had tables set aside for them as well.

Nikki and her friends arrived shortly after the adults and pushed more tables together so they could join the family.

"Was this the best day ever?" Nikki declared, her eyes shining.

The next day might bring tears when they had to leave, but today Nikki was happy, and that was what mattered most to Allie.

Tess arrived looking for Wendy, and a place was immediately made for her at Barney's table. She'd attended the theater opening with Justine, who'd spent most of the afternoon steering Tess away from anyone whose last name was Hudson. If anyone had wondered if Justine had told her daughter who her father really was, Justine's behavior was answer enough.

"Tess, we still have to make that climb up to the falls together," Allie reminded her.

"What are you doing tomorrow morning? I didn't bring my hiking shoes, but I think my running shoes would work just as well," Tess replied.

"We're leaving in the afternoon, but I think we could rally for maybe nine?"

"You're on. I'll be there," Tess assured her. "I'm looking forward to it."

"What are you doing tomorrow morning?" Des asked, having only heard part of the conversation.

"Something you've been bugging me to do for months," Allie said. "I'm climbing up to the top of the falls and Tess is coming with me."

"Is it a private party, or can anyone join in?"

"Everyone's welcome," Allie told Cara. "Feel free to come with us."

It's just like a big holiday in here, Allie thought. Family and friends, eating and talking and laughing, that air of triumph when you've completed a task you weren't sure could be done. Even Ben had slipped in to join them for what little time he had. Allie wanted to kiss every face around that family table, from Barney to Ben to Seth to Nikki and even to Mark. And Tess. Their secret sister, Tess.

Knowing what she knew now, Allie could see the resemblance to a young Barney. The features were similar, the eyes the same shade of blue. It must have driven poor Justine crazy, watching her daughter grow up to look so much like the sister of the man who'd dumped her for another woman, who'd left town without a backward glance, not even long enough for Justine to tell him she was having his child.

Allie didn't blame Justine for being torn. She was between a rock and an even bigger rock. Surely Justine knew the Hudsons would welcome Tess into their family circle, and just as surely she must be wondering how that would affect the relationship between mother and daughter. At the same time, Allie could see that Barney was dying inside, so eager was she to embrace Tess as her niece, her brother's first child. But they would all honor Justine's wishes and wait for a day that might not come.

Ben checked his watch, and apparently finding it time for him to go back on duty, walked to the desk where Allie had been quietly observing the group at their table.

"Think maybe I could stop over when I get off later?" he asked.

"Sure." She touched the side of his face where his five o'clock shadow had appeared. "I like this look. A little scruffy. A little casual."

He ran a hand over his face. "Really?"

"Oh yeah. Really." She leaned a little closer and couldn't help kissing him full on the lips. He looked so perfectly kissable and not just a little sexy with that scruff.

She pulled away, still admiring his new look, and he cleared his throat and said, "I guess I'm going to have to take another look at that clean-shaven regulation."

"So what time later?" she asked.

"A little after midnight. Unless some fool wraps himself around a tree between now and then."

"I'll meet you on the front porch. But you can't stay long. I'm making a big climb in the morning."

She was still watching him through the window as he walked across the street to his cruiser when Nikki and her friends decided to leave. "We want to go back to Aunt Barney's and sit outside, just for a little while, okay?"

"Sure. Just remember we have a flight to catch in the afternoon, so you don't want to stay up too late."

"Do we have to go?" Nikki made a face.

"I'm afraid so. But we will be back for Thanksgiving."

"I guess that's better than never."

Nikki and company filed out onto the sidewalk, walking in that slow way kids did when it's Saturday night and there's no place to go but home.

And then it was time to lock up the café, send the staff home, and start the walk back to Hudson Street. Tonight, instead of a lone walk, or having Ben for companionship, Allie was part of a small crowd. Barney and Tom. Des and Seth, who'd been sharing their wedding plans only to discover that everyone had their opinion of how things should be done, and where the wedding should be held, since the happy couple had to concede that the end of December probably would be too cold for a pond-side wedding. Cara and Joe, who'd be the next to wed, Allie was certain of that. And Tess, the other singleton in the group.

Allie locked the door behind them and fell in line with Tess. All the way back to the house they talked about their girls, the single life, their plans for the holidays. Tess had just finished reading a book she'd fallen in love with.

"I'd love to send it to you," Tess said. "I think you'll love it, too."

"I'll write my address down when we get back to the house," Allie told her. "It's only temporary, but we'll be there at least through the end of December."

"It's a shame you don't live closer." They'd reached the porch, where kids were draped on the railing and lounged in rocking chairs. "Wendy and Nikki are like two peas in a pod. And it's funny, I usually take a while to warm up to people, but with you and Des and Cara and Barney, I've felt right at home right from the start."

"We feel the same," Allie said, wishing she could say more.

"Well, I guess I should gather my child and go back to my mom's." Tess waved to Wendy to get her attention, but Des stepped outside and stood in the light from the sconces that stood on either side of the front door.

"Tess, Allie, come in. We're having a little extended celebration. Seth brought champagne. You don't want to miss out on a chance to tell us how to plan our wedding."

"It's hard to pass up an offer like that," Tess said. "It isn't every day you get to shove your ideas of the perfect wedding off onto someone else. I'm in."

"Al?"

"In a minute, Des." Allie watched her daughter, who was laughing and talking a mile a minute, enjoying the company of friends who, as Nikki would say, "really like me."

It was good to see Nikki being herself again, disheartening to know her good humor would come to an end tomorrow when they had to board the flight for Los Angeles. But she'd keep reminding her daughter they'd be back in a month for Thanksgiving, then Christmas, because that's what she will need to hear. Allie went into the house, wondering what would happen when the promise of a future trip back was no longer enough for either of them.

Sunday morning was cooler than it had been, and Allie had to borrow a sweater from Des before they began their climb to the top of the falls. The path led from the woods behind Barney's house all the way to the top of the hill from which the falls flowed into a wide pool below. Tess was at Barney's, Wendy in tow, at nine on the dot. Nikki, Des, and Cara joined the group and they started out with water bottles, sunglasses, and their phones.

"We need to take pictures, Mom," Nikki told her. "So we can have them always and remember what fun we had."

"Sweetie, climbing to the top of this hill is not my idea of fun," Allie replied.

"This is nothing," Cara said. "Wait till we get to the steep part."

"You mean . . ." Allie paused on the path.

"This is level ground compared to what lies ahead," Des added.

"Oh God, what am I doing here?" Allie moaned.

"Buck up, sister." Des poked her in the back. "There's a long way to go."

"Why did I think this was going to be easy?" Allie pretended to grumble, when in fact she was determined to reach the top. It was a goal she'd set for herself, and she wasn't going to back down.

"Just look at all the pretty trees and the wildflowers on the way up," Cara suggested. "That way, you won't notice how far you've gone."

"And before you know it, we'll be standing at the top listening to the water," Nikki added. "It's like the coolest thing ever. And we can stop and take pictures whenever you want."

"Good idea. Let's do that right now." Allie lined up a shot with Nikki and Wendy flanking Tess on either side. Then Nikki took a picture of Allie and Tess, then one of Allie, Des, and Cara.

"See, Mom? This is fun. Think about all the cool pictures we're going to have. I'm going to start an album of my pictures from Hidden Falls so I can look at them when we're back in California and remember all the great times I had." Nikki linked an arm through her mother's. "I took lots of pictures yesterday at the theater, and I took some at dinner and later when we were all back at the house. It helps to have something to look at when you're away, you know?"

Allie knew. She'd take a few pictures now and some when they got back to the house. She had no photos of Ben, and few of Barney and her sisters. Nikki was right. It helps to preserve the good times so you could look back when things weren't as good.

The higher they climbed, the denser the foliage and the narrower the path, and soon they heard the first hint of the falls. As they drew closer to the summit, that hint became a rush. When they finally reached the top, the entire group came to a sudden stop, stunned to find someone else had come to see the falls that morning.

"Uncle Pete, what are you doing?" From where Allie stood, she could see the man sitting near the edge of the largest rock overlooking the falls. In his hands, he held an urn. "Are those Dad's ashes?"

Pete didn't turn around. "Your dad loved this place. We used to come up a lot as kids. I thought I'd just toss a little bit of his ashes from here before I gave them to you. I didn't want to give them to you yesterday, since it was such a happy time for you all. I was going to stop at the house on my way down and leave them with Barney. I don't know where else you want them to go. Maybe you don't want them to go anywhere." Pete shrugged as if the thought had just occurred to him that they might want to keep the urn intact. He turned back and looked at them with eyes that appeared haunted. "Unless you don't want me to . . ."

"No, no. I think it's fine. Allie? Cara?" Des asked the others. "Since Dad spent a lot of time here, why not leave a little of him here?"

"Fine with me." Allie nodded.

"Sure," Cara agreed.

"Do you want to . . ." Pete held up the urn.

"No, you go right ahead with what you were going to do," Des told him.

Pete nodded and opened the urn, pouring out just a handful of ashes, which he scattered over the rock and down into the water below. He put the lid back on, then turned and said, "Did you know this is the rock my brother fell from? I guess you heard that story."

"Aunt Barney was going to marry him," Nikki said. "She loved him very much."

"Yes, she did. And he loved her." Pete smiled.

"I remember seeing the newspaper articles about his death," Allie said. "I didn't understand how he fell. Do you know, Uncle Pete?"

"I guess after all these years, it doesn't matter." Pete sighed deeply. "We were just talking, the three of us. Fritz, Gil, and me." He stopped, as if debating with himself. "Fritz had a tennis ball with him and we were tossing it back and forth. He tossed it to Gil, and it went over the rock. Gil stretched out to catch it but he reached too far. He lost his balance and . . ."

"We're all so sorry, Uncle Pete. But the story in the newspapers didn't say anything about you playing catch. It said you told the police you didn't know why he fell."

"Cara, your father felt so guilty. He knew how much his sister loved Gil. All they ever talked about was how they were going to get married as soon as he graduated from law school. He couldn't bring himself to admit it was his fault Gil fell."

"But it was an accident," Des protested. "Dad didn't mean for him to fall."

"No, of course he didn't. But Fritz thought if he hadn't thrown it so hard, Gil wouldn't have had to lean out to catch it. He never wanted Barney to know what really happened. He made me promise, and I did, and I've kept that promise, until now."

"Are you going to tell her the truth?" Allie asked.

"I guess since I just told you, I don't have much of a choice."

Pete stood, the urn in his hands, and started back down the hill.

Pete was still at the house with Barney, behind the closed door of the sitting room, when the group of six traipsed back down the hill.

"I wonder how she's taking it," Allie whispered as they passed the door.

"No way of knowing till they come out," Des said. "But I hope she's not too upset. It seems almost wrong to spring this on her after all this time."

"But she probably should know. I'd want to know," Cara said.

"I'm not so sure. From all we've heard, Fritz disappointed Barney in so many ways. I hope this doesn't put her over the edge to, you know, hating his memory." Allie frowned.

They were all hanging around the kitchen, drinking iced tea to cool off, when they heard the sitting room door open. Des, Allie, and Cara exchanged anxious looks. Should they say something? Should they pretend not to know? Had Pete told Barney what he'd told them?

Barney's laugh echoed down the hall, and seconds later, Pete joined in.

"What the . . . ?" Des went to the kitchen doorway. "What's going on, guys?"

"Oh, Pete and I were just talking about some of the outrageous things he and your father used to do." Barney noticed Nikki and Wendy sitting at the kitchen table. "Some things not suitable to be repeated in front of the C-H-I-L-D-R-E-N."

"Very funny, Aunt Barney." Nikki didn't even bother to glance up from her phone. She and Wendy were busy looking at the photos they'd taken that morning.

"And yes, Pete told me, and he said he'd told you, so there's that," Barney said. "I always knew there was something more to the story. Fritz was always juggling that damned tennis ball."

"You don't hate Dad, then?" Cara asked.

"I'm sorry that Fritz carried that guilt with him for so long, but it was Gil's fault as much as it was Fritz's. He should have known better than to sit at the edge of the rock like that." She smiled at Pete with the affection shared by old friends. "We've been remembering some of the good times, the better times. It helps, you know, to look back on the happy and try to ignore the sad."

"That's just what I said this morning, Aunt Barney." Nikki jumped off the window seat, her phone in her hand. "I said we needed to take pictures so we could remember the fun we had together climbing up to the falls. See, here's my mom and Wendy's mom and Wendy and me. And Mom and my aunts. I took as many pictures as I could. That's what you mean, right?"

"Ah, my smart girl," Barney said as she viewed the photos. "That's exactly what I meant."

"So hold still and I'll take a picture of all you guys and Uncle Pete." Nikki snapped a few shots, then showed them off. She turned to Pete and said, "I can send you some if you like, if you think you might like to remember today, too."

"I'd like that very much, Nikki." Pete looked over her head to Barney. "This is a day I'll want to remember for a very long time."

CHAPTER TWENTY-FOUR

The first two weeks Allie and Nikki were back in L.A. were relatively calm. Allie looked at several houses to buy and a few that were available to lease long term, but nothing appealed to her. Nothing felt like home. *Maybe when we get back after Christmas,* she told herself. *Maybe then it'll seem more important to find something permanent when we don't have trips to Hidden Falls to look forward to.*

When she was not looking at houses, she was at the dining room table in the townhouse putting together photographs in a manner meant to tell the story of the Sugarhouse, from its first days to the most recent. The pictures of the theater she and her sisters had worked so hard to bring back to life made her want to cry. She was already bored with the project, but then again, everything bored her. She'd thought about painting, but she'd have to wait until she had a place of her own to set up a studio. There was no room in her two-bedroom townhouse for an artist's studio.

She'd been so busy in Hidden Falls, between the theater and the Goodbye, that having nothing of real substance to keep her busy made her cranky and restless.

Some days she found herself so homesick for Hidden Falls she called her sisters individually to see what they were doing. She'd even called Barney when she knew her aunt would be at the Goodbye, so she could catch up with the waitresses who'd become friends and the customers she'd enjoyed the most.

"Allie, I'm busy," Barney told her one morning. "I can't talk right now."

"Well, then put Ginger on so I can see how Ava's doing." Allie had kept her on the phone so long Ginger finally had to hand the phone back to Barney so she could take care of her tables.

"Allie, dear, this is a busy morning. There was a meeting of the library board and everyone's come in for lunch. How 'bout I call you later?"

"Okay." Allie'd hung up feeling much like she imagined Nikki felt when she had to end a call with Wendy.

She looked forward to her nightly phone calls with Ben as much as Nikki looked forward to talking with her friends. Until their truce, Allie'd never given Ben credit for being anything more than a boneheaded pain in her butt. Now she saw him in a totally different light. When she was depressed about being on the other side of the country, Ben's sense of humor pulled her through. On nights when she felt particularly lonely, he cheered her by talking about all the things they'd do and the places they'd go when they were together again.

Nikki'd said little about Courtney since they'd come back from their weekend in Hidden Falls, but Allie suspected things were probably about the same. Nik was still reluctant to spend weekends at Clint's, and all but ran out the front door on Sunday nights when Allie arrived to pick her up. But since Nikki'd stopped complaining about Courtney, Allie had stopped asking, thinking perhaps the worst was behind them.

Until the day it all hit the fan.

"How'd it go?" Allie asked when she picked Nikki up from auditioning for the sophomore play.

Nikki merely shrugged.

"What's that supposed to mean? How'd you do?"

"I guess I did okay." Nikki brushed it off.

"Do you have much homework tonight?"

"Some." Pause. "Yeah, I guess a lot."

When they arrived at the townhouse, Nikki went right upstairs to her room, where she stayed, the door closed, until Allie went up to tell her dinner was ready.

"I'm not hungry." Nikki didn't look up from her phone.

"Well, there's dinner downstairs if you change your mind."

Nikki whispered thanks, but Allie heard the quiver in her voice.

Oh crap. Not this again. Allie knew without asking it was Courtney.

When Nikki went in for a shower, Allie did something she hated doing. She went into her daughter's room and looked at her phone. The text messages Nikki'd been reading were still open.

Hey, Nik—how do you like this picture of Mark? He sent it to me. You know he likes me more than he ever liked you, right?"

And:

Here's one more. He said I'm the hottest girl he ever met. That includes you, in case you think he likes you. You might as well just go hang yourself because your BF isn't yours anymore.

The next text was merely a picture of a rope.

Allie tried to catch her breath, but her lungs felt frozen.

There was no way she was giving this a pass. It was obvious to her that the photos of Mark were the ones Courtney had been sneaking to take in the Goodbye. But the last sentence had made Allie's blood run cold:

You might as well just go hang yourself because your BF isn't yours anymore.

Courtney had taken her bullying to a whole new level, and Allie was going to make sure no one ignored it this time.

She left the phone where she'd found it, but the next morning, before Nikki got out of the car in front of the school, with silent apologies to her daughter, Allie lifted the phone out of the top of Nik's school bag and tucked it under her leg. She'd kept her daughter talking the entire four blocks between the house and the school so Nikki wouldn't be texting. She practically pushed

Nik out of the car before driving around the school's horseshoe-shaped driveway, then headed directly to the street where Clint and Marlo lived. She rang the doorbell at Marlo's several times, but there was no answer. Nikki had told her that both Clint and Marlo often worked from home, so Allie walked the few houses to Clint's. He opened the door looking slightly rumpled, wearing sweatpants and a USC sweatshirt.

"And here all these years I thought you'd gone to Arizona State," Allie said.

"It's Marlo's school. She gave it to me for . . . What do you want, Allie? I'm trying to work."

"I need to talk to you and Marlo. Is she here?"

"If this is more nonsense about Courtney and Nikki—"

"Clint, who— Oh, Allie. Clint, don't just stand there. Invite her in. Allie, would you like coffee?" Marlo was cheery and friendly, and for a moment Allie almost regretted what she was going to do to her morning—to her life. Almost.

"No coffee, thank you, Marlo. I just wanted to have a few words with you both." Clint moved out of the way so Allie could enter.

"Well, actually, we were going to call you this week. Clint, do you want to tell Allie the news?" Marlo was beaming, and Allie had a feeling she knew what the news was going to be.

Clint cleared his throat. "I've asked Marlo to marry me, and she's said yes. I hope you'll wish us well."

"Of course I do. I'm very happy for you, Clint, and Marlo—" *Run like the wind, Marlo*, probably wasn't appropriate. "Marlo, I'm happy if you're happy."

They'd gravitated to the living room, where Marlo, already assuming the duties of hostess, gestured for Allie to sit.

"Are you sure you wouldn't like coffee?" Marlo asked again.

"No, really. But I do need a few minutes of your time. You're both aware that there's been . . . well, bad feelings between Courtney and Nikki."

"We've discussed it with Courtney every time you've brought

it to our attention," Marlo hastened to say. "She's denied that it's ongoing except for some mean-spirited text messages from Nikki while she was away. I'm at a loss to understand this. They used to be such close friends."

Allie had to bite her tongue. It wouldn't help anyone if she were to fly off the handle now.

"Actually, Marlo, I'm afraid it's the other way around. Courtney's been sending texts to Nikki almost nonstop since the summer."

"Allie, I know that as Nikki's mother you feel it's your duty to stick up for your child, but—"

"I have proof, Marlo."

"Allie, I asked you to let me handle this," Clint protested.

"And how have you handled it, Clint? By taking Courtney's side against your daughter?" When he started to protest again, Allie ignored him, instead looking at Marlo. "Have you looked at Courtney's phone?"

"No. Why?"

"I've looked at Nikki's." She pulled it out of her pocket. "She's going to be livid when she finds out I took it, but I know without showing you proof you won't believe what Courtney . . . Well, here. See for yourself."

Allie pulled up the texts Nikki had received from Courtney and let them read the entire conversation.

Clint read over Marlo's shoulder for a few seconds, then said, "So Nikki's boyfriend is texting Courtney and Nik's nose is out of joint. It's girls being girls."

He'd looked at the screen for less time than it would have taken him to view the entire conversation. Allie knew he'd dismissed the texts without having read them all.

"You are such an asshat, Clint. Read all the way to the bottom. Mark didn't take those pictures. Courtney did, at the Goodbye. Look at the background." She took the phone back and pointed to the edge of a photograph that had hung next to the table where they'd sat and ate lunch.

"Okay, okay, I see it." Clint shrugged. "So she's playing a joke on Nik, that's all."

"Clint. Look at the last photo!" Allie all but shoved the picture of the rope in his face.

Clint looked at the screen again, then at Allie. "Wait, you don't think she really meant—"

Marlo's face had lost its color and she lowered herself to a chair.

As gently as she could, not for Clint's sake but for Marlo's, Allie asked, "Is there something going on that's upsetting her?"

Marlo pointed to Clint, then to herself. "She hasn't been happy about Clint and me getting close, and she's angry that we're getting married, but is that reason enough to suggest that Nikki kill herself?"

"Maybe, if she's hoping it would break you and Clint up so you and her father could get back together."

Marlo had tears in her eyes, the full extent of her daughter's bullying irrefutable.

"She's never accepted the fact that we're divorced." She blew out a very long breath. "This is serious stuff. Dangerous stuff. I'm going to have to discuss it with her father, and we're going to have to do something about this. We'll need recommendations for a counselor." Marlo stood, and for a moment Allie thought she was going to fall apart. "Allie, thanks for letting me know about this. I hate what you've told me, but thank you all the same. I can't even begin to imagine how you felt when you read those texts. I'm sorry. I'm very, very sorry we didn't take this more seriously from the beginning." She kissed Clint lightly on the cheek as she headed toward the front door. "I'll see you later. I need to make some phone calls."

Allie remained where she was after Marlo left the house and closed the door behind her.

"I'm sorry, Clint. But she had to know."

"Why didn't you just come to me?"

"Because every time I did, you either didn't believe Nikki or you'd sweeten it up a little before you'd tell Marlo, and you let

Courtney lie her way out of it. Bullying is serious, Clint. This wouldn't have escalated to this point if you'd taken it seriously and trusted Nikki right from the start. That's why I wanted to talk to Marlo directly. I wanted her to see the truth because she hasn't been hearing it from you."

Clint ran a hand through his hair and it flopped back into his face. "What do you want me to do?"

"I want you to admit this custody arrangement isn't working. Oh, it's working just fine for you and Marlo, but it's not going so well for the girls. Courtney needs serious help. Thank God Marlo's smart enough to be willing to get her what she needs. Now you have to man up and let Nikki have what she needs."

"What is that supposed to mean?" He rose defensively and squared off with Allie.

Allie softened her voice to an apologetic tone. "Clint, I'm not attacking you as her father. I know you love her. But I'm asking you to consider what she needs most right now. She's miserable at school because Courtney's turned every one of her old friends against her by telling lies about her and she's totally ruined her reputation." Allie took a deep breath. "Nikki has anxiety every morning when she gets out of the car to go into school and every time she comes into your house because Courtney's so often here. With you and Marlo getting married, she'll be living here, and Nik won't be able to avoid her."

"Are you asking me to call off our wedding?"

"Of course not. Anyone could see you and Marlo love each other. This is not about you."

"So what should I do?" He sank onto the sofa, his head in his hands.

"I want you to let me take Nikki back to Pennsylvania to live. Before you say anything, hear me out. Nikki is happy there, happier than I've ever seen her. She needs the security of being surrounded by people who love her. The friends who love her, the family that loves her."

"I love her, too, Al."

"I know that. But you also love Marlo, and Courtney is her daughter. I'm not asking you to choose between Marlo and Nik. But I think we can agree Courtney and Nikki can't live under the same roof, especially until Courtney gets some treatment. She's got problems, Clint, and if you love Marlo as much as I think you do, you'll help her to help her daughter. Just as you need to help your own."

Clint appeared to be thinking it over. Moments later, he said, "Fine. But I get school holidays, time in the summer, and every other Christmas."

"Sold." Allie fought as hard as she could to keep the smile off her face. "Thank you, Clint, for putting Nikki's needs ahead of your own." And with that, Allie walked out the front door.

It was all she could do not to jump up, click her heels, pump her fist, and shout *Yes!*

It took Allie exactly four hours to pack their things and call the Realtor to let her know she was turning in the keys to the rental and wouldn't be buying a house after all. She called the airline to make reservations for the earliest flight she could get them on and lucked out with cancellations that would take them to Philadelphia International Airport later that night. From there they could drive to Hidden Falls, though Allie thought a stopover in Philly to see the Liberty Bell and Independence Hall might be a suitable substitute for Nikki's American history class. Maybe they'd take their time and visit Valley Forge before they headed for Hidden Falls.

Then she called Barney.

"Hey, did you rent out our rooms yet?" Allie asked.

"Don't be silly. What's going on?" Barney asked.

Allie told her what Courtney had done.

"Why, that horrible girl! You're so right, she needs a lot of help."

Then Allie told her how she'd talked Clint into letting Nikki come back to Hidden Falls to live.

There was dead silence on the phone before Barney said, "You know it's not good to tease old ladies. You could give them a heart attack."

"Barney, did you just call yourself an old lady?"

"Of course not. I was speaking in generalities. Now, tell me again."

Allie did.

"Oh, that is the most unbelievable news. I can't wait to tell the others. But our poor Nikki. Was she frightened?"

"By Courtney? Barney, this is Nikki we're talking about. Do you really think she'd be influenced to do something like that by the likes of Courtney?"

"No, of course not, but . . . Oh. I get it. You used it to make Clint let her come here to live."

"Sort of. I didn't make light of the situation—I would never do that—but I did point out how much happier both girls would be if they weren't living under the same roof."

"So when might we expect you?"

Allie told Barney her plans to take a few days to drive there from Philadelphia so she and Nikki could have a little time just to breathe.

"Make sure you take your time driving up through the mountains," Barney told her. "The foliage is just spectacular this year. You won't want to miss it."

"Mom, I can't find my phone," Nikki said when she jumped into the front seat of Allie's car later that afternoon.

"Oh, you're sitting on it. It was on the seat after you got out this morning." Half truth, Allie told herself. It was on the seat—after Allie put it there when Nikki got out of the car.

"I felt like I'd lost a limb, you know?" Nikki grinned. "So I guess it's true, what they say about kids and their phones, right? We're on them so much that we—"

Nikki looked at her phone, then looked up at Allie.

"It's still open," she said quietly. "You saw, didn't you?"

"I did." Allie silently debated whether to tell her the whole story. Oh, damn, of course she had to, and she did. "I'm sorry, because you trusted me, but I'm not sorry that I discovered how much this thing with Courtney has escalated. I promise I'll never do that again."

"I would have ended up telling you. She posted the pictures on her Facebook page and on Twitter and on her Instagram account, too, and said Mark was her boyfriend. Everybody in school saw them."

Allie muttered a curse under her breath.

"Mom, Mark didn't send Courtney those pictures. He doesn't know how she got them, but he swears it wasn't from him."

"Courtney took them herself, Nik. The morning of the weekend Dad and Marlo and she came out and you all had lunch at the Goodbye. I saw her taking pictures with her phone and now I wish I'd called her out on it. This probably wouldn't have happened." Allie pulled into a parking lot and put the car in park. "But it's the other picture she sent that has me concerned."

"Oh, the rope?" Nikki rolled her eyes. "Like I'm stupid enough to do something that dumb? Please, Mom, give me some credit. I thought it was the dumbest thing I ever saw."

"I wasn't concerned about you actually doing it. But I was concerned that Courtney had taken her bullying to that level. You know that some kids aren't as strong as you are, right?"

Nikki nodded.

"Suppose Courtney started bullying someone else who'd gotten under her skin, someone who isn't as strong as you. What do you think might possibly happen?"

The color drained from Nikki's face.

"Right. Exactly."

"Mom, are you going to show Dad or Mrs. Davenport?"

"I already did. Right after I dropped you off."

"You did? What happened?"

"We had a talk—a really good talk—and both your dad and

Courtney's mother agreed that this was the dangerous act of a troubled girl."

"What's going to happen to Courtney?" Nikki looked worried.

"Her mom's going to talk to her father, and they're going to send Courtney for counseling to work out her problems."

"Why is she having problems? And why is she taking it out on me?"

"Your dad and Mrs. Davenport have decided to get married, and apparently Courtney isn't happy about it. She was hoping her parents would get back together again. And that's why she started being so mean to you. At least, that's my theory. I think she thought if she was mean to you, her mother and your father would stop seeing each other."

"I know Courtney wants her mom and dad to get back together. She talks about it all the time."

"So if your dad was out of her mother's life . . ."

"Her parents would never get back together, Mom. They're nice to each other and all, but that's not going to happen. So it doesn't matter who her mother marries. Except to me, because he's my dad and that would mean she's my sister and we'd have to live together."

"Well, that's what I wanted to talk to your father about. I told him that you and Courtney could never live under the same roof."

"You got that right. That would be the worst. What did he say? Is he not going to marry her mother?"

"Oh, he's going to marry her all right."

"Then Courtney and I are going to be living together."

"No, you're not." Allie smiled, anticipating her daughter's reaction when she heard the news. "Because you are going to be living with me. And we are going to be living in Hidden Falls."

"Huh?" Nikki frowned as if confused. "What? We're . . . what did you say?"

"We are going back to Hidden Falls to live."

"With Aunt Barney? Like before?"

Allie nodded. "At least for a while, until we find a house of our own at some point, but yes. With Aunt Barney, just like we were."

"Please tell my you're not teasing me, Mom, because that would be, like, the meanest thing anyone ever did."

"I wouldn't do that."

"So, okay, we're going to move to Pennsylvania." Allie could tell Nikki was trying to remain calm while she sorted through the information her mother was giving her. "So, like, we're going to go next month for Thanksgiving and we're staying there?" Nikki's eyes held a hopeful shine.

"Nope."

"Then when?"

"Now."

"What now?"

"Now as in today. So we'd better get back to the townhouse and pick up our things so we can get to the airport on time." Allie put the car in gear and drove to the parking lot exit, still waiting for Nikki's reaction.

"We're going to the airport tonight," Nikki repeated. "Wait, we're going to the airport tonight? This night?"

"Yup."

"For real?"

Allie nodded. "Here's the deal. We're flying into Philadelphia . . ." Allie laid out her plans.

"We were just studying about the Revolutionary War in history class. All the stuff about how George Washington led the troops and they lost at Brandywine and they retreated, and they crossed the Delaware and they stayed at Valley Forge in the winter and some of the soldiers froze."

Nikki sat back against the seat, the widest smile Allie'd seen in a long time on her face.

"This is the coolest, most wonderful thing that ever happened to me." A moment later, "Will I go to the same high school as Hayley and Mark?"

"I think it's the only high school in the area, so yes, that's where you'll go."

"I can't stop pinching myself, Mom. I never even thought something like this could happen, that we'd go back to stay. I knew holidays and stuff, but not to live. I never even prayed about that or wished about it."

"Sometimes you get your wish without even wishing for it." Like a family you never knew you needed, and a man you never thought you'd find.

Allie parked in front of the townhouse and told Nikki, "I've packed all your clothes I could find, but you need to go through your room. Pack up your books except the ones you're going to want to read on the trip and we'll drop them off at UPS to be mailed to Aunt Barney's, along with the photos and things I've been working on for the theater book. We're going to have to move pretty quickly, though. Our flight is at ten, but you can never predict how heavy traffic will be."

Nikki practically ran through the entire house gathering belongings that Allie had missed, but since Allie had packed her clothes, there wasn't much more to do. "But I still have things at Dad's."

"We'll ask him to ship them. Though it's going to be cold out there soon, so we'll have to shop for coats and heavy jackets and warm boots."

"This is going to be awesome," Nikki declared. "We'll get to see snow."

They packed the car and Allie went back into the house and took one last quick look around.

"There's stuff in the fridge," Nikki reminded her.

"I know. The Realtor is sending someone over tomorrow to clean."

Nikki stopped in the doorway. "I didn't say goodbye to Dad."

"I called him while you were pulling socks out from under your bed. He's going to meet us at the airport."

"With Mrs. Davenport?"

"No. Just your dad."

Nikki stepped outside, her book bag and her purse over one arm. "Well, I guess that's everything."

"I guess it is." Allie locked the door behind them and tucked the key in her pocket to drop off at the Realtor's office on their way.

"Come on, Nik." Allie put an arm around her daughter's shoulders. "We're going home."

EPILOGUE

Barney poked along the sidewalk leading to the house, her pace dictated by the very sore toe she'd managed to break when she tripped over Buttons two days before. The emergency room doctor—whom Barney'd known since she was twelve and whose student loan application Barney had approved years ago—had taped the toe, then fitted her for a boot, telling her, "Might be a nice change for you to take it slow for a while, Miz Hudson. Stop and smell the roses."

Hmmph. More like stop and pick up the daffodil heads the damned squirrels had chomped off their stems.

Still, it was nice to have an excuse to let others take over now and then. Allie'd been going into the Goodbye to take Barney's shift most mornings after promoting Ginger to evening hostess. Barney was also left to read a favorite book while someone else made her tea and brought it to her. While she staunchly professed she hated being fussed over, secretly she had to admit it wasn't so bad.

She bent over and picked up another broken daffodil bud, this one a favorite pink variety, and she cursed softly. A car door slammed, and she looked up to see a young woman carrying a yoga mat up the driveway. She and Barney exchanged a wave as the woman headed to Cara's yoga studio in the carriage house. There were other cars parked along Hudson Street, as Cara's business had taken off. These days, Cara was teaching three mornings and three evenings every week. She had plans to offer classes for couples and Mommy and Me yoga in the fall.

There were lights on on the second floor of the carriage house as well, where Allie had set up a studio of a different sort. Having found the light in the big room to be perfect, she'd set up the space to test herself as an artist. She'd painted most mornings until Barney's accident, but now claimed the afternoon light was just as good if not better. Barney was pleased her girls had found purpose for the old building. She was pretty sure the Hudsons who came before them would heartily approve.

A horn honked loudly, and she turned to the road where Des had pulled over to the curb in the SUV she'd treated herself to.

"I'm taking a new dog to the vet's, but I wanted to see how you were getting along," Des said.

"I'm doing fine, thank you." Barney peered into the back seat, where a dirty beagle mix panted anxiously. "How was your trip to Montana?"

"It was wonderful. I was so happy to see all my old friends again, and the shelter's doing great, so I came home a happy woman. Everyone was relieved to know I'd still be bankrolling the shelter, so they could continue their work." Des grinned and looked upward. "The doggies thank you, Dad."

"I'm glad to see Fritz's money working for good causes."

"Me, too." Des looked down. "Are you supposed to be walking around with that boot on your foot?"

"I broke my toe, not my leg, dear. And the purpose of the boot is to allow me to walk around."

"Okay, then. I'll see you later." Des rolled up the window and took off.

It did Barney's heart good to see Des so happy. Her wedding last Christmas Eve had not been at the pond on the farm she now shared with Seth, but on the stage at the theater. The lights had been set low, and there were candles and flowers and greenery everywhere. She'd come down the steps through the balcony on Barney's arm and met her groom at the entrance to the audience, where a bower of evergreen branches and white roses had been built by Joe and decorated by Allie. The simple, heartfelt ceremony had been attended by family and friends on both sides, which meant the whole affair had been larger and louder than Des had imagined, because Seth had lived in Hidden Falls forever, and as mayor, he knew everyone. The bride had worn a beautiful off-the-shoulder dress of ivory lace with long sleeves, and she'd carried a bouquet of roses in myriad shades of white and ivory. Around her neck she wore the emeralds that had long ago been presented to an ancestor by a Spanish prince.

Soon that same necklace would drape Cara's neck, when she and Joe were married here in a few weeks in the backyard of the house the Hudsons had built and lived in since the 1800s. Barney'd been tickled that he'd asked not only for her approval but for Allie's and Des's as well.

"Fritz, sending your girls to live with me was the smartest thing you ever did, even if I had to give you a little push," Barney muttered as she walked toward the house. "They've found their hearts and they've found their own places in life just as we'd hoped they would. Aren't you glad you listened to me and plunked that little clause I concocted into your will? Of course you are. Your girls are here, where they belong, and they're staying, and the theater has been brought back to life—though only you and I know that was just the vehicle to bring them home. You may thank me when we meet up on the other side. Hopefully, that won't be too soon. There's still so much I need to do." She stooped to pick up a small piece of paper that the wind had blown onto the lawn. "We all missed you terribly at the theater's open house. You would have loved it. Everyone in town was there, oohing and aahing over the renovations. Your girls did you proud, Fritz. They brought new life to the Sugarhouse, and to Hidden Falls as well. They're already planning—summer stage this year, and the dance school in town has already asked to have their *Nutcracker* performance there in December. I think things are going to work out just fine.

Better than fine. Someday the old girl might be able to support herself. And no, I wasn't referring to myself there." She paused. "But I'm wondering if there are more of your wild oats yet to come home to roost." She rolled her eyes at her mixed metaphors. "For pity's sake, what were you thinking, carrying on with Justine and Nora at the same time? Tess was your firstborn, and you should have known her. You should have looked back, Fritz, at least once."

In spite of everything, Barney couldn't have been more pleased with the way things had worked out. All three of her girls were thriving and happy and exactly where they were supposed to be. They were a tight family now—a tribe, as Nikki would say—just as they were meant to be, though it hadn't always been easy for Barney to guide the process.

And it had been touch and go where Allie was concerned, but things had a way of working out. She and Ben were practically joined at the hip these days, and Barney wouldn't be a bit surprised if there was another wedding in their future.

Nikki was doing wonderfully in school—no surprise there—and was happy and healthy and making the world a brighter place for everyone she met. It still annoyed Barney that they'd had to put her on a plane to California last weekend to spend her spring break with her father and his new wife, but, as Allie'd pointed out, it was a small price to pay for having her daughter live in Hidden Falls year-round. Nikki'd called the night before, and much to everyone's relief, reported that Courtney had been seeing a therapist and was apparently getting the help she needed to work out her problems. Courtney was acting like her old self again, Nikki'd told them, and had apologized "a million times" for all the horrible things she'd said and done.

Reflection was good on a beautiful spring morning, Barney thought, the squirrels and their annoying habit of lusting after her flowers aside.

Voices from across the street reminded her that Tom's sister and her children were there for the week. Barney should go over and say hello to Emily. They hadn't spoken since they were in high school, but she couldn't remember why. Tom's children were due anytime now. He and Emily had agreed their kids could select what they wanted from their grandparents' home and hoped there wouldn't be any arguments or disagreements. After the house was sold, Tom would probably be moving into the Hudson house with Barney, though she had no intention of marrying him at this stage of the game. She'd lasted this long without a husband, and she wasn't sure she wanted one, but she hadn't quite made up her mind about that. Tom had asked and she'd demurred. For now, Barney was pleased to know that once Tom moved in, she'd be the target of salacious gossip. At her age, she found it amusing, and in fact, she looked forward to it.

Barney was almost to the end of the walk when movement on the porch caught her eye. A figure sat in one of the rocking chairs, a visitor Barney'd been expecting—and praying for—for months.

"Hello, Tess."

Barney stopped on the top step and studied the young woman's face. Her puffy red-rimmed eyes, her pallor, all told of the confusion she felt.

"Would you like to come in?" Barney asked as gently as possible.

Tess nodded, and burst into tears.

"Come now, dear." Barney put her arm around the sobbing woman's shoulders and opened the door. She would find the way to help Tess through this. That's what she did for her girls. "Come inside, and I'll make you a cup of tea, and we'll talk . . ."

THE
GOODBYE
CAFÉ

MARIAH
STEWART

This reading group guide for The Goodbye Café includes an introduction, discussion questions, and ideas for enhancing your book club. The suggested questions are intended to help your reading group find new and interesting angles and topics for your discussion. We hope that these ideas will enrich your conversation and increase your enjoyment of the book.

INTRODUCTION

California girl Allie Hudson Monroe can't wait for the day when the renovations on the Sugarhouse Theater are complete so she can finally collect the inheritance from her father and leave Pennsylvania. After all, her life and her fourteen-year-old daughter, Nikki, are in Los Angeles.

Allie's divorce left her tottering on the edge of bankruptcy, so to keep up on payments for her house and her daughter's private school tuition, she packed up and flew out east. But fate has a curveball or two to toss in Allie's direction—she just doesn't know it yet.

She hadn't anticipated how her life would change after reuniting with her estranged sister, Des, or meeting her previously unknown half sister, Cara. And she'd certainly never expected to find small-town living charming. But the biggest surprise was that her long-forgotten artistry would save the day when the theater's renovation fund was threatened.

With opening day upon the sisters, Allie's free to go. But for the first time in her life, she feels like the woman she was always meant to be. Will she return to the West Coast and resume her previous life, or will the love of "this amazing, endearing family of women" (#1 *New York Times* bestselling author Robyn Carr) be enough to draw her back to the place where the Hudson roots grow so deep?

TOPICS AND QUESTIONS
FOR DISCUSSION

1. When we pick back up with the Hudson sisters, Allie is feeling eager to prove herself in hopes of inspiring her daughter to do the same. If you have children, what are some things you've done mainly to set an example for them? If you don't, are there things you've done only to prove to someone else that you could?

2. Early on, as Allie paints the ceiling of the theater, she is not only terrified of the height but feels like a fraud and an impostor (page 5). But as the project nears completion, she barely notices the height of the scaffold and lets herself acknowledge that her work is good (page 276). What factors helped contribute to this change? And in what other areas of her life is that new confidence felt?

3. Ben Haldeman is introduced as "the very bane of Allie's existence, the gigantic thorn in her side" (page 10). Even if you haven't read the previous books in the Hudson Sisters series, did you immediately suspect from that description that they would end up together? Do you think romance can blossom out of animosity? Why do you suppose Ben decided it was time to stop the bickering?

4. At times, Allie worries that she is overprotective of her daughter. What kind of mother do you think she is? Did you question any of her parenting decisions?

5. Barney decides to buy the Goodbye Café on the spot. Have you ever made a major life decision on impulse or gut feeling? Did it turn out to be a good one?

6. Ben thinks there's a "West Coast Allie" and an "East Coast Allie" (pages 257 and 259). Have you ever made a significant move like Allie's from L.A. to small-town Pennsylvania? What was it like? Did you adjust? How did you feel differently—about both the places and yourself—over time?

7. The Sugarhouse Theater and the Goodbye Café share similar story lines in this novel. How do their restorations work in tandem with each character's development throughout the book (especially Allie's)?

8. Allie recognizes she has a problem with alcohol. What were the factors that enabled her to stop drinking? Do you think she'll eventually fall back into her old patterns of behavior?

9. Do you think Ben can fully accept being in a relationship with someone who has a drinking problem, after his wife and son were killed by a drunk driver? How has he been able to remain friends with Joe, when Joe's father was the driver who caused the accident?

10. Allie is admittedly the family diva. When did you first notice that her attitude was changing in a more positive direction? Allie wakes up the morning after the "Goodbye at the Goodbye" party, having worked harder than she'd ever worked in her life, and feels exhausted but invigorated. What is she starting to realize about herself?

11. Have you ever had a "friendship" that resembled Nikki and Courtney's? If someone betrays your trust (as Courtney did when she spread lies about Nikki), can you ever really trust that person again?

12. Did you agree with how Allie handled Courtney's bullying of Nikki? How did you feel when Allie confronted Clint and Marlo about the texts she'd discovered on Nikki's phone? If you suspected something was very wrong in your child's life, would you resort to looking at his or her phone, or do you consider that too much of an invasion of privacy?

13. Nikki says she's never felt as much at home anywhere as she does in Hidden Falls (page 312). Do you think that has more to do with the place itself or the people surrounding her? Are some people just more suited to small-town life, or do you think most people can feel at home anywhere as long as they are surrounded by loved ones?

14. What are some of the signs that Allie might be changing her mind about moving back to Los Angeles? What is the breaking point, and why does she ultimately decide to return for good?

15. Fritz was a man of many secrets, one of which Pete reveals near the end of the book. Do you think Barney may have suspected her brother had an accidental hand in Gil's death?

16. Were you surprised to learn Barney had orchestrated the clause in Fritz's will that brought his daughters together? Do you think she'll ever tell her nieces the truth?

17. When did you realize that Tess was Fritz's daughter? Were you as shocked by the revelation as Allie, Des, and Cara? Or had you suspected that even before Barney announced Tess was her niece?

18. If you were in Justine's position—faced with potentially damaging your relationship with your daughter by telling her the truth after all these years—what would you have done?

19. Of all three Hudson Sisters books (*The Last Chance Matinee*, *The Sugarhouse Blues*, and *The Goodbye Café*), which was your favorite and why? What do you think will happen next in Hidden Falls?

ENHANCE YOUR BOOK CLUB

1. Allie studied art in college but hasn't used that skill since. What is a skill you have or a hobby you haven't tried in a long time? Try it out with your book club!

2. Choose one of the books on Nikki's TBR list and read it with your book club: *The Lost Queen* by Signe Pike, *The Nightingale* by Kristin Hannah, *The Crystal Cave* by Mary Stewart, *The Night My Sister Went Missing* by Carol Plum-Ucci, *Fly Girls* by Keith O'Brien, or *Code Girls* by Liza Mundy. Why do you think the author chose this list of books for Nikki? What do they say about what her family thinks of her?

3. Try out a new Mariah Stewart series that you haven't yet read! Dive into the Chesapeake Diaries series or the Dead series, or pick up one of her many stand-alone novels.